ALEXANDER McCALL SMITH

The Perfect Passion Company

Alexander McCall Smith is the author of the No. 1 Ladies' Detective Agency novels and a number of other series and stand-alone books. His works have been translated into more than forty languages and have been bestsellers throughout the world. He lives in Scotland.

alexandermccallsmith.com

BOOKS BY ALEXANDER McCALL SMITH

In the No. 1 Ladies' Detective Agency Series

In the Isabel Dalhousie Series

In the Paul Stuart Series

In the Detective Varg Series

The

PERFECT
PASSION

Company

The
PERFECT
PASSION
Company

Alexander McCall Smith

VINTAGE BOOKS

A DIVISION OF PENGUIN RANDOM HOUSE LLC

NEW YORK

A VINTAGE BOOKS ORIGINAL 2024

Library of Congress Cataloging-in-Publication Data
Name: McCall Smith, Alexander, [date] author.
Title: The Perfect Passion Company / Alexander McCall Smith.
Description: First edition. | New York : Vintage Books, 2024.
Identifiers: LCCN 2023050434 (print)
Subject: LCGFT: Novels.
Classification: PR6063.c326 p48 2024 (print) | DDC 823.92—dc23
LC record available at https://lccn.loc.gov/2023050434

Vintage Books Trade Paperback ISBN: 978-0-593-68832-8
eBook ISBN: 978-0-593-68881-6

Book design by Nicholas Alguire

vintagebooks.com

Printed in the United States of America
10 9 8 7 6 5 4 3 2 1

Contents

PART I

Cook for Me

CHAPTER ONE

No. 24 Mouse Lane

They were two young women, lingering over a cup of coffee in a slightly shabby Edinburgh bistro. Both were thirty, or thereabouts; both were dressed, unintentionally, in matching outfits: well-cut jeans and white linen blouses.

There were differences, though: Katie had dark hair, with that combination of green eyes and almost translucent skin that sometimes goes with Celtic ancestry; Ell was a blonde, or almost; Katie had a red scarf thrown casually around her shoulders; Ell wore pearl earrings—each a large, single pearl at the end of a delicate gold chain. Both had that particular confidence that suggests that somebody has a right to be there.

"You said, three husbands? *Three?*" That was Ell, who was busy wiping a thin line of latte foam from her lips.

A woman at a nearby table overheard this. A delicious snippet, she thought. Three husbands? She would tell her friends.

Katie nodded. "She's my cousin—or second cousin, shall I say—and she's had three husbands." She raised three fingers. "Three. Seriatim, of course."

Ell smiled. "Seriatim." She rolled the word around her tongue.

"My father always called her his colorful cousin—mostly because of the men, you know. She's fond of them."

"Oh well," said Ell. "It can happen to anyone, I suppose. Mind you, to have had three husbands sounds a bit greedy. Especially to those of us who've had none . . ."

Katie smiled. "You'll find him. You've got plenty of time."

"Not that I'm looking," said Ell, adding, "this week."

"Ness is now just into her fifties," Katie went on. "She's my father's first cousin. She acquired the first husband when she was twenty-one. Barely out of school. And he was only twenty. A mere boy."

"Ness," mused Ell. "I like that name."

"It's short for Inverness," Katie explained. "Her father—my grandfather—came from the north of Scotland. He called her Inverness, and his son was called Aberdeen. Inverness Macpherson. Quite a name, don't you think?"

Ell agreed.

"Of course, from the start her first marriage had no future," Katie went on. "They were far too young."

"Young lovers," said Ell. "There are plenty of precedents. Tristan and Isolde."

"Oh, yes."

"And Pyramus and Thisbe. That's even before we get to Romeo and Juliet."

"Yes," agreed Katie. "But who gets married at twenty these days? He hardly needed to shave."

"And Daphnis and Chloe," Ell added. "Two innocents who were brought up together and who fell in love."

"I've heard of them vaguely," said Katie. "Very vaguely."

"I actually read the book," said Ell. "I was on holiday in Cyprus, and I found it beside my bedside. They were young lovers, but eventually were able to marry. I thought it a touching story, in spite of everything that happened to Daphnis. Much of it somewhat unlikely."

"Oh?"

"He was abducted by pirates—standard stuff for the times, perhaps. But do you know a single person who has been abducted by pirates? I don't. Not one."

Katie laughed. "That first husband lasted a few years and then said that he wanted his freedom. Ness told my mother all about it."

"He left?" asked Ell.

"Yes. He went to Dublin, and was never heard of again. Did he find what he was looking for, I wonder? Possibly."

"Oh well."

"Ness was resilient. She's never been put off by minor setbacks, such as discovering one's husband has gone off to Dublin. *Worse things have happened* is what she says in such circumstances. And I suppose she's right. There's always something worse happening elsewhere. It's worth reminding ourselves of that, I suppose."

"Possibly."

"And then, in her mid-twenties, with her first divorce out of the way, she met Max."

"Husband number two?"

"Yes. He was stunningly good-looking, and that, it turned out, was a problem. He was a complete narcissist."

Ell rolled her eyes. "We've all met him, haven't we?"

"He was a model for men's clothing catalogues. You'd recognize him: purposeful chin, eyes focused somewhere in the middle distance. Very discreet designer stubble. He went off with a photographer called Mae, eventually."

"Oh well. These things happen. As long as they found what they wanted. Narcissists like photographers."

"Yes. And photographers like narcissists. It worked for everybody, I think." Katie took a sip of her coffee. "Mae published a book—*Max in Sepia*. You know those old-fashioned photographs. Ness showed me a copy. She was actually quite proud of it. She was pleased that Max was happy. She said: 'Max used to be mine, you know. Isn't he beautiful?' And he was—particularly in sepia."

Katie took a sip of her coffee. "Ness's story gets better. There were plenty of boyfriends, and then eventually she ended up with husband number three. He was a parachutist called Sidney. If I were called Sidney, I'd jump out of a plane, I suppose. Anyway, he did free fall jumps. I actually met that one when I was a student. I rather liked him."

Ell's eyes widened. "But I don't think I'm going to like the ending."

"No, it was one of those worse things she talked about, I'm afraid. He was doing a charity jump—a fundraising event. He did the jump wearing his kilt. His sponsors loved the idea, but unfortunately, the kilt blew up over his head the moment he entered the slipstream, and he couldn't see what he was doing. He couldn't find the ripcord. Or that's what they think happened. It was very sad." Katie sighed. The lives of others often seemed so susceptible to derailment. "And so, Ness found herself a widowed double-divorcée in her early forties, with nothing much to do. Sid had been heavily insured—a wise move for a parachutist—and, as the icing on the cake, he had owned a dry-cleaning business. He left her the lot. So, that's how she started her business."

"Which was?"

"The Perfect Passion Company. A sort of dating agency, or introduction bureau, as Ness likes to call it. I suppose she wanted to make the most of her experience with men."

"You should play to your strengths." Ell frowned. "But isn't an introduction bureau a bit old-fashioned these days? Anyone can go to one of those apps . . ."

Katie interrupted her friend. "No, not everybody wants to meet online. There are people who prefer to be match-made, so to speak. They like the personal approach. They want a bespoke service."

"And that's what she's giving to you?"

Katie hesitated. "Not exactly giving outright. She's been running it for ten years now, and she wants a break. She's keen to take a grown-up gap year. She's off to Canada."

"And asked you to be in charge?"

"Temporary owner was how she put it. She said that I can have the business on a trial basis. If I like it, she'll pass it on to me. She says I need to see if I like bringing people together."

Ell shuddered. "Matchmaking? Some of these people will be . . ." She searched for the word as a series of images of defeated-looking people came to mind—a shuffling line of the unsuccessful in love. The word came to her. "Tragic?"

"Aren't we all?" asked Katie. "In our way? Aren't we all a bit tragic? But . . ." She thought for a moment. She had already accepted, and it was now too late. She was due to meet her cousin in town the following day to pick up the keys and get her instructions about running the business. It was too late for doubts.

"Actually," she said, "I'm looking forward to it. This is charitable work, Ell. It's like working for some sort of relief agency. It's a *calling*."

Ell stared at her friend. She had always known that Katie was an idealist, but there were limits. This, she thought, is not a good idea, whichever way one looked at it. "Be careful," she said. "Dates don't always work out."

Katie nodded. "Of course. But some do."

"I'll worry about you," said Ell. "Taking over a business you . . . well, to be frank, a business that you know nothing about."

Katie reassured her. "No need for you to worry," she said. "What can possibly go wrong?"

"Everything," said Ell.

"Defeatist," said Katie.

Ell laughed. "We'll see."

The woman at the nearby table finished her coffee and rose to leave. She shot a glance at Katie and Ell, and then looked away. She had managed to hear most of it, and she disapproved.

"That's what I like about this city," whispered Ell. "It can still actually look disapproving. Where else does anybody actually bother?"

CHAPTER TWO

Hope becomes conviction

Katie made her way along the back lane with its neat progression of mews houses. It was not a street that she was familiar with, being tucked away at the edge of Edinburgh's Georgian New Town, at a point where the city sloped away to the Firth of Forth below. The fortunes of the street would have fluctuated over the one hundred and fifty years of its existence: after providing cheap accommodation for domestic servants attached to larger establishments, the houses had been converted into private flats, and then into premises for architects, studios for commercial artists, offices for accountants. This mix of domestic and business use had continued into the present, with the result that at night the street still had a certain life to it. And here and there in the neighborhood, there were bars and restaurants, a delicatessen, shops selling stationery and office supplies, and, at No. 24 Mouse Lane, up a rickety stair entered through a shared front door, *THE PERFECT PASSION COMPANY*, its name announced in discreet black lettering on a brass plate.

Katie pressed a small button at the side of the door. A bell sounded inside, and then she heard a voice call out, "One moment." She smiled: the voice was familiar, a slightly high-pitched voice, the vowels drawn out in the way in which genteel Edinburgh once spoke. Every city had its ancient accents, obscured over time by layers of accretion, but still heard now and then in odd surviving corners.

Ness stood before her at the door, her arms outstretched, her lips parted in a broad smile.

"I knew it was you," she said. "Or rather, I hoped—and there's a point, isn't there, where hope becomes conviction."

Katie was absorbed in her older cousin's embrace. *Hope becomes conviction*: this was typical of Ness, who delighted in such observations.

"Well, I did say I would arrive round about now."

Ness released her younger relative from her embrace. "Let me look at you," she said. "It's been . . . what, a year? Perhaps more. And you've only been in London, of all places. London! The horror, the horror, as Conrad put it. Still, you're back in Scotland now, for which we must all be intensely grateful."

Katie laughed. Ness overstated everything. "London's all right," she said.

Ness looked at her reproachfully. "But not for the whole weekend, my dear . . ."

Now they both laughed, and Ness led her visitor into the office that lay beyond the small entrance hall. She gestured to a comfortable-looking armchair while she herself returned to the office chair on the other side of an expanse of desk.

"Your desk is impressively neat, Ness," Katie remarked.

"That, I should point out, is immensely important. People judge others by their desks—and their shoes. That's all you need to know in the first impressions department."

Katie smiled, and Ness gave her a discouraging look.

"I'm absolutely serious," she said. "Desks reveal an attitude to order." She paused. "Do you know that haunting Wallace Stevens poem? 'The Idea of Order at Key West'? An impossible poem to get to grips with, but utterly fascinating nonetheless. I would have loved to have met Stevens and asked him outright: What on earth were you thinking about? But not to be. Mortality is such a spoilsport. As is morality, come to think of it . . ."

Katie laughed. "And shoes?"

"Shoes," said Ness, "tell you about self-respect. And self-respect tells you everything you need to know."

"I see."

"When somebody comes in here and sits in that very chair on which you're sitting, I discreetly look at their shoes. And it's all there: not only self-respect—or its absence—but also aesthetic sense, attitude to tradition, boldness, bravado, timidity. The whole range of psychological possibilities are displayed in a person's shoes."

Katie thought about this. That Ness should say this was no surprise to her: her cousin was given to the extravagant statement, the grand theory. That was what she was like.

"But what about trainers?" she asked. "Or running shoes? Or sneakers? Or whatever you like to call them? Everybody wears those these days—or just about everybody."

Ness made an airy, dismissive gesture. "Not the people who come here," she said. "The online people wear trainers. Not *our* clients. We are *supra-trainer* here. Distinctly so."

Katie looked at her cousin. It occurred to her that Ness might simply be a snob. Edinburgh had a reputation for being a bit haughty, and it was only one short step from haughtiness to disdain. And if that was the case, then what was she, who prided herself on her non-elitist views, doing getting involved in this strange enterprise?

"Don't smile like that," Ness scolded her. "If you think my views peculiar, please laugh outright. It's better to be laughed at than smiled at." She thought of something, and paused. "Have you ever heard of a man called Maurice Bowra? I suppose there's no reason that you should have. These great figures fade, as is only to be expected. He was a translator of ancient Greek poetry and famous for his conviviality and mots justes. He's the one who said, *I'm a man more dined against than dining*. Isn't that just superb?"

"I've never heard of him," said Katie.

"Ah well, but trainers . . . I know what you mean: everybody wants casual footwear these days—or almost everybody. But it's so characterless, isn't it? It's all the same. Men's and women's shoes are becoming interchangeable pieces of moulded rubber. All made in remote sweatshops, I believe." She sighed, before continuing, "Even the Italians are wearing them now—even the Italians, who always believed so deeply in elegant shoes. The Italy of Bellini and Botticelli in trainers . . ." Ness faltered, her expression becoming slightly wistful. "But enough of that. Down to business, as they say. You're staying with a friend, you said?"

"Yes, Ell. She and I were at school together. I don't think you ever met her. We lost touch for a while, as you do with school friends, but we're catching up."

"But you're still happy to move into my flat? The day after tomorrow perhaps? Just before I leave for Toronto."

"Of course. If that's all right with you."

"More than all right—a great relief. I didn't fancy tenants—one has to put everything away, or they break it—and you can't leave a place unlived in for long. So . . ."

"I'm really looking forward to it. To everything." She tried to convince herself that this was really so. It was too late to change her mind, after all, and she felt a certain obligation to her cousin.

Ness seemed pleased. "There are some arrangements that seem just perfect. I wanted to go away; you wanted to return to Edinburgh." She paused, and looked at Katie quizzically. "Why did you want to come back? I don't think I ever asked."

Katie hesitated. People came home—they just did—and sometimes they were not at all sure why they did so. Was she tired of London, even after only a few years? Had she had enough of crowds and rush and the sixth-hand air? Edinburgh, after all, was so beautiful, so close to a hinterland of hills and water, surrounded by one of the most romantic landscapes in the world. Or was it just *home*, and a place to return to because that was where, for her, it had all started?

Her answer was brief. "I missed home."

Ness understood. "Of course you would. Anyway, my wanting to go away for a while and you wanting to come back made us a perfect match—and perfect matches are, as you know, what this business is about."

Katie swallowed. The idea had seemed so attractive, but now she was not so sure. This was a real business, with paying clients who expected something for their money. And she would shortly be sitting behind that desk interfering in their private lives, because that, ultimately, was what this business was all about. It was full, she thought, of psychological risk.

Ness sensed the unexpressed reservations. "No need for cold feet," she said. "When I started this business, I, like you, knew absolutely nothing about it. But that's how everything starts, don't you think? Everybody starts from a position of complete ignorance and proceeds to one of slightly attenuated ignorance."

"But . . ."

"Believe me," Ness interrupted. "Believe me, Katie, you're going to *thrive* in this business. You've got everything it takes—everything."

Katie said nothing.

"And I am a good judge of these things," Ness went on.

Katie saw her cousin's gaze move to her shoes: They were made of supple dark blue leather and had white rubber soles. "Formal trainers?" she said.

She looked up, and their eyes met. They both laughed.

Ness became serious. "But tell me, Katie: Do you have any current emotional entanglements?"

Katie shook her head. "I've decided that I don't need men."

Ness clapped her hands in delight. "My dear, who does?"

"I used to," Katie added. "But not any longer."

Ness looked at her. "Am I meant to believe that?"

"Not really. And I suppose I don't either."

Ness nodded. "Aspirational," she said.

Ness showed her round the office, which did not take long, as it was no more than two medium-sized rooms, a kitchen, and a minuscule bathroom lit by the tiniest of windows. The main room, in which clients were received, was tastefully decorated, having more the air of a study than a place of business. The paintings on the walls were not the usual reproductions to be found in offices, but were carefully chosen drawings and watercolors by Scottish artists, one or two of whom Katie recognised. One was a Peploe drawing of a child; another a Fergusson pastel of one of his angular women dancing naked under a palm tree. Opposite the desk were several shelves lined with books. Katie glanced at the spines—a glance intercepted by Ness, who said,

"The books are mostly psychology and Greek mythology. My two weaknesses. Don't lend them to the clients—they *never* return them."

Katie peered at a slender volume into the top of which various scraps of paper had been inserted as bookmarks. She read out the title: *Did the Greeks Believe in Their Myths?*

"Interesting."

Ness peered at the book. "Oh, that. Yes, I read that a couple of months ago. It's by a French professor of philosophy. Usually, French philosophers are not immensely readable, but I was intrigued by this one."

"And did they?"

"The Greeks? Yes, in a sort of way, which is what this book is all about, actually. He suggests that we can believe in things in different ways. So you may know that something is unlikely—or even manifestly impossible—but you can still act as if it's true."

"You pretend?"

"You could call it that. We compartmentalise, you see. There are certain things that we are very careful only to believe if we can demonstrate them to be true—scientific facts, for instance. Then there are . . ." Ness paused, and gave Katie a bemused look. "Am I going on excessively?"

"You never go on excessively," said Katie.

"And you'd never be so rude as to say yes," Ness retorted. "But it is an interesting question, isn't it? Whether we all have to believe in things *in the same way*. There are plenty of things that we realise are not true, but that we believe in because they stand for something important. So, we believe in them without really believing in them—if you see what I mean."

"Such as?" asked Katie.

Ness smiled. "Love. What this business does. We believe in

something that might elude most people, but that we know is important, that people need in their lives. So, we carry on as if it weren't true that people get tired of one another but stick together because they need to. And they may call that determination to see the whole thing through *love*—that's the word they might use—while at the same time they know that it may not be that at all."

Katie stared at her. "Isn't that a bit cynical?"

Ness shook her head. "Not at all. Because if you believe in something, then it may have the effect you want it to have, even if it isn't there in the first place. Take love—since I brought the subject up. It grows, it develops, and eventually you have something that looks pretty much like the thing you wanted to believe in in the first place."

Katie thought about this. She said, "So what you're talking about is *hope*. That's what you . . ." She gestured to the desk and to the filing cabinet beside it. "That's what this is all about?"

Ness touched her arm gently. "Yes, my dear, exactly. You understand it perfectly." She paused. "I wouldn't have asked you to take over the business if I didn't think you were capable of grasping that. And you are. So, all you need to do is to be careful not to overestimate what you can achieve. Little things: achieve those. Small moments of happiness. Remember the big picture. And use your own experience to help other people. When you're listening to somebody telling you how they feel, remind yourself of how *you* once felt."

How had she felt on that first date with James, the boyfriend she had yet to tell Ness about, and perhaps never would? Would her own experience be of any use to anybody else? She remembered their first date—in that restaurant in Soho where the tables were so close together that any conversation of necessity involved the couples on either side of them; where the food was served cold, but the white wine was warm; where they had exchanged unambiguously evaluating glances; and where she had paid the bill because James, quite genuinely, had forgotten to bring his wallet. She was drawn to him physically, and he became a sort of addiction, an intoxication. She delighted in his touch, and in the touch of him. She felt guilty about that, as if she had taken the first draft of the poppy, knowing it would be impossible to break away.

Their lives had quickly become intertwined, and they had become accustomed to doing everything together. "I never thought I'd get so deeply involved," James had said. "Don't take that the wrong way, please, but I just didn't see my life becoming so *integrated* with somebody else's." He was careful in the way he spoke, picking his words so as not to give offence and showing elaborate concern for the niceties of social life. But there was no heart to the way he looked at the world. There was no empathy.

She had not thought much more about this until later, when after living together for six months in a cramped flat in Pimlico, she had suddenly become aware of how little space, both physical and psychological, she had to call her own. And then, towards the end, as they approached the first anniversary of their meeting, she had realised that there was a lot about James that she simply did not like. It was not just disagreement that opened up between them—many couples fail to see eye to eye on various subjects—what she felt was an actual antipathy to some of the views that he expressed, to many of them, in fact; no, to most. James was a libertarian. Schools, hospitals, libraries—all the things that Katie believed made society bearable—were, in his view, best left to individuals to provide for themselves. She had tried arguing with him, but he could not be shifted.

"People can't expect the government to do everything for them," he said. "They just can't." And that attitude of robust individualism was applied to everything, including, and in particular, the use of fossil fuels. If people wanted to use internal combustion engines, then they had the right to do so without being lectured on pollution by the state. Similarly, if they wanted to smoke in public places, they should be permitted to light up when they wished. That was their right.

"And the rest of us can just hold our breath?" said Katie. "Through the smoke?"

He had looked at her in surprise. "I never said that. Nobody's stopping you breathing."

And that was the point at which Katie realised that the differences of attitude between them were so profound that she simply could no longer bear him. She had no idea why she had stayed with him so long, until, in a moment of bleak self-realisation, she came to admit that it was no more than physical attraction. The thought depressed her in its sheer reductionism. Was that the essence of any attachment between people? Was that all it was?

He said to her, "You've gone off me, haven't you?"

And she replied, "Yes." She felt a flood of relief. He had done the difficult work with his question. He had done it for her.

"May I ask why?"

She had taken a deep breath. Her tone remained civil, matching his cold politeness. "Because I dislike everything you stand for. I'm sorry, but I do."

He looked at her, as if astonished by the disclosure. But he must have known, she thought; he must have.

"But you've been happy enough."

She held his gaze. "Not at all," she said. "Couldn't you tell?"

"No."

"Well, I was. Almost all the time. Listening to views I really don't share. In fact, you may as well know it, James, but I disagree with everything you say—on any subject."

He shook his head in disbelief. But then he said, "If that's what you want."

"It is, I'm afraid. And I'd add something. You never cleaned the bath. Not once."

And it had been that easy. She had moved out of the flat in Pimlico, spent two weeks on a friend's couch in the dreary reaches of London suburbia, and then had received that telephone call from Ness in which the offer had been made. She had taken an hour to mull over it and then had telephoned with her response. She had not been happy in her work in an expensive art gallery off Cork Street. She handled relations with clients, who could often be extremely demanding. Nor did she always see eye to eye with her boss, for whose tactlessness she found herself constantly having to apologise. They would have no difficulty replacing her, as there were always plenty of people wanting to work in a gallery. She would not have to give much more than a couple of weeks' notice, and, once she had done that, she could return to Edinburgh. She would run the intriguingly named business. She would look after Ness's flat. The decision taken, she felt nothing but relief. Being single was so much simpler; so much less messy; so much more . . . *dignified*.

The contradictions in her situation did not strike her then, although they did much later on. She was assuming, sight unseen, the running of a business that sought the very opposite of the clean singularity she had just discovered for herself. She was about to help people in their quest to involve themselves with others—to become part of another's life. But perhaps that was not all that unusual, she told herself. Not everybody practised what they preached: somewhere there must be vegetarian butchers, or pilots with no head for heights, or atheist priests. If these existed—as they must do—then a matchmaker who thought it better to be free of romantic attachments was not an impossibility.

Ness showed her how the business side of the company worked. "We have a very good accountant—Dan," she said. "He keeps the books. All you have to do is issue invoices. It's all there in that drawer. Letterheads. Bank details. Everything. And if there's anything you don't understand, phone Dan—that's what he's there for."

She led Katie to the filing cabinet and opened one of the drawers. "Here's the raw material. We work with old-fashioned paper files. The name of the client is on the outside, and inside . . ." She extracted a brown manila folder to show it to Katie. "And inside, we have my notes. I give everybody who comes in here at least an hour to tell me about themselves. I make notes, of course, and they go in here. That's what I call the information."

Katie glanced at a page in the open folder. There was a photograph, and underneath it a series of notes in Ness's characteristic handwriting.

"We take care," Ness continued, "to ask people what they're looking for. Sometimes they're not sure, and it helps them to discuss it. Sometimes they're pretty unrealistic, and we can help to reduce their expectations—gently, of course. The Perfect Passion Company is not here to destroy illusions completely. We all need one or two to keep us going."

She replaced the file in the filing cabinet. "I'll tell you now how we go about bringing people together—once you've decided that they're right for one another. I've found it helps to be proactive. A lot of people dread making the first move out of the blue, so to speak. They prefer an old-fashioned introduction—something that mimics the introductions of the past."

"So, they don't just agree to meet in a bar?"

Ness shook her head. "Definitely not. I go along with one of the parties—usually to a coffee bar or somewhere like that. Then I make a natural introduction. 'Helen, this is John.' That sort of thing. I then stay for a short while before I look at my watch and say, 'Goodness, is that the time?' and I leave. It's all very natural."

Katie's eyes widened. "And you think I should do the same?"

"Yes, if possible. But you decide what seems natural to you, and do it that way. You'll be the boss—as from five o'clock this evening."

Katie caught her breath. "I'm not sure . . ."

"You'll be fine," said Ness, reassuringly. "This is skilled work, of course, but I think that they are skills that you happen to have. And that's because of natural talent—something that can't always be learned. You don't need a degree in . . . What was it you studied, by the way?"

"History of art."

"Well, you don't need that to do this," said Ness. "Common sense, tact, and a sense of humour. That's all that's needed. Mind you, I suppose that it could be helpful to know the difference between Monet and Manet—which I assume you do."

"Or Peploe and Fergusson," said Katie, looking at the walls. Then she continued, "What do you need a sense of humour for?"

Ness thought for a few moments before responding. "Because

the results are often very funny," she said. "And you have to keep a straight face while inside you're doubled up with laughter."

"At?"

"Human nature. The things people do. The things they expect."

"I hope I'm going to be up to it. I'm a bit worried about being on my own. And I don't want to keep bothering you for advice on what to do."

"You don't need to bother me," said Ness. "There's William."

"Somebody else works here?"

Ness shook her head. "No. In the flat next door. There's a young man called William—an Australian. He runs a design studio there—knitwear and so on. But he's got a very good instinct for people, and he won't mind giving you advice if you need it. No, you're not on your own, Katie. Anything but."

"Could I meet him?"

"He's a phone call away," said Ness, lifting up the telephone. "Or if you bang on the wall loudly enough, he'll hear you and come through."

Ness dialled, and spoke briefly into the receiver. Then she rang off. "William's coming round to say hello," she said. She gave Katie a thoughtful look. "One thing, by the way, just to give you a bit of background. William is highly desirable, but I'm afraid there are complications. You ought to know about them."

Katie nodded. She had made what she thought was an obvious assumption. Sympathetic men who ran design studios were unlikely to be available to her. But she felt a certain resentment that Ness should imagine that she assessed every man in terms of his availability. That was not the way it was with her—or with most people, she thought. The problem, of course, was that Ness belonged to a different generation. The twenty years or so that lay between them had produced a shift that had transformed the social landscape. Men and women thought differently now. They could be friends without being potential lovers. And friends just as easily could become lovers and then revert to being friends. Fluidity was all: it was all much more relaxed, much less . . . starkly binary. But how did you explain all this to somebody who clearly viewed the world in the light of its potential for old-fashioned romance between men and women?

Ness had raised an admonitory finger.

"Don't think that I think . . ." she began.

"I wasn't," Katie protested.

Ness looked at her reproachfully. "Don't think that I think that men who design jumpers aren't interested in women."

Katie protested again, more weakly now. "I didn't."

"You did, Katie, darling. Not that I hold it against you. Of course, you imagine that I think in conventional terms. I don't. I'm as modern as the next person. And I know being interested in knitting and clothes has nothing to do with one's orientation." She paused. "Except sometimes."

Katie waited.

"In William's case," Ness continued, "I have absolutely no doubt but that he's interested in women. Even me, perhaps. Or shall I say: I wish. But the problem is that he's engaged."

Katie nodded. "Nice men often are."

"Unfortunately, that's true. However, there's a glimmer of hope. William's engaged to a girl in Melbourne. That's a long way away, and in my experience these distant affairs are never very satisfactory. So . . ."

Katie smiled. "I told you, Ness. I'm not thinking in terms of picking up a man any time soon."

"Yes, you did. But if you were to change your mind . . ."

"Does being a matchmaker mean you're always on duty? Twenty-four seven?"

The bell rang.

"That's him," said Ness. "So, the subject's shelved. But who knows? It's always a good idea to be open to new developments. Life, after all, is an unfinished narrative, the plot of which is constantly subject to revision." She moved to the door. "And a drama in which we discover our roles by playing them." She looked back at Katie as she opened the door. "And here we have William. William enters stage left."

"Drama queen," said William, planting a kiss on Ness's cheek.

CHAPTER THREE

Even Lotharios need love

Katie moved into Ness's flat the following morning, two hours before Ness was due to leave for the airport.

"These are the keys," said Ness, handing her a small leather key-wallet along with a sheet of paper. "And these notes I've made will tell you everything you need to know about . . ." She waved a hand airily, "About everything. Switches. Fuses. My somewhat eccentric hot water system."

Katie took the keys gingerly. It seemed to her that she was assuming an entire life—what with having agreed to run the business and to look after Ness's flat. She was stepping into the other woman's shoes, and she was not sure whether that was what she really wanted to do.

Ness was looking at her intently. She understood. Katie was younger and less experienced; she would have the natural reticence of youth. She would be concerned about what people thought of her; at what age did we stop caring about that? Forty? Fifty?

Katie tried to smile. "I know. But, it's just that . . . I feel such a fraud."

Ness made a dismissive gesture. "A fraud? Why on earth would you feel that?"

"Because I don't know the first thing about running a business like yours. I'm completely ignorant of what it entails. And I'm expecting people to *pay* for the privilege of my utterly inexpert advice." She paused. "What's the expression? The blind leading the blind?"

Ness shook her head. "But I was in exactly the same position," she said. "And nobody ever complained. The Perfect Passion Company was a success from the word go—day one. We never looked back."

"Well . . ."

Ness put a sisterly arm about her. "Look, Katie, I'm prepared to bet anything you like that after a day or two you'll be enjoying every moment of it. What's not to enjoy? You'll love making a difference to people's lives. I promise you."

Katie struggled. She did not want to put a dampener on Ness's departure. Her trip to Canada was, after all, a major undertaking for her, something she had been looking forward to for some time, and it would be churlish, she felt, to make her anxious about what she was leaving behind. Summoning up such optimism as she could manage, she said cheerily, "You're right. I'll be fine. You mustn't worry."

"Good," said Ness quickly. "So tomorrow you'll be making a start with your ten o'clock appointment—the one I mentioned to you. One David Bannatyne. Forty-four. Airline pilot—or he was. He's a farmer now. Wants a wife. Simple." She paused. "You saw his photograph in the file."

Katie nodded. "He looked all right."

"Yes," said Katie. "He's presentable enough."

"So why is he coming to us?" asked Katie. "Why can't he

find a wife himself? Don't pilots have women hanging all over them? Cabin crew and so on. Aren't they spoiled for choice?" She paused. "Is there a problem?"

Ness looked at her watch. "That's what you need to find out tomorrow. When a man looks good in his photograph, is solvent, is not actually wanted by the police, then there's likely to be a snag. I don't say definitely—but the odds are that there's a problem."

"I see."

"And that's what you need to find out tomorrow. It's a bit like buying a horse. Look at his teeth, so to speak. Find out whether everything is as Mr. David Bannatyne would like us to believe it is."

Ness looked at her watch again. "I find it hard to believe," she said, "in fourteen hours I shall be in Toronto."

Katie squeezed her cousin's forearm. "Excited?"

"Very. I'm planning some very big adventures."

Katie grinned. She liked the idea that a woman in her early fifties could be planning a big adventure. She felt proud of Ness. She was the opposite of those people who let life happen to them; she had spirit.

"This Mr. Bannatyne," she said. "Will he know that I've never done this before?"

Ness shook her head. "I told him that he would be being looked after by my new associate."

"Associate," mused Katie.

"Yes. And I told him . . . Well, I said that you were joining us from London, and that you had a great deal of experience."

Katie looked reproachful.

"Well, I didn't say *what* experience. I didn't mislead him."

Katie said nothing. She was imagining herself in the office, inviting Mr. David Bannatyne to take a seat.

"Please make yourself comfortable, Mr. Bannatyne. Then we can have a little chat and see what we can do for you . . ."

And he would sit down and say, "Just tell me: Do you have anybody you think may suit me?"

"But, Mr. Bannatyne, I need to find out about you. I need to know . . ."

And now the real David Bannatyne, seated in the chair in front of Katie's desk, legs crossed, easy in his manner, smiled at Katie as he said, "You know, I felt almost furtive coming up your stairs. People know about this place. They talk about it."

Katie studied him as he spoke. At least the photograph was an honest one—Ness had warned her that many people deliberately used photographs taken years earlier. The David Bannatyne in the chair looked exactly the same as the David Bannatyne in the photograph, if anything, more youthful. He could be thirty-five, Katie found herself thinking; he could even be my age.

"No need for embarrassment, Mr. Bannatyne," Katie heard herself saying.

"David. Please call me David."

"Right. David. And I'm Katie."

David played with the cuff of his jacket. "I suppose you're right about there being no need for embarrassment. It's just that people might think I'm one of those types who can't cope with life—you know, a social inadequate."

Katie adopted her most reassuring tone. "It's quite natural to feel slightly awkward." What do I know about it? she asked herself. How do I know what's natural? "But let's not worry about any of that. Nobody saw you. Nobody's going to be doing any whispering."

David sat back in his chair and smiled. "Good," he said.

He looked at Katie expectantly.

Katie glanced down at the file in front of her. "So, you're forty-four," she said.

"That's what I said on the form I filled in," he said. "It's all there. Forty-four. Born in Stirling. Strathclyde University, mechanical engineering, and then pilot training. One or two long-term relationships that . . . that fizzled out. No kids—obviously. Then I inherited the farm owned by my uncle, who had nobody else to pass it on to. Left the airline to start farming. That's it. And now I'm sitting here." He looked at her as if to challenge her to ask for more detail.

"Interesting," said Katie, not really knowing why she said it.

"Do you think so?" he asked. "Why?"

"Well, being a pilot must be interesting."

He shrugged. "A lot of people think that. But the reality is that for much of the time planes fly themselves these days. Computers do the work."

"But you get to go all over the place," said Katie. "Exotic destinations."

"Liverpool?" he said. "Southampton? Rotterdam?"

"But surely the job has taken you further afield?"

"Not in my airline," he said. "If you fly with some of the others, perhaps. You might find yourself going to the Bahamas, Tokyo, Honolulu, and so on. But not with my bunch."

"Do you like flying?" asked Katie. "I read somewhere that it's a job that most people who do it actually love."

He nodded. "I love it. I've always loved it."

"And yet you've given it up?"

He sighed. "Flying gives people up rather than the other way round. I was getting too expensive for the company. They edge people out when you get a bit more senior—then they can employ younger people—and pay them far less. That's what happened to me."

"But you still enjoy it—if you get the chance?"

"I do," he said. "I'm never happier than when I'm up there. I do some microlight flying."

"And that helps?"

"It satisfies the craving." He gave her an intense look. He was opening up, and he had not expected to do so. There was something about this young woman, he thought. He wanted to speak to her.

"It's hard to explain why flying does this," he continued. "It's like a drug, in a way. Once you've tried it, you find that you need it."

Katie glanced at the file. "Do you mind telling me about the relationships you've had so far?"

He shook his head. "I don't." He looked a bit puzzled, and asked, "But why do you need to know about all that?"

Ness had given Katie her instructions on that. "It's because we need to know about you if we're going to introduce you to somebody. We owe both of you a duty."

He saw the point. "To protect the woman?"

"Yes—and the man. It works both ways. We wouldn't want to introduce you to a woman whose motives we suspected."

He looked thoughtful. "So, if you have a man who's a complete Lothario, you'll hesitate to introduce him to somebody?"

"Well," said Katie, making up policy as she went along. "I suppose that depends. Even Lotharios need love . . ."

But then she remembered something that Ness had said

about screening out *undesirables*. Katie had smiled at the word, and yet now she said, "We're careful about undesirables."

David gave a snort of laughter. "That's a great word, that. *Undesirables.*"

Katie blushed. "I know it sounds a bit old-fashioned, but it says it all, doesn't it? There are some people you don't want to get mixed up with."

David shifted uncomfortably in his seat; only briefly, and it might have been missed. But she noticed it. And the thought occurred to her that her first client was an undesirable. And if that were the case, then what did one do? Should she decline to take the matter further? There must be a way of doing that tactfully—by simply saying that unfortunately they had nobody on their books to whom an introduction might be made. That could lead to a confrontation, though, and she realised that she had no idea of what to do in the event of a disagreement with a client. This was real life that the Perfect Passion Company was engaging with, and real life could become messy.

She struggled to contain her suspicions. She should concentrate on the task in hand—which was to find out more about David Bannatyne and reach a considered conclusion. She was relieved now that he seemed to take the initiative.

"You wanted to know about my past?"

"Well . . ."

"It's not very eventful—or, shall I say, very successful. I've been involved with several women—two for some time, actually. In each case, I hoped it would come to something, but it didn't. In one case, we couldn't agree about children . . ."

She felt that he looked embarrassed. Then he said, "It's probably the opposite of what you think."

She raised an eyebrow.

"I was the one who wanted them. She didn't. Normally it's the other way round, isn't it? The woman wants to start a family and the man doesn't."

He was right: she had not expected it to be that way round. She admitted that she had thought that. "I suppose that's true," she said. "The biological clock is ticking, and the man isn't ready to commit. Yes, that's common enough." Listen to me, she thought: the expert.

He looked at his hands, and suddenly she felt sorry for him. This was real regret.

"People don't realise what a pilot's life can be like," he said. "It can be very unsettled. The hours are odd. You're never in one place for all that long. You're sleep-deprived half the time, even if you're not crossing time zones; you have to get up at unearthly hours."

"And yet you said that you loved flying."

"That's right. The flying bit was fine, but it's the rest . . ." He sighed. "I wanted to lead a steady, suburban life. I wanted to have somebody to come home to. I wanted to lead the life that I saw being led by the people I used to load into my plane and fly off to mundane destinations for their boring meetings." He paused. "I wanted somebody to look after me."

He stopped, and looked up at her. She held his gaze for a few moments, and then looked away. She had been wrong about him. This man deserved her sympathy.

"And the other woman?" she asked gently.

"We were together for six years," he said. "I should have married her, but I didn't. I thought everything was fine as it was. But then she met somebody else, and he asked her to marry her more or less straightaway. She accepted him, and that was that."

Katie asked him whether they had ever discussed marriage. Had he known that this was what she wanted?

David shook his head. "No. Believe it or not, we never talked about it. I don't know why. It was an awkward subject perhaps. Or I was too tone-deaf to realise that she wanted me to say something." He paused. "I know all that sounds ridiculous, but a lot of what we do looks ridiculous when we look at it afterwards—in the cold light of day."

Katie said, "It sounds to me as if you've had a lot of misunderstanding in your life."

This produced a grin. "That's a good way of putting it." He fiddled with his cuff again, but stopped when he noticed that she was watching him. "I feel nervous," he said. "Not with you. Not about being here, but about my life. I feel that time's slipping through my fingers, and I'm getting nowhere. That's why I got in touch with you people." He looked at her helplessly. "I'm not looking for anybody glamorous," he said. "It's not that."

She inclined her head. "I didn't think that."

He seemed grateful that she understood him. "I want somebody . . . I want somebody to . . . ."

To love you? she thought. The desire expressed in any number of popular songs: that simple wish, perhaps the commonest human yearning there is.

David hesitated. "Actually, I would like a wife who would be able to cook. I know that may sound a bit odd, but that's what I'd like."

It took her a few moments to react. Then she said, "Just that? You want somebody to . . . to make your meals?"

He hesitated. "Yes. That's what I want. I suppose it's because I want to be looked after. Having somebody to cook for you . . . well, that seems to be the very summit of being looked after."

Katie could not help but smile. "It's a bit basic, don't you think?" She thought, though: He's looking for stability and consistency; he was looking for a mother. She had a theory that many men were doing just that: looking for a mother.

"Life's basic."

"I suppose so."

He looked at her imploringly. "It's what I want. It just is. A person who cooks my meals for me. Who makes me feel . . . I don't know. Maybe, who makes me feel secure. Or who just cooks for me. I know that sounds ridiculous, but it's what I want."

Katie frowned. "A domestic skivvy?"

He reacted quickly. "That's unfair. I didn't say that. I'd do my share of everything else. I'm not lazy."

She apologised. "I'm sorry. It's just that there are an awful lot of men who seem to think that a wife or partner is there to dance attendance on them. And women don't necessarily see it that way."

"I just said cooking," he protested. "I'd pull my weight. I really would. I'm handy enough round the house living on my own."

For a short while, neither said anything. Then Katie broke the silence. "Let's get this clear," she said. "As far as you're concerned, you want somebody who's a good cook. Is that right?"

"Yes. But nice as well. And a non-smoker."

Katie looked at his file. That had been mentioned in a note that Ness had made. "Nobody wants a smoker," she remarked. "Not even smokers."

"And prepared to live in the country," he said. "Not everyone's happy with that, but I live on a farm now."

Katie thought about this. "Would she have to milk the

cows?" And then added, "When she's not doing the cooking, of course."

"No cows," he said. "I grow barley." He looked down at the floor. "I take it you're being sarcastic."

The accusation hung in the air for a few moments before Katie replied. "I'm not. And I'm sorry if I gave that impression." She paused. She had been unprofessional, and now she was not telling the truth. His apparent sense of male entitlement had jarred. "Actually, I was—but I shouldn't have been, and I apologise."

He shrugged. "If you think that you can't do anything for me, then just tell me. It would be better that way."

She was quick to reassure him. "David, I don't think that. Let me have a look through our files. I'll see if there's anybody with the qualities on your list, and then we can have another meeting."

He seemed satisfied with her response. He glanced at the bookcase, turning his head to read the vertical titles on the spines. "Greek myths," he said. "You're obviously interested in Greek mythology."

"My colleague's," she said. "The books belong to her."

"What is it about Greek mythology that people never seem to let it go? Troy? Diana? Icarus?"

"You're a pilot," she said. "Icarus should interest you."

He appreciated the joke. She noticed his eyes: they became bright when he smiled. He should have no trouble, she thought. Not with those eyes.

"I suppose so," he said. His gaze returned from the bookcase. "When will you let me know?"

"The day after tomorrow?"

He rose from his chair. "You've made it very easy for me,"

he said. "I was dreading this. But it wasn't so bad. You made it easy for me."

The client is thanking me, she thought. I must be doing something right.

"Don't thank me until we've found somebody."

He gave her a searching look. "Do you think you will?"

"I'm sure we will."

Her answer seemed to reassure him. "Well, I suppose you have the benefit of experience—of this sort of thing, at least."

She hesitated, and then decided that honesty required her to set him right. "I wouldn't want to mislead you," she said.

He frowned. "Mislead?"

"To tell the truth, I'm not all that experienced."

He waited.

"In fact," Katie continued, "I should tell you something—you're my first client."

He was clearly taken aback, and Katie was about to tell him that if he wanted to withdraw, she would understand. She would refund any fees he had already paid. But that was not what happened. Instead, David's face broke into a broad smile, and he said, "Everyone has to do a first solo flight. I remember mine vividly. My instructor got out after we had landed, and he said, 'Okay, you're ready to go up by yourself.' And so I did. And . . ."

"And?"

His smile broadened. "I nearly crashed."

CHAPTER FOUR

Pâté and sympathy

Katie spent the following hour browsing through client files. There were sixty of these, divided more or less equally between men and women. Ness's system was an eccentric one, with the clients arranged according to degree of difficulty involved in successful introductions and also as to outcome. At one extreme there were several files labelled *Completely Hopeless*, while at the other there were those on which she had scrawled such phrases as *Utterly Charming* and *Successfully Placed*. Her further observations in many cases made amusing reading, with feedback on dates faithfully recorded, sometimes in scandalous detail. *Made a premature and unwelcome move*, read one note; *client asked me to warn others.* And then there was *Behaves like Napoleon on a bad day*, and *needs to attend to teeth: raise the issue tactfully at some point*, and *eighteen-carat mother's boy if ever there was one.*

Then there were the occasional references to the figures of Greek mythology. One client, successfully introduced and soon married off, was described as reminding Ness of Penelope, the wife of Odysseus, who spent the years of her husband's absence weaving and discreetly undoing the same piece of work. *Penelope-type*, Ness had written. *Rather worthy, but probably loyal.* And another was described as looking *just like Athena—grey eyes, dignified, somewhat classical.* Katie tried to picture the female chartered accountant to whom that description had been given. She would be a bit severe, she thought, and . . . She read further down the page and saw that several introductions had been made, but none had been taken further by the men involved. *Too classical, perhaps?* Ness had written at the foot of the page. And then, in an aide-mémoire to herself, her cousin had gone on to write: *Any Greek men? Must check. Even half-Greek, faute de mieux.*

She found the files completely absorbing, and was only brought back to reality by the ringing of the doorbell. She got up from her desk to open the front door, her mind still on the classical-looking woman and her disappointing romantic life.

It was William.

"I wondered if you'd like a cup of coffee," he said.

She looked at her watch. "Oh, I see it's that time already. I've been looking at client files."

"Are you going to invite me in?" he asked.

"Of course. I'm so sorry. I'm . . ."

He interrupted her as he came in the door. "Oh, I can imagine. First day. No need to apologise."

"Thank you. I'm finding my way. It'll be . . ."

"It's going to be fine," he said reassuringly. "And I make the coffee, by the way. I usually come down round about this time to make it for Ness—unless she had one of her people in with her—her fleet, as I call them."

William went into the small kitchen adjoining the office. Katie watched through the open door as he took two cups out of a cupboard, and then tipped beans into a coffee maker. "Do you take milk?" he asked. "I do a pretty mean latte with this milk-frother. Ness loved it."

That would suit her too, she said.

He had his back to her as he ground the coffee. When she had met him two days earlier, she had been uncertain about his age and had later asked Ness, who had told her he was twenty-six, which made him four years Katie's junior. She had been slightly surprised to learn of his age, as he had struck her as possibly being a year or two younger than that. But then she had decided that he was one of those people whom it is always difficult to date: they might still look thirty on their fiftieth birthday, and even beyond.

He was certainly good-looking; she had noticed that immediately. His features were regular, a bit boyish, perhaps, and there was a litheness in the way he carried himself. But what was most striking, she thought, was the woollen pullover he was wearing. She could now take a closer look at that, as he had his back to her while making the coffee. It was rather like a Fair Isle sweater, with its intricate rows of lines and diamonds and its color scheme of autumnal shades—browns, greens, light greys. But there was something about it that gave it a markedly distinctive appearance—an unusual pattern that she liked immediately.

He turned with the first cup of coffee in his hand and saw that she was staring at him. "Do you approve of the sweater?" he asked.

She nodded. "It's beautiful. It really is." She paused. "Did you?" She gestured towards the pullover.

"Did I knit it? Design it?" he asked. "Yes to both. It's one of my designs—in fact this was the prototype of a sweater I designed for a big mail-order catalogue based in London. They like my work. It'll be in their next collection."

"It reminds me of something," Katie said. "It's gorgeous."

"Reminds you?"

"Of patterns I once saw in a book. A book about the work of . . ."

"Kaffe Fassett?"

"Yes, that was the name. I remember it now. It's the first time I saw his work—in that book. I was pretty taken by it."

William handed over her cup of coffee. "He's been a big influence on me. I'm not sure that I would have ended up doing what I do if I hadn't seen what he did."

They sat down. She felt immediately at ease with William; she felt that they had become friends, even after only one previous meeting, which had been dominated, anyway, by Ness. Now that they could get to know one another better, she found herself looking forward to the prospect. She stole a glance at him, and noticed that his skin was slightly tanned. Was that the lingering shadow of Australia? Relatively few people were tanned in Edinburgh, with its misty, northern sunlight, so atmospheric but so lacking in real heat. No, she thought, it was his natural coloring, and nothing to do with the sun.

He was sympathetic. That was another thing that she had picked up at their first meeting, and was now being very much confirmed. You could tell whether somebody was sympathetic even before they said anything; it was a quality that somehow manifested itself in their movements, their overall disposition, the way they looked at the world. It was always readily apparent, even when, for whatever reason, a person might be trying to appear tougher than they really were.

And a sympathetic attitude was something that Katie was ready for after James. Not that she was thinking of William as a replacement for him—she had convinced herself that she was not ready for a close relationship—but as a sympathetic friend; she was definitely ready for friendship.

The thought of James made her say something without thinking.

"Do you like libraries?" The question came out and was hanging in the air before she realised it.

William was about to take a sip of his coffee, but his hand, holding his coffee cup, was stayed by her unexpected question. "Libraries?" he said, his surprise evident in his voice.

Katie felt flustered, and again without thinking, broadened this to a larger question. "And museums too? Free museums, that is: ones that don't ask you to pay. Do you like that sort of museum?"

William took a sip of his coffee. "But of course. I love libraries. I always have. And museums too. I like the museum here in Edinburgh—you must know it. And the Scottish National Gallery, while we're about it. I like all these things."

"Good," she said.

He was looking at her enquiringly. "Why do you ask?"

She hesitated. But she felt that she wanted to tell him the truth. William was not the sort of person one wanted to conceal anything from.

"I had a boyfriend," she said. "In fact, quite a recent one . . . Very recent. He didn't believe in these things—or, rather, he didn't believe that the state should pay for them. He thought that we could have them if people who went to them were prepared to pay the whole cost."

She saw that William was listening intently, and it helped her to talk. She had not spoken enough about James, and it was part of the process of getting him out of her system.

"He also had views on things like smoking," she continued.

"He was a non-smoker?"

"As it happens, yes. But he didn't think smoking was any-body's business but the individual smoker's. He thought that it was not the government's business to tell people not to smoke or try to get them to give it up."

William frowned. "But if they don't tell them to stop smok-ing, who will?"

"That's what I thought," said Katie. "I never said that peo-ple couldn't smoke in their own space, but I thought that people should know about the risks."

"It's called health education," said William. "And of course, the state has the right to spend money on that. After all, it's the state that picks up the bill for lung disease and the clogged-up arteries."

"That's what I told him."

"And he didn't listen?"

She shook her head. "No."

William shrugged. "This guy's past tense, you said?"

"Yes."

He gave her a searching look. "Do you miss him?"

She took a while to answer, but eventually she said, "I sup-pose I did—for the first few days. But I'd decided, you see, that I didn't like him."

William looked thoughtful. "We can still miss people we don't like, you know. You get used to thinking negative thoughts about them, and then suddenly they're not there, and you feel as if something's not quite right. No negative thoughts."

"I'm going to try not to think about him," said Katie. "So, let's talk about something else. Your knitting, for instance. I find it hard to imagine that that's how you earn your living. Knitting. It seems so unlikely."

William put down his cup. "I know. But it's the same as being any sort of designer. There are people who earn their living designing cars and birthday cards and . . . well, all sorts of things. I design woollens."

"Yes," said Katie. "I see that. And there are stranger ways of earning a living . . . Such as what I'm doing at the moment." She waved a hand about the office. "This is not exactly mainstream work."

William gazed around the office. "It's worthwhile, though. And if there's a demand for it, why not?"

"And people will always need sweaters and so on."

"They will," he agreed. "And I make them as well as design them. For special clients. That's the high-end stuff, but there are plenty of people prepared to spend a thousand pounds for a knitted jacket or a pullover."

Katie found her eye drawn again to the pattern of his pullover. How did he do it? How did you get that intricate effect? She was filled with admiration.

"Did you always knit?" she asked. "When you were a boy?"

He nodded. "I started when I was eight. I had an aunt who was a keen knitter. They had a place on the coast, about two hours from Melbourne. We went there for weekends. There's this terrific beach and a river that I used to go fishing in. We would go down on a Friday and stay with them until Sunday evening. I loved it. My cousins and I used to go out into the bush. Sometimes we camped out on the riverbank. We caught fish and cooked them on a fire. My cousins made damper. Do you know what that is?"

She did not.

"It's an unleavened bread you make when you're camping. You bury it in the sand next to your fire and cook it that way. You put butter on it while it's still warm, and then you add whatever you like. Jam. Vegemite. Or you dip it in gravy or whatever."

"I love the sound of it."

"Food always tastes great in the outdoors, when you're camping. Simple things seem delicious." He paused. "And at night, the sky down there was full of stars—thousands of them. I used to stand in the mouth of the tent and look up and feel dizzy at the sight of them. I loved the Southern Cross. We thought of it as being our special constellation—something just for us, hanging there, looking after us, it seemed. I felt sorry for people who didn't have stars—we did."

"So . . . knitting. This aunt of yours taught you?"

"Yes. I watched her, and then one day I said, 'Can I try that?' She was a bit surprised because her twin boys, my cousins— Ned and Tommy, and they suited their names—were very different. They never asked to do anything like that; they just broke things and threw stones at the cat—that sort of thing. And here was I asking to knit. But she said yes, and she showed me how to do a few simple rows. It's not hard—that basic stuff."

"And that was the beginning?"

"Yes. I remember the first thing I made. It was a scarf for our dog, Harris. He was an Australian cattle dog. They sometimes call them blue heelers. They often have one eye a different color from the other. I loved him to bits, and I think he loved me back. I knitted this scarf for him and wound it round his neck."

"What did he think of it?"

"He ate it. But I didn't mind. Harris could do anything he liked, as far as I was concerned."

"Oh well."

"And so I started on other things. And I found that I really liked it. My aunt encouraged me; my father was a bit against it at the beginning, I think. He thought it effeminate for a boy to knit. That generation did, but that was the way they were. It wasn't their fault. Australian boys were meant to be tough—interested in sports mainly. Cricket, footy, so on. My old man was a bit dubious about knitting."

"That's changed here too," said Katie. "Boys are encouraged to sew and knit. They teach them at school."

"We didn't learn it at school," said William. "I went to an all-boys' school, you see. No sewing or knitting. Lots of cricket. A testosterone-endowed education."

"So you had to hide it?"

William's face fell. "I don't like to think about it," he said. "When I first went to that school, I hated it. There was institutionalised bullying—more or less. And if your face didn't fit, then you had a difficult time. Have you ever watched a group of boys together? Look at them. They punch one another. They push. There's a lot of aggression, even if it looks like friendly aggression. It's really odd, but it explains a lot about how males are. And about the world, I suppose. About wars and ecological irresponsibility and bad behaviour generally."

She knew what he meant. Boys were physical.

"I never told anybody about my knitting," William continued.

"I can understand that."

"I suppose I could have been called a secret knitter—a closet knitter, if you like. But I didn't give it up. I knitted at home, and became better and better. I knitted sweaters for everybody in the family—they couldn't believe it. And then it got out. One of the teachers let it slip, and people got to hear about it."

He told her what happened. The teacher knew his aunt, and had been told that he had knitted himself a sweater. She mentioned this in class, in the course of a discussion of hobbies, unaware of the fact that he did not want anybody to know. Some of the other boys had sniggered, and one made snide remarks. William, though, had been going to judo lessons, and he responded by flooring the principal author of these taunts, fracturing the other boy's arm in the process. That landed him in trouble with the school authorities, but it ended any unwanted remarks about his knitting. "After that," William said, "I didn't care if they knew. And a few of them were even envious. One started to learn himself, but gave up when he discovered he was no good at it. But the point was made, I think: boys can knit."

"And then?" asked Katie.

"I did a degree in textiles at a place called RMIT," said William. "It's in Melbourne, and it's probably the best place in Australia to study textiles. It was a terrific course, and I enjoyed every moment of it."

"How did you end up in Scotland?"

William looked at his empty coffee cup. "Ness always likes a second cup," he said.

"I should do whatever she did."

While William prepared their second cup of coffee, he continued talking over his shoulder.

"I worked for a few years with a firm that imported textiles. It was okay, but a bit boring most of the time. In my spare time—and I had quite a lot of that—I started marketing my own designs. I took commissions—and there were quite a few of those. Then I decided that I wanted to travel, and I ended up in Scotland, after the usual spell in Thailand and so on. I have an Irish passport, courtesy of my mother, who's Irish, as well as an Australian one. That means it's easier to work here. I decided to offer my designs to a couple of firms here in Scotland, and they said yes right away. So I set up next door."

He paused. "That's me—more or less. Nothing much to add, really."

Katie decided to ask about the fiancée. "Ness said you were engaged."

William sucked in a cheek. "Did she? Well, I suppose I am."

"Who to?"

He looked away, and Katie wondered whether her question was too obtrusive. William's manner was easy, but he might not be as open as she imagined. There were limits to intimacy in any conversation, even one as seemingly relaxed as this one.

"I'm sorry," said Katie. "It's none of my business."

He reassured her. "Oh, I don't mind. There aren't many secrets in my life." He put on an expression of mock regret. "In fact, none at all."

"Everyone has at least one secret," she said. "Everyone."

"Well, maybe . . . Yes, now that you come to mention it. But let's not go there, as they say. Alice isn't a secret, anyway. She's a medical student in Melbourne. She was a radiographer and then decided to get medical qualifications. She's got another three years at medical school. It seems to take forever to become a doctor. We've known one another since we were ten, by the way."

"A childhood sweetheart?"

He laughed. "It wasn't quite like that. We started going out when I was still at uni. It felt a bit strange at first."

"Changing from friend to lover? That can be difficult."

He agreed, and asked why she thought that should be so.

"Because it's different, I suppose. With friends there's a sort of unspoken understanding about sex. It's not there, if you see what I mean; it's *unshared*. Then suddenly it is there, as part of a mutual experience of the world."

"And that can be awkward?" William pressed.

She grappled with the idea. She found it hard to define exactly what she felt about this. It was to do with *otherness*, she thought. The friend remained an *other*, close, but not *in* one's intimate life; the lover became something quite different, was admitted to a distinct room in the private suite of one's existence—somewhere that we kept out of the sight of others. It was to do with privacy, then; or so she thought. It was something to do with that, but she would have to give it further thought, because she had not really tried to analyse these things to any degree.

"Yes," she said. "It's about privacy, I think. Something to do with that."

He seemed to weigh this. And yes, he thought she was probably right. But then he returned to Alice, to his distant fiancée. "We went out together for three years before I left. When I said I wanted to spend some time abroad, she suggested that we get engaged before I left—as a sort of gesture that we wanted it to carry on. I said yes . . ." He broke off. There was a note of doubt in his voice, Katie thought. "I'm not sure it was the right time, but I agreed with her."

"So, she proposed?" said Katie. "You didn't?"

William said he was not sure that formal proposals mattered all that much any longer. "People drift into these things. The idea of somebody asking formally is a bit old-fashioned."

"But it was still her idea?"

He shrugged. "I suppose so. But I went along with it."

"It must be hard conducting a relationship at that distance."

He said that he thought so too. "But eventually we'll get together. Once she's finished medical school, she could come over here. Or I could go back to Australia. It's all open one way or the other."

She was not sure how convinced he sounded. She also wanted to ask him what the point was of having a relationship like that—one in which they would only rarely see one another. But she did not, because she thought that a question along those lines might seem crude—as if there was no point in nurturing feelings for somebody from whom one is separated by life, by history, by geography. There were many love stories of star-crossed lovers who kept faith with one another and were eventually united—sometimes after decades of separation. It was a common romantic theme—indeed, rather touching. That was all about long-term loyalty and persistent devotion—values that were not always thought too much about in a world accustomed to immediate gratification. She remembered her grandfather telling her about a man he had served alongside in the Second World War who did not see his fiancée for five years, the length of time he was posted abroad. And yet the fiancée waited for him, as people did in those days, without making much of it. But that was then, and this was now, when it seemed that people were different. They put up with less; they were more impatient than earlier generations. Why? Because now we were used to getting what we wanted—and getting it quickly, whether it was something ordered online, or happiness itself . . .

So she did not ask him what she wanted to know, and instead she told him about her meeting with David earlier that morning. William listened. When it came to David's request for somebody to cook for him, he burst out laughing. "My God, nobody thinks in those terms," he said. "Those are old ocker attitudes. Nobody—except a completely unreconstructed man—thinks that way these days. Is he unreconstructed?"

"I imagine so."

William shook his head. "And yet that's what he wants—and I suppose your job is to find him somebody who fits the bill."

"I suppose it is. My feelings—our feelings—don't really come into it. You and I may disapprove, but he's the client."

"Yes," said William. "He is." He gestured towards the filing cabinet. "Have you done a trawl through the files? Through Ness's interview notes—her forms and so on?"

Katie told him that she had gone through most of them. A few remained, but she did not have any great hopes of discovering what she was looking for in them. "None of them says anything much about cooking. One or two of them actually say that they prefer to eat out, if possible. Not promising."

William sighed. "So, what are you going to do?"

Katie thought for a moment. "I was going to ask you," she said. "I was going to ask you if you had any bright ideas—because I don't. Ness said you sometimes helped her."

"Sometimes. I'm not sure how much use I've been."

"She said that you were often a lot of use."

William said that Ness tended to be too generous in her assessments. "She may have thought I was being useful, but I'm not sure that I was." He paused. "Although now that you come to ask . . ."

"Yes?" said Katie, encouraging him.

"I'm going to cookery classes. Right now. Tuesday and Thursday evenings. There's a cookery school here in Edinburgh. They offer all sorts of short-term courses. I've enrolled in a two-month course, held two nights a week, and covering, well, just about everything. We're doing knife skills tomorrow evening. Chopping an onion and so on. Filleting a fish. Last week we had a session on pâtés and mousses. I made chicken liver pâté—with lashings of Grand Marnier in it. I'll make it for you some time."

The offer gave her a curious sort of pleasure. It was a small thing, but it excited her, and she thought: Why should I be so thrilled that somebody should offer to make me chicken liver pâté? And the answer, of course, was because the offer came from *him*. She closed her eyes. Be careful. Don't. Just don't. This is *not* in the new plan. And then she went on to think: James never made me *anything*, let alone chicken liver pâté with Grand Marnier in it. That was because he was not simpatico, and a man who is not simpatico never thinks of offering to make chicken liver pâté for his lover—or for anybody, probably.

"Why don't you get him to enrol in that course?" William said. "You can join at any time because it's just goes on and on. They cover the syllabus in a couple of months, but then they just start over again, and so you can get all the sessions by just staying on."

"But he says that he wants to get somebody to cook *for* him. He didn't say that he wanted to cook himself."

"Yes, I know that," said William. "But the point is that almost everybody in the class is a woman. There are thirty people altogether, and I think there are only four men, apart from me. And a lot of the women are single, because one of the organisers said something to me about that. So, if you want to meet somebody who's interested in cooking, here's your pool of people, so to speak. Right there. Go to a cookery school—that's where they'll be. Simple."

Katie stared at him. It seemed a long shot, but she could see what he meant. A cookery school was exactly where a man might meet keen cooks. And all it would take would be one of these people to like the idea of marrying a man with a farm in East Lothian, with rather attractive eyes . . . and who was financially solvent, too, although nobody liked to admit to such considerations.

William seemed convinced. "I can take him along," he said. "You can enrol at any of the sessions."

"Tomorrow is knife skills, you said?"

"Yes. Haven't you always wanted to slice an onion like those television chefs do. *Chop, chop, chop* and the onion's sliced in thirty seconds. You'll have seen it on television. *Bang, bang, bang*. And no fingers lost. I can't wait."

"You'll take him—if he agrees to go?"

"You tell him that it's all part of the service."

"But he'll have to pay a fee?"

William looked pensive. "Maybe. But what I could do is this: I'm on good terms with our instructor. She's one of the owners of the school. I could come clean with her at the outset."

"And tell her why he's there? To find a wife?"

William nodded. "What I might say is that he wants to meet people. I don't think I have to spell it out. I think she'll be happy to help. I gave her one of my sweaters the other day: one of her helpers let slip that it was her birthday. She was seriously pleased, and I think she'll want to reciprocate in some way. This gives her the chance. I don't think the issue of a fee will arise."

"So we really can tell him it's all part of the service we offer?"

"Yes," replied William. "You can."

It did not take long for Katie to agree. William seemed pleased, and said that he would telephone the school once Katie had ascertained that David would be willing to try what they proposed. She called him about that before William went back to his studio, explaining that they did not have anybody particular on the books who might be suitable, but they had had an idea. She went on to tell him about the cookery school and William's suggestion. David, although slightly bemused, agreed that the idea was worth trying. "You people certainly think outside the box," he said.

"Boxes are there to be thought outside of," said Katie.

It was rather an apt thing to say, she thought, and she would try to remember it. It was not every day that one said anything memorable, and this, she thought, was a good sign. Running the Perfect Passion Company was going to be fun, and, she hoped, it might just bring happiness to a few people—just might.

CHAPTER FIVE

Knife skills

Arrangements were made. The cookery school class was due to begin at six in the evening; David would arrive at the offices of the Perfect Passion Company in Mouse Lane at five-thirty and would walk with William to the cookery school, which was in Broughton Street, a couple of Georgian blocks away. William had already spoken to Julia Macfarlane, who was part-owner and deputy-principal of the school—a title that she herself described as too grand by half.

"I am a teacher of cookery skills, pure and simple," she said. "They think that having a deputy-principal raises the tone. I don't, but there we are."

Julia was the instructor to whom William had given the sweater, and, as far as she was concerned, he could do no wrong. His results had been disappointing, for some reason, on the evening on which the class had practised the art of making a light and airy soufflé, but she had blamed the oven for his flat and discouraged-looking concoction; then he had burned his onions when he should only have softened them—so easily done, if one's attention wandered, and the heat beneath the pan became too fierce, but she had said that this was due to inferior butter; and as she stood at the top of the class and demon-strated some aspect of the culinary arts, her eye, if it wandered at all, inevitably seemed to wander in his direction. She knew, though, that he was off-limits. The age gap was too wide, and she had a sharp nose for the ridiculous; she was in her early forties and there yawned between them a chasm of eighteen years. May and December romances were tricky—they could work—but then she had heard from one of the other members of the class that he was engaged—"some girl in Australia, such a tragedy"—and so she put all thought of a closer friendship firmly out of her mind.

Not that it was theoretically out of the question, of course; she was a divorcée whose ex-husband, Colin, had been the edi-tor of a classic car magazine—and incapable of talking about anything other than classic cars. She had never worked out why she had married him in the first place—it was, she con-fessed to friends, in a fit of temporary absent-mindedness, and for reasons she could not recollect. The old adage, *Marry in haste, repent at leisure*, an ancient piece of folk wisdom, applied without qualification in her case; such truisms irritate us with their well-worn banality, but are so often irritatingly true. And yet, in spite of her realization of her mistake, she was loyal to Colin, and, unlike so many who are dissatisfied in their mar-riage, she did not try to blame him for what went wrong. In her account of the marriage, she was the one at fault for being unable to take a proper interest in classic cars. "I should have tried harder," she said. "I let Colin down. I should have made more effort."

In the result, it was Colin who made the first move. Julia began to suspect—or, rather, hope—that he was seeing some-body else, and eventually he made a clean breast of the affair, confessing that he was involved with a well-known rally driver

called Tanya Turnbull. Julia had seen Tanya's photograph crop-
ping up rather frequently in the pages of the classic car magazine, and that had made her wonder whether there was
anything between her and Colin. When he wrote an article
singing the praises of Tanya's performance in the Sahara Challenge, a major event that took place in Morocco every three
years, she became suspicious; and when she examined more
closely the accompanying photograph of the prize-giving ceremony, her suspicions were confirmed. Colin was pictured
standing in a group of rally drivers, all wearing white rally
outfits festooned with advertisements for car part firms and
oil companies. Tanya was not next to him, being a couple of
places away, but the photograph caught the moment when the
two of them were looking at one another with frank adora-
tion. The picture must have been chosen for inclusion by the
magazine's picture editor, as Colin would surely have realised
that it gave something away; but it was published nonetheless.
He assumed, perhaps, that Julia did not read the magazine and
would not see it, but on this occasion she did.

It required very little effort for her to unearth his private
credit card statement. It told the story clearly enough: there
were several payments for restaurants in Casablanca and for
a hotel in the foothills of the Atlas Mountains. He had told
her that the trip was entirely a working one and involved little
more than attendance at the ceremony at the end of the rally.
If that were the case, then he would have used his business
credit card rather than his personal one. She challenged him,
and he made his admission. "I didn't plan it," he said. "It's just
somehow happened." Then he added, almost apologetically,
"You know how it is."

She was relieved. "I fully understand," she said. "But look:
no recrimination. None. No, seriously; I mean it. I promise

you: I'm not cross with you. And you might as well introduce me to her if we're going to do this in a civilized manner. I don't hold this against you, Colin. All I want is for you to be happy." She did not say that her own chances of happiness were now markedly improved by his thoughtful embarking on an affair.

He had been astonished by her readiness to accept the end of the marriage—and grateful too. He took Julia to Tanya's garage outside Perth, and the two women met. Julia noticed that Tanya's fingernails had a layer of black grease beneath them. That was to be expected, she imagined, from her calling as a restorer of classic cars, but she had had to suppress a slight shudder. Tanya had said very little, and there had been several lengthy silences, but Julia was relieved that the meeting had taken place.

"She's really interesting," she had said to Colin on the way home. "The two of you will make the perfect couple."

"Do you think so?" he asked. "Do you really think so?"

"Well, you have a lot in common, don't you?"

"I suppose so." He paused. "You've been so good about it all. You really have. And I didn't want to hurt you, you know. I never wanted that."

"Very few people want to hurt other people," she said, which was untrue, she reflected, because she thought there were many who were perfectly content to do just that, and actively sought that precise goal.

"That's true," he said. "Yes, I suppose that's true."

She wanted to say something positive about Tanya because she felt grateful to her. And Julia, through an entirely natural kindness, unlearned but intuitively felt, was not one to be uncharitable. "She must know a lot about cars."

"She does. She drives a 1969 Chevrolet Camaro. It's a beauty."

She disliked cars that ended in a vowel. It was, she had

always felt, a bad sign. "There can't be many of them around." Fortunately, she thought.

"You can say that again," said Colin. He paused. "I hope that you're going to be all right."

She made an effort not to answer too quickly. "I'll be fine," she said. "I've got my job. The school takes up a lot of my energy. And it's rewarding work. I'll be all right." She might even have said, "I'll be better": her world had shrunk during their marriage; now her horizons, she hoped, would enlarge.

"Cooking is so creative," he said. "You can put your soul into it, can't you? Just like cars. You can put your soul into a car you're working on, you know. Lots of people don't seem to understand that."

She nodded. "They don't, do they?"

"No, they don't. They think cars are just . . . well, just cars." He gave a look that invited her to join him in his exasperation over the failure of people to understand. She inclined her head in agreement: people obviously did not understand—that was clear enough.

There was very little else to say. The divorce was easy. Everything was split down the middle, apart from the two classic cars, both of which went to him. "They mean more to you than they do to me," Julia said.

"You're really kind," he said. "If only other people could bring their marriages to an end in such a grown-up way."

"Yes," said Julia. And sighed.

"I think you should have the dog," he said. And then, reacting to her response—the dog, an insecure Cavalier King Charles spaniel, was difficult—he went on, "No, don't object; please don't. I really want you to have him."

That was three years ago, and was an increasingly distant memory. Now Julia thought only very infrequently about her marriage, and immersed herself in the affairs of the cookery school. That had been a success in every way, including in the commercial sense, and this had enabled them to spend money on the refurbishing of the large demonstration kitchen in which they conducted the courses. The equipment was modern, the stainless steel food preparation surfaces smooth and gleaming, the rows of gas cookers all installed to the highest and most expensive specification. Julia was proud of it all, and it was in this kitchen that William introduced David to her.

If David had been at all ill at ease, Julia very quickly reassured him. When he began by saying that he knew nothing about kitchens and cookery, she told him that that was the whole point about going on a course. "You won't be alone," she said. "Quite a few of our students are starting from scratch—particularly the men."

She looked apologetic as she said this. "I'm sorry; that's a bit tactless. It's just that some of the men who study with us haven't had the chance to do much in the kitchen."

William laughed. "That's not tactless—that's putting it extremely tactfully. They don't know the first thing because they've been spoiled by being cooked for by their mothers, and then by their wives."

David said nothing.

"Tell me," Julia asked, "what are you particularly interested in learning?"

David shrugged. "Everything, I suppose. Starting with how to boil an egg."

Julia smiled at that. "There's an element of skill even in that," she said. "And we do actually cover it in our syllabus. Eggs can be over-boiled, you know."

"Just like lobster," said William. "Lobster mustn't be over-cooked, or it becomes rubbery."

"We covered that, didn't we?" said Julia. "It's a very important bit of cooking lore."

"Well, I don't know anything," said David.

Julia had fixed him with an enquiring stare. "But you're keen to learn?"

He hesitated, but only for a moment. "It would be useful," he said.

Julia's phone rang, and she saw that it was a call she had to take. She excused herself, leaving William to take David to a spare stool beside one of the work surfaces. In front of each place, a set of knives had been laid, like a surgeon's tools on a theatre trolley. On a plate at each station, a whole fish had been placed, ready for filleting.

"She's going to throw us in at the deep end," said William. "Filleting fish isn't easy. It's far harder than chopping vegetables, which is what we'll do later on."

David picked up a knife and tested it against his thumb. "Not all that sharp," he said.

"We're going to be taught how to sharpen knives," said William. "We'll learn all that."

Other members of the class drifted in, and soon all the places were taken. William saw that David was observing the new arrivals, summing them up, he thought. This was a good sign: the whole scheme was a long shot, but at least David was going to take it seriously.

Julia returned from her phone call, and the class began. Knives and their different uses were discussed. Weight and balance were compared, and then, as a preliminary, sharpeners, looking to all intents and purposes like toolbox files, were distributed. The techniques of sharpening were demonstrated amidst the sound of steel on hardened steel. William watched as David followed the demonstration and tried his hand at preparing blades. He watched him, too, as the technique of handling knives was explained. Grip, said Julia, was all important: on how one held the knife hung everything else. Then there was posture. One had to stand correctly to handle a knife the right way: one was not to slouch. Throughout the class, people stood up straight. William saw that David pulled his stomach in and squared his shoulders, as if on parade. He was taking knife skills seriously.

Onions were distributed, and then carrots and large, peeled potatoes. As the class watched, Julia reduced these ingredients to small chopped and julienned piles. Her knife moved with such speed that it was hard to follow. She slowed down, and they all peered at the vegetable under the perfectly controlled blade.

"She knows what she's doing," whispered David.

"Yes," said William. "She does."

The chopping of the vegetables was followed by a demonstration of the filleting of fish, and then it was the turn of the class to try. William saw that David wielded the knife with confidence and control. He saw him glance at Julia, and then stand up straight; that was interesting. All about them was the sound of metal blades on chopping boards.

"You're not bad," said William.

David seemed pleased with the compliment. "It's rather enjoyable," he said. "I like the feel of it."

Julia walked round the class to look at people's results. She offered encouragement here and suggestions there. When she reached David, she was impressed by what she saw: neat, unjagged fillets, with very little loss of usable flesh. It was a perfect result.

"Very professional," she said. "Are you sure you haven't done this before?"

"Not in this life," David answered.

Julia grinned. "Well, you've done it extremely well."

"Beginner's luck," said David, modestly. But he was clearly pleased, and now he washed the blade of his knife under a nearby cold tap, drying it carefully with a pristine white tea towel.

"Try another onion," she said. "Show me."

David peeled the onion and then placed it on the chopping board.

"There's a poem about this," said William. "Have you heard it?"

Julia looked interested. "A poem about chopping onions?"

"Not quite. About peeling them. The poet says that onions are like memory—both make you cry. Onions have layers, and they make you cry as you peel them back, just as the layers of memory do."

David was more interested in the task before him. "Shall I chop?" he asked Julia.

She nodded, and he set about the onion, slicing it down the middle and then attacking each side—and attacking, too, the middle finger of his left hand.

The blood discolored the translucent white flesh of the onion.

"Stupid," muttered David, as he dropped the knife onto the chopping board.

Julia, uttering a sharp cry of alarm, leaned forward to examine the cut. It was a small red line, along which the dots of bright red were a tiny ellipsis. The staff of cookery schools are used to cuts, most of which are minor things, minute duelling wounds in the friendly daily battle against potatoes, fish, onions. This was no more than that, and she was relieved. "It's not too bad," she said. "It'll need a plaster, though."

"Really stupid," muttered David, wrapping his handkerchief around the injured finger. A red stain appeared through the fabric, spread out only very slightly, and then stopped. Julia had gone off to a cupboard at the side of the room and returned with a plaster and roll of surgical tape that she now gently, and expertly, applied to the affected finger.

"I'm so sorry," she said. "My fault. I should have . . ."

"Known I'd do something stupid?" interjected David.

The humour defused any tension in the situation. It made William, who had been surveying the scene nervously, burst out in laughter. He had been worried that he would have to report to Katie that the client had been badly damaged—lost a finger, perhaps; had been exposed to raging septicaemia; had died. Now he need say nothing, other than to pass on the news that there was a minor incident of friendly fire—and he might not even need to do that.

"I should have asked you to practise a bit more, before giving you that slippery onion."

"No," insisted David. "My fault entirely. Trying to run before I can walk."

"Well, I hope not too much harm done," said Julia.

"Very little," said David. "In fact, none. A cut finger doesn't count as damage—at least not in my book. I'm a farmer, you know, and farmers get knocked about a bit."

Julia looked concerned. "You're being very good about it," she said.

He smiled at her. "It's nothing. Nothing at all."

William continued to observe. There was a very detectable warmth in these exchanges between David and Julia, and it suddenly occurred to him that David's visit was proving successful in a way in which neither he nor Katie had imagined it would. He looked away. If what was between them was a tender plant—and it must be that at this stage—he did not want to inhibit it by blocking out the light. He thought: I feel a headache coming on—one that will require me to leave David here to get on with this at his own pace. And even if a real headache was not coming on—and it was not—a diplomatic headache would be justified in the circumstances. So he sidled up to Julia and explained that his sinuses were feeling a bit blocked, and he hoped she would not mind if he left David with her.

She was quick to assure him that this was perfectly all right; more than that, he felt, she brightened at the suggestion. From this, he concluded that Julia clearly liked David. And that meant that the Perfect Passion Company had succeeded—at least in the objective of making an introduction. He had not been thinking of Julia herself for David, but there was no reason why she would not do. David wanted a cook—well, that was what she was. They had found him somebody who was eminently well-qualified for the role that he had in mind. He would never find a better cook than Julia, no matter how far he searched. The thought lightened his mood. He felt ebullient. It was no more than an initial introduction, but there was something in the atmosphere that made him feel that this was going somewhere. It was an energy that one could not necessarily define, but was unmistakable. When two people are interested in one another, a light appears in their eyes. It can neither be measured nor described, but you know when it is there; it is obvious. It was there now. These two were going to get along. Love at first sight? People argued about that. Some said that it did not exist; that it was a fond illusion, the creation of songwriters and armchair romantics. Yet William believed in it even if he thought it would probably never happen to him: he was engaged to Alice. If you were engaged to somebody, you had made them a promise, and he believed in keeping promises. That had been drummed into him at home, as a boy, and it had lodged somewhere deep in his psyche. Besides, he could not hurt Alice; he could not hurt *anybody*, really.

He thought of Katie. No, he told himself. Don't think about it; put it out of your mind. Don't make a fool of yourself by saying anything to a woman who's older than you are, who knows that you are engaged, and whom you hardly know anyway. Be sensible—that's all, and, above all, don't complicate your life. You don't *need* to be involved with anyone else. You have enough to do, and Edinburgh, and all this, is temporary. Katie is attractive, and interesting, in a way in which a slightly older person may be. You like her sense of humour. She's sharp; she's witty. But that's it, so think of something else.

He remembered that as the advice that the chaplain at school had given the boys in one of what he embarrassingly called his fireside chats. "You may be tempted to think about the physical side of love, boys," he said. *Us? The very thought.* "But here's some advice for you. When that happens, all you have to do is think about something else. That's all. Simple. It works."

<hr />

Katie was impatient to hear how the lesson had gone. She resisted the temptation to call William that night, and waited until the following morning to get his report. She rang the bell beside his office door shortly after nine, but there was no reply. She did so again at ten, with a similar result, and she began to wonder whether something had gone wrong. Perhaps the whole thing had been a disaster, and William was now too embarrassed to tell her what had happened. She tried to think of possibilities, but could think of none. She would just have to wait.

He rang her bell shortly before eleven. "Coffee time," he announced. And then, seeing her expression, he went on, "I'm sorry. I was late in this morning. I couldn't sleep last night and only dropped off at about three. Sometimes I lie there and think—you may know what it's like. And the more you think, the more wakeful you become."

She told him she knew exactly what he meant.

"You'll be wondering about last night," he said.

"I was giving it the occasional thought—yes."

He caught her eye. "I should have phoned you. Sorry. It went really well."

She relaxed. This was very good news indeed. "Tell me," she urged, as he switched on the coffee maker. "Every last detail."

"He cut his finger."

Katie frowned. "There? At the cookery school."

William laughed. "I thought I'd give you the bad news first. Yes, but only a tiny cut. Not much more than a nick, actually. He was chopping an onion, and I suppose he was a bit too confident."

Katie shivered. She was squeamish about blood. Blood was fine in its appointed place, inside the veins. Beyond that, it was disturbing. She hated to watch men shave with anything but an electric razor. There could be blood; there often was. It was a miracle that more men didn't cut their throats, accidentally, of course, particularly when they went to Turkish barbers and the Turkish barbers got out those large open razors and . . . She shivered again.

"That was the bad news," William continued. "The good news is that he met somebody."

"First time?"

"Yes. Last night. Right there—under my eyes. He met the instructor—you know, the one I gave a sweater to for her birthday. Julia—as in Julia Child, the famous cookery writer. But Julia Macfarlane, in her case. They met, and wham! Electricity! Two hundred and fifty volts—at least."

Katie listened in astonishment as William described the feeling that he had detected between them. "Think in terms of magnets," he said. "It was like that. Same thing."

"And is she available?" asked Katie.

"Completely," said William. "She's divorced—I know that much. Some racing driver type, I think. Anyway, he's off the scene. All she has is a dog who's a bit neurotic, apparently. She's one hundred per cent available."

"And have they arranged to meet—outside the cookery class, that is?"

William was not sure. "I thought you should send him a message," he said. "Ask him how he thought it went."

"Possibly," said Katie. "Or we can leave it and see how it develops."

"Maybe do that," said William. "But I'm telling you, this is going to work. If you had been there, you'd have seen it yourself. Chemistry—pure chemistry." He had abandoned the metaphors of physics—electricity and magnetism—for those of the chemistry lab. "Instant reaction. It was like when you put potassium in . . ." He tapped his forehead. "The science bit never really stuck."

"Thank heavens for chemistry," said Katie.

"Yes," said William, handing her the mug of coffee. And

then, almost to himself, muttered "chemistry" this time, with a slight note of sadness, as if lamenting lost knowledge—equations once understood and now hopelessly confused in a jumble of forgotten symbols—or, alternatively, as if reflecting on the arbitrary nature of chemistry between people. We can fall in love with the wrong people because Cupid's darts are sometimes misplaced, or fired in a spirit of mischief.

But Katie did not hear him. She had seated herself behind her desk and was making a note in David's file. *Report from the field: initial meeting reported to be successful,* she wrote. And then added, *cautiously optimistic,* before striking out *cautiously.* She asked herself: Why be cautious? This peculiar business in which she found herself should, if anything, be bold, adventurous, heady. It claimed in its very name to be about passion, did it not, and passion, as everyone knew, was indifferent to caution—as everyone who had suffered from passion knew. *Suffered from . . .* Was that really the right way of putting it?

William was looking at Katie. She was lovely—but he reminded himself of what was possible and what was not. Sometimes virtue can be a burden—as it was now for him. But the virtuous tend not to complain about their lot, and so he set his lips in a firm line of determination and contemplated his coffee.

He's pursing his lips, thought Katie. Why? Is there something wrong with the coffee? Too bitter?

The lure of Italy for the Italophile

For a few weeks the cooking lessons came and went. David attended religiously. He bought a book on Scottish cuisine and both volumes of Julia Child's *Mastering the Art of French Cooking*. He also acquired, at considerable expense, a set of cook's knives, made in Japan, and sold with a special carrying case. The handles were made of cherry wood, and the knives were designed to balance in one's hand for perfect chopping. They were used, their leaflet claimed, by chefs in all the great kitchens of the world. Chefs left them to their friends in their wills; culinary museums lined up to display them.

He showed Julia these knives at his next class, and the book on Scottish cuisine too. She said, "I can see you're getting bitten by the bug. I'm so pleased." And then she added, "There is a cook within each and every one of us. Few people are without an internal cook."

If she was pleased, then so, too, was he. He had been indifferent to cooking before he started the course; now he found himself fascinated by it. He began to try at home some of the recipes he had read about in his newly acquired books, or in *The Creative Kitchen*, one of the cookery magazines that he picked up from the local newsagent. He began to take an interest in the source of food, and engaged in long and detailed conversations with the butcher in Haddington, the town a few miles from his farm. The butcher knew exactly which herd his beef came from, and how long it had been hung. In the supermarket, he began to look with disdain at the generic sausages and the olive oil marketed as being "from more than one country," as the bottles put it in their small print. He started to seek out oil from single estates, garlic from particular regions of France, and obscure cheeses from parts of Italy he had never heard of—hilly regions in which hardy shepherds tended their goats.

William was bemused. It was clear to him now that the interest that David showed in Julia was entirely reciprocated. He noticed that during the coffee break they drifted into each other's company, and that their conversation was animated in the way in which the conversation of lovers may be. And yet, when he asked David about whether he and Julia were seeing one another outside the cookery school, he was answered with a shake of the head of sufficient curtness to indicate that he was being cautious. William reported this back to Katie, who said that she thought this was a good sign. "Some people who have fallen in love don't necessarily want to broadcast the fact in case they jeopardise their prospects. Let them get on with it."

William asked Katie about how she would bill David for the introduction. "Will you wait until something happens?" he asked. "Will you do something when it becomes . . . official?"

Katie said she would wait and see. She had been studying the company's billing system, and it seemed to her that there were wide variations.

"I think we'll stand back and see how it develops," said

Katie. "There are enough funds in the company accounts to keep us going for a long time."

She had been puzzled by that. Ness had told her that the company had a substantial working capital, but had not said how much it was. When Katie looked at the bank statements, she saw that substantial was possibly an underestimate: the operating account was awash with cash. So she did not feel under any pressure to levy a further fee on David—nor did she feel the need to canvas for further work. Each week, she saw one or two existing clients and arranged a new introduction for them or listened to their verdict on an introduction that had already been made. The pace of business was slow, but Katie rather liked it that way. In the gallery in London there had been times when she had struggled to keep up with the demands of the job. Now, by comparison, the day's routine was perfect: a late start, a few letters and phone calls to deal with, and then coffee with William. That lasted an hour, and they got through a wide agenda. William talked a bit about the news from Australia. His twin cousins, Ned and Tommy, were getting married—at a joint wedding. They were marrying two sisters, and they were going to spend the honeymoon together in Bali. Katie was not sure that she liked the idea of a double honeymoon, but William seemed unfazed by it. "As long as everybody remembers who's married to whom," he said, and then blushed. Katie laughed. "I'm sure they will," she said, but she was not.

And William had his misgivings too. "Those girls," he said. "I'm not sure that they're the best choice for Ned and Tommy, but their parents are putting a brave face on it. The sisters may be all right now—they weren't when they were teenagers. They were both arrested once for fighting. That doesn't happen all that often."

"Fighting with one another?"

"No, with two other women in a bar."

Katie raised an eyebrow. "They sound a bit tough."

"They are," said William. "They both go to body-building classes. That's where Ned and Tommy met them."

"Do they knit, I wonder?" said Katie.

William, who missed the irony in her question, snorted, "Definitely not. They wear leather, not wool."

"I see."

"But Ned and Tommy seem happy enough," he went on. "I had an email from Ned the other day. He said that he and Billy—that's his fiancée—have found a place they're going to buy. It's part of an old house in Fitzroy North. He's very pleased with it. Melbourne can be expensive, but they're getting this at a reduced price because it's being sold by a cousin of Billy's mother. She owns a big hairdressing place out there."

"Billy is a woman, is she?"

"Yes, she's definitely a woman. The name's misleading. I think she's called something else on her birth certificate. Wilhelmina or something like that. Her sister's called Norm. But that's short for Norma, not for Norman."

There were other things to talk about. There were the new designs that William was working on. There was the impending visit of a buyer from one of the London fashion houses. She wanted to talk about knitted evening wear and had also expressed an interest in taking some of what William called high-end creations. "She's pretty high-end herself, this woman," he said. "Very plummy voice. I can't understand a lot of what she says."

"The opposite of Billy and Norm?"

William laughed. "It would be interesting to see them all

together." He paused. "Getting back to David: he's going to have to make a move sooner or later. I'm sure the time is right."

"Declare himself?"

William laughed. "You sound seriously old-fashioned. People don't declare themselves. They call it hitting on somebody. That's a bit more direct, I'd say."

Katie stood her ground. "Not here," she said. "Not in the Perfect Passion Company. Nobody hits on anybody here. That's not the way we put it." Even as she spoke, she reflected on how quickly the Perfect Passion Company had become *we* and *us*. If corporate culture had to be learned, she had done that remarkably quickly.

"What do you do then?" William asked. "Make a pass? Do people still say that: Do they still make a pass?"

"They do. All the time. Or they ask other people out. Or they get to know one another better. Or, possibly, become an item."

"All the same thing," said William. "But I wonder when he's going to do any of that."

"In his own good time," said Katie.

Which, as it happened, was the following Friday, when David and Julia met for dinner in a small Italian restaurant off Leith Walk, not far from the cookery school. Julia had suggested it when David had first issued the invitation. "Could we have dinner together?" he asked. "You choose the place—I'm happy with whatever."

She accepted. "I love going out to dinner. It's a relief not having to cook."

He hesitated. He was not sure what to say. Did she dislike cooking? Or did she just have too much of it?

"It's just that I spend my entire day cooking," Julia went on. "The last thing I want to do is cook at home."

The last thing I want to do is cook at home. He pondered this. Then he said, "Yes, I imagine you get fed up."

"I do," she said. "Can I let you in on a little secret? I order a lot of takeaways. Thai stuff. Indian curries. Pizzas. All delivered to the house. My own kitchen at home is more or less empty—virtually unused."

"I see," said David. He could not hide his disappointment.

Julia was looking at him quizzically. "Are you shocked?"

He was, but he did not say as much. "I thought that you would spend a lot of time in your own kitchen. I imagined that the meals at your place would be something special."

This prompted her to laugh. "Well, you thought wrong. I'm a real slouch at home. Never cook. Hardly ever hoover. Oh, I know I should make more of an effort, but when you have to do what I do in the cookery school all day—and on several evenings a week with your classes—well, you can imagine that I just want to put my feet up."

He said that he could. He was the same, he said. He had never really cooked at home. "I was hoping one day . . ." He stopped himself. He had almost let it all slip out, but of course he could not confess to what he had been hoping for. Besides, something had changed—and now he confronted that change. David wanted to cook now: he had discovered a real interest in cookery. And that meant, he suddenly realised, that everything was suddenly different. He did not want somebody to cook for him—he wanted somebody for whom *he* could cook.

They went to dinner. The restaurant made much of being Italian. "Return to Sorrento" was playing when they went in, and still playing when they left, after an intermezzo of assorted Neapolitan pieces. The dishes were suitably obscure, and were featured under unpronounceable dialect names. Squid and octopus appeared in varied guises: there was not a pizza nor a bowl of spaghetti carbonara in sight. The wine was all southern Italian: Puglian and Calabrian, or from the dark soils on Etna's slopes. There was a picture of the volcano on the wall, and below it, by accident or design, an antique Italian sign, *VIETATO FUMARE*, no smoking, in elaborate script.

"It's a few years since I was in Italy," said Julia. "I first went there as a student. I travelled with a girlfriend. We started in Rome and travelled south to Calabria and then right down to the deep south. Then we went to Bari. I've been back many times since then. I love Italy."

"Who doesn't?" said David.

"I'd like to go back soon," said Julia. "I'd like to go back and try all sorts of dishes I've never tried. Sample wines that never make it out of the country but that are utterly wonderful. Go for walks through hills with cypress trees and olive groves."

"Perfection," said David. "I must go too. I really must."

There was a brief silence. Then he went on, "I really need to get myself organized. The trouble is that one talks about all sorts of things one wants and never seems to get them done."

She took a sip of wine. "My trouble too."

He took a deep breath. "Can you get away? Does the school keep you tied down?"

"I can get away all right," she said. "We're well-staffed."

He fiddled with the menu. "Perhaps you might care to accompany me. We could make it something of a gourmet tour—something like that."

She did not hesitate. "That's a wonderful idea, David."

He felt a flood of relief. "Let's make it soon."

"Good idea."

It was their first date, and yet there they were, he reflected, arranging to go off together. But why not?

They talked a bit more about Italy. There were other things to discuss: the striped cathedral in Siena, hill villages in Tuscany, the Dolomites. Then they got on to flying, and he told her about the microlight aircraft he kept on the farm. "It has one of those fabric wings," he said. "The seats are suspended underneath, and the engine's at the rear. It's dead simple. You need hardly any runway to take off—it's really a motorised kite, but it's a real thrill." He paused. "I'll take you up if you like."

"That would be a thrill. Thank you."

"Next Saturday?" he asked.

She had to think for only a moment before she said yes. Next Saturday would suit her very well.

"Provided the weather's all right," David warned. "But it's settled at the moment, and the forecast is good." He looked at her. "You're not frightened, are you?"

She said that she was not. But she asked him what would happen if the engine failed. "Would we drop like a stone?"

He shook his head. "Not at all. We'd become a glider. We'd glide down perfectly safely."

"That's reassuring."

He laughed. "I wouldn't want to lose you."

He bit his tongue. He should not have said something like that, he thought. It was too early. He did not want to frighten her off. But she did not seem to mind. "Nor I you," she replied.

He cast his eye up, at the picture of Etna. *C'è la luna mezzo mare*, sang a tenor, infectiously, in the background; through a glass panel in the kitchen door, he saw a chef beating time with a spoon.

Ell had said that she would drop in to see Katie in her office. "I love the idea of you sitting there," she said, "in your Perfect Passion Company office—dispensing happiness like some benevolent Cupid."

"It's not like that," said Katie. "It's very ordinary. There's a desk and some filing cabinets and a chair for the client to sit on. That's about it."

Katie suggested that her friend should drop in at coffee time. "I have a sort of colleague," she said. "He doesn't exactly work there, but he sort of does. He gives me advice and helps a bit. He makes the coffee too."

Ell worked in an investment firm, and enjoyed flexible working hours. She suggested that Katie name a day, and she would be there. And when she rang the bell on the agreed morning and made her way into Katie's office, she stopped and clapped her hands with delight. "Where the magic is worked. Romance HQ."

"We do our best," said Katie, with a wry smile. "And now that you come to mention it, we've just had a bit of success."

"Really?"

"Yes. Something we arranged worked. Two people have found one another in . . . well, I suppose one would call it midlife."

Ell sat down in the client's chair. "How about me, then?" she said. "Got anybody for me?"

Katie laughed. "I didn't know you were looking?"

"On and off," said Ell. "You never know when a nice guy will turn up. You have to keep an open mind."

Katie wondered about the investment firm for which Ell

worked. It was a large concern, and there must be a good number of eligible men. Weren't large offices just the sort of place to find a man? Ell shook her head. "No such luck. It's packed full of actuaries and physicists who have given up on string theory and gone into financial model making. They're a particular type—heads full of figures. Where's the romance in that? Not for me, I'm afraid."

"What is your type, Ell?"

Ell smiled. "Are you going to put me on your books?"

"No. I'm just interested."

"Gentle," said Ell. "Artistic, but not precious about it. A good sense of humour. Civilized. Is that enough—or is it too much?"

"No," said Katie. "There are men who fit that description, I imagine." It was her own list, too, but she did not say that.

"I don't seem to be meeting them," said Ell.

Katie looked at her watch. William was slightly later than usual, but now she heard his key turn in the lock. She had given him a key to the office to save herself the trouble of having to let him in. And she regarded him as staff now, in spite of the fact that he was not on the payroll.

He came in and, not realising that Ell was there, immediately blurted out, "You know what David told me at the class last night? He's taking Julia up in a microlight. He's . . ." He broke off when he noticed Ell. "Oh, sorry."

"This is Ell," said Katie. "And don't worry—she's not a client."

Katie saw that Ell was admiring William's sleeveless pullover. She said to her friend, "This is William. And yes, he actually knits those himself. And designs them."

Ell said, "It's lovely. It's the most beautiful jersey I've ever seen."

Will accepted the compliment gracefully. "It took a bit of time."

"I bet it did," said Ell. "It should be in the Scottish National Gallery. Framed."

"Oh, it's not that good," said William. "I've done more complex pieces than this." He paused. "Are we all for coffee?"

"We are," said Katie.

She watched Ell, who was looking at William as he prepared coffee. It was obvious: Ell had noticed William. Katie could see it in her expression. *Interest.* That described it perfectly.

Ell realised that Katie was watching her, and she turned back to face her friend. She looked slightly sheepish—like a child caught doing something forbidden. Katie mouthed a word soundlessly, "Engaged."

Ell turned back to look at William again through the open door of the kitchen. It seemed to Katie as if she was mentally undressing him. She shook a finger at her friend; William could not see—he had his back to them.

Ell smiled. "I'm going to the theatre tonight," she said. It was a statement but also, Katie thought, an invitation—and it was left hanging in the air.

William returned with a cup of coffee that he passed to Ell. "I hope it's all right," he said.

She took the mug of coffee from him, and for a second or two their wrists touched. William withdrew his hand. Had he noticed? Katie asked herself. Could one be indifferent to that sort of obvious interest?

William could not stay long. He had a deadline to meet, he said, and he had to have something ready. Within ten minutes of his having arrived, he was closing the front door of the office behind him, leaving Ell and Katie alone together.

"Well," said Ell. "He's rather nice."

"Yes," said Katie. "He is. Very."

"What were you mouthing to me back then?" asked Ell.

"Engaged," said Katie. "William's engaged to some medical student in Melbourne." She paused, and then continued, "I'm sorry about that."

"Oh well," sighed Ell, and then, with a smile, added, "It's ever thus. But Melbourne's a long way away, isn't it?"

Katie gave her a challenging look. "It's no use," she said. "He really is engaged."

"Then why is he over here?" asked Ell. "If he's so committed to this medical student, why is he in Scotland? Doesn't that suggest to you that he might be just the smallest bit lukewarm? And if that's the case, then isn't he available?"

Katie felt a flush of anger come over her. Available? Sweet, gentle William was not *available* to anybody. Ell had no business flirting like this, doing this ridiculous moth to the candle dance. It was simply not appropriate. Now she felt protective of William, in the face of this shameless statement of intention from Ell.

"He's younger than you. He's only twenty-six," Katie said.

"Nothing wrong with that," said Ell quickly. And then she said, "Do you fancy him yourself? Is that why you're trying to put me off?"

"I told you," Katie retorted. "He's engaged. Taken. Reserved."

"No man is engaged, taken, reserved until there's a marriage certificate," said Ell. "And all I'm saying is that I find him rather dishy. One glimpse, and that was it. Oh, weak and foolish me." She stressed the final sentence like a bad actor.

"Drop it, Ell," said Katie. "Please just drop it."

"Somebody just experienced a sense of humour failure," said Ell. "But seriously, I did rather like him. There's nothing wrong with that, is there? We're all human. I wouldn't mind putting him on the mantelpiece of my flat—just to look at."

Katie looked serious. "You were flirting with him. I could tell."

"Was it that obvious?" asked Ell.

"Yes," Katie replied. "Extremely obvious. And I think he might have noticed."

Ell shrugged. "I don't care. For all you know, he may like the look of me. Not all men run a mile if they detect female desire. Some do, I'll admit. It can make some men feel anxious. But that's all to do with male insecurity, isn't it?"

"Is that what you call it? Female desire?"

"Well, what else is it?" asked Ell. "Remember: we can be just like men now—if we wish. No need to be coy." She suddenly grinned at Katie. "Look, I'm not serious. I'm only having a bit of fun. I haven't fallen for him. Your young friend is perfectly safe. I was only winding you up, Katie. Female desire and all that. Big cliché."

"You weren't . . ."

"Of course, I wasn't," said Ell. "He's nice enough—in his woolly, Fair Isle sort of way. But I wasn't seriously eyeing him up, for heaven's sake. What do you take me for?"

They both laughed.

"Sorry," said Katie. "Let's talk about something else."

"Tell me about your success story?"

Katie hesitated. "I can't give you their names. Confidentiality."

"Of course," said Ell. "But what made it work?"

"An interest in cooking," said Katie. And she told Ell the story, including the parts related to her by William. Katie listened with interest. Then she said, "That's going to work. It's obviously going to work. It's a great story."

"I think so," said Katie.

The conversation drifted. The ease of their relationship—the comfort of an old friendship—seemed somehow to have been strained by their brief exchange over William. Ell said that she had not been serious, and perhaps that was true, but Katie told herself now that she had not misinterpreted the look that Ell had given William. That had not been simulated—that was real. And it was a look of *interest*—she was positive about that. Of course, she reminded herself that one should not lay too much store by that. William was strikingly good-looking, and the most common reaction to beauty in any form was a sort of surprise, a look of wonder, in a sense, that such harmony should exist. That was what our aesthetic response to beauty was all about. And that, of course, was as innocent as it was unavoidable; there was nothing untoward in that. No, Ell had no plans in relation to William; Katie felt that she could reassure herself about that. But even as she thought that, she reflected on her own motives. Was it a jealous desire to stop somebody else thinking about something that, if she were to be truthful, she wanted herself? Was *she* the one who wanted to put William on her mantelpiece, as Ell had put it, and was that why she should have felt so uneasy over her friend's light-hearted bit of flirting?

In spite of her flexi-hours, Ell had to get back to her office. "A very tedious meeting lies ahead," she said. "Compliance issues. We have to be so careful about everything we do now—everything."

Yes, thought Katie. You should be careful. There were compliance issues in friendship, just as there were in the world of finance and business. Everyone had to be careful—about everything.

They made a vague arrangement to meet for lunch at some

point in the following weeks. And there was a party that Ell had been invited to and had been told she could bring a friend. Katie, Ell thought, might know some of the people who would be there and might like the chance to reconnect. Katie said she would, and they said goodbye at the office door, which Katie then closed.

For some reason she stood there for a while, just inside the small entrance hall, thinking. And after a few minutes, she heard voices outside, on the common stair that linked the various offices and flats. She heard William's voice, and she wondered whether he was talking to Bobby, the postman, whom they all liked and who was always ready for a few friendly remarks about the weather or the state of the world. There was another voice, though, and she now recognised it as Ell's. Ell was talking to William on the stairs; he must have been going out or coming in just at the time that she chose to leave.

Katie felt the back of her neck go warm. This always happened when she became upset or anxious. It was warm now. She moved closer to the door, conscious, as she did so, of the fact that she was like that parody of the eavesdropper, ear glued to a keyhole or a crack.

She could hear them. She could.

Ell said, "Could you give me your phone number then?"

Katie drew in her breath.

And William said, "Sure."

Then Ell said something else that Katie could not catch, but she heard William mutter something that sounded like *no problem*, which was something that he often said. And then silence, except for steps on stone, and then a door opening somewhere, and more silence.

CHAPTER SEVEN

Microlight descending

"It's so small," said Julia. "Tiny. And flimsy. Isn't it a bit flimsy, David? Are those wires strong enough?"

They were standing before David's microlight aircraft in its shed. The shed was on his farm, at the edge of a field of mown grass. From the outside, one might have expected to find that it contained some piece of agricultural equipment, or bags of fertiliser, or, as many sheds do, nothing at all. But this one contained a working microlight aircraft, with its kite-like wing stretched above its two seats, its rear-mounted engine, and its small aluminium propeller. Rigging of taut plaited-metal wires held the whole thing together. There was a smell of petrol in the air, and on the floor beside the aircraft an open toolbox and a large can of engine oil.

"Everything's very strong," said David. "The rigging is checked every time I use it, and the whole thing is serviced by a good mechanic."

"So, it's . . . what do you say? Fully airworthy?"

"Precisely. That's the term. Yes, it is." He paused. "You don't have to go through with this, you know. You can change your mind, and I won't be in the least bit offended." He smiled at a memory. "I brought a friend out here once, and he changed his mind just as we were beginning to taxi out onto the field. He said that he wanted to get off. We cancelled the flight. Pity, but I didn't mind. This is meant to be fun—that's the whole point of it."

He looked at her. He did not want her to feel that having said that she wanted to come, she could not now call the whole thing off. Yet, somehow, he felt that she did not want to do that. And now she said, "No, I'm really keen on doing it. I love the idea. I've seen people in these and thought how exciting it must be, to be up there, with the wind all about you and the whole world down below. I imagined it must be like being a bird."

"It is," he said. "That's exactly what it's like. You're a bird. Soaring. Nothing around you but the air. It must be exactly how birds must feel. Naturally they take it for granted."

"Just as we take it for granted being people," said Julia.

He looked at her, and suddenly, at that exact moment, he realised that he loved her. Up to that point, he had liked her; he admired her; he thought that there was a future for them. But all of that had been selfish, in a way, because he had been thinking of himself, and of how she fitted in with his world. He had wanted her to cook for him. It was like employing a nursemaid or, indeed, a cook. That was all. It was human—and understandable—enough, and yet he was vaguely ashamed. Now he felt that he wanted this for her, not for him. As these thoughts came to him, they were almost as a reproach. He wanted to do something *better*: he wanted to embrace her, not to kiss her, but just to hug her, to protect her, to hold her close to him. That was all. He felt a tenderness: that was what it was, he thought, a tenderness. And that, surely, was much the same thing as love—not that he had thought about these things before. He had never thought about the meaning of love, and there were many reasons for his failure to do that. He was a pilot, and now a farmer, and he had always concerned himself with ordinary, practical things, and he had never looked much below the surface of the tides that carried us through life. They were just there; they existed; and he had gone along with them, as most of us do.

He gestured towards the plane. "I'll push it out, and then we can strap ourselves in."

"Those wheels look like pram wheels," she said.

David laughed. "They probably are. Nobody uses those old prams any longer, but their wheels are much in demand."

He pointed to a flimsy-looking contraption suspended immediately behind the pilot's seat. "That's yours," he said. "I'll strap you in."

She manoeuvred herself into position, and David, leaning across her, helped her fasten the cross-straps of her safety belt. Stepping back into the shed, he brought out a helmet, that he adjusted and gave to her. Then he put on his own helmet and climbed into his seat.

The engine was directly behind her, and she gave a start as it stuttered into life. She felt the wind being sucked past her and the vibrations of the rigging and the canopy above them, the wing with its stretched fabric. Their lives would depend on that thin surface, the tightened wires, the tubes that were the veins carrying fuel into the engine; everything relied on fixings remaining in place, on nuts and bolts continuing to do their appointed job, on David continuing to be conscious while at the controls.

She remembered reading a newspaper report of a passenger in a light aircraft who had been obliged to land a plane when

the pilot had a heart attack. He had been talked down successfully by the control tower; how would she cope if she had to
do a similar thing? Could she even reach past him to take control of the levers by which he was now steering them out onto
the grass of the make-do airstrip? As she thought of this, they
began to pick up speed. The aircraft bumped and rattled as the
engine propelled them faster and faster, until, with a sudden
jolt, they were airborne. She gave a little cry, an exclamation,
but it was quickly swallowed in the rush of air and the din of
the engine. She looked up, towards the taut, stretched material
of the wing that was now taking the strain of their ascent. It
was rippled at the edges, where it was joined to the bars that
were the wing's skeleton.

The ground fell away below. They were over the line of a
hedgerow, and then over a stand of trees, the green of the fo-
liage moving in the breeze. Then they hit a pocket of rising air,
and she felt its warm hand beneath them, pushing them up
further. There were clouds off to their right, and somewhere
there was the flat blue surface of the sea. She did not have time
to work out exactly where they were, to look for familiar land-
marks, because they were banking over to the left, and there was
nothing beneath her on that side but the ground down below,
getting smaller. She saw a tractor crossing a field; it looked
like a child's plaything, with a toy man seated on it, driving
across chocolate-brown earth. David pointed at the tractor
and shouted something that she did not catch. She assumed,
though, that it was his tractor, the earth his field, the toy man
the man who helped him on the farm. She waved, and smiled,
and shouted *yes*, which would cover everything, she felt.

The aircraft levelled out, and they began to fly to the west.
Edinburgh was before them, Arthur's Seat, the hill that domi-

nated the city, a crouching lion. Cars crawled along the motor-
way to Glasgow, a never-ending stream of traffic; and there,
straddling the Firth of Forth, were the three bridges, each a
steel poem of arches, towers, strung-out wire cables. Over his
shoulders, she watched his hands at the controls, making tiny
adjustments to their progress through the air. She suddenly
felt the urge to put her hand upon his shoulder, and she did.
He half-turned round to see if there was anything wrong, but
she simply smiled and mouthed the words *This is so lovely*. He
made a thumbs-up sign and turned back round.

They were heading, he had said before they took off, for a
place he knew, not far away, barely twenty miles or so, in the
hills to the south of Peebles—a quiet glen where there was a
field on which they could land. He knew the farmer there—
they were friends. They could go for a walk, perhaps, before
they took off again. There was a burn nearby they could explore.

Now they were approaching Peebles, and she saw the bridges
and the great Victorian bulk of the Hydro Hotel. Then the
road snaking off to the south and the glen that was their destination. She looked up at the sky, beyond the wing, and she felt
that she was part of it. On the ground you did not feel that—
the sky was above you, distant; now that sense of separation
was simply not there. She was part of the sky, part of the wind
about her.

They flew over the field before he began his approach to
land. There were a few sheep clustered at one end of the field,
and they looked up, confused by the sound of the engine,
before returning to their grazing. David indicated, by a movement of a hand, that he was going to circle round before he
came down to land. She nodded; she understood. She looked
at the hills. They were closer now, and lower than the sum-

mits about them. It would be so easy, she thought, to fly into a hillside if there was mist or darkness. But David knew what he was doing, and everything was clear in the bright unfiltered sunlight of morning.

They dropped down further. Now objects below seemed to speed up as they passed by: a stand of trees, a drystone dyke, a trailer filled with sacks, parked by the side of a road. And then the field itself. It seemed to be coming up at them so quickly, and she could see clumps of grass, with reeds growing out of some of them; and the sheep that had seemed like grey stones when viewed from above were now sheep once more, and were moving about, disturbed by the intrusion.

They touched down. The aircraft bounced back up, and then dropped again, landing more heavily this time. She gave an involuntary cry at the jolt—a suppressed *oh*—but now they were rapidly slowing down as the engine note changed, coughed, and then became silent. David turned round to her and smiled. "Landed," he announced.

She laughed. "It was so easy."

"It is," he said. "Even birds can do it."

They freed themselves from their harnesses and climbed out of the seats. Julia looked about her, at the field and at the hills beyond the stone dyke. The sheep had stopped moving about, but were staring at them, trying to make sense of this strange visit from above. David pointed to a small stone building beyond a gate.

"That was an old bothy," he said. "Shepherds used it. Jack— he's the farmer—did it up for hikers. Not many people use it, but some do." He unwound the scarf he had been wearing. It was warm in the sun. "Let's go and take a look."

She followed him across the field. Beside the gate there was a stile, that they both climbed. He held her hand as she clambered over, but then he let go of it. She had hoped that he would not.

They approached the bothy. It was the simplest of buildings—a single room, under a slate roof, strong enough against the weather. The door was black and had been painted recently. Beside it was a small sign, which she bent down to read. YOU ARE WELCOME IN THIS BOTHY. THERE IS FIREWOOD AT THE BACK. PLEASE EXTINGUISH ANY FIRES BEFORE YOU LEAVE.

"I love that tradition," said David. "The idea of having a shelter for people is such a kind one."

She agreed. "That sort of thing is disappearing, I suppose. The Scottish idea of welcoming strangers . . . well, it's become rarer, I suppose."

"I don't want Scotland to become like everywhere else," said David.

"No," she said. "Neither do I."

He pushed open the door.

She stepped through the doorway. She stopped. She looked at David. He said, "I think they must be expecting us."

She took another step forward, towards the small trestle table that had been set up in the middle of the otherwise empty room. It was covered with a white tablecloth. There were several plates on it, knives, forks, a serving dish. There was a basket of bread rolls.

David said, "I think this is our picnic." He pointed to the serving dish. "That quiche," he said. "I made it."

"You?"

"Yes. I got the recipe from that book I showed you. It's my second quiche—I did a trial run."

She struggled to find words. "You mean . . ."

"I brought all this over yesterday. I left it with Jack at the farmhouse. His daughter set this up for us. I thought you might like the surprise."

She reached out and touched his forearm. Then she kissed him on the cheek, and he put his arms about her. She said, "Oh, my goodness." She could not think of anything else to say, and so she repeated, "Oh, my goodness."

There were two folding chairs. They sat down and had their picnic. The quiche, she said, was perfect; she could not fault it, even had she wished to do so, which of course she did not.

There was a flask of coffee. He poured some out for her. She said, "I loved being up there, you know. I loved every moment of it—even that bumpy landing."

He said, "Would you like to learn how to fly one of those things?"

She nodded. "I think so."

"I could teach you," he said. "You taught me how to cook—I could teach you how to fly."

"All right."

"Provided that you marry me," he added.

CHAPTER EIGHT

A salmon roulade

William lived in his work studio. Although on the same landing as the office of the Perfect Passion Company, he had a different configuration of rooms, an extra one at the back being used as a bedroom. Most of his living, though, was done in the large room used as a studio, one end of which had a sofa and easy chairs, a dining area, and a low table covered with books, magazines, and papers.

They sat facing one another from opposite ends of the sofa, William, wearing a kaftan shirt and jeans, his legs tucked underneath him, Katie in a loose Indian-print dress that she had bought on her last trip to Kerala. They held glasses of chilled white wine and before them was a plate of small round oatcakes on which William had arranged slices of smoked salmon.

"I've prepared something special," William said. "Everything we're going to have this evening I learned from the course."

Katie said that she was looking forward to the meal. He had not given her much notice—the invitation had been extended the day before—but she was free and had accepted it.

"I get a bit bored cooking just for myself," William said. "I like having somebody to share things with."

"I feel the same," said Katie. "Occasionally I just make scrambled eggs on toast. Or I open a can of soup. Simple things that require next to no cooking."

"I used to live out of tins," William said. "And those ready-made meals you get in supermarkets. That's all changed since I started the course. I hardly use convenience food any longer."

"That's probably a good idea," said Katie. "Those ready-made meals are full of salt and sugar, aren't they?"

"So we're told. Do you read the lists of contents printed on the packaging or the tin? So many grams of this; so many of that. Carbohydrates per hundred grams and so on. It doesn't make cheerful reading."

"No. But . . . but I suppose if people are too busy to cook."

He was unconvinced. "We're all getting lazier."

She took a sip of wine. "What about Alice? Is she keen on cooking?"

She had no sooner asked the question than she regretted it—a shadow had crossed William's face. It was clear to Katie that he did not want to talk about his fiancée.

"I mean," Katie continued hurriedly, "if you're a student, then you don't have the time. I didn't cook all that much when I was a student. I did sometimes, but the temptation was always just to get a pizza or something like that. Scotch pies—we loved those, and they were dead simple."

But William wanted to answer. "She does a bit. When she has the time, she can cook fairly fancy things. She likes making hot dishes. I'm not so keen on curries. I can take them, of course, as long as they're not too spicy. She goes in for really hot ones. Vindaloo. Have you ever had that? There's a government health warning on that one."

"I heard of an Indian restaurant," Katie said, "where you have to sign a consent form before they serve their hottest curries."

They both laughed, and the moment of danger seemed to have passed. Or so she thought.

"We don't always see eye to eye on everything," William said.

Katie said nothing.

"On some quite important things," he continued. "Not just curries."

She waited. If he wanted to speak about this, she would let him, but she was keen that he should not think she wanted to learn about their differences. She remembered James, and how they had disagreed about virtually everything. It could not possibly be that bad between William and Alice.

Eventually she said, "Politics? Do you disagree on politics?"

He shook his head. "No, not really. I think we both vote the same way—in fact, I know we do. That's never been an issue."

"Do you think that it's possible to be happily married to somebody of a very different political persuasion—or even to be in a relationship with them, let alone marriage. For example, if you were a communist—a real Marxist—planning the revolution, or a fascist, say—could you get into bed . . ."

"Literally into bed?"

She smiled. "Yes, and metaphorically: Could you get into bed with somebody who believed in liberal democracy? It could be difficult."

William considered this. "It could be. But it would be more difficult the other way round, I think. If you were the democrat and the other person was a fascist or whatever. Fascists probably find it easier to be involved with liberals because fascists will quite happily use people." He paused, and took another sip of his wine. "No, it's not politics. It's more . . . I suppose, intellectual matters. Alice hardly reads anything. She doesn't get fiction. I love novels. I love Shakespeare. She's never, ever read a Shakespeare play or been to see one. Never—as far as I know."

Katie was careful to choose her words. "That's a bit of a gap. But people can still get on even if they entertain themselves differently."

This seemed to discomfort William. He shook his head. "No, I really don't agree with that. I think you have to have *some* common ground in these things."

"Does she read any novels at all?"

He looked thoughtful. "I don't think so."

"What about films?"

"We have different tastes. She doesn't like anything historical."

"No Jane Austen?"

"She won't watch that sort of thing at all."

Again, Katie was cautious. "But surely you must have some things in common. You're not Jack Spratt."

William looked blank. "Jack who?"

"Jack Spratt. It's a nursery rhyme. *Jack Spratt could eat no fat; his wife could eat no lean*."

"I see," said William.

"It's about incompatibility—at least on the surface of things. Most of these things have some sort of little moral in them, or refer to an actual event. *Ring a ring o' roses* was all about the plague, I gather. Pretty sinister."

Other lines came to her, unbidden. *The farmer needs a wife, the farmer needs a wife / Heigh-ho the derry-o / the farmer needs a wife.* And then, *The wife needs a child, the wife needs a child / Heigh-ho, the derry-o / the wife needs a child* . . . And then the child needed a dog, and the dog needed a bone, and then we all patted the dog.

Would children be allowed to sing that these days? She was not sure that the social reality it portrayed would be approved of: farmers needing wives and so on—this was all too patri-archal, too conventional for modern tastes. And yet farmers, if they happened to be men, did want wives, and they often hoped that their wives would help run the farm. And many of the wives would say yes, we do need a child, because that's what many women—and men too, of course—wanted. And then it occurred to her that this is exactly what the Perfect Passion Company was doing for David. He wanted a wife who could cook for him. They had tried to provide just that. As it happened, they had inadvertently reversed everything. They had introduced him to a potential wife who did not want to cook, while, equally inadvertently, they had sparked his interest in culinary matters. At the end of the day, everything worked out; they had created the set-up that he had in mind any-way: a comfortable domestic arrangement centred in a warm farm kitchen somewhere. What was wrong with that? Noth-ing, she thought, even if there were those who would consider it stifling.

William answered her question about interests. "Yes, we do have interests in common. We definitely do. And I do love her."

As William said this, he cast an anxious glance at Katie. She wondered whether he was trying to convince her, or him.

"I'm sure you do," she said. "You're engaged to her, after all. You're going to marry her."

"Yes."

There was no enthusiasm in his voice, she thought.

He rose to his feet. "I'd better go and get things ready in the kitchen. I haven't got much to do—it's mostly ready."

"I can't wait," said Katie. She was pleased that this awkward conversation had come to an end. She had formed the impres-sion that he wanted to unburden himself, but that he was not quite sure how to go about it. Or he wanted to share his feelings, but felt ashamed of the way he felt. This was his loyalty, she imagined. He had made his bed, and he was going to lie in it because he did not want to disappoint Alice.

As he rose to his feet, she said, rather quietly, "Loyalty is an odd thing, you know. It shouldn't necessarily tie you to something that's not right for you."

She feared that she had gone too far, but it was almost as if he had not heard her.

"I'm happy," he said.

She was not sure how to take that. She thought that it was sometimes the case that people who said *I'm happy* were not. It was like whistling in the dark. You did it to convince yourself of something that you were not at all sure about.

They made their way to the table, where William served the first course, a salmon roulade. "Julia taught us to do this," he said. "The first time I tried, it was a failure. It was too floppy. Then I got the gist of it. I hope this is better."

Katie sampled it. "Perfect," she said.

He sat back in his seat. "I've been thinking about our first case together," he said.

She was pleased that he said *our.* That was what she wanted: the Perfect Passion Company to be a *company.*

"Yes," he went on. "If you look at it, everything went the opposite way from how we intended. David wanted a cook, and he got one, but cooking at home—for him—was not what she had in mind."

"So it would seem."

"And then he, being the non-cook, discovered that he was a cook after all, and presumably he'll do the cooking for her."

"Probably."

"And then he takes her up in his plane and offers to teach her to fly. That's what he said he did, anyway. And now they're planning to get married."

"Success? I think so. And I suppose we can send a bill now. It'll be the first fee I've earned since I took over."

He smiled. "I wonder how our next case will go."

Katie thought for a moment. "It could hardly be more surprising."

"No, I suppose not."

He looked at her fondly. "May I ask you something?"

She held her breath. And then she said, "Yes, of course."

"One of these days, may I knit you a sweater?"

She said she would love that.

"Natural colors?"

"Of course."

He said that he would not be able to start it just yet. "I have rather a lot of orders stacked up. Do you mind?"

She did not. "I'll wait as long as it takes."

"Fair Isle pattern?"

"I'd love that."

He refreshed her glass of wine. She raised it to her lips. The light was in it.

PART II

*A Laborer in the
Vineyard of Love*

CHAPTER ONE

Friends, lovers, etc.

The growing appeal of William's knitwear could have meant that he had no time to do much else other than to design and knit. Yet he seemed increasingly keen on involving himself with the Perfect Passion Company, and Katie regularly sought his advice on a whole range of issues. Sometimes, though, they simply chatted, as they were doing now, over a cup of coffee when nothing else was happening.

She enjoyed these moments, as did he. William was younger than she was by almost four years, but the disparity between their ages seemed to make little difference. There were some twenty-six-year-olds who were still surprisingly immature, Katie thought, but William was certainly not one of those. He *understood*, she told herself; he empathised. He was one of those people who could sense what it was like to be you—it was as simple as that. People who had that gift gave you their full attention, which, after all, was what most of us wanted. And we did not like the opposite of that: it was particularly annoying, Katie thought, to find yourself talking to people who patently could not be bothered to listen to what you had to say, or, if they listened, were clearly indifferent to what they heard.

She remembered somebody she had met in London who was just like that—a minor art critic who seemed to be at every gallery opening and who had made a point, it seemed to her, of forgetting her name.

It was this issue of attending to others that, as it happened, Katie and William were discussing that morning as they sat in the office, Katie behind her desk, and William leaning against a filing cabinet. William, Katie had observed, liked to lean, which he did with an appealing nonchalance. Everything about him was appealing, though, as far as she was concerned, and so it was no surprise that when it came to leaning, he should lean in an attractive manner.

"You could always sit down," said Katie, gesturing towards the chair before her desk. "You might be more comfortable."

Nursing his mug of coffee in clasped hands, William shook his head. "No," he said. "When I'm in my studio, I usually sit down. I like to stretch a bit."

"You should do yoga," said Katie. "Lots of stretching."

"I've done it in the past," said William. "Back in Melbourne. I went to yoga classes for two years. Our teacher was amazing. She could bend herself right over until she was the wrong way up—or most of her was upside down. You found yourself talking to her feet, which were where her head should have been." He paused. "You know something? You can say things to a person's feet that you can't say to their face."

Katie burst out laughing.

"Not that I ever did," said William, with a smile. He took a sip of his coffee. "You were saying this critic would come into the room and look about him to see if . . ."

"If there was anybody worth talking to," said Katie. "Yes, he came to the gallery openings. People like that love gallery openings."

William made a face. "I can't stand those things," he said. "You can't get anywhere near the paintings because the place is full of people drinking wine and chatting to friends. The pictures might as well not be there."

Katie agreed. For two years she had attended monthly openings at the gallery in which she worked in London, and she had seldom enjoyed them. She felt sorry for the artists, who were sometimes completely ignored on these occasions. At one opening, she had seen the artist mistaken for a waiter and asked to fetch a glass of wine; at another, she had heard somebody delivering a scathing criticism of the work on show without realising that the person he was addressing was the artist herself. Those were egregious examples, but there were many lesser humiliations in store for artists at their openings, especially in the earlier stages of their career.

She pictured the critic she had been describing to William. She had not thought about him for a while, and now he came back to her, dressed in his habitual blue-striped seersucker suit, his salt-and-pepper hair swept back into a slightly ridiculous ponytail, his expression one of bemused superiority.

"He churned out art crits for a London magazine," Katie said. "But apart from that, nobody really knew what he did. He was everywhere—at all the openings—and he seemed to know everybody. But his real interest was talking to people he thought were influential. If he spoke to you at one of the openings, he would look over your shoulder to see if there was anybody more interesting. It was so obvious."

William shared her distaste. "Awful," he said.

"Yes. But it made me think about how the rest of us manage friendship. We have our faults. The way we choose friends, for instance—is it always . . . on the basis of who they are, or is it sometimes to do with what they have?"

William frowned. "Surely not. Because they're well off? No."

"No," said Katie. "Life isn't a Jane Austen novel. But if you think about it, are we really indifferent to whom our friends are? Does it matter if they're rich or broke? I'm not saying that I'd seek out the friendship of people simply because they have money, for instance."

William looked at her reproachfully. "I should hope not."

"Although there are lots of people who do just that," said Katie.

"Maybe. But then they're . . . they're just that sort of person."

Katie nodded. "Yes, they are. But, if we're honest with ourselves, don't we choose friends because of what we think we might get from the friendship?"

William waited for her to explain.

"I mean, we like people who *mean* something. At least, I do. And maybe that's because we think that some of the things our friends do will rub off on us. We think that being around interesting people makes us more interesting ourselves."

William looked doubtful. "I don't see how that works. You don't get to play the violin by hanging out with a famous violinist."

"No, you don't. But the truth is that we *feel* better when we're in the company of people with something to say, people who are fun."

William thought about this. Then he said, "Blondes have more fun. Did you know that?"

She laughed. "So they say. But I'm not sure."

"David Hockney thought they did. He saw a commercial that said exactly that, and he went off and dyed his hair blonde. He never looked back."

Katie thought of her friend Ell, who was one of those people who were on the verge of being blonde, depending on the light. Was Ell's hair color natural, she wondered? And did she have more fun? She remembered Ell's play for William—her flirting and the overheard conversation on the landing outside the office door. William had not mentioned her since then, and Katie had no idea whether or not he and Ell had been in touch. She did not like to ask, though, nor even to think of it, because it made her feel hot and bothered. Perhaps it had all blown over. Perhaps there had been no phone call between them.

She said, "I could ask my friend Ell. She's a blonde—sort of."

William looked away, and Katie realised that she had touched a nerve. She should not have said what she said—she must have sounded sarcastic, even sharp, which had not been her intention. William was gentle: he seemed to dislike barbed remarks, and she had just made one.

"Actually, I didn't mean that," she said quickly. "I'm sure Ell doesn't touch up her hair. It's natural, I think—and it is quite blonde, I suppose."

But once again, the *I suppose* had sounded a jarring note. She tried to backtrack. Now she said, "I'm very fond of Ell, you know. Very fond." She swallowed. Half-truths, or even things that she wanted to be true even if they might not be, had always made her swallow. She understood the expression *to choke on a lie*. She would be hopeless, she felt, on a lie detector. "We go back a long way. We've known one another since we were eight." That, at least, was true. She and Ell had played Snakes and Ladders together, and now she remembered something: Ell had cheated. But that was a long time ago.

She hoped that this recollection of their long friendship would make up for what had gone before. Now she asked, "Do you think one might become blonder by spending more time with blondes?"

William laughed, and the tension dissipated. "Seriously,

though, when people—your clients—tell you that they're look-ing for somebody with some characteristic or other, are they doing that because they feel something will rub off?" He paused. "You were telling me the other day about a man who was looking for an artistic woman. He was very insistent about that, you said. Why?"

"I assume he was looking for common interests," said Katie. "People like to be interested in the same things. It gives them something to talk about."

"But what if he wasn't artistic himself?"

"Then it might be because he admired artistic people," said Katie.

"So, she could be making up for some perceived inadequacy in himself?" said William.

"Possibly," Katie replied.

"Do you think that people feel they can be . . . what's the right word? Improved? They feel they can be improved by meeting somebody who represents what they'd like to be—but aren't?"

Katie hesitated. She could see what he meant, but she felt that it was an odd view to take of what went on between peo-ple in a relationship. She was not sure that she saw anything wrong in admiring somebody for qualities that you yourself might not have. And if admiration then went on to a desire to possess, then that, again, was just how things had always been, and would continue to be. Human nature was not always what we wanted it to be.

William looked at his watch. "You said you had somebody coming at eleven?" It was already ten minutes to.

Katie finished off her coffee. "Yes, thanks for reminding me."

"Anybody interesting?" asked William.

Katie told him she knew nothing about the client who was

shortly to arrive—other than that his name was George and that he had sounded secretive when he phoned to make the appointment. "His voice was lowered," she said. "It was as if he was frightened—as if he was expecting to be interrupted and the phone snatched away from him."

William was intrigued. "Could I sit in?" he asked. "I feel I sort of work here now, and I won't interrupt."

"Of course," said Katie.

She was pleased with his offer. She liked being in his company; she liked to share with William. He's one of these people who rubs off, she thought, and smiled at the idea of it.

"Something funny?" William asked.

Katie shook her head. "No, not really."

The bell rang.

"I'll answer it," said William. "I'll bring him through."

He put down his coffee cup and moved towards the door. Katie watched him. There was something in the way he walked that struck her. She tried to think of a verb to describe it, but failed to find one. She liked it. It might not suit just any man, but it suited William. William was not *just any man*; there was nobody quite like William, Katie thought.

CHAPTER TWO

Sharks and emails

William showed George into the office, where Katie was already standing beside her desk, ready to shake hands with her new client.

"This is . . ."

George looked ill at ease. "George Fane," he said. "I hope you were still expecting me."

"Of course I was," said Katie. "And I'm Katie."

George nodded. "We spoke on the phone."

Katie introduced William. "You two have already met, of course."

William smiled at George, and gave him a little wave. George inclined his head slightly in acknowledgement.

"William works with us," Katie went on.

There, she thought: I've said two important things. William *works*, and he works with *us*.

William nodded. He turned to George. "How are you doing, mate?" he asked.

Katie struggled not to show her surprise. It was a quintessentially Australian phrase from William. Australian men addressed one another as mate as naturally, and as frequently, as

Frenchmen called one another monsieur. *Mate* was a term that carried a whole hinterland of significance—of friendliness and lack of formality. It made a statement. But she had not expected that quite so soon from William, who did not fit the stereotype of the Australian male. He knitted, for a start. But that stereotype was outdated, of course—Australia had changed.

George replied formally. "I'm fine," he mumbled. "I'm doing fine."

Katie invited George to sit down, and then went behind her desk to sit down herself. William leaned.

"William prefers to stand," she said, in an effort to put George at his ease. "He likes to stretch, don't you, William?"

"Yes," said William. "I like to stretch."

George glanced from Katie to William, and then back to Katie. He waited.

Katie fiddled with a piece of paper in front of her. Then, making eye contact with George, which was difficult, as his gaze moved away nervously, she said, "I don't know if you're fully aware of what we offer here in the Perfect Passion Company. You may have read a bit about us." She looked at him enquiringly. "Have you?"

George inclined his head. "There was an article in *The Evening News*. I read that."

Katie smiled. "That said some of it. But perhaps I could fill you in with a little more."

"All right," said George. He had come in with a scarf, a light silk scarf of the sort that suited the cooler summer weather that had settled over Edinburgh. Now this dropped from his hands, and he reached down to pick it up off the floor. Katie took the opportunity to give him an appraising glance. He was a man somewhere in his thirties, she thought. He was reasonably well built—not weak or skinny—and he had one of those comfortable faces that while not being entirely unmemorable were nonetheless not the sort of face to be easily brought to mind. He had brown hair, cut fairly short, and he was clean-shaven. His clothes were, like the man himself, nothing remarkable. The word *timid* came to Katie's mind. George was too large to be truly timid, but timidity was a matter of manner and attitude, as much as physical presence, and Katie sensed a slight air of mousiness about George.

She remembered Ness's advice and looked at his shoes. They were brown brogues, well-polished, which told her something—if Ness was to be believed. They looked like Church's shoes, she thought—the English footwear company that proclaimed the virtues of solidity and reliability—once again, if Ness was to be believed.

The scarf retrieved, George looked up, and his eyes met Katie's briefly and, she thought, apologetically.

"The first thing I'd say is that we do our best," Katie began. "We do our best, but we can't guarantee anything. We may be able to introduce you to somebody we think you may get on with, but we aren't miracle workers."

George grinned weakly, and Katie, in a moment of embarrassment, realised that what she had just said was, in one interpretation, tactless. It implied, she thought, that George would need a miracle.

"In the sense that we can never be certain if people are going to get on," she said hurriedly.

William came to her rescue. "What Katie means," he said, "is that although you may be the sort of guy really to appeal to women, as I bet you are, there's no telling how things will work out. Chance plays a role, you see."

George had not taken offence. "Chance comes into everything," he said. "You never know, do you?"

Katie gave William a thankful glance. "No, you don't, do you? Some people seem to get all the luck, and then some get none at all."

"That's right," said William. "I knew somebody who went swimming back home and had a shark bite his leg. Not a great white or anything like that—one of those smaller, nippy sharks you get. Anyway, he got this bite and had to have a whole lot of stitches. He got better, and then he went swimming again—and there was a shark scare. Everybody had to get out of the water."

George winced. "That's bad luck."

Katie thought, absurdly, of a note for her profile of George: doesn't like sharks. She tried not to smile.

"Too true," said William.

"Perhaps it's safer not to go back in the water," said Katie. "Once you've been bitten, that is."

"That's what I pointed out to him," said William. "But you know what he said to me? He said that statistically he stood a much smaller risk of being bitten by a shark after he'd been bitten that first time. He could swim with impunity and not have to worry. The reason is that the odds on being bitten twice by a shark are infinitesimally small."

George looked thoughtful. "Are you sure about that?" he asked. "I would have thought that anybody going into the water, whatever has happened in the past, faces the same risk. The risk at that point is unaffected by what's gone before."

Katie nodded. "That sounds right," she said. "Maybe you should do a course in statistics, William."

She took the initiative once more. "But the odds of our finding somebody we can introduce you to are pretty good."

"Yes," said William. "They are."

"We need to know a bit about you, of course," Katie went

on. "We have a sort of questionnaire I can give you, but a personal chat is, I think, a bit better."

"I don't much like questionnaires," said George. "Ticking boxes and so on. It's too much like work."

"All right," said Katie. "But you don't mind my asking you questions?"

George did not. But then he frowned. "This is just between us?" he asked.

"Of course," Katie reassured him. "You, me, William. That's it."

George still looked concerned. "And you won't try to get in touch with me at home? Or at work?"

"Not if you don't want that," said Katie.

"And no emails?"

Katie hesitated. "We have to be able to communicate, you know. And email is the obvious way. Or texts. We could do texts, if you'd prefer."

George twisted the scarf in his hands. Katie noticed. This was the body language of anxiety.

"Email is pretty confidential," Katie suggested.

George looked at her, and she saw that in his eyes there was an unspoken appeal. "Other people read mine," he said quietly.

Katie raised an eyebrow. "Do they know that you know?"

George did not answer. "Texting might be better," he said. "But please don't put anything too sensitive in a text." He paused. "If you don't mind, that is."

Katie found herself feeling sorry for this man. And then something occurred to her, and immediately she felt foolish. Of course! She should have realised it right at the beginning. *George was married, and his wife read his emails.*

She felt a sudden surge of anger. That was a very basic rule, she thought, and she should have spelled it out to him. The Perfect Passion Company did not exist to help married men to find somebody with whom to have an extramarital affair. How dare he.

She took a deep breath. When she spoke, her tone had become icy. "I take it that you're single."

William looked up sharply. Perhaps he had reached the same conclusion about George, Katie thought.

George looked back at her in complete surprise. "Of course, I am."

"Have you ever been married?" Katie pressed. "You aren't in the process of getting divorced or anything, are you?"

George shook his head vigorously. "I told you. I'm single. I've never been married. Ever."

Katie felt that she had to explain. "It's just that you said some-body reads your emails. I thought that might be your wife."

"I haven't got a wife," protested George. "I told you that."

"A secretary then?" asked Katie. "Do you have a secretary who reads your emails?"

George looked miserable. He shook his head. "It's my mother," he confessed. "She reads them. My mother."

This disclosure was followed by silence. Katie glanced at William, who was staring at George in disbelief.

"I know it sounds a bit odd," said George. "But the situation is this: I live in our family hotel. It's the family business. There's a computer in the hotel office. That's where my emails go, and my mother comes into the office and looks at emails. I've seen her. She reads mine as well as the ones that are addressed to the hotel."

"Does she know that you mind?" asked William.

George looked down at the floor. "I don't know," he said. "I don't want to upset her." He paused. "Maybe I should tell you a bit about us—about the family."

"It would be helpful," said Katie.

CHAPTER THREE

You don't know my mother

"We have a hotel," George began. "It's been in the family—on my mother's side—since 1926. During that time, it's been run by the family, sometimes with the help of a manager; most of the time, it's been run by one of us. My great-grandfather, my grandfather, my father, and then my mother: it's a long tradition."

"Like a farm," interjected William. "Same thing. Farms stay in families, don't they?"

George did not seem to resent the interruption. "Yes," he said. "It's pretty much the same thing. It makes a business special, I think. It means more to everyone that way. Our hotel is called the Hutton, by the way. You may have seen it."

Both Katie and William had.

"After the inventor of geology," George went on. "Remember? The man who looked at the rocks below Arthur's Seat and decided that the earth . . ."

"Was really ancient? Yes. He was a Scotsman, wasn't he?" asked Katie.

"Yes," said George.

"I know the hotel," said William. "I walk past it when I go over to the deli on Elm Row. It's the building set back from the street. I've often wondered about it."

George asked him why.

"Because it's not what you expect," explained William. "The New Town is so regular—those lines of Georgian buildings, and then suddenly what looks like it must have been there before everything else was built."

George nodded. "It was. It used to be a country house, you know, and then the city grew up around it. There were others, of course, but they were knocked down in the early 1800s when the New Town reached them. They left us, for some reason— probably because it belonged to an earl. That sort of influence counted for more in those days.

"Anyway, the building survived. It was used as a school for a while, as far as we can make out, and then it became a private house once more—a big one. Then my great-grandfather acquired it in 1926. He was still quite a young man then, but had made a bit of money. He bought it and ran it for some time, knocking the building about a bit—the rules were more flexible in those days—before he handed it over to my grandfather at the beginning of the 1950s. He passed it on to my mother as a twenty-first birthday present. She's still . . ." He hesitated, before continuing, "she's still the boss."

Katie knew immediately. The way a word is uttered can carry a whole hinterland of meaning. *The boss.* That was the problem.

She took advantage of George's slight hesitation to ask, "Do you work there yourself?"

He nodded. "Yes. There's me and my twin sister, Angela. We have a couple of receptionists, kitchen staff, and so on, but the three of us are the management team."

Katie thought that he used the expression *management team* almost ironically—as if the real management was done by only one member of the team—by the mother, she assumed.

"So, there's you and Angela," Katie said. "And . . . What did you say your mother's name was?"

"She's Margaret," George answered.

"So Margaret—your mother—is the manager, and you and your sister do what?"

George took some time to answer. "Angela's really good at dealing with catering and staff matters. It's hard enough to get people, but she has a real talent for keeping them. We've had one waitress for fifteen years and another for eleven. That's something, these days." He paused. "I handle the business side. Bookings. The accounts. Wages."

"And Margaret?"

Again, he was slow to reply. "She keeps an overall eye on things. We have a meeting every day. She likes us to keep her informed of . . . well, of everything, I suppose."

Katie watched him. He seemed defensive—as if ready to forfend any criticism of his mother. She thought of another note she might make, which would simply say *Mother*, and perhaps be underlined in red.

"I imagine that your mother must know everything there is to know about running a hotel," said Katie.

"Ma always knows," muttered William.

George half-turned, to throw a glance in William's direction. Then he turned back to face Katie.

"I need to tell you something," he said.

Katie encouraged him.

"I'm very fond of my mother," he said. "Angela is too. She means a lot to us."

"Of course," said Katie.

"But I can't pretend that things are always easy," he said. "Mother depends on us, I think. She brought us up single-handed, you see."

Katie waited. She glanced at William. He was looking at George sympathetically.

"My father left us, you see. Mother met him when my grandfather took him on as manager of the hotel. My grandfather died, and left the hotel to Mother, as I already told you. Then she married the manager, our father. When I was three, he went off with somebody else, leaving Mother to do everything—run the hotel, look after us, and so on."

"I'm sorry," said Katie. "That can't have been easy for anybody."

"No," said George. "It wasn't."

"And your father dropped out of your lives completely?"

George nodded. "Completely. He went to work in the Netherlands, I believe. To Rotterdam. We had no contact with him. Mother didn't want it—and I don't think he did either.

"Mother was an only child," George went on. "That means we have no cousins or anything—on her side. I don't know whether there are any on my father's. That's all theoretical, anyway.

"So, she has no family, really—apart from us. She has friends, of course—she plays bridge, and she has a season ticket at the Lyceum Theatre. She gets out. And, of course, she has the hotel to keep her busy. She runs what we call the special side of the business."

"Which is?" asked Katie.

"Our hotel has strong literary associations," said George. "In the days when it was a private house—a country house, really, because the city hadn't spilled over this far in the eighteenth century—it was lived in by a woman who ran a sort of literary salon. Not a big grand one, but there were readings and so on.

Robert Burns was definitely there one evening when he was in Edinburgh in 1786. There's something about it in a letter somebody wrote at the time. He was probably meeting one of his lady friends."

"He had an eye for women," said Katie.

George smiled—for the first time since the conversation had begun. "I love his poems—I really do. If I could choose somebody to meet—from whatever period—I'd choose Burns. Even ten minutes in his company would be enough."

"I like him too," said William. "That poem about the mouse . . ."

"Yes," said George. "And . . . and all the rest."

"So he came to the house," said Katie.

"Yes. And then, much later on, Walter Scott used to come for dinner. He knew the family who owned it then, and he was a regular visitor. He mentions it in one of his letters. He said that he wrote part of *Waverley* when he was spending a weekend there."

"That's a very distinguished pedigree," said Katie.

George nodded. "It is. And it gets better. Robert Louis Stevenson visited it too. We think he may have discussed *Kidnapped* with the man who owned it then. He was a great authority on the Jacobites—he knew everything about them, apparently, and so Stevenson probably got some of the background for the novel from him. It's perfectly plausible, even if there's no actual evidence."

Katie wondered what the significance of all this was.

"There's that staircase in *Kidnapped*," William interjected. "What's-his-name goes to stay with that wicked uncle of his . . ."

"Ebenezer Balfour," said George. "Who tries to get him to go up a staircase that drops off into a void."

"Yes," said William. "Some uncle."

"So, the hotel caters for literary pilgrims?" asked Katie.

"Exactly," said George. "They account for at least a third of our business. We hold regular Burns Suppers."

Burns Suppers were a feature of Scottish life—dinners held towards the end of January each year, on the anniversary of the poet's birthday. There were recitals of his work, performances of his songs, and speeches about his life. They were occasions for tartan and licensed nostalgia, and were particularly popular with visitors.

George had more to add. "We don't just have a Burns Supper in January," he said. "We have one every month throughout the year."

Katie raised an eyebrow.

"Why not? People love it," said George. "We have guests from all over. The US. Germany. India. You name it. Robert Burns reaches the parts other poets can't reach. They love him." He paused. "And there are plenty of people who still read Scott and Stevenson. They turn up throughout the year too. We have a Scott bedroom and a Stevenson one too. We don't claim that either of them slept in the actual room, but they might well have done. There are ways of suggesting things without actually claiming them."

William laughed. "So-called Shetland-style sweaters," he said. "Shetland-*style*. People sell those knowing full well that people will think they were knitted in the Shetland Islands. Or that the wool is from Shetland sheep. In actual fact, they might be made in the Philippines."

George looked interested. "They do that with whisky too. One of our guests showed us a bottle he'd bought in South America. It had a very Scottish-looking label—mountains, a stag, and all the rest, and it was called Highland Mist. Right down at the bottom of the label was the small print. *Distilled in Venezuela.*"

Katie tried to get the conversation back on track. "You said that Margaret runs that side of things? The Burns Suppers and so on?"

"Yes."

She looked at him expectantly.

"My mother is somewhat possessive," he said.

Katie made a gesture of acceptance. "Mothers often are."

"She has our best interests at heart," said George. "But she doesn't . . ." He broke off, and it was a few moments before he resumed. "She doesn't find it easy to let go."

Katie was gentle. "That must be difficult for you and Angela."

George nodded. "Very. We've tried to get our own lives going, but I'm afraid Mother does everything she can to make that difficult." He was staring down at the floor, and now his discomfort was too obvious to be ignored.

"I understand," she said. "It must have been hard for you to form relationships if your mother . . ." She trailed off. She was not sure how to put it tactfully.

He nodded glumly. "And it's been the same for Angela. Mother knows how to make us feel guilty. Angela has had three boyfriends—all driven away by Mother. Subtly, of course, but she sees them off every time. Angela's more or less given up." He paused. "You'd think she might want to encourage her to produce grandchildren for her, but she hasn't shown any signs of that. Not so far."

"And you've had to put up with the same thing?" said Katie.

He nodded again. "I met somebody I liked, and it was all going well. Then she told me that she couldn't cope with Mother. She was freezing her out. She said she would only stay with me if I moved out of the hotel and found a flat somewhere. I looked around and was going to do something about it, but Mother heard about it. She said she became sick with worry. How was she going to cope with the hotel if I went off? She even accused me of being selfish." He sighed. "I know I probably seem weak to you. You're probably thinking: Why doesn't he . . . what's the expression? Why doesn't he show a bit of backbone?"

Katie interrupted him. "I wasn't thinking that at all," she protested. It was true; she had not been thinking in those terms. Her reaction, rather, had been one of anger at his mother for her manipulation. For that was what it was, really. It was manipulation, or, even, bullying behaviour. Parents could behave that way. They rarely saw themselves as bullies, but that was what some of them were.

"Nor was I," said William. "Quite the opposite, in fact. It's only too easy to be selfish. You weren't being selfish."

George smiled weakly. "You're being kind."

Katie shook her head. "No, we're just telling you what we really think." She fixed her gaze upon him. "What you've said explains why you want to keep this private. You want to keep it from Margaret."

George nodded. "I thought it might be easier if I had a relationship away from the hotel. Then I wouldn't worry about Mother, and what she felt."

"But eventually?" Katie asked. "Eventually you'd have to face up to her finding out."

George shifted uneasily in his seat. "Yes, but by then it might be too late for her to wreck anything. If I get engaged—or even married—and then tell her, there's not all that much she can do."

Katie thought about this. There was still a lot a determined mother could do. After a while, she said, "Wouldn't it be simpler just to have it out with your mother? To tell her that you'd met somebody, and that was that? To tell her that you resented her interference and just would not accept it? To call her bluff, so to speak?"

George looked at her wistfully. "You don't know my mother," he said.

There was a brief silence. Then George turned to face William; he seemed to have remembered something. "That man who was bitten by the shark," he began. "Was he bitter?"

William looked puzzled. "Bitten?"

"No, bitter. How did he feel about sharks afterwards?"

William shrugged. "I don't think he likes them," he said.

George nodded. It seemed to have been the answer he was expecting. "And I don't blame him," he said. "People say you have to forgive, but I'm not sure I'd find it that easy—if I'd been bitten by a shark and then almost encountered another the first time I went back in the water."

William grinned. "There's no point in worrying about these things," he said. "There's a lot of wildlife in Australia that bites. We don't let the thought of it prey on us."

"But *they* prey on you," said Katie. "These various creatures. Saltwater crocs, for instance."

"We don't get those in Melbourne," William said. "It's too far south. Most of Australia is pretty safe."

"What about those snakes?" said George. "I read about a snake called the western something . . ."

"Western taipan," said William. "Yes, they're pretty lethal, but I wouldn't worry about them, if I were you. You only get them in a very small area, Northern New South Wales, I think, or Queensland—somewhere up there."

"And box jellyfish?" George asked.

"Very local," said William. "You just keep out of the water in the affected areas—it's nothing to panic about."

Katie became businesslike. She reached for the list in front of her. "Perhaps you could tell us what sort of woman you'd like to meet, George. Then we can see if there's anybody."

George blushed. "Somebody about thirtyish? I'm thirty-two, you see. Maybe twenty-eight. Anywhere round about there."

"Fair enough," said Katie. "A contemporary. That's always a good idea."

"Tall, if possible," said George.

Katie made a note.

"I like tall girls," said William. "Actually, I like short girls too. I don't think height makes that much difference."

George gave him a reproachful look. "You asked me what I'd prefer. I was just telling you."

Katie kept her eyes on the file. She considered herself tall enough. Ell was taller. "Of course," she said. "We asked you."

"And thin," George added. "I haven't got anything against people being fat, but . . ." He stopped; he was clearly embarrassed.

"No need to apologise, George," William said. "I like thin girls too. Although, you don't want to be too thin. I knew a girl who had a really thin boyfriend. She tried to feed him up. She kept giving him fried food—high calorie stuff. He left her eventually. He said he didn't want to put on weight. And I can see his point. People should be allowed to be what they're comfortable being."

Katie took a few more details. George liked hill walking, and he would prefer it if any partner shared that enthusiasm. He enjoyed folk music. He sometimes played tennis in the summer. He went to the gym once a week. He liked watching Scandinavian crime series. He preferred white wine to red.

At length he stood up, and William showed him to the door. Katie heard what William said when they parted. *We'll fix you up. She'll find somebody. Hang in there.*

William returned to the office. "Poor guy," he said.

Katie sighed. "Yes, exactly. Poor guy." Then she said, "That mother of his . . ."

"Oh, yes. That mother. He's going to have to cut the apron strings."

"Do you think he will?"

Katie was unsure. But she was sure of one thing: she was keen to do whatever she could to help him. This was different from the case of David Bannatyne, the farmer who had been their last success story. David could probably have got by without their help; George needed them to do something for him. He needed to be rescued.

"Poor guy," Katie repeated.

"Yes," said William. "I think we both agree on that." He paused. "Did you see how nervous he was? Not just about coming here, but about other things, including box jellyfish. He's in Scotland, and the nearest box jellyfish is ten thousand miles away, or whatever."

"I think that may have something to do with his mother," said Katie.

"It always does," said William. "Or that's what the Freudians say. I don't. I actually love my mother—or loved her, rather."

William had not spoken about his parents before. Was his mother dead? He had said *loved* in the past tense.

"What happened to your mother?" Katie asked.

"A box jellyfish . . ." William began, and then dissolved into laughter. "Actually, nothing at all. She's still in Melbourne—alive and well."

Katie gave him a disapproving look. "You don't joke about your mother," she said.

"I do," said William. "And she jokes about me. We get on very well, laughing at each other."

Katie now asked, "Does she get on with your fiancée—with Alice?"

William was silent.

"I'm sorry," said Katie hurriedly. "I shouldn't have asked."

"No, it's all right," William assured her. "I don't mind talking to you about it. I don't think she's too keen on Alice."

Katie waited to see if he would add anything. And he did. "They're different types, maybe."

"But she's not like George's mother, I take it? She's not going to try to interfere?"

William shook his head. "No, she's not like that at all. But I know one thing for sure: she'd be much happier if I broke off the engagement."

"I see."

Katie realised that she was pleased with his answer. She knew that she should not be, but she was pleased.

The silence that now ensued had an awkward note to it, and Katie was relieved when William stroked his chin and asked, "So? Anybody come to mind? Anybody wanting a slightly anxious man with a potential mother-in-law from hell?"

"We'll see," answered Katie. "I think he needs someone who will fight his corner—who'll stand up to her. What's the Scots expression? A *bonnie fechter*?"

William was pleased. "Have you got one of those on the books?"

"I think so," Katie replied.

CHAPTER FOUR

A dark green house

Ness had had her second thoughts as early as Edinburgh Airport. As the taxi dropped her off to catch her flight to Toronto, it occurred to her that she was asking too much of her younger cousin. It had all happened too quickly: Katie had accepted within hours of the offer being made; the handover had taken place in the space of a single day; and then Ness had finished her packing, ordered her taxi, and set off. It was the opposite of the good business practice she had seen described in the only management manual she had ever read. That had recommended a period of shared responsibility so that those who were taking over could ask for advice and support. Katie had been given very little advice, and the agency had been handed over rather quickly. It was no way to run a business; in fact, it was probably the quickest way to *ruin* a business.

On the other hand, Ness had always been of the view that life was short, that the time to put plans into effect was the present, rather than some indeterminate future, and that things had a way of sorting themselves out. She herself had always risen to a challenge with enthusiasm and gusto, and she suspected that Katie, although much younger and more inexperienced than she was, was made of much the same stuff. If she were not, then would she have accepted the offer so quickly? Ness thought it unlikely. And if willingness to take on a challenge was a genetically determined characteristic—and why should it not be?—then she and Katie, with their shared genes, might be expected to be not all that dissimilar in their approach to life.

Ness was, in fact, something of an amateur geneticist. Her understanding of the science involved was at best shaky, but she was a keen devourer of books and articles on the workings of heredity. Her personal views, though, were quirky, and often out of step with the articles she read. Environment might play a part in the development of character, but the old saw that you could not make a silk purse out of a sow's ear had, in Ness's view, been proved time and time again. If the genes were not up to it, then no amount of effort would make anything but a superficial difference. Selfishness and a lack of consideration for others would sooner or later come to the surface.

This apparently deterministic view of human nature did not make Ness censorious. She was, in fact, more tolerant than many, believing, as she did, that those who behaved badly could not really help themselves all that much. If your genes made you what you were—and she firmly believed that to be the case—then how could you be blamed for acting as those genes dictated? You did not choose the genome with which you were endowed in that early, invisible moment of conception—that was allocated to you by a biology you neither asked for nor controlled. This did not mean, of course, that you could not be taken to task for your failures and misdemeanours—people had to be called to account—it was just that those failures and misdemeanours, Ness believed, should be greeted with a sigh, rather than with real anger. The timber of humanity was crooked; it always had been, and probably always would be.

By the time her plane took off, and Scotland was unrolling silently beneath her, she found herself thinking more of what lay ahead rather than what she was leaving behind. Katie would be all right. She had William to advise her if she were to feel out of her depth, and she could easily contact Ness should any really serious issues arise. Ness had stressed to Katie that she was not to hesitate to make a phone call, and that Ness would make sure that she was contactable. She qualified that, though. "Of course, if I'm in the real wilds, that might be a little difficult—in fact, impossible—but give it a try anyway."

She did not linger in Toronto. Having left one city behind her, she had no desire to be in another, and so she lost no time in travelling to Kingston, a few hours to the east. At Kingston train station she was picked up by the man with whom she had negotiated at long distance to drive her to the small town further north in which she had rented a house for a couple of months. The house had been chosen from the offerings of a leasing agent in Kingston. It had been singled out on the strength of its description, and its suspiciously low rent. There had been a caveat, to which Ness, with her optimistic nature, had paid only passing attention. *This property,* the advertisement said, *is awaiting modernization, and renters should not expect a modern standard of finish in all departments.* Ness had smiled at that. The language of real estate agents was the same the world over. *Awaiting modernization* meant that nothing had been done to maintain the property for decades, and it would be years before anything would be done—if it ever would. *In all departments* meant that nothing worked. But then for the small rent that was payable, almost any inconvenience, Ness thought, was bearable. Shabby places, she felt, were often more comfortable than their smarter equivalents. Ness, in short, was prepared to take whatever rough came her way; the smooth would be the sheer pleasure of being in a place that was remote enough to offer her a real sense of getting away from things.

They made the two-hour journey to Murdoch, a small town on the edge of a placid lake, bypassed by both the main highway north and history. The lake was fed at one end by several springs and drained at the other by a sluggish river. The river was dammed at several points by beaver lodges, creating deep ponds and reed beds in which wildfowl bred. In every direction, an arboreal landscape stretched out to the horizon, interrupted here and there by low rocky outcrops.

"You hear wolves round here," she was told by a woman in the local store. "They come close to town in the winter. Their howls are full of sorrow. I guess that's because it's hard being a wolf."

The town itself consisted of a handful of stores, one selling hardware and one selling liquor. There was also a grocery store and a gift shop-cum-gallery that catered for summer visitors. Apart from that, there was not much more than a small elementary school, a roadworks depot, a police post, and a run-down hotel. Dotted round the lake were the summer cottages owned by the well-heeled Torontonians who each summer doubled the town's population. The sky above was empty and echoing.

If anything, the house was slightly better than its description in the advertisement. It was true that work was needed, but the hot water system worked, the rooms were dry, and the kitchen, though basic, had been kept spotlessly clean. Ness bought from the general store the provisions she needed and introduced herself to the immediate neighbors. They were welcoming, if initially guarded. "Nobody stays here long," they said. "Except us locals. We're here because . . . well, because this is where we've always been."

It was clear to her that they thought she was running away from something, but her explanation that she was on an adult gap year resulted in a quick thawing. They gave her a basket of vegetables from their own garden—carrots, onions, and potatoes still moist from the earth—and a small flask of maple syrup from a producer in Quebec.

That was the neighbors on the one side. On the other, just visible through the trees, was another house, painted dark green, in front of which a battered truck was parked.

"That's Herb la Fouche over that side," said the neighbor who brought the vegetables. "Herb runs traplines up north. He's away right now, but he turns up with his pelts, and you'll see him about the place then. Herb's a good man. Causes no trouble."

She stared at the dark green house. The dark green house of a man who causes no trouble, she thought.

That first night in the house, she went to bed early but had difficulty falling asleep. The summer evening was light, and the sky did not darken properly until well after eight. Her neighbor's light could be made out through the trees; a square of yellow that was suddenly extinguished behind the latticework of branches. For the first time she felt that loneliness that the Canadians talked about—the feeling of human absence in nature. The voices of the dead, the works of man; these things we were used to having about us.

Ness thought of Katie. She thought, too, of William and his smile and the scarf he had promised to knit her. "If you ever come back," he had said with a smile, adding hurriedly, "which you will do, of course, once you have had your adventures."

In the darkness of her silent house, Ness wondered what she was going to do. She had planned nothing, other than that she would come to Canada to spend some time in a small and remote community. You did not want to plan your life in too detailed a way. It was better, she thought, to let life happen to you in an *organic way,* whatever that meant, which was probably nothing much.

She drew the blankets over her head. They were rough against her skin; they had come with the house, and she would replace them the following day with bedding from the store. Blankets that had been used by others, she had read somewhere, would have fragments of their previous owners' DNA in the fibres, however well they had been washed. Such blankets could tell the story for generations, she told herself.

She thought of Herb la Fouche. She was not sure what was involved in running a trapline, and perhaps he might explain to her what it entailed. Perhaps he would ask her to accompany him when he went off to check his traplines. She saw herself sitting in a camp somewhere further north, a fire crackling in front of her, and Herb la Fouche stirring some concoction in a pot. It was a comforting scene, human against the emptiness of this wooded landscape. Then, after dinner, they would sit under a night sky across which the constellations would dip and swing; Cassiopeia, with its recumbent W-shape; the Bear; Orion and his belt; Castor and Pollux. That might happen, she thought, if she liked Herb la Fouche, of course, but she imagined she would. She liked the idea of a man with a dark green house and a life altogether elsewhere in the snow, not that there was any snow yet, nor any man yet for that matter.

CHAPTER FIVE

A bit too keen

Cumberland Street was a residential street in the Georgian New Town. It was considerably more restrained in its proportions and ambitions than the streets adjoining it, consisting, as it did, of a line of modest four-storey stone tenements without much adornment or flourish. It was popular with young professionals at the start of their careers—a springboard to the larger flats in the more expensive streets only a block or two away. It was exactly the right place, Katie thought, for a young woman like Emma Henderson to live. It would not be too pricey for her to manage to live there alone, although there would normally be a flatmate to share the cost, or, possibly, to provide companionship. There was nothing in the file about that, although there were several notes in Ness's handwriting here about other things, as there were in most of the files. *Can look after herself,* one said. And another expressed the view that Emma might possibly be *A bit too keen—might be advised not to frighten men off. Tricky.*

Katie was not sure about that last note. Meaning sometimes depended on punctuation or the taking of a breath, and these words scribbled by Ness were an example of that. In one reading, this meant that it would be tricky to advise Emma that she would frighten men off if she were to appear too keen; in another reading, it might be taken as suggesting that Emma herself was tricky. Katie decided that the first of these was the more likely. And Ness was right; it was something that Katie had often observed: women who were manifestly too eager to encourage a particular man could end up discouraging him. Men, she felt, liked to see themselves as leading the pursuit. She knew that such things were questioned today; that there was meant to be equality in relationships, and that traditional ideas of courtship were outdated. She knew that either party in a relationship could make the running, could propose when things got to that stage. That was the theory, and yet she also knew that there were many women who liked the idea of the man making the first moves and, in due course, if it came to that point, being the one to propose. That may not have sat well with proponents of equality in relationships, but it was still an observable fact. And although more and more people followed principles of equality in their private lives, there were still some people in whom some vestiges of older attitudes still prevailed. Ness was probably one of those, as might be many of her clients. After all, they were a self-selecting group: they were people who were prepared to enlist the help of an introduction agency, and one, moreover, that had an unquestionably romantic name. The Perfect Passion Company: What could be more idealistic than that? Who believed that perfect passion was actually *possible*? Well, the answer to that would be a business that chose to call itself the Perfect Passion Company.

Katie did not take long to identify Emma as a possible match for George. It had not been a large field, as there were few people in the files who matched the age requirements. There were plenty of forty-something-year-olds—the company's particular demographic bulge, as Ness had described it to Katie—but markedly fewer in their early thirties. There was currently nobody at all in their twenties, which did not surprise Katie, as there would not be many in that age group, she thought, who would not be using online dating. Nor would disappointment—or caution—have brought them to the point where they might think an introduction agency was necessary.

The photograph in the file before Katie was a good likeness, and she recognised Emma immediately when she opened the door to her. Katie was expected, and was invited into the airy sitting room that led off the flat's rather gloomy entrance hall.

"We don't get enough light in the hall," Emma said, as she showed Katie the way. "But the main rooms have these long windows—see—and they make up for it."

Katie glanced at the other woman. The first thing that impressed her was her bearing. Emma was tall and held herself in that erect way that unapologetically tall people sometimes manage. Recalling George's comments about height, she felt a flush of self-satisfaction: so far, so good. Then her gaze passed briefly over Emma's clothes. Again, there was nothing to worry about there. A soft-colored blouse and ordinary, unripped jeans would, she thought, appeal to George. If he had had any colorful tendencies, then these, she had decided, would long have been suppressed by his mother. Emma, she thought, was suitable—but there still remained the issue of whether the two of them would get on. That brought her back to earth: it was hard to work out what anybody might see in George, but then many dull men—and George probably would be regarded by many as dull—managed to find somebody who was happy enough to put up with their dullness. Shortly before they had parted, Ness had said, "One conclusion I've reached from doing what I've been doing is that there is always someone for everybody—and I mean everybody without exception." And she had given Katie a look that suggested that she thought that she might not be believed. "You may think this is unlikely, Katie, but I believe we can place *anybody*."

That made Katie wonder why Ness herself did not appear to have anybody in her own life. Perhaps having been married three times before, she had decided to call it a day. Or had she been so busy bringing others together that she had not done anything about herself? That was possible, she decided. And yet Katie still agreed with the observation that Ness had made, because she had reached the same conclusion herself on the basis of what she had seen of life. It was simply a question of compromise. All you had to do was to lower your expectations sufficiently, and, with each notch they were lowered, the range of possible partners expanded. But now, as she accompanied Emma into her sitting room, she found herself wondering why this poised, confident-looking young woman should need her help at all, and, moreover, why would she even bother to look at poor George, with his issues, and his slightly diffident manner.

Emma made coffee for them both.

"I would have been happy to come to the office," she said to Katie as she handed her a cup. "You're close enough."

"But I wanted to get to know you a bit better," said Katie, placing the cup of coffee on the table beside her. "As I told you on the phone, I've only recently taken over the running of the business. I want to meet all our clients." She picked up the cup and took a sip. "Meeting somebody in their own home gives one a far better idea of who they are, don't you think?"

Emma agreed.

"But I'd still like to ask you a few questions," Katie continued. Emma nodded. "I don't mind."

There was a directness about Emma that appealed to Katie, and now, on impulse, she decided to match it with directness of her own. "Why did you come to us—to the Perfect Passion Company?"

Emma seemed surprised by the question. "Because I wanted to meet a man. Isn't that why people come to you?"

Katie smiled. "Of course, it is. But there are plenty of other ways to meet somebody—more common ways—and far less expensive too."

"You mean online?" asked Emma.

"That's one," said Katie. "Then there are bars. Clubs. There are plenty of ways."

Emma sighed. "Oh yes. There are plenty of those."

"You disapprove?"

Emma shook her head. "No. They may work for some people—for a lot of people, in fact." She hesitated. "I tried them, you know. I went to one of those dating sites. It wasn't what I wanted."

"Oh?" said Katie.

"Yes. I went on two dates. One in Edinburgh and one over in Glasgow. In Edinburgh it was with a guy who had lied about his age. He said he was thirty-seven, but he was at least fifty—probably mid-fifties."

"Appearances can be deceptive," said Katie. "Perhaps he . . ."

Emma cut her short. "No. I was able to work out his age. We went to see a film at the Cameo Cinema, and before we went in, when we were having a drink at the bar, this woman came up to him and reminded him about sending in a reply to an invitation. She apologised to me for interrupting. She said that she was organising the thirtieth reunion of their graduation from university. Now if he graduated at, say twenty-two, then that made him fifty-two—at least. He could have been more. He tried to interrupt her, but the cat was out of the bag."

"Not a success?" said Katie.

"No. Not a success at all. And then there was Glasgow, which was the experience that really put me off. In this case, it was the opposite. We had arranged to meet in a hotel bar and then go out for dinner. I turned up and I saw this . . . this *schoolboy* sitting in the bar. He had said that he was twenty-eight, but I think he was probably eighteen—at the most."

Katie gave an involuntary gasp. "The *cheek* . . ."

"Yes. I wasn't sure what to do. I should have walked straight out, but I didn't. I sat down, and he went off to fetch me a drink. When he came back, I asked him outright how old he was, and he repeated the lie. He said he had just celebrated his twenty-eighth birthday. He pretended to be surprised that I asked him."

"The gall."

"Yes. Anyway, we went off to dinner, mainly because I felt sorry for him and did not want to embarrass him too much. We went to a Thai restaurant. He said that he had been to Thailand earlier that year. He said that he had gone trekking in the Himalayas. He actually said that. I said that I thought that the Himalayas were in Northern India and Nepal, and he looked at me as if I'd accused him of lying—which I could have done. It was pathetic.

"But then he started to talk suggestively. He had had a couple of glasses of wine, and I think they had gone to his head. He started to boast about the girlfriends he had had and the weekends away he had enjoyed with them. That's when I decided that enough was enough, and I said that I was leaving. He said that I should have left before he ordered the dinner because now he would have to pay. So I gave him twenty-five pounds. I put it down on the table, and he reached out and took it. That was my second experience of online dating."

Katie said, "They aren't all like that. You had bad luck."

"Very bad luck."

"Well," said Katie, "that's where we come in, I suppose. We'll think very carefully before introducing you to somebody."

Emma said that she liked the idea of that. "No liars," she said, adding, "please."

"No liars," said Katie.

They looked at one another, each waiting for the other to take the conversation forward. Eventually Katie said, "What sort of man would you like to meet?"

Emma thought for a while before she answered. "One in his early thirties?"

Katie laughed. "I'm not surprised—after your earlier experience." She paused. "And apart from the age requirement?"

"Somebody kind," said Emma. "Somebody reliable. Somebody who won't let me down."

"All that is very important," Katie agreed. She hesitated, and then went on to say, "Are you looking for somebody exciting?"

Emma replied immediately. Shaking her head, she said, "No, I don't think so. The trouble is that I find myself a bit . . . how shall I put it? A bit exhausted when I'm with exciting people. I think I'm more suited to the quiet type."

She could not have come up with anything more calculated to please Katie. Hardly believing her luck, Katie said, "So you wouldn't object to a man who's a bit . . ." She struggled to bring herself to say it.

"Yes?"

"A bit dull?"

"You could put it that way," said Emma. "Although the

interesting thing about people who *seem* dull is that they often *aren't* dull once you get to know them."

"I couldn't agree more," said Katie. "In fact, we have on our books somebody who might be considered a bit dull . . . not that I'd say that of him, of course, but who, yes, might be *thought* to be dull. He's a nice man, though. I like him. It's just that . . ."

Emma looked at her expectantly.

Katie made her decision. She would run this business on an honest basis. It was not in her nature to do otherwise.

"One consideration," she said, "is that the person I have in mind has a possessive mother—a seriously possessive mother."

Emma's reaction was unexpected. She laughed.

"Actually," said Katie, a note of reproach in her voice, "it's a real problem for him."

Emma looked apologetic. "I'm sorry. It's just that *all* mothers are possessive. Or at least most of them are. It's perfectly natural."

Katie conceded that while there was a natural possessiveness in the maternal role, mothers nonetheless had to be prepared to let go. "You can't run your children's lives forever," she said. "That leads to problems."

"And there are problems in this case? In the case of . . . what's this person's name?"

"George."

"So, George has a mother who won't let him get on with his life?"

Katie nodded. "And it gets worse, I'm afraid. Her possessiveness means that she discourages his girlfriends."

Emma's eyes widened. "Yes, that's possessiveness all right." She looked thoughtful. "And dangerous. Poor guy."

Katie remembered that was what she and William had both

said: poor guy. "I felt I had to tell you. I wouldn't want to introduce you if you felt that . . ."

Emma cut her short. "If I felt that I couldn't face this mother of his? No, if anything, that makes me more eager to meet him."

Katie remembered what Ness had written in the file. *A bit too keen—might be advised not to frighten men off.* She was not sure whether this was the time to say something about that, but she decided that she would.

"I think it might be best to tread carefully," she said. "Sometimes men get put off if women are too direct—perhaps, too forceful. And men can be odd about their mothers, you know."

She watched Emma for a reaction.

It was one of insouciance. "Of course they are. That's what Freud's all about, isn't he? Oedipus and so on." There was a brief silence. Then Emma continued. "I can handle a mother. In fact, I rather like the idea. It's a bit of a challenge."

"Well, yes, I suppose it would be. But I still think a bit of caution might be a good idea."

Emma was dismissive. "Yes, okay, that's fine. But his mother's not the point. The point is: Do you think George is a nice man? It's that simple. And if he is, do you think he might like me?"

Katie thought for almost a minute before she answered. Then she said, "Yes, I think that George is a nice man—yes, I do think that—from what I've seen of him. He's a bit under his mother's thumb, but he wants to escape from that. And yes, I think that he would get on well with you. We can at least try."

"Then let's do that," said Emma. "Let's try. Will you arrange a meeting?"

"I shall," Katie replied.

CHAPTER SIX

A kiss in the air

William was knitting when Katie returned to Mouse Lane. She knocked at the door of his studio and then, as he had invited her to do, let herself in with the key he had given her. William's front door opened onto a corridor leading to his studio. From the studio there drifted the sound of an operatic duet. William listened to opera and early music, and Italian composers were his favourite. "Rossini, Verdi," he explained. "Even Wagner, if it's a Saturday. Or the early stuff. French troubadours. That's the music that helps me work. Anything else seems to make me drop stitches."

He looked up from his needles as she entered the studio. "Verdi," he said. "*Aida.* I feel so sorry for her. And for him too. I have to listen to something light afterwards, or I end up feeling pretty low. Yesterday I tried *Carmina Burana,* and that helped, but then I was working on a design, and Carl Orff is all wrong for that. Too stirring."

"What about silence?"

"Always possible," said William, reaching out to his laptop computer.

"I didn't mean now," said Katie.

William smiled. "I know, but I wanted to hear what you have to say without competition from the late Giuseppe Verdi. I'll turn it right down. There. All ears—if you came to tell me something, that is."

Katie seated herself on the sofa opposite William's work chair.

"Hand knitting," she said. "It must be important."

"A commissioned piece," he said. "This is going to go down to London—to a terrifically important client. She gets together a whole new wardrobe for herself every year."

"A bit wasteful," said Katie. She was Scottish, and shared the general Scottish dislike of profligacy or showy displays of wealth. "In fact, rather sad. She must be unhappy with herself, don't you think? To *need* new clothes all the time . . ."

"Yes," agreed William. "I think she feels she has to look for ways to spend her money. Do you like rich people?"

Katie considered this. "I don't know all that many," she said. "One or two, maybe. And they're all right, I suppose. Actually, one of them is more than all right—she's very generous. She does these charity lunches all the time and gives large amounts of money to a charity that does cataract operations in places where they otherwise wouldn't have them. She's serious about that."

"I like her already," said William. "Perhaps I should knit her a scarf."

Katie stared at him. "Are you serious?"

He nodded. "Why not? It would be to make up for knitting this top for this wealthy person who doesn't know what to do with her money and who, I suspect, doesn't give all that much of it away." He put down his needles. "Yes, I like the idea of doing something for somebody who does lots for other people but probably has very little done for her. I suspect nobody ever thinks to give *her* anything. I'll do a scarf for her, whoever she is."

"I think that's a really great idea." She felt a surge of affection for William. There were not many men like him. There were kind men; there were charming men; there were good-looking men; but there were not all that many men, she imagined, who were kind and charming and good-looking, all at the same time, as well as being able to design and make garments that were the sort of thing that angels would knit, if they ever knitted.

"You'll pass it on to her?"

"Yes, I can do that," said Katie. "And I imagine she'll be really touched."

In the background, lower now, but still audible, the victorious Egyptians sang throatily after their victory over the Ethiopians. In the opera, Aida watched, her tears falling for the defeat of her people.

"I went to see her," Katie began.

"Who?" asked William.

"Emma Henderson. I mentioned to you that I had somebody in mind for George."

William remembered. Katie had shown him Emma's file. "Ah, yes. And?"

"She's tall. You'll remember that George said he would prefer somebody tall."

William nodded. "Well, that's a good thing. But you don't base a whole relationship just on height." He looked bemused. "At least, you don't if you have any sense."

"No," agreed Katie. "Nobody would."

"And so, other things? Is she suitable for him? And is he suitable for her?"

Katie looked up at the ceiling. "Possibly." Even as she said this, she realised the slender foundations of the whole exercise. How could she pronounce on something as complex as human compatibility on the basis of a single encounter with each person? The whole idea suddenly seemed ridiculous. And yet it was what the two people involved were asking her to do. It was her job. They wanted her to do this, and if she was intervening in their lives on this shaky basis, she was only doing so because that was what they looked to her to do. Life was far from perfect. Life was a rickety, haphazard business, and too close a scrutiny of the way things worked was not always helpful.

William gave her a sideways look. "You don't sound all that certain."

For the moment, she put aside her doubts. Get on with it, she thought. But be frank. "Well, I'm not. And can you be certain with this sort of thing? All you can do, surely, is look at the possibilities. And there are one or two things worrying me."

He asked her what these were, and she told him that the first of her concerns was that Emma might be in too much of a hurry. "I just had a feeling," she said. "I just had an impression that she was extremely keen to get a partner. And that gives rise to a few issues."

"Such as?"

"She could scare men away by being too keen. Ness wrote something about that in her notes."

William looked dubious. "Some men don't mind that."

"Some may not," said Katie. "But a lot do. Nonetheless, they take fright when they realise a woman has them in their sights."

William looked amused. "It's not a hunt."

"Isn't it?" said Katie, wryly. And then continued, "But my real fear is that she'll regard George's mother as a challenge.

She made a remark to the effect that she would encourage a showdown. She wasn't explicit, but that's the way I read it."

William thought about this. "And that's a bad thing."

She shrugged. "It might come to a simple choice—from George's point of view. If there's a showdown, he's going to have to choose, isn't he? Mother or girlfriend?"

William looked thoughtful. "Probably."

"And whom will he choose?" asked Katie.

William picked up his knitting and examined it as he weighed the possibilities. Then at last he said, with some conviction, "Her."

"Which her?"

William had made up his mind. "Girlfriend. Emma."

"Why?"

He put down his knitting. "Because I think he's decided that he simply has to do something. I think George realises that this is the fork in the road. If he doesn't do it now—stand up to his mother, that is—he's never going to. That's what I think. What about you?"

Katie sighed. "I don't think he's got the courage. I think he's too weak. Look at the way he approached us—all that business about not emailing him. If he had plucked up the courage, he wouldn't have cared if his mother found out about what he was doing. He would already have shown signs of questioning his mother's authority. But he hasn't done that, has he? She's still the boss, you see. Mother is." She gave William a look of regret. "I wish it weren't like that, but it is."

"We'll have to see, then," said William. "What's planned?"

"I'm going to invite them both for coffee in Valvona & Crolla. Then I'll suddenly realise I have to be somewhere else, and I'll leave them to it." Valvona & Crolla was the Italian deli where both she and William shopped. There was a café at the back where Katie had briefly worked in her student days. On her return to Edinburgh, she had been delighted to find it unchanged.

"That's what Ness did," said William.

"Company procedure," said Katie, with a smile.

William picked up his knitting.

"I'm interrupting you," said Katie. "I must let you get on."

He looked up—and blew her a kiss. She stood quite still. He had never done that before. The kiss hung between them, a tiny, invisible thing. She wanted to reach for it, and hold it to her. But kisses blown on the air fade quickly, and in a moment, it was gone.

CHAPTER SEVEN

Angela asks

The following morning, shortly after she arrived in the office, Katie received a telephone call from George's sister, Angela.

"I hope you don't mind my approaching you out of the blue," she said. "But I know that George has been round to see you."

Katie was hesitant. She knew that everything that passed between her and her clients was confidential, and if Angela was hoping to discuss her brother with her, she would have to decline. Her reply, then, was guarded. Yes, George had come to see her, but . . .

She got no further. "He knows I'm calling you. He gave me the go-ahead."

Katie relaxed. "I see."

"And he knows that I want to see you. He says that it's all right for us to meet."

Katie wondered whether Angela was hoping to be taken on as a client too, although it was difficult to see why she felt she needed George's approval for that.

"So, I wondered if I could make an appointment. Would that be possible?"

They arranged a time. Angela would come to the office at eleven that morning. "I won't take up too much of your time," she said. "But I would like to discuss one or two matters with you. If you're going to help George, there are certain things you should know."

Katie wondered what these might be, but did not prolong the conversation. "I'll see you at eleven then," she said, and rang off. Without hesitating, she went into the kitchen area where William made coffee and banged on the wall. From the other side of the wall came an answering thump, and a few minutes later Katie heard the sound of the front door opening.

"You rang?" William said. "Or rather you thumped?"

"I have to tell you something," Katie said. "Angela Fane— that's George's sister—has just called. She's coming here to talk to me about her brother. She's coming at eleven."

William raised an eyebrow. "Is that allowed?"

"He's given her permission," said Katie.

William glanced at his watch. "And do you want me to be there?"

"If you're free," Katie said.

He looked again at his watch. "I have one or two things to do, and then I'll be back. I'll make coffee when she comes."

She looked at him with gratitude. "I really appreciate your help," she said. "This job would be a bit lonely without having somebody to talk to. You make it so much easier, you know."

"Me too," he said. "I love being involved. I like the human interest."

"And you're the one with the ideas," Katie went on.

He looked away modestly. "No, you are."

She laughed. "All right: we both are. What's the saying? Two heads are better than one?"

"Except sometimes—when you need to make a decision. Two heads can complicate things."

He was right, she thought. And she would have to remember that she ran the Perfect Passion Company and would have to make decisions herself. "Possibly," she said.

She looked at him. There was a certain ease in their friendship—something that had grown, had flowered, so quickly—and that made her feel that they had known one another for much longer than the few weeks they had actually spent in one another's company. In spite of that ease, though, she was still wary of the difficulties that might lie ahead. She could easily become too fond of him, she realised, and then, very rapidly, the whole situation could become an ordeal. The boundary between being friendly and being in love was not always well marked; it could be crossed over suddenly and unwittingly. And the first thing you knew was that you were feeling that dull ache that is attendant upon love; that yearning that is quite unmistakable. You fell—and the language of falling was completely appropriate for love; you fell for others, and you wanted nothing more than to be with them; to have their attention; to possess them. There was no mistaking love: that is what it did to you. She could easily feel that about William, and then she would be miserable because William was unobtainable. He would not allow himself to become involved with her, even if that was what he was tempted to do. She had wondered whether that was what he secretly wanted, but had put the thought out of her mind: an affair between the two of them, she felt, would spoil everything, although she wished that he would recognise the pointlessness of his continuing his relationship with Alice. He did not love her; Katie was sure of that. He would be unhappy. And so, perhaps, she should rescue him from his enmeshment. She should help him to be free, even by doing something small and insignificant—such as returning the kiss he had blown her. It would not be an act of selfishness on her part—it would be one of liberation.

Except that it was not, and she stopped herself from thinking along those lines. She should not get too involved in the life of this young man, in spite of his appeal—his shy smile, his artistic flair, and his sympathetic manner. You don't need any of that, she told herself. And then another thought occurred: Was there something about William that did not quite ring true? Was he really engaged, as he claimed to be? Was there really a medical student called Alice in Melbourne, committed, like him, to a long-distance relationship, and then to marriage? It was easy enough for people to chat online in spite of geographical separation, and yet she had not seen, or heard, him doing that with Alice—not once. Why had there been no phone calls, no sudden alerts on the laptop computer that he often brought with him into Katie's office? Of course, there were awkward time differences with Australia, but even taking those into account, more contact might have been expected.

But why would William create a story of a non-existent engagement? A fantasist might do that, of course, but there was nothing to suggest that William was that. Fantasists spun stories in all sorts of contexts: William seemed grounded in everything he said. She considered possible motives. A fiancée might be invented as protection of some sort, and this protection was most likely to be against unwanted involvement. Alice, of course, had existed prior to Katie taking over, and that meant that the deception, if that was what it was, started when Ness was there. It was possible—just possible—that William had invented Alice to forfend unwanted interest from . . . Ness.

Katie was uncomfortable with the idea. That Ness was some sort of romantic who would allow herself to imagine a younger man might be interested in her seemed inherently unlikely. And yet why should a woman in her early fifties not feel attracted to somebody like William? A woman should not be expected to be a nun just because of her age. For a short while, Katie played with the possibility, before dismissing it. No, it just seemed wrong to her. Somehow it lacked credibility.

She returned to the idea that William had created Alice as cover. That had happened a great deal in the past when gay men felt the need to dissemble to protect themselves. It was a sad note in the long and painful history of oppression, and although things were much better than they had been, there were still some who might feel the need for that sort of camouflage. Katie was entirely comfortable with people being gay, but she did not feel that William was. She was determined that she would not make the facile assumption that a man who knitted was more likely to be gay. That was a crude, rather offensive assumption—exactly the sort of thing that Katie felt should be resisted. And if William was not gay, and if it was unlikely that he felt pressurised by Ness, then the whole idea of a non-existent engagement made little sense, and she decided to put it out of her mind. And anyway, she did not like speculating as to where people fitted on the spectrum of human sexuality. There was no need to pigeonhole people, she thought. Labels were neither here nor there; what mattered was that people should be accepted for who they are.

Alice existed. There was a real medical student in Melbourne who was really engaged to William, and there was something distasteful in questioning the engagement. William was not dishonest. That would be apparent to everyone, she thought.

He was considerate, amusing, and honest. He was all of these things—and more—and she would not do him the disservice of doubting him.

———

"Did he tell you that we're twins?" asked Angela.

She and Angela were sitting in the office—William was leaning against the filing cabinet—and the mid-morning sun was falling, a yellow square of light, on the bare floorboards beneath the window.

"He did," said Katie, adding, "And he told me all about the hotel."

Angela sighed. "Yes, the hotel . . . We're all bound up in that."

"It sounds like a rather special place," said Katie.

She looked at Angela. Like her brother, there was nothing striking or memorable about her appearance. She was the sort of person one would not particularly notice when one walked past her in the street: not the sort of person to make waves; the sort of person one might meet at any number of school gates picking up young children at the end of the school day. And for a moment, Katie wondered whether that was the destiny Angela would have liked to have had, the quiet suburban life with a husband and children—instead of which there was the hotel, with all that it entailed.

Angela shifted uneasily in her seat. "My brother . . ." she began.

Katie nodded. "He came to see me. He told you that, you said."

"Yes. He said that you were very helpful. That was kind of you."

Katie smiled. "I hope that we can introduce him to somebody he likes. We'll do our best."

She waited.

"Yes," said Angela. "I don't know if he told you, but the real problem is our mother. It's not him—it's not anything to do with my brother. I'm sure he'd be able to find somebody . . ." She hesitated before continuing, "If only our mother would let him."

"I suppose that she's . . ."

Angela did not let her finish. "She's extremely possessive. She won't let go. She plays on his loyalty."

"I see."

"George is a really good person, you know," said Angela. "I know he's my brother, and one might be expected to be loyal to one's brother, but I know what sort of man he is. He's really kind. And my mother takes advantage of that."

Katie said that she had picked that up from George.

"I don't like to sound disloyal to my own mother," Angela continued. "In fact, I try to understand her. And I think I do . . . now."

Katie said nothing. She noticed that Angela's voice was becoming strained with emotion.

"There's something I know that George doesn't know," Angela said. "Did he tell you about our mother's background?"

"A bit," Katie answered. "She said that your father left her and that she had to bring the two of you up alone."

Angela inclined her head. "That's true enough. And that's what George believes. He thinks that our father was the hotel manager at the time. He believes that he went off with somebody else."

"And didn't he?"

"He did. The hotel manager did go off, but he wasn't our

father. When he married our mother, she was already pregnant with George and me. Our real father was somebody else—also named George—George McIntyre—a boyfriend she had who was married to somebody else and wouldn't leave his wife. The manager stepped in and married her out of . . . well, I suppose he was fond of her, but he probably married her out of charity. Or, and I don't like to be cynical, but he might have married her because he saw marriage as a chance to get his hands on the hotel."

Katie asked Angela how she had learned all this.

"It was through our solicitor," Angela explained. "There was a pay-off agreement when the manager—our apparent father—left our mother. There was a note that the solicitor had made about a conversation he had had with my mother. She had given the lawyer the background to her marriage and its break-up. She told the solicitor that we were really the children of her lover. Unfortunately, this note got caught up in another set of papers that were delivered to me from our solicitors. I shouldn't have seen it, but I did."

"And you didn't discuss it with your mother?"

Angela seemed surprised to be asked this question. "Of course not. You don't know my mother—she's one of these people who doesn't like to talk about personal matters. She'd be mortified if she found out that I knew that she had had a lover who wouldn't marry her. She's a very proud woman. I can't see myself talking to her about it."

Nobody is talking to anybody, thought Katie. It was not a good way to run a family—or a hotel for that matter.

"And George?" Katie asked. "Have you taken this up with George?"

Katie shook her head. "George has enough to deal with. I

don't want to burden him with this. It could send him into a real spin."

Katie thought about this. She was not sure what Angela expected of her, and now she asked her.

"What exactly do you want me to do about all this?"

Angela replied immediately. "If you want to help George . . ."

"Which I do."

"Well, if you want to help him, then the best thing you could do would be to sort our mother out. I want you to do something to get her off our backs."

Katie was taken by surprise. "I don't see what I can do—I really don't."

Angela saw it differently. "You can do something. It's something that I could do myself, but I just can't bring myself to do it."

Katie looked at her expectantly.

"My mother needs somebody. At the moment, all she's got is us. And so, if she lets go of us, then she's left with nothing." She looked at Katie, as if willing her to understand. "If she had somebody, then she might feel that she could let us get on with our lives."

Katie sat back in her chair. "So, you're wanting me to find her a partner? Is that what you're asking?"

To Katie's surprise, Angela shook her head. "Not in the way you think I'm asking."

Katie frowned. "I'm not sure I understand what you mean."

Angela leaned forwards. "My mother's life was messed up a long time ago. When she had that affair, when she was young, and her lover, who was married, left her to have us on her own, her heart was broken. I think that was the trauma that made her so clingy, so possessive of her children."

Katie thought about this. She could imagine that something like that could have a profound effect, but wondered whether it was the sort of loss that would be ameliorated through the passage of time. Time cured—the old folk wisdom about that was absolutely right. It did its work patiently, content to be in the background, until suddenly, like a conjuror who we always knew would pull off the trick, time pulled the rabbit out of the hat, and we felt better.

Angela now looked miserable. "I feel so sorry for Mother. She's been carrying this . . . this *thing* about with her for years. This . . ." She searched for the right words. "This emotional burden."

Katie nodded. She wanted to make Angela feel she was not alone in her evident distress. We all had our problems, and it sometimes helped if those who felt they were singled out for suffering were convinced they were not, in fact, alone. If the world was a vale of tears, then it was a vale of tears through which we all, without exception, had to make our way. "We all have that," she said. "We all have that—to an extent. We all have bits of the past that drag us down. Everyone does." She glanced at William for support.

"Yes, we do," said William. "I had a friend who couldn't get over something trivial he'd done. He set fire to his uncle's shed when he was twelve. It haunted him. He kept talking about it."

Angela looked at him briefly, and then looked away. She did not seem to have been comforted. "My mother," she continued, "needs to speak to our father—our real father, that is. She needs to confront him."

Katie drew in her breath. "Will that help?"

Angela was certain that it would. "Closure," she said. "That's what people talk about, isn't it? They need closure."

From his side of the room, William agreed. "Yes, closure is the thing. Definitely."

Angela glanced again at William. "Yes. If she had closure, then she could . . ."

"Move forwards?" suggested William.

Angela nodded. "Yes. She needs to move forwards."

Katie suppressed a sigh. Of course we *all* needed to move forwards—who did not? And what were the alternatives? Moving backwards? Or sideways? Or staying where you were? The last of these was probably where most people were: where they had been the week, or the month, before. She was tempted to smile. One could have fun with popular psychology.

But William was serious. There might be a bit too much easy talk of closure and moving forwards, but what they referred to was real enough. Katie put aside her frivolous thoughts. Now she wondered how Angela knew that this was what her mother needed.

"You say that you haven't talked to her about your father," she said. "If you haven't, then how do you know that this is how your mother feels? How do you know that she's been carrying the whole thing round with her all this time?"

"I just know," Angela said, a note of stubbornness in her voice. "I just know it's that. Sometimes you do, you see—you know things and you can't say why you do."

William intervened at this point. "Yes," he said. "When you're around people for a long time, you can read their minds. They don't need to say anything. You pick it up."

Katie was not sure whether she agreed. You may think that you know what another is feeling, and sometimes you might be right. But as often as not—perhaps more often than not—you might simply be projecting your own thoughts onto the other.

You may think that somebody feels something because that is what you feel, and what you wish the other person would feel too. And quite apart from this, it occurred to Katie that there was a significant problem. Where is he? Could she even find him?

"I know where he is," said Angela.

Katie was surprised. "You've seen him?" she asked. "You've spoken to him?"

Angela shook her head. "No. I haven't. I could, I suppose, but I haven't. I just can't bring myself to do it." She paused. "Once I found out about him, it was not hard to trace him. Scotland isn't a big place, you know. It's hard to get lost here." She paused. "That's what I've come to ask you to do. To speak to him about all of this."

Katie looked uncomfortable. This was not what she envisaged herself doing. This was therapy, or something close to it, and she was worried about being drawn in. And that was precisely what Angela seemed to propose the next time she spoke.

"If we could arrange a meeting between the two of them . . ." she began.

And Katie thought: What does she mean by *we* here?

". . . if we could arrange a meeting between the two of them," Angela continued, "it would give them the chance to sort it out. For him to apologise, maybe. For her to tell him how she's been feeling all these years. And maybe for us to meet him."

"Do you want to do that?" asked Katie. "Do you want me to bring him back into your mother's life—and into your life too?"

"I'm not sure that I want him in my life. Not fully. But in my mother's? Yes, I think so. Just to help her get over him—to unblock the logjam. They might even become involved with one another again—who knows? And that might—just might—get her to let George and me get on with our own lives—or have our own lives even." She looked at Katie. "Doesn't that seem reasonable to you?"

Katie was quick to say that it did.

Angela continued, "I can't face making the first move, but if somebody else sorted it out—yes, I would, I think. And it would be good for George, too, because he needs to get over the past. It might help him to develop a bit more confidence. That's what I want you to do." She looked apologetic. She wanted to make a request, not give an order. "Or rather, that's what I'd like to ask you to do."

Angela stopped. She sat back in her chair while she waited for Katie's response. She looked defeated, as if she did not anticipate a positive response.

But that is what she got. Faced with this appeal, Katie found her resolve not to become involved was simply no longer there. This was a plea—a direct plea—from a person who needed her help. How could she resist? Glancing across the room at William, she realised that he, too, had been affected by what Angela had said. He gave her a hopeless look, unspoken encouragement to say yes to this unhappy woman. And Katie had begun to realise that the work of the Perfect Passion Company was going to have to be a little broader in its scope. If its goal was to bring happiness to people, then there were other aspects of their lives in which it would need to become involved. She had signed up for something bigger than she had imagined. But why not? If the agency had to help in other ways, then that was because help was needed. And sometimes people had no idea where to turn. She would talk to Ness about it at some point, she decided, as it would be helpful to hear what she thought about expanding the scope of the agency's mission.

"All right," said Katie. "If you think it's going to make a difference."

Angela put her hands to her face. "Thank you so much. Thank you. Thank you."

She was near to being overcome, and they could see that she was close to tears. Katie watched her, and reminded herself that Ness had said, *By the way, keep a box of tissues in the office,* and she had not paid much attention—there was so much to deal with at the time, and it seemed no more than a passing remark. But this was the reason behind it—of course it was the reason.

William came up behind her and offered her a clean handkerchief. "Use this," he said. "And you can keep it."

"You people are really kind," Angela said, recovering herself. "And it's a great name you have for the business, by the way. Fantastic."

CHAPTER EIGHT

Old Chrysler

Ness bought supplies at the general store in the town. It was an old-fashioned concern, seemingly unchanged for decades, in spite of the conversion of most businesses in such places into more fashionable delicatessens and gift shops. This store still sold things in bulk—and unpackaged, as if the individual parcelling out of nuts and beans and the like had yet to be invented. She noticed, with satisfaction and approval, that there was less plastic in evidence than elsewhere, and that brown paper bags were still used. There was a counter, too, covered at one end in ancient tin, and shelves that reached right up to the ceiling, stacked with indeterminate items. There was the smell that was an inevitable concomitant of such places—a smell that had notes to it of candlewax and cheese and carrots and a hundred other constituents. It was a place in which most people, other than the most irredeemably modern, would feel immediately at home—as Ness did on her first provisioning visit.

Her third trip to the shop was the first occasion of which she saw her neighbor, Herb la Fouche. He came into the shop behind her, and she heard him talking to the proprietor while she was bending down to examine a box chaotically filled with winter overshoes. She glanced over her shoulder, and saw a man in his fifties, wearing a dark tartan shirt, standing at the counter. He turned his head at the same time that she looked towards him, and their eyes met. He said something to the proprietor before stepping away from the counter to come over towards her.

He extended a hand. "I guess you might not know who I am, but we're neighbors."

Ness stood up. "You're Herb la Fouche, I imagine."

He smiled. "You're probably right. And you're Ness, they tell me. You're the person who's moved here for a while. I was up at Campbell's Bay when you arrived. Sorry I wasn't around to welcome you." The smile broadened. "Not many folks come here. They visit, of course, but that's not quite the same thing. Or they stay in cottages further out on the lake. But we don't get many here in town."

"Well," said Ness, "I thought I might stay awhile."

This seemed to please Herb. That anybody should think it worth spending more than a short time in Murdoch appealed to him. "That's good news."

He offered to take her back to the house with her purchases. "You need a car round here," he said. "You will have had a bit of a walk, I guess. I can drive you anywhere you need, of course. Just ask."

She told him that she had no plans. "I thought about a car, but I haven't decided."

"I know a guy who has an old car you could have. Six or seven hundred dollars is all it's worth. An old Chrysler. But it still goes." He paused. "Would you like it? I can tell you something about that car—it'll never let you down. Starts first time, and keeps going until you tell it to stop."

Ness thought about the offer. "Well . . ."

"Look," said Herb. "Five hundred. No questions asked."

"But . . ."

"He might take four. I could try four. And a full tank of gas. And a spare tyre."

"It could be useful," said Ness.

"Done," said Herb. "You've got yourself a car."

Ness started to object. She wanted to say that you shouldn't buy a car unseen, but she was cut short by Herb.

"There's nothing to see," he said. "It's just a car. Blue, I think. Maybe brown—I can't remember what he said. But underneath, they're all the same."

"I don't know. I was . . ."

"I'll get him to bring it over. He's called Jacques, by the way. He was originally from Trois-Rivières. His father was an engineer on a freighter on the St. Lawrence. Jacques is a diesel engineer. Or was. He lost an arm in an accident. Then he worked as a logger. Nasty business. He does a bit of freelance logging now. He's the only one-armed logger in Canada, I think."

"He's a lumberjack?"

"You could call him that. He maintains telephone poles too. How he manages with his one arm, goodness knows—but he does. He has a place about five miles outside town. He breeds fancy dogs. Wins prizes."

He looked at his watch. "Look, you finish buying what you need. I'll come back in fifteen minutes and give you a ride home."

It was not presented as a suggestion, but as a decision.

―――――

The following morning the car was brought round to Ness by Jacques, with Herb la Fouche in the passenger seat. It was blue.

It came to a halt in front of Ness's porch, although Jacques kept the engine running until Ness came out to greet them.

"Your wheels!" exclaimed Herb, as he got out. "You see. Runs sweetly."

Jacques emerged from the other side. He grinned at Ness. "Jacques Fontaine," he called out. "Herb tells me you want my car."

Ness greeted him, but quickly turned to Herb. "I was hoping to take a look at it beforehand."

He brushed aside the objection. "Everything's in good condition, Ness. Everything. Lights. Muffler. Doors. Tip-top condition." He patted the bodywork. "You heard it just then. The engine runs as if it was made yesterday."

"Can't beat these old Chryslers," said Jacques. "Built in Canada. American design. Solid as a rock."

Ness sighed. "It looks as if I've no choice." She needed a car. This was a car—and it appeared to function as such. She managed a smile. "All right." And then, lest she should appear churlish, added, "Thank you."

"Wise choice," said Jacques.

The transaction was completed inside, where Jacques was paid in the cash she had drawn from the bank that day, which he immediately tucked into his shirt pocket. Ness noticed the dexterity with which he used his single hand, the fingers unbuttoning the pocket while still holding the wad of notes. Her eye went to the empty sleeve on his left side, pinned in against his side so that it should not hang loose.

"Lost an arm ten years ago," Jacques said suddenly. "I was surprised at how little I missed it."

Ness was embarrassed to have been caught staring. "I'm sorry," she muttered.

Jacques shook his head. "No need to apologize. If I see

something unusual, I always look. I saw a really short guy this morning at the gas station. You know the guy I mean, Herb? Lives over at Partridge Lake."

Herb nodded. "He's easily missed, that guy."

"He saw me staring at him, and he didn't like it," said Jacques. "I looked away, but he came over and said something about how he couldn't help being the height he was, and I should know better than to stare, having only one arm myself."

"Oh well," said Herb. "None of us is perfect."

Ness invited them to sit down while she prepared coffee.

"Don't drive that car too fast," Jacques called out to her as she disappeared into the kitchen. "It gets a bit unstable. It's good at lower speeds—but drive it too fast and it likes to drift to the left. You have to keep correcting the steering."

"You should have had that fixed," Herb reproached him.

"None of us is perfect," Jacques retorted.

Ness brought them coffee. As she sat down, she was aware of their eyes upon her. She felt uneasy. There was something about Jacques that unnerved her. It was nothing to do with his missing arm; it was something to do with his facial structure, his eyes. He had a sharp nose and high cheekbones. His hair was slicked back and was shiny, presumably from pomade. His hand was small, more the hand of a woman than of a man. He wore a curious ring—a tiny silver snake curved round one of the fingers. He was, she thought, somewhere in his late forties, although the outdoor life had taken its toll on his complexion.

"It's a snake," he said. "I bought it in Vancouver. It's Malahat First Nation."

Once again, he had noticed her staring. She blushed.

Whether it was because he had noticed the awkwardness of the situation, or for some other reason, Herb loudly changed the subject.

"Do you fish?" he asked.

Ness shook her head. "Not really."

"You've got plenty of fish over there in Scotland, though," Herb said. "I saw a programme. Salmon. They showed people catching salmon. And trout too. Nice fish."

"We have them," said Ness.

"We could take you fishing," said Jacques. "We might catch a pike. Lots of people think pike make good eating."

"Too bony for me," said Herb. "All those little harpoon-shaped bones. No, sir. But they're great fishing. I caught a big guy two weeks ago. Twelve pounds."

"The Germans like them," said Jacques. "It's a big delicacy over there in Germanland."

"Germany," corrected Herb.

"Yup," said Jacques. "That's the place."

Ness said that she would like to go fishing. And she would; she had nothing to do, and she had deliberately come to a place where, having no major plans, minor activities might fill the day. She wanted an ordinary life of the sort that these people seemed to lead. She wanted to be away from her previous life—and that, she thought, was the whole point of an adult gap year. She wanted to have a year *off*.

Sitting in her kitchen a few nights later, she sent an email to Katie, her first message to her since arriving in Canada. She began,

I know I should have written before, but you know how it is when you're settling in somewhere new. But I suspect that you have had so many other things to think about than how I'm faring over here. But were you to ask me that question, the answer I would give is that I have found exactly the place I had been hoping to find. Canada has its sophisticated cities, like everywhere else. It has Montreal and Toronto, for a start, that have a little bit of Paris and New York to them, but without some of the drawbacks that go with being that iconic. But that is not what I'm looking for. I could get a lot of that in Edinburgh, after all, which is a city that can hold its head up in any company, including that of Venice and Vienna (just to think of the *V*s). No, I wanted a small town—a place where you can encounter the beating heart of a country. And so here I am staying in a small wooden house in a small wooden town in the most gorgeous setting. The Canadian Shield, a geological formation, comes up near here, and there are lakes and rocky outcrops and mile upon mile of pristine forest. It goes on and on forever until it meets the sky. At night, that sky is wide and almost white in part with fields of stars. I heard a wolf the other night, howling in the forest. A wolf! I cupped my hands and howled back to him, but he saw through me, I think, and did not reply.

I have made a few new friends. My neighbor, Herb, has been good to me. He is a trapper. I am not romanticising: he is a real trapper. He's straight out of *Rose Marie*, which is a film that nobody watches any longer, but I did when I was younger. Nelson Eddy and Jeanette MacDonald. You know about the Royal Canadian Mounted Police, I take it. Red jackets. Hats. Lances. A very romantic bunch. If you have to be arrested, you may as well be arrested by people with style. Anyway, *Rose Marie* was the Mountie movie to end all Mountie movies. Did you know, by the way, that there was a whole genre of films involving Mounties? Such heroes.

And then there is Herb's friend, Jacques, who has one arm—he lost the other one in an accident. He breeds what Herb describes as "fancy dogs," but I have yet to meet them. Jacques has sold me a car—an old Chrysler—with only four hundred thousand kilometres on the clock. I know that sounds like a lot, but remember they are kilometres. It is a sort of blue, but in certain lights it looks green, or even brown. The seats are covered with cracked blue leather, or artificial leather, rather. It has a strange, not entirely unpleas-ant smell to it—garlic, I thought, when I first got into it, but I may be wrong.

Jacques and Herb are going to take me fishing on one of the lakes next week. Jacques says he knows where very large pike like to lurk. He says that there's one pike there who is a real monster, and he's hoping to catch him either this year or next. I would prefer to let him be—what harm is a pike doing, other than eating every fish it ever comes across?

Jacques has invited me to a party at his friend's house next week. She's called Patty, and she lives with her friend Maddy, who drives a steamroller for the road maintenance people. Jacques tells me that they are both strong-minded women. He says Patty and Maddy drink a lot, but it's mainly because of the cold. People drink a lot in the winter, Jacques says, and then, when the summer comes, they forget to stop. It's much the same in Scotland, I think. All northern countries have that issue: look at the Russians, and their penchant for vodka. Jacques says that Patty and Maddy make their own whisky. He says it's best not to drink it, and if they give you a glass, you should discreetly pour it into a flower bed or put it down the sink if you're inside. He says that it's against the law to run a still—just as it is in Scotland—but that nobody is too keen on the law up here. He says that French Canadians have a different understanding of the law, anyway. Quebec's law is based on the Code Napoléon, which is more broad-minded than English law, which he says has always been so strait-laced about everything. Jacques has many other theories. He is one of these people whom you might call a "professor of many subjects." Jacques knows a lot about wolves, Herb said.

I am very happy here, Katie, and I'm so grateful to you for making this all possible. Please pass all this news on to William, as it will save me writing separately to him. And I almost forgot—the business: I take it that all is going well. You will be bringing great happiness to people—that's what the Perfect Passion Company is all about. I miss it, but I already feel that I have a new life here, and it's one that promises to keep me more than busy. There are more ways than one of skinning a cat, I always say. And there is certainly more room in this place than one needs to swing the same unfortunate feline.

> Your devoted, although absent, and remote, cousin,
> Ness

Katie read out the email to William. When she finished, he stared at her for a few moments before he began to laugh.

"I don't see what's so funny," Katie said. She was concerned about this Jacques. Ness kept strange company—in Edinburgh she had always enjoyed the exotic and the bohemian—but this was in a different league. A one-armed lumberjack? Maddy and her steamroller? The hunting of the large pike?

"Everything," said William. "Herb. The ancient car—and its garlic smell. Garlic! Jacques. The two ladies. Complexities ahead?"

She thought for a moment. "Possibly. But I imagine that Ness can look after herself."

"I hope so," said William. He looked at Katie, and smiled. "It must be nice to be looked after."

Her heart skipped a beat. Oh, please let me look after him, she said to herself, or to whatever fate or deity might be listening. Let me look after William.

But Katie said, simply, "Yes, wouldn't it?" and William said, with a sigh, "I must get back to my knitting."

CHAPTER NINE

Hyperventilation

"I'm hyperventilating," said George. "I can feel it. I'm not imagining it. I can tell."

He was standing outside Valvona & Crolla, the delicatessen that Ness had recommended as an ideal place for introductions to take place. There was a café at the back, a long room lined with family pictures, where the tables were sufficiently far apart to allow private conversations. "You don't want people listening in on such occasions," Ness had explained to Katie. "You know how nosey people are."

Katie did. She liked overhearing snippets, truncated though they may be, and Edinburgh streets were a fertile source of those. *I didn't think I'd done anything wrong,* she had heard a man say that morning, as she waited for a pedestrian crossing-light to change. *But she took a totally different view, would you believe it?* And his friend had said, *No! But then she . . .* And the light had changed, and the drama of which she had briefly been vouchsafed a glimpse would remain forever a mystery.

But now there was this sudden note of alarm from George, and she was not sure what to do. She had a vague idea that hyperventilation was to do with stress, and that in a state of extreme anxiety, people might breathe too quickly and too often and . . . and . . . She had no idea what the consequences were. Did they collapse? Did they lose consciousness? She looked at George: he appeared to be doing neither of these—at least not yet.

"It's carbon dioxide," stuttered George.

Katie frowned. "Too much carbon dioxide?"

"No, too little."

She reached out to take hold of his forearm. "Take a deep breath."

"No, I'm taking too many," he panted. "That's the problem. I have to hold my breath."

She watched powerless as he closed his eyes and held his breath. Then he pinched his nose, so as to block his right nostril.

"You need to allow carbon dioxide to build up in the body," he said. "We all need carbon dioxide."

"Should I call an ambulance?" asked Katie. Perhaps they carried carbon dioxide, as well as oxygen.

George shook his head. "I'll be all right. Just give me a few minutes."

Katie looked about them. They were standing just outside the door to the delicatessen. People came and went, walking down the street; a few came out of the deli. But nobody paid any attention to them. One might be really low on carbon dioxide, Katie thought, and nobody would be any the wiser . . . That was the sort of thing William might say. She would tell him about this. In fact, she wished that William were there with them. This was her first attempt at this sort of introduction, and it would have been reassuring to have him there beside her, especially if George was going to hyperventilate . . .

George seemed to be becoming calmer. He let go of his nose and looked at Katie. "It's because I'm nervous," he explained.

"If I get nervous, or too stressed, I have a tendency to hyperventilate. It's just the way I am."

Katie released his arm. "You had me worried," she said.

"I used to do it in exams," he said. "History exams, in particular, made me hyperventilate. I'd look at the exam paper and see questions I knew I could answer, but I'd still hyperventilate. I still hyperventilate if people start talking about the Scottish Reformation and the Covenanters. That really brings it on."

"Or a date?" asked Katie.

"Yes. A date. Not always, but it can—not that I've had many dates."

That, thought Katie, is because of your mother. She had yet to meet Margaret Fane, but she imagined that she would be enough to make anybody hyperventilate.

"I'm much better now," said George. "It goes away after a few minutes, and it tends not to come back."

"Good," said Katie, and reached out to open the door into the deli.

They walked past the cabinets of pasta and hams, of Italian cheeses, of panforte, of jars of sun-dried tomatoes and anchovies, to the café at the back. George was calmer now, but Katie could tell that he was still nervous.

"It's going to be fine," she whispered.

"Is she here already?" he asked, glancing nervously along the rows of tables.

Katie glanced about the restaurant. "No. We're first."

Katie had reserved a table, and they sat down. George said, "What if she doesn't like me?"

Katie smiled. "Of course she'll like you. You're a nice man, George. There are hundreds of women who'd love to go on a date with you. Hundreds."

He stared at her, trying to ascertain whether she was serious.

"I mean it," she said. "All you need is to work a bit on your confidence."

"I know," he muttered. "I'm trying. I really am."

"I can tell that."

"And what should I talk to her about?"

Katie shrugged. "You could ask her whether she likes Italian food. That always breaks the ice."

He frowned. "Always? If you meet somebody, you ask them whether they like Italian food? Is that what you're saying?"

"Well, not on every occasion," said Katie. "It depends on the context. But sitting here in Valvona & Crolla, I'd say it was a pretty obvious way of getting the conversation going."

"And if she doesn't?"

Katie laughed. "That's highly unlikely."

He nodded. He was watching the entrance to the café, and now he reached out to tug at Katie's sleeve. "I think that might be her," he whispered.

It was, and Emma soon spotted them and came down the line of tables to join them. As she arrived, George sprang awkwardly to his feet.

Katie made the introductions. She noticed that neither George nor Emma looked at one another. As he sat down, George fiddled with his table napkin; Emma seemed interested in something on the floor.

"Well," said Katie, "here we are."

They both looked at her, and then, for a few moments, at one another. Of the two, Emma seemed more confident. She gave George a smile, and to Katie's relief he returned it.

"It's quite warm today, isn't it?" said Katie breezily. One could always talk about the weather, in whatever circumstances.

George nodded. "Warm," he said. "But there's cooler weather coming our way—according to the forecast."

"Rain," said Emma. "I think it might rain." She paused. "Or it might not. One never can tell."

"No," said George. "One can't."

Katie looked at the menu. "Do you like Italian food?" she asked Emma, glancing briefly at George as she posed the question.

"I was just about to ask the same thing," George blurted out.

"Not particularly," replied Emma. "Not that I dislike it, but I wouldn't go out of my way to find an Italian restaurant."

"Of course, in Italy, you might have no choice," said George.

Both Katie and Emma looked at him.

"Possibly," said Emma.

A silence followed.

Katie glanced at her watch—rather obviously, she felt. "I have to keep an eye on the time," she said. "I've just remembered I have a hair appointment. I mustn't keep the stylist waiting."

"No," said Emma.

And then Katie noticed Emma's breathing. It was quick, coming in short spurts, rather as if she had run upstairs. "Are you too hot in here?" she asked. "I could ask them to open a window."

Emma shook her head. "It's not that. It's just that . . ."

"Are you hyperventilating?" asked George, his voice full of concern.

Emma nodded mutely. George reached out and put his hand on her nose. He blocked a nostril. She did not struggle.

"Try to hold your breath," he said. "Big breaths, kept in. Slowly, slowly."

Emma took a deep breath and made a conscious effort to hold it in. After almost a minute, she exhaled. "Better," she said. "I'm so sorry."

George let go of her nose. "I have the same problem," he said. "You don't have to apologize."

Emma stared at him. "You mean, you hyperventilate too?"

He nodded. "Not all the time, but on occasion. I had a bit of an attack just before we came in here, didn't I, Katie?"

"But that's amazing," exclaimed Emma. "I mean, here we are with the same problem. What sort of coincidence is that?"

"A very nice one," said George.

"I really must go," said Katie.

It was as if nobody heard her. George and Emma had launched into a discussion of hyperventilation, and she felt that she was needed even less than before. She rose to her feet. So engrossed in each other were they that she concluded that they had not heard what she had said about having to get away. They looked up as she began to leave. George half-rose, but Katie indicated that he should remain seated.

"Don't worry about me," she said.

Emma looked at her briefly, and smiled, before she turned again to George.

Chemistry, thought Katie. Chemistry.

It was a week before they saw George again. Katie deliberately left him to make his own arrangements with Emma—it was not part of her job, she thought, to nursemaid the relationship through its initial stages. The Perfect Passion Company was an introduction agency, and although she was beginning to see its role as being a broad one, it should only intrude, she felt, where needed. She knew, though, that there would be more involvement needed from the agency if George and Emma should take to one another as she—and indeed they—had planned.

Then they would have to address the issue of Margaret, who was the rock upon which George's previous relationships had foundered.

The more she thought of Margaret, and of her baneful influence, the more outraged Katie felt. She had never met her, of course, but her dislike of the other woman had become intense. She discussed that with William one morning, as they sat over their companionable coffee. William had shown her a design he had just finished, and she had admired it, even if somewhat absent-mindedly.

He had noticed. "You're somewhere else this morning," he remarked. "Not that I particularly mind. You don't have to talk to me if you don't want to."

There was no reproach in his voice, but she quickly apologised. "Sorry, William. I wasn't ignoring you. I like that pattern. I really like it."

He laughed. "I wasn't fishing for compliments. I was only showing you because, well, because you've got good taste."

The tribute pleased her.

"But there's something on your mind," he went on. "What is it?"

She hesitated, and then said, "Do you think it's fair to dislike somebody you've never met?"

He reached for his mug of coffee. It was a mug she had found for him the previous week, and he liked it. It was blue, with *WILLIAM* printed round it in large letters. "It's *my* mug," he had said. "Look. Mine. It was waiting for me in the shop where you bought it. It was waiting for me."

"Solipsism," said Katie, and laughed.

"What-ism?"

"Something I read about—somewhere, I don't remember where. The belief that everything exists only for you."

William looked at the mug. "But it's just a mug," he said. "And I wasn't being serious."

"Nor was I."

Now, holding his eponymous mug, William returned to her question about disliking people. "I think it can be reasonable to take a view of someone else. If somebody tells you about somebody else who's really awful . . . If they spell out the horrid things a person's done, then, yes, you can dislike them. As long as what you've been told is true."

Katie agreed. "Some people in public life, for example. You hear about some bully whose position has gone to his head. You hear about him intimidating staff. You hear about him making some junior person cry—I've heard that, you know, about some politicians right here in Scotland."

William rolled his eyes. "Oh, that's a familiar enough story. We've got those guys at home too. Australian politics can be rough." He took a sip of coffee. "I hate bullies. There's something about them that's just . . ." He searched for the right word.

"Detestable?"

"Yes. Detestable. There was one at school. He was called Eddie Fraser. He was what I'd call a career bully. I was at school with him from the age of eight onwards. I had years of Eddie Fraser—not that he bullied me. He even liked me, I think, although I couldn't stand him. I gave him no encouragement."

"What did he do?"

"He'd pick on anybody who was vulnerable," said William. "If you lacked confidence, he'd suss that out. Then he'd start mocking you, challenging you to do something about it. There was a boy who was a bit effeminate. He was called Julian, but Eddie called him Julia. He made Julian's life a misery, and his parents withdrew him from the school."

"And he got away with it?"

"Most of the time," said William. "Boys don't like to inform on others. In Australia, we call that dobbing somebody in. There's a sort of omertà, down among the boys, you know." He shook his head. "It carried on until he was killed."

Katie caught her breath. "Eddie was killed?"

"He was hit by a train," said William. "Nobody knew what he was doing on the line, but he was killed by a train. He was sixteen. There was an article in the local paper about him. It said what a popular boy he was and how he would be missed."

"I suppose they were just trying to provide some comfort," said Katie. "Even bullies have families."

"Yes," said William. "But you know something? They had a service at school—a sort of memorial service for him. And I remember crying. I actually cried for Eddie Fraser. And after I went home, I cried again, and my mother came into my room and said, 'I'm so sorry—you must be so sad about your friend, Eddie.' I didn't say anything because I actually was sad."

There was a silence. Then Katie said, "Poor Eddie. He must have been unhappy. I know that sounds trite, but it's true, isn't it? People like that are unhappy, which is why they feel they have to make others unhappy too. It's that simple, I think."

"Is it?" asked William. He thought for a moment, before answering his own question. "Maybe it is. I think I might have realised that—even then. That might have been why I was upset when he was hit by the train."

For a short while nothing was said. William remembered Eddie, and Katie thought of the train, and its warning whistle, and the Australian sky above, which she pictured as a wide one, and empty.

"The reason why I asked," Katie said, "is that I found I've been thinking very negatively about George's mother."

William was pleased to move on from the memories of Eddie. "Oh, her! Yes. I'm not surprised. She sounds ghastly."

"But she probably isn't. Because a lot of the people we think are ghastly are not so bad when you get to know them. And maybe it'll be like that with George's mother."

William shrugged. "Possibly." And then he asked, a note of mischief in his voice, "Are you suggesting we should keep an open mind?"

"Perhaps we should. I know it's easier to be prejudiced than to be open-minded, but . . ."

William finished his coffee. "I'll try then."

"So will I."

He asked her whether she had a plan, and she told him that she was waiting to hear from George. "If he and Emma are all right with one another, then I think he wants us to handle his mother. Emma said she wanted to meet her. I explained that George might be unhappy about that, but she insisted. She seems very determined."

"And what does George think?"

"I've spoken to him on the phone. As I had imagined, he was not all that keen about it, but I'll work something out once I know that he's happy with Emma."

William drew in his breath. "It'll be a bit risky bringing Emma and George's mother together, won't it?"

"That's what I thought. But that's what she wants."

"I see," said William.

Katie smiled at him. "Yes. And then we sort out Margaret. We have to try to get her to talk to George the First. That's so that she can let go of George—her son, that is—not the original George." She thought for a moment. "She has to let go of two Georges, I think. George after George. She needs to let go of both."

"I assume the other one—George the First, so to speak—has a family." William looked at Katie enquiringly, and she wondered why he asked.

"Probably. We know that he wouldn't leave his wife back then. They're probably still married."

"Unless he started carrying on with someone else after Margaret," said William. "After all, he had done that sort of thing before. What do they say about leopards?"

Katie pretended to puzzle over this. "That they can see in the dark?" Her straight face failed, and she laughed. "No, their spots. They can't change them."

"Can't or don't?" asked William, with mock seriousness.

"Both," Katie replied. "Leopards can't change, but I don't think that applies to people—particularly now. People are more and more open to change. The idea that you stay the same is old-fashioned." She looked at William. "Haven't you changed? Surely, if you look back, you must see some change in . . ." She thought she should be careful. "In the way you see things?"

What she wanted, of course, was for William to realise that he had grown out of Alice, but even as she recognised the direction her thoughts were taking, she blushed for the sheer shame of it. That was nasty: you should not will other people's relationships to fail. It was not quite as bad as wishing others dead, but it was heading in that direction.

William repeated her question. "Have I changed? In what respects?"

"Tastes. Attitudes. Things like that." She waited.

Then William shrugged. "I used to like heavy metal music. Now I don't."

"You grew up."

He smiled. "Possibly. And I used to like sugar in my coffee."

"Once again, you grew up," Katie repeated.

He grinned. "Possibly. I used to be intolerant too. I dismissed people I disapproved of."

Katie threw caution to the wind. "And in relationships? Have you changed in what you're looking for in a relationship?"

Katie saw the glance that William gave her. It was not hostile, but it was surprised, perhaps even a bit suspicious. It was a look that suggested that he knew that her question had more to it than met the eye.

"I don't know about that," he said evenly. "I think that by and large one should try to stick by people. You make a decision, a choice, and then you try to make that work." He paused. "I don't think that people should be treated as disposable."

"Absolutely," gushed Katie. "Of course. I completely agree." Her heart, though, had become a cold stone within her. He was not going to give up Alice. He was engaged, and he meant it.

William now changed the subject. "The whole situation with George is a bit complicated, don't you think? And I've been wondering whether we should really be doing all this. Is this our—I mean, your—job?"

"Yes," said Katie. "This is what I think we might call the premium service."

"Oh well," said William, reaching out to relieve Katie of her empty coffee mug. "I need to get you a mug with *KATIE* on it. Would you like that?"

"Yes. But you don't have to."

William made his way to the kitchen. "I'd like to," he said over his shoulder.

She looked out of the window. There was nothing particularly significant, she thought, in buying somebody a mug with her name on it. And yet she was touched, and she gave William a fond look that he did not notice, as he had his back to her. Her gaze stayed upon him, and then moved away—with a touch of regret.

⁓

Shortly before lunch that day, George telephoned. He had seen Emma several times, he said, and they were getting on well.

"You made a very good choice for me," he said. "I'm really grateful."

Katie told him she was pleased.

Then George said, "You haven't breathed a word about this to anybody else?"

Katie assured him that the only people who knew, apart from him and his sister, were herself and William.

"But what are you going to do about your mother?" she asked.

He answered quickly. "Angela said you were going to do something."

"We are," said Katie. "We haven't done it yet, but we will."

"Well," George went on, "Emma wants to meet her anyway."

Katie drew in her breath. "As your girlfriend? Isn't that a bit . . ."

He did not let her finish. "No, she wants to meet her without anything being said. She wants to meet her as somebody unconnected with me. Or even just see her. She says she doesn't have to meet her—if she can just see her." He shrugged. "It's what she wants."

Katie was cautious. "Do you think that's wise?"

"It can't do any harm. She's very curious about her." He paused. "And I was wondering whether you could arrange that. I was wondering whether you could bring her to our next Burns Supper. At the hotel. If she came with you—just as two members of the public—then Mother won't be suspicious. There'll be no reason for her to think that Emma and I are seeing one another."

Katie sighed. "I must say that I don't like this deception. It's ridiculous."

There was a silence at the other end of the line, and she realised that she must have upset him. She began to apologise. "I'm sorry. I understand how difficult it is for you . . ."

He cut her off. His voice was strained, and she wondered whether he was about to hyperventilate.

"I really don't want her to find out. Not just yet. I'm really keen on Emma, you know—really keen. And I don't want my mother to put her oar in and wreck it. I couldn't bear that . . ."

"Look," she interjected. "Don't worry. I'm perfectly happy to go along with your plan. We'll come with Emma. We'll buy tickets and book a table. We won't give any impression of having anything to do with you. I promise you that."

He sounded calmer now. "Thanks. I know it sounds pointless, but I want this to work. I want this to work with Emma."

"I'm pleased," said Katie, and, as an afterthought, added, "And is Emma happy too?"

There was a short silence, before George replied, "Emma said something to me last night. She said . . . Well, she said that she and I were ideally suited. She said that she was already very fond of me. She said that."

Then he added, "You know something? Nobody has ever said that to me before. Nobody has ever said that they loved me."

Katie tried to say something, but the words caught in her throat.

"I'm so happy," he went on.

Katie pulled herself together. "That's really great, George. I'm so pleased. I really am."

"I'm walking on air," he said. "That's what it feels like—walking on air."

He gave her the details of the unseasonal Burns Supper and said that he would make a reservation in her name. Then he rang off.

Katie sat at her desk. She had been moved by George's account of what Emma had said to him. It was simple, and unexceptional. People regularly declared their love—there was nothing unusual or special in that. But this touched her because George deserved a bit of good luck. He was not a vain or demanding person. He did not appear selfish. He had been a dutiful son and brother. He deserved this romance, and she was determined that insofar as she could help him, she would try to do so. And if Emma was pleased with George, as it appeared she was, then the Perfect Passion Company had contributed to the overall happiness of humanity. Not every company could do that, but if any could, then it was appropriate that it should be one called the Perfect Passion Company that should do it. Nominal determinism, she thought: perhaps that applies to companies as much as it does to people. We fulfilled the destiny that our names had in store for us. It was an absurd notion, she reminded herself—of course it was—but then one met carpenters called Sawyer, dentists called McCavity, and mechanics called Ford. There was no shortage of these—each one, of course, a coincidence.

CHAPTER TEN

The memory of a poet

Katie spoke again to Emma as she and William walked with her to the Hutton Hotel. It was one of those settled, benign nights that an Edinburgh summer can occasionally conjure up, when latitude seems immaterial, the air is still, the sky is clear, and darkness, even at eight in the evening, is still almost three hours away.

"I'm not entirely comfortable with this," Katie said. "In fact, I think the whole thing is slightly ridiculous. But . . ."

Emma and William both turned to look at her as they walked along.

"But?" prompted William.

"But George wants it," Katie went on. "He doesn't want his mother to interfere. He's jumpy. He knows that you have to see her at some point, Emma. And you want that too, I suppose."

"Yes," said Emma. "I do. But, like you, I don't like the idea of a relationship—any relationship being concealed. It goes against the grain."

"Poor George," said William. "He's scared stiff of that mother of his."

"I can't wait to see what she's like," said Emma. "A real dragon, do you think? Fire-breathing?"

"We'll soon see," said Katie. "But Emma, I think it's really important that you keep a low profile. Don't be tempted to do or say anything that could make her suspect that you and George are an item. Please don't."

Emma bit her lip.

"She may still feel she can see off anybody who threatens her relationship with her son," William said. "People like that can be pretty confident of their powers."

"And she's done it before," Katie pointed out. "She probably imagines she can do it again easily enough."

They continued with their journey in silence. The Hutton Hotel was only twenty minutes or so from Cumberland Street, where Katie and William had met Emma at her flat. Now they were only a few minutes away.

"You've never been to a Burns Supper before, have you, William?" Katie asked.

William shook his head. "I went to a St. Andrew's Night Dinner in Melbourne once, but that was different. They had a piper and so on, and somebody sang 'Jock of Hazeldean,' but that was about it. My father likes to go to those things. He loves formal dinners. He can't get enough of them." He paused. "What happens at a Burns Supper?"

Katie explained. She started by reminding him that to have a Burns Supper in a month other than January was highly unusual, so it was possible that the format could be quite different. But if it followed the normal pattern, she said that there would be a piper who would pipe in the haggis. "The chef brings it in, held high on a plate," she said. "And then the person addressing it, sticks a knife in through the casing, which I'm sorry to say was traditionally a sheep's stomach."

William made a face.

"Nowadays," Katie went on, "it's a sort of artificial sausage skin."

"And then?" asked William.

"Then we get our haggis, served along with turnips—or neaps, as we call them. And there are more addresses. There's something called the Immortal Memory, where somebody speaks about Burns, and there are usually songs and so on. It's all very Scottish. You'll enjoy it. It's very sentimental."

Emma agreed. "I used to go to them," she said. "When I was at university in Glasgow. I was in a club that used to have them. We had a speaker once who went on for almost an hour."

"I doubt if that will happen tonight," said Katie. "This is mainly for tourists. I suspect many of them won't know that Burns's birthday was back in January and that this will be the only Burns Supper in Scotland taking place off piste."

"But what you don't know, you don't fret over," said William.

"Precisely," agreed Katie.

They arrived at the hotel, where there was already a small crowd in the entrance hall. The dinner itself was to be in the large dining room that had been added to the side of the house in late Victorian times. This room was effectively a very large conservatory, with French windows giving out onto an expanse of lawn and a walled garden. There was a top table, set for twenty or so, and a further twelve tables at which six guests would be seated. Because of the light still visible in the sky above the glass roof, there was no real need for lighting, but candles had been lit at each table. Near the open door onto the garden, these candles guttered, and in some cases had been extinguished.

There was a seating plan, and because they were among the last to arrive, they went straight to their table and did not help themselves to the drink that the other guests had been offered. There were two spare seats at their table, but a waiter came and wordlessly removed these.

Katie looked around for George, and eventually saw him ushering guests into an anteroom off to one side. These were those who were to be seated at the top table, and when the piper struck up, these guests were piped in, all walking in a long line with a tall, rather imperious-looking woman at their head. All the other guests stood up to welcome the official party, clapping in time to the pipe tune.

"Margaret," whispered Katie, nudging William, who was seated beside her.

William followed her gaze. "Yes," he whispered back. "That'll be her all right."

Katie glanced at Emma, who had reached the same conclusion as she had. Emma gave her a half-smile, a conspiratorial acknowledgement. She mouthed a word silently, that Katie thought was probably *Mother*.

The haggis arrived, greeted with a cheer by some of the guests. The visitors were conspicuous by the photography in which they now engaged: every moment of the ceremony was accompanied by small flashes from phones held above heads. Then the platter was carried off by the chef, steam rising from the spilled entrails, to be divided out in the kitchen. An excited buzz of conversation now arose, as the foreign visitors discussed what they had seen.

Margaret rose to pronounce the welcome. "This supper is one of Scotland's great traditions," she said. "This is how we recall the memory of our great national poet and pay him homage. We are honoured to share this with all of you—wherever in the world you come from."

She sat down to polite applause. Waiters appeared with

plates that were placed before each diner. This was cock-a-leekie soup, another traditional Scottish dish. William sniffed at it suspiciously. Emma glanced over his shoulder towards the top table, where George was engaged in conversation with an elderly woman in a red dress. She grasped his arm to emphasise a point. Next to him, on the other side, a young man in a dark blue suit looked into space; the woman in red turned to him, said something, and then turned back to face George.

And then Emma looked at Margaret. It was at the exact moment that Margaret, who had been surveying the guests from her position in the centre of the top table, turned her attention to Emma's table. Their eyes met, and Margaret smiled at her. Flustered, Emma looked away, and when she looked back in that direction, Margaret's gaze was elsewhere.

Then George cast a glance in Emma's direction. She thought that he smiled, but she could not be sure. Katie leaned over to Emma and said, "Be careful. Don't make it obvious. Please."

The haggis was served. William picked at his helping suspiciously, and then smiled. "Actually, it's rather good. Peppery. Yes, I like it. What's in it?"

"It's best not to say," said Katie.

Emma asked. "Don't ask. Just eat it. It's considered rude to ask what goes into haggis."

"Really?" asked William.

Katie laughed. "No. That's nonsense. It's lamb and beef. Oatmeal. Onions. Spices—including nutmeg and pepper. That's it."

At the coffee stage of the meal, the Immortal Memory was proposed. A man in a kilt, grey-haired and scholarly, who had been sitting at the top table a few places away from Margaret, rose to his feet. The hubbub of conversation died away as people turned in their seats to face him. Katie glanced across the room at George and saw that he was looking at Emma. She, too, looked at Emma, who, looked guiltily away, muttering, "She's not paying any attention." Katie felt like saying, "She could be, for all you know," but did not. And then she thought, not for the first time that evening: this is ridiculous—this is like two teenagers, two sprigs of the Montagues and Capulets, conducting a secret courtship, away from disapproving adult eyes. But these were two adults, in an age when no parent should dream of interfering in the romantic choice of their grown-up offspring.

Katie realised that her mind had been wandering and that she had missed the speaker's opening remarks. Now he was in full flow, and she gave him her full attention.

"We might remind ourselves," he said, "that Burns, our poet, was a simple farmer, and that he had, like so many young men of his time, to occupy himself with the day-to-day cultivation of a farm—in his case, the farm of Mossfield, in Ayrshire. And it was there, in 1785, while ploughing a field with a young helper, that he disturbed a tiny field mouse. The boy with him would have despatched it with a spade, but Burns told him not to do that: for him it was a moment of inspiration, and it is said that it was in that field, on that very day, that he composed one of his most appealing poems, that still speaks to us today, and that says so much about how we may feel about nature."

The speaker stopped. There was silence. He began the poem.

Wee sleekit, cowerin, timorous beastie,
Oh what a panic's in thy breastie!
Thou need na start away so hasty
Wi bickering brattle!
I wad be laith to rin and chase thee
Wi murdering pattle!"

He paused. Katie closed her eyes. She could not hear this poem but see before her the cowering mouse—and the pattle, the shovel, that might have been its nemesis.

"And then," the speaker continued, "Burns shifts so easily from Scots into English, and we do not feel the transition—we barely notice it—because his mastery of language is so sure-footed, and while Scots is so effortlessly good at conveying the poignancy of that first encounter, English can easily bear the burden of the formal sentiments that now need to be expressed:

> *I'm truly sorry man's dominion*
> *Has broken Nature's social union*
> *And justifies that ill opinion*
> *Which makes thee startle,*
> *At me, thy poor earth-born companion*
> *And fellow mortal!"*

Katie kept her eyes closed. *At me, thy poor earth-born companion, and fellow mortal!* It was a statement of fellow feeling more powerful than any she knew. She thought: Yes, yes.

And the speaker thought so too. He now said, "I would like you to think for a moment about those words *earth-born companion*, and of the work that they do in telling us of the sympathy that should link us each to one another—and that doesn't do that in our fragmented and divided world, because we prevent it; by the hardening of our hearts, we prevent it. Burns reminds us of that. Even today, all those years after that incident in that field, when we have done so much more to scar our earth than any eighteenth-century plough could do, his words make us sit up and think."

She opened her eyes. William was looking at her, and he smiled. It was as if he had been thinking exactly the same thing himself and wanted to share the insight. He leaned towards her. "Yes," he said. "That's it, isn't it? That's true."

The speaker finished, and the toast to the memory of Robert Burns was made. Then people sat down; most were affected in some way by what they had heard. Some knew the poem, had heard it recited before on an occasion just like this, but even they were moved.

Now, Angela appeared, ushering into the room a singer and a player of a clarsach, the Scottish harp. Two Burns songs were sung, "Ae Fond Kiss" and "John Anderson, my Jo." These were followed by another toast, and then the coffee cups were cleared. This signalled the end of the evening. Margaret stood up and thanked everybody for their presence. She was enthusiastically applauded, and the party began to break up.

Katie said, "Well, there you are, William. Your first Burns Supper, even if it's at completely the wrong time of year."

William smiled. "It doesn't matter," he said. "I get the idea." He looked at Emma. "You said you used to go to them at uni. You said you were in a club."

"Yes. A rowing club."

Emma said that she had not been to a Burns Supper since she had gone to one held by her rowing club in Glasgow, when she was a student there.

"You row?" asked William.

"That's what rowing clubs do." She laughed. "I used to. The rowing club always had a Burns Supper every January."

He grinned. "Of course. It's just that rowing and . . . poetry . . . well, the connection isn't obvious."

Katie moved her chair back from the table. She felt tired, and did not want to linger, but at that moment she saw that Margaret was making her way towards them through the throng of guests that was now preparing to leave.

She glanced at Emma, who was looking over towards the other side of the room, where George was engaged in conversation with the singer and the harpist. Angela was with him. Emma had not seen Margaret approaching, and now it was too late: Margaret had stopped, and she was speaking to them.

"Thank you so much for coming. I do hope you enjoyed yourselves."

Emma turned round. If she was surprised to see Margaret, she disguised it. "No, thank *you*," she said. "That was great."

Margaret gave her a look of appraisal. "You're local. A lot of our guests are overseas visitors."

Emma made a gesture of understanding. "This must have been very nice for them. A bit of Scottish culture. Haggis and whisky and . . . Robert Burns."

Margaret laughed. "It's what we do. People come to Scotland, and they want these things."

Katie detected a note of defensiveness. There was an undercurrent there, she thought, and it alarmed her.

"I enjoyed it," she said quickly. "I've been to plenty of these occasions, and I still enjoyed it." She reached out to touch William's arm. "As did William. He's Australian."

"Yes," said William. "I liked those songs. And the mouse poem." He paused. "Mouse Lane. That's where I live."

Margaret turned to him. "Mouse Lane? Here in Edinburgh?"

"Yes. You know it? It's only a few blocks away."

Margaret said that she knew it well. "One of our chefs lived there." She was speaking to William, but she was still looking at Emma. Noticing this, Katie felt even more uncomfortable. She wondered whether Margaret had intercepted a glance between George and Emma. If she was as possessive as George and Angela had described her, then she might be expected to be watchful of any sign of interest in others on the part of her children. But surely not, Katie thought: Nobody went through life like that.

"William's a knitwear designer," Katie blurted out. "His studio's next door . . ."

She stopped herself. She had not intended to say that.

But Margaret was mainly interested in what William did. "You do those jerseys?" she asked him.

William inclined his head modestly. "Yes. And other things."

"I read an article about your work," Margaret said. "Like Kaffe Fassett?"

"I'm not him," William protested. "I wish I were."

"I walked past your studio the other day," said Margaret. "I think I know where you are. You're next to that . . . what's the name of it? The Perfect Passion Company. That marriage bureau place?"

William stared at her. He did not answer. He glanced at Katie, who met his gaze for a brief moment before she said, "Yes, that place. Actually, that's me. I run that."

Margaret turned to her. "But there was another woman there, wasn't there? I met her at a bridge evening."

"My cousin," said Katie. "She's away at the moment. I'm running the business for her."

Katie spoke in a tone of resignation. She felt that she had to say what she said because it would have been impossible to do anything else, once she had revealed that William was her neighbor.

Emma had been silent. But now she said to Katie, "I'm going to have to slip away."

Katie turned to her gratefully. "Of course. Actually, we all need to go. It's later than I thought."

Margaret smiled benignly. "I'm glad you enjoyed yourselves."

She gave a last glance at Emma, who muttered her thanks again. Then Margaret left them, to speak to the guests about to leave another table.

"Sorry," Katie whispered, to nobody in particular, but perhaps to Emma more than anyone.

"Not your fault," said Emma.

"I hadn't planned that," Katie went on.

"She didn't see anything," Emma reassured her.

"I think she did," said William.

There was no sign of George as they made their way out of the hotel.

"Was that what you wanted?" she asked Emma, as they stepped out onto the street.

"I met her," Emma replied. "I wanted to do that." She paused. "I felt that I had to. I wanted to know what I was up against."

William said that he understood. "Of course, you needed to do that," he said. "You do see that, Katie—don't you?"

"I suppose so," said Katie.

"You aren't cross with me, are you?" asked Emma.

Katie shook her head. "No, I'm sorry. I just feel a bit foolish. We go there to see and not be seen. I then go and almost give the game away."

"You didn't," protested William. "You didn't give anything away. You were terrific."

"Yes," said Emma. "William's right. You were."

She wanted to kiss William. *Ae fond kiss* . . . Robert Burns would have said, "Kiss him, kiss him." William was so . . . What was it? He was so . . . kind. Burns would have approved. His poetry was all about kindness and love.

"Oh, well," she said.

"Yes," said William. "Exactly. Oh, well."

And with that, he linked his arm in hers. Emma smiled. She had guessed correctly how Katie felt about William. Another woman can always tell, she told herself. It's only too obvious if you watch the way people look at others, at what their eyes say about what they are thinking. There is no great art in it— simply an awareness of how we give ourselves away.

CHAPTER ELEVEN

A day out with Herb and Jacques

Herb came round to collect Ness in his truck. Jacques was with him, having left his own older and even more decrepit truck outside Herb's house. Ness had seen them from her window and had watched as Herb came out to greet his friend; she saw that Jacques had something with him—a small sack of some sort—and he handed this to Herb, who looked inside it, appeared to say something to Jacques, and then took it inside. Jacques lit a cigarette while he waited for Herb to return. Ness watched the small clouds of smoke rise above his head, like breath in winter. Then Herb came out of the house, and the two men climbed into the other truck. She hoped that Jacques would not smoke as they drove to the lake. People sometimes said, "Do you mind if I smoke?" even as they lit up. She would say she did. She believed in telling people that she objected, and she would do so if Jacques asked her.

Herb came to her front door and knocked. There was a bell, but it did not work, and Herb appeared to know that.

"Your bell hasn't worked for years," he said. "You knew that? I always knock when I come here. The last people to rent this house were deaf. I had to knock real loud to get them to answer."

"I'll fix it," said Ness. "I'm going to be living here for a while."

"There's a guy called Bill who does these things," Herb told her. "He's not exactly an electrician—but he behaves like one."

Ness laughed. "That's an interesting way of putting it."

"He'll fix your bell," said Herb. "Bill's got electricity tape."

She locked the front door behind her and walked with him back to the truck. Jacques had moved to the back seat.

"We haven't got far to go," said Herb. "I've got the rods in the back. Also, some sandwiches. Fishing can be hungry work."

Jacques greeted her from the back seat as she got into the front of the cab. "We're going to catch a pike today," he said. "Maybe two or three. You never know."

"That big one," said Herb.

"You said that last month, Herb," said Jacques. "And the month before. He's still there. Watching us. Laughing."

"I've been trying for a long time," said Herb.

Ness gazed out of the window as they moved off. Trees, she thought. All these trees.

"We've got trees, all right," Herb said.

She looked at him from the corner of her eye. He appeared to have read her mind. And then she asked herself, What do I think I'm doing? Going pike fishing with two men I barely know? *Pike fishing!*

From the back, Jacques said, "No shortage of trees."

Ness decided that she should say something. "I like trees."

"You like trees?" asked Herb.

"Yes. I love forests. I love the way they smell. And the quiet. I like the way that trees deaden sound."

Jacques made his contribution. "You don't want to get lost in all those trees out there. You could wander around indefinitely."

"It's happened," said Herb. "Last winter there was somebody from Ottawa who came out here. He wanted to go snowshoeing. He went off by himself. They never found him."

Ness frowned. "Never?"

"No. They found one of his snowshoes, but there was no trace of him."

"Froze," said Jacques. "You freeze, you see. You don't know it's happening, but you freeze. Doesn't take long, especially if there's wind. Goes through you like a knife."

"Another guy disappeared the year before," Herb continued. "That was in the summer. You can get lost summer and winter. Fall too. Any time, really. You go off and you become disorientated."

"That means you don't know where you are," offered Jacques from behind. "You think you're going north, and you're actually heading south. Then you start walking in circles."

"Climb a tree," Herb pronounced. "That's what I say. Climb a tree and see if you can see anything."

"More trees," Jacques muttered. "You see more trees, often as not."

For a while they travelled in silence. The road they were on was narrow and winding. There was little traffic: a car that passed them dangerously close to a blind summit—"Idiots," muttered Herb; a truck with a swaying trailer—"That guy's going to lose his trailer," remarked Jacques; and a motorcyclist on a Harley-Davidson, going in the opposite direction.

"Bob van Voort," said Herb over his shoulder. "Do you reckon that was Bob, Jacques?"

"Could be," answered Jacques. "It looked like his bike."

"Trouble is," said Herb, "you can't see their faces under the helmet."

"Bob's been sick," offered Jacques. "He went to Toronto and ate something. Came back sick."

"He owes Jim Howard two hundred bucks," said Herb. "Hasn't paid for nine, ten months. Jim's getting impatient. He said he won't lend him money next time."

"Speeding fine," Jacques said.

Herb half-turned to Ness to explain. "Jim's kind, you see. He built old Martin Gregor's patio for him. Made a really good job of it and didn't charge him a cent. That was after Martin lost his wife."

"She went to Toronto," Jacques added from the back of the cab. "Ate something down there."

Ness's eyes widened. "Like Bob?"

Herb looked thoughtful. "Yes. But different, I reckon. She had cancer before she went."

"So it wasn't something she ate?" asked Ness.

"Probably not," said Herb. "But you never know, do you?"

Ness was not sure what to say. She looked at Herb, who glanced away from the road for a moment or two to smile at her. "Life," he said. "It's an uncertain business, isn't it?"

She hesitated, and then relaxed. Herb saw the humour in what he had said. She thought that he might be gently making fun of Jacques, who seemed to be far more literal than he was. This was a world that was quite different from the one which she had inhabited in Edinburgh. These people lived in a small town, deep in the country, a long distance from the city; this was a world in which Toronto did indeed seem distant; a world in which if you went off to a city, with all its exotic cuisines, of course you would be at risk of food poisoning. This was a world in which not much happened, even on a busy day. And yet, even as she thought this, she realised that the life that people led here had far greater depth than the life of the city: in Toronto or Montreal you might sit in a café and see from your window more people go past you than lived in a hundred square miles of rural Ontario, but you would not know, nor find out, a single thing about them. Cities were populated by strangers, whereas a small town was full of people whom you recognised, whose personal history you would know or would soon have explained to you, whose faults and failings and dreams and triumphs would be only too familiar to others. That appealed to Ness, as did the sheer physical reality of Canada—the scale of the landscape, the sense of space above and about you, the awareness of a hinterland that stretched to the very limits of the habitable world, to an edge of tundra and ice and frozen seas.

It took them no more than half an hour to reach the lake, the last stages of the journey being on an unpaved road through the low scrub that grew on granite outcrop. Then, by the lakeside itself, the trees returned, thick and mysterious to the very edge of the water, which was dark and deep even at the shore. Where the track descended to the lakeside, a small, rickety dock ventured out a couple of yards; beside it, drawn up onto a narrow beach, were two small rowing boats and an upturned canoe. Herb explained to Ness that one of these boats belonged to Jacques, and the other to his friend Tom, who was happy for them to use it. It was a friendship that went back years: Jacques had given Tom a dog some years earlier and had also fixed his borehole pump. "It's quid pro quo in the country," Herb said. "You know that expression, Ness?"

Ness said that she had heard it.

"Greek," said Jacques. "It's Greek for *tit for tat*."

Ness checked herself, but Herb did not. "It's Latin, Jacques," he said.

"Yup," said Jacques. "It's Latin all right."

"You said it was Greek."

"I meant Latin. That's what I meant."

Ness said, "Favours come back, don't they? You do something for somebody, and then they do something for you."

"Too darn right," said Jacques. "And you never know when it's going to happen."

"You never know when *anything* is going to happen," observed Herb.

"Not much happens round here," said Jacques, as he fitted oars to one of the boats. "But when it does happen, then I reckon it really does happen. No half-measures."

Herb helped Jacques to push the larger of the two rowing boats into the water. Then, tethering the first boat, he turned to help with the launch of the other.

Jacques had brought a small electric outboard that he now installed on the boat he was to use. "We'll have to split up," he said. "Neither of these boats will take three people. So you go with Herb, Ness, and I'll take the smaller boat. I've got my outboard. We can fish different ends of the lake—we'll cover the options that way. Sometimes fish like to swim to one end; sometimes they hang about the other. You never know with fish."

"I find it difficult to imagine what goes on in a fish's mind," Ness mused.

"Nothing," Jacques said. "Fish haven't got much of a brain. They don't know what's going on half the time."

Herb laughed. "I could name a few people like that. And you could, too, Jacques, I suspect."

"Sure could," said Jacques. "My ex-brother-in-law, for

instance. Poor guy doesn't know which way is up, half the time. He runs a pet-food franchise down in Kingston. He's done quite well. Drives a large Mercedes-Benz now."

"He must have known something to get where he did," suggested Ness.

Jacques shook his head. "Wallace knows nothing," he said. "A very ignorant man."

"As long as he's happy," said Ness.

"No, he ain't," said Jacques.

Herb sighed. "Oh well. Lots of guys are unhappy when they don't need to be."

Jacques thought about this. "True," he said. And then he asked, "What's the name of that guy?"

Herb frowned "Which guy?"

"That guy. The one who said we all want to marry our mothers. That guy."

"Freud," said Ness. "Sigmund Freud."

"That's him," said Jacques. "Well, just look at him. He said that we're all mixed up inside. He had a point, I think."

"A lot of people agreed with him," said Ness. "They still do."

The second boat was now launched, and was safely tethered to a rock on the shore. Jacques addressed Ness. "We can meet. In two hours—that suit you? Meet back here?"

They agreed, and set off. Ness was at the stern of the boat, while Herb rowed from the thwart. The sun was on her face; she was warm and comfortable. The air was scented with pine. The water lapped at the side of the boat. A dragonfly darted across the surface of the lake, a flash of blue and yellow.

Herb spoke as he rowed. "Yes, I've been coming to this place ever since I was a boy. I came here with my uncle in the old days—then he went to Guelph. He had the record for a trout in this water—he was always talking about that. Pike eat the trout you know—they're predators. Mind you, most fish are, come to think of it."

Herb shipped the oars and reached for a fishing rod, which he handed to Ness. "And what about you, Ness? What did you do back in Scotland?"

She took the rod, dropping the lure into the water.

"You'll need to cast that," said Herb.

"I had a business," she said, in response to his question.

"What sort of business?"

"An introduction agency. I introduced people who were looking for partners."

Herb smiled. "And it worked? You fixed them up?"

"Some took some time," Ness replied. "But we prided ourselves on being able to find somebody for everybody."

Herb looked thoughtful. "Do you think you could find somebody for someone like me?"

She was surprised, and it was a moment or two before she responded. "In theory, yes."

"No, not in theory—for real."

She looked at him. "You want me to . . ."

"I want you to help me," he said. "Me and Jacques. Both of us. We could both do with a wife, but you know how it is."

CHAPTER TWELVE

The man in the kitchen

Katie looked at her watch. It was now ten minutes past eleven, which meant that William was ten minutes late for morning coffee. He was normally scrupulously punctual, letting himself into the office at five minutes to the hour and serving her a steaming cup of light roast Arabica—the lightness of the roast, he said, allowing for the subtlety of the beans to come through. "Dark roast, cheap beans," he had explained, through the hiss of the milk steamer.

She wondered whether he was out. When she had arrived at Mouse Lane that morning, she had looked up and seen a light at one of his windows; on the landing she had heard, too, the sound of a radio drifting out from behind his door. She remembered that because it had been nine o'clock, and she had heard the sound of the announcer's voice reading the brief news bulletin that was always broadcast at that hour. There was an air traffic control strike, and there were recorded interviews with a Scottish family stranded in Florida. A woman was complaining volubly about lengthy delays; they had waited six hours for a substitute flight, which brought a wry smile to Katie's lips. The crossing of a continent or an ocean was now such a routine matter that a brief delay of that sort was cause for irritation and annoyance. That journey had previously taken weeks, and during those weeks, one faced the risk of perishing from any number of reasons and never making one's destination. That put a six-hour delay in perspective.

So William was in, or at least had been in. She looked at her watch again, and then made up her mind. She would seek him out. She did not want him to get the impression that she was watching over him—she would *not* be a mother hen—but she thought it important to check. People sometimes slipped in their flats; they tripped up over a carpet or on a polished floor, and then they might lie for hours before a friend or neighbor happened to come by. William was young, and strong enough; he would not consider himself to be at particular risk, but accidents in the home could happen to anyone, and at any time. She would go and check up—discreetly—and satisfy herself that all was well. If William was safe and sound in his flat, then there might be momentary embarrassment when he realised that she was watching over him, but that surely was far better than leaving somebody on the floor, unconscious or with a broken leg.

Leaving the office, she made her way to William's front door and rang his bell. She heard the bell ringing deep within the flat, and then the sound of an interior door being opened. He was alive. Good. She almost turned round to slip back into her office unobserved, but he would guess it had been her, surely, if he found nobody outside on the landing. So, she waited until he had opened the door and was standing in front of her, knitting needles in hand and a slightly surprised expression on his face.

"That time already?"

She nodded. "I was just wondering. If you're busy, don't

worry . . . or I can make coffee and bring you a cup. How about that?"

He told her that his mind had been elsewhere. "I'll come round," he said. "Give me a mo to deal with this."

Her eye went to his knitting. It was the front piece of a sweater, the design an intricate tribute to a Fair Isle motif, although the colors were altogether more vibrant. Yet they worked; William had an eye for harmony when it came to color. He was a peacemaker in color, she thought. No color fought with another color; everything took its place gently beside its neighbor.

She returned to her office and waited for him, leaving the front door open. A few minutes later he arrived, and made his way directly into the kitchenette in which he made coffee.

"You must be desperate," he called. "Caffeine on its way."

"You were busy."

"Yes. That's a commission. It's for a Swedish countess, believe it or not. I didn't realise the Swedes had countesses, but they do, apparently. This one saw my work at an exhibition in Stockholm. I had a piece in this show, you see, and she went along and saw it. She gave me free rein. I could do anything I wanted."

He came out with two mugs of coffee, and deposited one on her desk. Holding the mug with its *WILLIAM* motif, he leaned against the filing cabinet. She saw that he was staring out of the window, over the rim of the mug.

"Are you all right?"

He looked back at her, before putting his mug down on the top of the filing cabinet. "Not really."

She had not expected this. In her experience, people usually answered the question as to whether they were all right positively, and then, if they were not, added a rider, explaining what was wrong. Now William went straight to an admission that not all was well.

"Can I . . ." she began.

"Can you help? I don't know. Maybe."

Katie's mind raced. It was Alice. Or it was his parents: William had mentioned that his father had a heart condition. That would be it.

"Is everything okay back home?"

William shook his head. "Not exactly."

"Your father? Is he . . ."

"Not him. No, it's nothing like that. He was a bit unwell earlier this year, but he's fine now. He has angina, but he has these pills that keep it under control."

"You mentioned that."

"Yes, but he's fine. It's Alice."

Katie was silent.

"We had a row."

Katie took a sip of her coffee. She avoided looking at William.

"I called her on FaceTime," William continued. "I speak to her every other day. I probably told you that."

He had not, and Katie felt a momentary disappointment. She had imagined that they rarely talked to one another.

"It's a bit difficult because of the time difference. But we've managed."

"Good," said Katie. She did not know what else to say.

"Anyway, when I called her at the time we agreed, she wasn't there. I tried again an hour later, and then an hour after that. Eventually I got through to her, and she was . . . well, she was very short with me. Snippy. She said that she had her own life to consider—those were her exact words. She said, 'I've got my own life to consider, and I don't have to be at your beck and call all the time.' That's what she said."

He gave Katie an injured look.

"That's a bit hard," she said. She weighed her words carefully. You interfered in a lovers' tiff at your peril. Everyone knew that. Lovers closed ranks.

He did not take offence. "I thought so too. I asked her whether I'd done anything to offend her—I didn't think I had, but I wanted to make sure. And she said that she didn't think I cared. So I asked her what she meant by that, and she said that I had gone off to Scotland and didn't care about what happened to her."

"I don't think that's fair," Katie said, mildly.

"No, I don't either. But I offered to come back."

"To Australia? To Melbourne?"

He nodded. "I said that I'd come back if she liked."

Katie caught her breath. She did not want William to go. He couldn't. "What did she say to that?"

"She said that she didn't want me to come back. She said that we needed more space."

Katie thought that the ten thousand miles, or whatever it was, between Edinburgh and Melbourne should be space enough for anybody. She did not say this, though, but gave, instead, an ambiguous shrug.

"We left it at that," William went on. "I said that I'd get in touch with her in a few days' time, and I was about to say goodbye when I saw something." He paused. "She was speaking to me from her flat. It has a small living room, with a kitchen off at the end. Normally you can't see the kitchen on the screen—there's a sofa, and Alice sits on that when we talk. The kitchen door, which is in the wall behind the sofa, is normally closed.

But suddenly it opened. There must have been a breeze or something, and I . . ."

Katie waited. There had been a man in the kitchen. There must have been a man.

"There was a man in the kitchen," said William.

"Oh."

"I saw him before he reached out to close the door."

"And did Alice realise that you saw him?"

He shook his head. "I don't think so."

Katie looked up at the ceiling. She would have to be very careful. She felt so pleased. "What sort of man?" she asked, and then, immediately, realised how odd her question sounded. "I mean, was it somebody you knew?"

But William did not find her question at all ridiculous. "He was the same age as us, I suppose."

"Wearing?" asked Katie. As she asked this, she thought: Men don't always notice what people are wearing; women do. William, perhaps, as a designer, was different. And he had noticed.

"Boxers," he replied. "That's all."

~~~~~~

After William went back to his studio, Katie found that she could not settle down to work. She had no appointments that day, and the only pressing matters were a couple of bills to be sent out and a letter or two to be written. Ness had given only a brief explanation of how the financial side of the business worked, but Katie had been helped to understand it by the accountant, and it was now reasonably clear to her. Clients paid a significant registration fee right at the beginning, and a further sum became payable after each introduction. That seemed to be enough to keep the current account healthy, and the business had no difficulty in finding enough for Katie's salary and for everyday running expenses. The Perfect Passion Company, she was pleased to discover, was more than solvent—it was, in fact, cash-rich.

She dealt with these bills and with a few items of correspondence. Then, still rehearsing in her mind what she had said to William, and what she thought perhaps she should have said, she decided to close the office and go off for lunch at her usual bistro on Queen Street. She would enjoy a solitary lunch, reading a book, undisturbed, and there was a novel that she had to finish before the next meeting of the book group she had recently joined. It was not an easy group—there were several members who seemed to delight in being highly critical of every title chosen for discussion, but she wanted to persist. Eventually, she saw herself resigning, in favour of a less author-hostile environment, but for the time being she was persisting. The latest novel, in which the heroine had suffered a litany of misfortunes, including being stuck at the hips when crawling through a window, was testing her resolve, and by the time she reached the bistro and took her place looking out onto the street, she realised that she was too affected by what had happened that morning to pay any attention to the novel in question. She laid the book aside and gazed at the day's menu. There was a *soupe du jour*, which she usually ordered, as long as it was not fish-based. That would need enquiry, although there would be no need for the debate she had entered into with the *patron* the previous week over the distinction between a *soupe du jour* and a *potage du jour*. That, apparently, was a fine point. *Soupe*, he said, was a generic term to cover everything, whereas *potage*, strictly speaking, was made of vegetables. *Soupe* was usually thicker than *potage*, which could, of course, be a consommé. Then there were *veloutés*, he went on to point out, that contained more finely liquidised ingredients, added to a base of melted butter and flour. It was not simple.

But neither was life. Prior to her conversation that morning with William, Katie had decided that she would be careful not to become too involved in William's life. His engagement was his affair, and she should steer well clear of any discussion of Alice, whom she had never met and knew little about. But now, since twenty minutes past eleven that morning, things were different. Twenty past eleven . . . it was like that refrain from the Lorca poem when the time is intoned as a solemn chorus . . . twenty past eleven and everything had changed. William was in a difficult situation, and she could not, as a friend, pretend that nothing was happening. Whether she liked it or not, she was being drawn into his private life.

Katie had expressed sympathy. After he had made the disclosure that the man was wearing only boxers . . . and she had been unable to stop herself imagining what Ness might have said about that—*one does not wear boxers in other people's kitchens, dear; one just does not*—even after that fact had been added to the *velouté*—no, she told herself, this is *not* funny—this is a grade one moral dilemma—even after that, William had said, "Poor Alice—I suppose she's lonely."

Katie had been tempted to say, "But she isn't lonely, William. You are *never* lonely if you have a man in your kitchen, particularly one who is wearing nothing much, or just boxer shorts, as in this case. The definition of *lonely* does not include such situations, I think." But she did not say that. She just looked at William and thought: How kind, or . . . and here she reproached herself for her lack of charity as she thought how *weak*. And it was weak. You did not condone something like that if you were prepared to stand up for yourself. You did not return to your knitting and comment on the loneliness that had driven Alice to conceal a man in her kitchen. By contrast, you asked, with genuine indignation, what he was doing in the kitchen in the first place. But William had not. And he had finished his coffee and said, "Let's talk about this some other time—I'm a bit upset right now."

A bit upset? She wanted to say, "You have every right to be *very* upset. Alice is your *fiancée,* for heaven's sake." But once again, she said none of this, and had merely agreed that they could talk on some other occasion. And then William had returned to his studio, and she had been left staring at the space immediately in front of her desk, thinking about what had happened. It was obvious to her that William was blaming himself for this situation and that he wanted to repair the relationship with Alice. And this meant that she now had to decide what to do. Should she encourage him to respond with proper outrage to the deception that Alice had practised on him, to accuse her of unfaithfulness and bring the whole thing to an end, or should she support him in his desire—if there was indeed a desire on his part—to sort out their difficulties? In other words, should she help to bury a failed engagement, and have more of William's attention herself—even if only as a friend. Or should she try to be dispassionate about it, and think only of the happiness of these two temporarily estranged lovers?

The *patron* was at her side. "*Soupe du jour?*" he said. "I think you like artichokes, don't you?"

She nodded. It was a distracted nod. She was thinking of the man in the boxers. Was there an innocent explanation for that? Was it *that* hot in Melbourne? A thought came to her: It was summer in Scotland—winter in Australia.

CHAPTER THIRTEEN

Stuck at the hips

Katie went to her book group that night. The two members who always found fault with the choice of book were in hypercritical mode, trying to outdo one another in the strength of their condemnation of the author's pale efforts.

"I can tell you one thing," said one of them, a tall, bespectacled woman named Eleanora who taught French history at the university and who had written a book, some years earlier, on Mallarmé, "Leavis would have considered this book to be . . ."

"Worthless?" offered her friend, a small woman in her fifties with straggly hair that Katie had decided was in need of a good shampooing.

"Exactly, Dawn," said Eleanora. "Without any discernible merit at all. None."

Dawn, thought Katie. The name seemed just right, somehow, though she had known Dawns who did not have straggly, unwashed hair—who were, in fact, rather glamorous. But Dawn still suited this Dawn—perhaps even ironically.

"Oh, I don't know," said Katie hesitantly. "I rather enjoyed it." She had not, but she was determined not to agree with these two—and she felt that the other members of the group were on her side in that respect.

"Loved it," said the woman in whose flat they were meeting that evening. "I agree with Katie."

Dawn gave her a baleful look, but said nothing.

"For example," Katie continued, "when that woman gets stuck at the hips while going through that window, I thought, Precisely! That sort of thing happens only too often."

Eleanora was staring down her nose at Katie. "You aren't serious, surely? I know of nobody—nobody at all—who has *ever* got stuck at the hips."

Katie dug in. "Well, I do," she said firmly. "Several, in fact." She knew nobody who had experienced that fate, of course, but Eleanora and Dawn were so irritating that Katie would be prepared to invent anything to oppose them.

Eleanora continued to stare at her. "Leavis said—and T. S. Eliot held much the same view, I'd point out—that the function of literature was not to entertain . . ."

"With stories about people getting stuck at the hips," interjected Dawn.

"Precisely," agreed Eleanora, "but to help us to understand the moral issues in our lives."

"Which is why he starts off *The Great Tradition* by saying that there are only four great novelists in the English language: Jane Austen, George Eliot, Henry James, and Joseph Conrad."

Eleanora nodded approvingly at each name.

"Nonsense," said Katie. The Devil could quote F. R. Leavis for his own purposes. She had had enough of this . . . what was it? It was posturing, she decided. It was pure posturing.

"I couldn't agree more," said their hostess. "But let's not argue. Let's have a cup of coffee and a piece of cake. I've made two sorts: one is very chocolatey, and the other is a lemon drizzle. Those who are feeling a bit acidic might prefer the chocolate option." She glanced at Eleanora and Dawn as she said this, and then, briefly, at Katie, who exchanged a conspiratorial smile with her.

The book group broke up shortly after ten, and Katie returned to her flat on foot. The city was quiet, and there was a slightly eerie feel to the empty streets. Edinburgh was one great opera set, she felt, with its towering stone buildings, its eccentric, spiky skyline, and its ubiquitous historical echoes. And walking home now made her feel that she was back in the time when the streets of the Scottish capital were brimming with conspiracy. That group of four men at that corner, for instance, could be discussing the fate of Darnley, the unfortunate husband of Mary, Queen of Scots, and that man walking ahead of her could even be Bothwell himself, who plotted Darnley's death and then married the Queen. It did not require much imagination to think in those terms—not against this backdrop.

She did not stay up when she reached her flat, but took a quick warm bath, slipped into bed, and turned out the light. She could not get William out of her mind, and thought of him now. He had been in her thoughts all day, even at the book group while Eleanora and Dawn were parading their knowledge of literary criticism when all the other members were looking longingly at the last few slices of chocolate cake. What was so wonderful about William? His kindness? Yes. His willingness to listen to you, to make you feel that you were the only person he wanted to hear from? Yes, that too. His sheer loveliness? Was that it? Did one have to resort to a term like that—*loveliness*—an old-fashioned, catch-all term that nevertheless caught the essence of one who is beloved for whatever inexplicable reason; for that was a feature of those who were beloved—it was often difficult to say exactly why we loved them; we simply did.

She drifted off to sleep, thinking of him. Curling up with the thought of another, she thought, is often every bit as consoling, if not more so, as curling up with the person himself.

Shortly after ten-thirty the next morning, Katie's office doorbell sounded. She answered the door, half-expecting the postman, who often delivered letters at that time, but found an unexpected visitor instead.

Margaret Fane looked apologetic. "I don't have an appointment," she said.

Katie struggled to conceal her surprise. "No. I . . ."

"I was walking past," said Margaret, "and I thought I might just see whether you could spare me a few minutes."

Katie opened her mouth to reply, but was interrupted by Margaret, who continued, "I really would appreciate it. I know how busy you must be."

Why, wondered Katie, would Margaret imagine that she would be particularly busy? If there were any season in which an introduction agency should be busy it surely would be summer. The thought made her smile, and Margaret thought that the smile was one of assent.

"Thank you so much," she said, moving over the threshold. "I promise I won't take up too much of your time."

Katie led her visitor into her office and invited her to take a seat. Then she herself sat down. "I take it that this is a social call," she began. "I very much enjoyed the Burns Supper the other night, by the way. It was beautifully planned."

Margaret acknowledged the compliment with a smile. "That was one of our regular speakers, Professor Purdie. He's much in demand for these occasions."

"I'm not surprised," said Katie. "And the singer too. She had a lovely voice."

"The daughter of a friend," said Margaret. "She's studying singing at the Conservatoire in Glasgow. They have high hopes for her."

There was a brief silence. Then Margaret said, "I know I should have called you first. Or written, I suppose. But I felt a bit awkward about it, and I decided that it would be easier to speak to you in person."

Katie felt her stomach tighten. Margaret had found out about Emma and was here to interfere. She did not welcome the thought because she would have to bring their meeting to a quick end. George was her client, and she could not discuss his affairs with anybody else, even—and particularly—with his mother. "I'm sorry," she began. "I can't discuss anybody else's affairs. I hope you understand."

"But of course you can't," said Margaret. "And it's not anybody else's affairs that I want to discuss. This is about me."

Katie stared at her. "You mean that this is about you? About introducing you . . ."

"But of course," Margaret interrupted her. "That's what you do, isn't it?" She looked puzzled. "Or have I misunderstood the situation?"

Katie quickly assured her that she had not. "No, that's what we do. It's just that . . . Well, perhaps you should tell me what you have in mind."

"I'd like to meet somebody," said Margaret. "I'm a divorcée, you see. I have been for years, actually. And I've been busy with the family hotel—and with family too. Now I think it's time that I thought of finding somebody to enjoy my retirement with."

Katie drew in her breath.

"Do I surprise you?" asked Margaret, almost coquettishly. "Am I too old for this sort of thing? I'm in my sixties, which isn't exactly ancient . . . these days."

"Of course, it's not too old," said Katie. "We have clients who are older than that. And younger, too, of course. No, there's no reason why people in their sixties shouldn't start again."

"Well, I'm glad to hear that," said Margaret. "Ageism is a real problem, you know. Many people don't realise that they have ageist attitudes, but they certainly do."

"Well, we don't," Katie reassured her. She had overcome her initial surprise, and was now becoming more businesslike. It was an immense relief that Margaret had not come here to speak about George, and, with that threat disposed of, she felt she could start looking at Margaret's request.

"Perhaps you could tell me a little more about yourself," she said. "We like to build up a profile of each client so that we can match people intelligently."

"As I said," Margaret began, "I am divorced. It was a brief marriage. He went off, as men so often do. Fortunately, I had our family hotel to run, and that gave me financial security and somewhere to bring up my children. I have twins, you see—they are adults now. They work in the hotel with me."

Katie asked her about retirement. "You said that you were keen to give up working. Will your son and daughter take over the running of the hotel?"

Margaret frowned. "Did I mention that I had a son and daughter? Perhaps I did. Yes, they will. George and Angela. They're pretty much on top of it as things are."

Katie tried to sound bland. "Are they married?"

Margaret shook her head. "No. They're both single. I'd rather like them to find somebody, of course, but you can't arrange these things."

Katie swallowed. "You'd like them . . ." She broke off. She was not sure how to continue.

"Yes, my son has had one or two relationships, but they seemed to fizzle out. Likewise with my daughter."

Katie said nothing.

"Nothing would give me greater pleasure," Margaret now said, "than to see George with some nice girl—particularly one who could help with the running of the hotel. And Angela too—she's a very loving person, and she deserves to find somebody." She paused. She was looking at Katie in an intense way. "You couldn't . . . No, I shouldn't raise it."

"No, please do," encourage Katie. "You can speak quite freely. Nothing of what is said here will go any further."

Margaret looked sheepish. "I just had a rather ridiculous idea. I wondered if you might be able to introduce George to somebody . . . I know he can do these things himself, but he doesn't seem to get himself organised." The intensity of her stare increased. "The problem is Miss . . ."

"Katie."

"The problem is, Katie, that George is very dependent. He's dependent on me. He defers to me on everything, and although I try to get him to stand on his own two feet, he doesn't seem able to." She transferred her gaze to the ceiling. "That's why we shall have to be very careful if you do come up with somebody for me. George will probably feel threatened by it, and we shall need to be discreet."

Katie took a deep breath. "Discretion," she muttered. "Yes. Discretion is important in a place like Edinburgh. Absolutely."

Margaret seemed pleased. "I'm not sure how you people work," she said. "But I assume you'll arrange a meeting—if you have anybody who you think might be suitable."

"Yes," said Katie. Her mind was on other things. "A meeting. Usually in a hotel—for a drink or dinner. Sometimes in a deli that serves lunch. Valvona & Crolla's good for that."

"I know them," said Margaret. "That would be nice."

Katie decided to take a risk. "Your son," she said. "Do you think that he sees things in the same way as you do?"

Margaret looked puzzled. "I'm not sure that I understand you."

"What I was wondering was whether he sees himself as dependent on you or . . . whether he thinks that you're dependent on him."

Margaret considered this for a moment, and then laughed. "But that's just not the case," she said. "I know that there are some mothers who hang on to their children, but I assure you I am definitely not one of them. I've been trying for years to get them to be independent. That's why I'm keen to retire, you know. If I'm not around, it will be much easier for them to run their own lives—including their own emotional lives." She paused. "You do see that, don't you?"

Katie nodded. "Yes, I do."

"Poor George," said Margaret. "He's a terribly nice young man, you know, but he really needs to let me go."

Katie was aware that her astonishment must be registering on her face, but Margaret seemed not to notice. And at that point William came into the room. Seeing Margaret, he stopped in his tracks, and began to mumble an apology. Katie signalled for him to stay.

"This is my friend, William," she said.

"We met," said Margaret, smiling at William. "You're the man who makes those wonderful sweaters."

"He is," said Katie.

"I'll come back later," said William.

"No, please stay," said Katie. And to Margaret she said, "William not only makes excellent sweaters—he makes excellent coffee too."

"That's always welcome," said Margaret.

Katie exchanged a glance with William. Her glance said, "We'll have to talk later." He picked it up and understood it perfectly. "I'll make the coffee right away," he said, which meant, "I can't wait to hear what's going on."

Margaret stayed only long enough to finish the cup of coffee that William made for her—then, citing another commitment, she left. During the time that William was in the room, the conversation moved on to other matters. Margaret was interested in embroidery, and was asking William's opinion of a textile artist whose stitched panels she had recently read about. William knew the artist, and she offered to lend him the catalogue of a previous exhibition. It was clear to Katie that the two of them got on well. But who, she asked herself, could fail to be charmed by somebody who looked like William and was, at the same time, so sympathetic in manner?

William saw her to the door. Coming back into the office, he exclaimed, "Well, that was unexpected. Has she found out?"

Katie hesitated. She was still trying to make sense of what had happened, and one way of clearing her thoughts would be to go over possibilities with William.

"I don't think she knows that George came to see us," she said. "And I don't think she knows about Emma. Although . . ."

William raised an eyebrow. "Although?"

"Although I don't suppose I can be completely sure."

William shrugged. "Well, assume for a moment that she does know. Let's say that she intercepted some message between George and Emma in which they mentioned how they met. That's possible, isn't it?"

Katie agreed that it was. It was unlikely, she said, but she thought that it was possible.

"So," William continued, "if she had found out, then she might want to come and see whether she could get anything out of you. She might have thought that she could come and find out something . . ."

"I told her outright that I couldn't discuss other clients' affairs. She would have realised that she wouldn't get anything out of me." Katie paused. "But she had a pretext for her visit. She said she wanted me to provide her with an introduction."

William looked disbelieving. "She said that?"

"She did. She said that she was thinking of retiring and passing the hotel over to George and Angela."

William listened intently.

"And then," Katie continued, "she dropped the bombshell. She asked whether I could find somebody for George. She said that thought had just occurred to her while she was talking about her own request."

William whistled. "That's a trap," he said. "That's got 'trap' written all over it."

"Why?"

"Because she may have thought that you would then reveal if you had already done something for him. She might have hoped that you would say, 'Oh, but we've already done that.' Big coincidence, of course—but life is full of coincidences."

"Perhaps," said Katie. "But on the other hand, I didn't think she was lying. If she was acting, then she deserved an Oscar. She sounded completely genuine." She paused. "But then she said something that took my breath away. I probably showed it, but still."

"And what was that?" asked William.

"She said that George and Angela were far too dependent on her. She said that she wanted to encourage them to lead their own lives."

William's eyes widened. "She said that? She said that *they* are the dependent ones?"

Katie nodded. "She couldn't have made her opinion clearer."

William had been in his usual leaning position against the filing cabinet; now he came and sat down on the edge of Katie's desk. He leaned forward, as might one who was about to issue a warning.

"Listen, Katie," he said, his voice lowered, "that woman is bad news. She's seriously bad news. I wouldn't believe that if it came notarially executed, sworn before a judge, and then carved in stone by a monumental sculptor. No, definitely not."

Katie reached out and touched his wrist. It was a gesture intended to show him that she was taking his concern seriously. He looked at her hand, and then reached out and touched her on the wrist too. "I like your wrists," he said.

The moment was brief. Then she withdrew her hand, as did he. He rose from his perch on her desk.

"You may be right, though," he said. "And I may be wrong. I've been wrong before, you know."

They both laughed. "Haven't we all?" Katie said.

She thought of James, her last partner in London. Her judgement had been wrong on that occasion. And for a second or two she flirted with the idea of asking William whether he thought he had been wrong about Alice. But something stopped her from doing that.

William now asked, "One thing that I find hard to understand is this: If she's telling the truth—if she is genuinely not a possessive parent—then how can her family—her own children, after all—be so wrong about their mother? Why would they see her as being interfering and possessive? It doesn't make sense."

Katie sighed. "People read things completely differently. Listen to the account of a break-up or a divorce—as often as not, you get two totally different versions—two different histories. And the people encourage one another in their ideas of what's going on. That's folie à deux for you. People strengthen the common misconception. It's not uncommon."

"All right," said William. "But what do we do?"

Katie half-turned in her chair so that she could look out of the window. The office had a view of the hills of Fife, across the Firth of Forth. Fields yellow with a ripening crop. A sky across which isolated cumulus clouds were sailing eastwards. Sunlight on the slate roofs of a line of Victorian buildings in the foreground. It was so beautiful. It was Scotland.

She said, "Let's take what she says at face value."

She did not expect William to agree, but he did. She thought that perhaps once he had registered his doubts, he could consider other possibilities with a degree of dispassion.

"I don't want to walk away from them," she said slowly. "We took George on. We agreed to help." She paused. "I'd like to see that family sorted out."

"And that means doing something for Margaret?"

Katie looked thoughtful, and eventually said that she felt that it did. "If she has her demons . . ."

"Which she might have."

Katie nodded. "Yes, which she might have. If she's unhappy and if Angela thinks that it would help her to put her past to rest, then perhaps we should do what we can. I know we don't have to, but if it's easy enough for us to achieve something, then perhaps we should try."

"What exactly should we do?"

"We speak to their father. We see if he's willing to have any contact with them. If he is, then we can bring them together . . . After all, isn't that what we're meant to do in this business— bring people together?"

"I suppose so," said William. "Logjams have been known to loosen. And if this one does just that—if it shifts—then everybody might just end up happy?"

"I'm not saying that," protested Katie. "I don't think we can expect any miracles, but in any difficult situation, once people start talking to one another things usually get better."

William smiled. He liked the way Katie put things. "Yes, I think you're right."

"Well, we know how to find him," asked Katie. "Angela told me that he was living in a village called Doune. It shouldn't be too hard to locate him, small places being what they are." She looked at him enquiringly. "Will you come with me?"

William asked, "A trip into the country? With you? What's not to like?"

He left, and Katie sat at her desk, wondering what she could read into his answer. People said things without really meaning them, she reminded herself—especially somebody as kind as William. So, she decided not to think about it too much, dif- ficult though that might prove to be. All he had said was that he would like a trip into the country, and had added that he would like to go with her. That was all.

⸻

Angela phoned. "You're still going up to Doune, aren't you?" she asked.

Katie confirmed that she was.

"I see."

There was a brief silence before Angela continued, "I've told him now. I've told my brother about our father."

Katie waited. All families had their issues, but it seemed to her that the Fane family had rather more than their fair share. Was George now going to veto the approach to a father whom perhaps he did not want to meet?

But that was not what Angela had to say. "He didn't mind," she said. "In fact, he's very pleased. I don't think he liked the idea of being the son of the hotel manager. He likes the idea of George McIntyre. This is more of a love story, as far as he's concerned."

"So he wants to meet him?"

"Yes," said Angela. "Very much so."

CHAPTER FOURTEEN

A long time ago

They drove into Doune, with Katie at the wheel of the decrepit blue Jaguar she had brought with her from London, a car she had acquired for six hundred pounds from her former boss at the London gallery. "It may or may not get you as far as Edinburgh," he had said. "But you can give it a try."

It had, and she had been able to store it in the mews garage that Ness owned. Edinburgh was a walkable city, but she had managed to use it on occasions such as this. William approved of it. "Modern cars lack character," he observed. "Any old Jaguar is just so beautiful. Their lines are so much softer. More feminine."

They parked just off the village high street. William pointed at a small butcher's shop nearby. *Try our legendary pies,* a sign in the window proclaimed, while next to it a display of large pork sausages, bulging within their skins, tempted the passer-by. "We could ask in there," he said. "He looks as if he might know what's going on." He had seen the butcher, a stout man in a blue-and-white lined apron, attending to a customer.

Katie agreed and led the way into the butcher's shop. The

butcher greeted them with a smile, while completing the wrapping of a customer's order.

"Your pie," Katie began. "The sign in the window recommends them."

"It does indeed," said the butcher.

"Then I'd like to buy one," she said.

"Large enough for two," William interjected.

She felt pleased.

"Dinner tonight?" William whispered.

"Good idea."

The butcher retrieved a large pie from the shelf behind him. "Technically, this does four people. But it depends on your appetite."

"Healthy," said William, with a smile.

"That's good," said the butcher. "And anything else?"

Katie cleared her throat. "Actually, there is," she said. "You wouldn't happen to know George McIntyre, would you? I gather he lives here in Doune."

The butcher, having wrapped the pie in brown paper, was now tying it with string. Katie watched him carry out the time-honoured butcher's ritual. She remembered from her childhood small parcels of meat, tied exactly this way, being delivered to the house on the south side of Edinburgh. She remembered her mother checking them against the invoice before putting them away in the fridge. She remembered Ness coming to dinner once and announcing that she was planning to give up meat but would enjoy the lamb chops they were having that night. The conversion to vegetarianism never took place, although Ness said that it was a project for the future.

The butcher handed the package to her. "George? Yes, I know him well enough." He hesitated. "Nothing wrong, is there?"

"No, not as far as I know," said Katie. "We don't know him, but we'd like to talk about somebody who's keen to meet him."

The butcher frowned. "About?"

"It's an old friend wanting to get in touch." Katie thought this was true. It was exactly that—although in an unusual way.

"He keeps to himself," said the butcher. "Especially since his wife died."

Katie said she had not heard about that.

"A year ago," said the butcher. "Nice woman. Retired teacher, I think."

"George?"

"No—her. He was with the Bank of Scotland. He managed their branch in Bridge of Allan until he moved here a couple of years ago."

Katie asked where he lived, and the butcher, after only a moment or two of hesitation, said, "I assume he won't mind."

"I don't think he will," said Katie hurriedly.

The butcher explained. George's house, he said, is on the outskirts of the village, along the Callander Road. "There's a set of lights just as you leave, and then you see a sign on the right that says, *Fresh Hens' Eggs Always Available,* and then a short way after that, that's George's place. It's behind some trees— you won't see it from the road."

William wanted to pay for the pie, and Katie did not object. "I've got a nice bottle of South Australia Shiraz," he said. "That goes well with pies."

They set off in the old Jaguar. The butcher watched them from his window. He waved cheerfully.

"That was simple," said William.

"I told you it wouldn't be difficult," said Katie. "Everybody knows everybody in places like this."

"It's the same in Australia," said William. "I used to spend time at my uncle's place in the Grampians. Do you remember *Picnic at Hanging Rock*?"

Katie shivered. She had watched the film before she read the book. They both disturbed her.

"Eerie," she said.

"Yes. Very. My uncle's place was close to Hanging Rock. It's very attractive round there, but that particular story gives it a bit of an atmosphere. It wasn't true, by the way. Those girls never disappeared."

They were now on the Callander Road. As they passed the traffic lights and the sign for eggs, William remarked, "That could be a general observation, you know. It could just mean that hens' eggs are always available—in general. It might not mean available right there."

Katie laughed. "I always thought that about signs that say, *Don't Walk*. I thought that might be a general instruction."

"Bad advice," said William. "We should all do more walking."

"Well, there are signs that say, *Walk . . .*"

She turned the Jaguar off the road and onto the short driveway that led to what looked like an old farmhouse, faced in off-white harling that had, here and there, peeled off to expose the grey stone within. On a small patch of lawn, a couple of outside chairs had been placed around a wooden garden table; a wheelbarrow parked beside a rather neglected flower bed had a gardening fork protruding from it. The front door, beneath a small stone portico, was ajar.

"Somebody's in," William muttered.

Katie switched off the car engine and turned to face William. "I hope we're doing the right thing."

He seemed bemused. "Second thoughts?"

"Yes," replied Katie. She felt awkward, but did not reproach herself. There was never anything shameful in having reservations or second thoughts.

"We can't give up now," he said. "And anyway, I agree with what you said yesterday about wanting to help these people."

His support strengthened her resolve. "I hope so," she said.

They approached the house. Beside the front door, suspended on a twist of rope, was a ship's bell. William had reached out to ring this when a figure appeared in the doorway.

"No need to ring. I saw you drive up." And then, "That's a lovely old Jag."

Katie found herself faced with George McIntyre. He was a man somewhere in his late fifties or sixties, or so she imagined: he was one of those people, she thought, whom it would be difficult to date with any degree of certainty simply on the basis of appearance. It was something to do with fraying of genes, she thought: some people were fortunate in looking much younger than they were. George McIntyre appeared to be one of these. And then she thought: Yes, he looks like a bank manager; change the relaxed country clothing—the gardening trousers, the loose flannel shirt—for a white shirt and a dark suit—and the bank manager archetype would be unmistakable.

Katie introduced herself first and then William. George inclined his head politely, and waited.

"We were wondering if we could have a word," she said. "Sorry to arrive unannounced."

George smiled. His manner was formally polite; they could have been bank customers arriving to discuss a mortgage, thought Katie.

"I don't get many visitors."

"It's just that somebody—a client of my business," she continued, "has asked me to have a word with you. It's a personal matter."

"Then I should invite you in," said George. "Please." He made a gesture of welcome and led them into a small entrance hall. A Victorian hat and stick stand occupied one corner of the hall, a high-backed chair the other. Several pairs of Wellington boots were lined up along one wall. She saw a picture on the wall—a black-and-white photograph of a young couple standing on a harbour breakwater. She recognised George; and that, she thought, was the wife—the woman he had chosen to stick by in spite of his affair with Margaret. Was the photograph taken before the affair, she asked herself—or afterwards? And had his wife even been aware of his infidelity?

They accompanied him into a sitting room at the front of the house. It was comfortably furnished, although not at all smart. The chairs, covered in old-fashioned chintz, were in need of reupholstering, and there were shavings of firewood on the stone hearth. A newspaper was spread out on a kilim-covered ottoman—a copy of the previous day's *Scotsman*, opened at the Sporting section.

George invited them to sit down. Then, while still standing himself, he said, "Now who is our mutual friend?"

Katie met his gaze, and then turned away. She was on the point of changing her mind, when William, who had sensed her hesitation, said, "Your daughter."

George froze.

"Angela," said Katie. "Margaret's daughter too."

George's upper lip trembled. For a moment, Katie wondered whether he would collapse from shock. William should have been more circumspect, she thought. She had assumed that when he had left Margaret, she had been pregnant: he *must* have known that.

"Angela and her brother, George," William added. "They have both spoken to us."

George recovered his composure—but not entirely. When he spoke, his voice faltered.

"What are you?" he asked. "Are you . . . lawyers?"

Katie tried to sound as friendly as she could. "Oh, heavens no—nothing like that. We've been helping George in a personal matter." She paused. "We are aware of the circumstances of their . . . well, of their birth."

George sat down heavily on the chair opposite Katie. He was now avoiding her gaze, and when he spoke, his voice was strained and almost inaudible. "It was a long time ago. Thirty years. That's rather a long time."

"I understand that," said Katie. "But now they're keen to involve you in something."

"To do with the hotel?" asked George. "A financial matter? I'm not a wealthy man, you know."

"Nothing to do with money," said William. "They're not wanting money from you."

George stood up. "You must forgive me," he said. "This has come as a considerable surprise to me—a shock, in fact. But I shouldn't ignore my duties as host. May I make you tea?"

Katie accepted. Tea always helped—as did coffee. It was the ritual, as much as the warm liquid.

George retreated from the room. From beyond the hall, they heard the sound of a running tap and the clink of china. Katie turned to William.

"I've seen him before," she whispered, pointing towards the door through which George had disappeared. "I'm sure of it."

"Where?"

She shook her head. "It was recently. But I can't remember. I'm sure I've seen him somewhere . . ."

"In the street, do you think . . . or . . ."

She cut him off. "Oh, the Burns Supper. Yes. The Burns Supper. He was there, William—that's where I saw him." Her voice rose slightly, and William put a finger to his lips to remind her to keep it down.

"He was sitting a couple of tables away," she continued. "He was with another man and a woman. He was wearing a kilt, and I remember admiring the tartan."

William glanced towards the doorway. He kept his voice low. "Are you sure?"

"Yes. Positive. I was trying to work out where I'd seen him, and then it came to me. He was there."

William frowned. "But why? Was it a coincidence?"

Katie shook her head. She did not think George's presence at the Burns Supper was a coincidence. "I don't think so. No."

"Then why?" asked William.

Katie shrugged. "Stalking them?"

William looked doubtful. "He's a . . . was a bank manager. Bank managers don't stalk their former lovers and their children."

"People do all sorts of unlikely things," said Katie.

They were interrupted by the reappearance of George, carrying a tea tray with teapot and cups. He set this down on a table and asked them how they liked their tea. If he had been shocked by their blunt announcement of their mission, it now no longer showed. He poured tea and handed them their cups.

Katie glanced at William. She had made up her mind, and now she said, "I believe I've seen you before."

He took a sip of his tea. "I'm sometimes in Edinburgh. Perhaps we met somewhere. Do you go to the opera?"

She shook her head. "No, not that. I mean, I follow Scottish

Opera, but it wasn't there. It was at that Burns Supper a few days ago. At the Hutton Hotel."

He put his teacup down on a table beside. He stared at her, as if uncertain how to respond. Then, after a few moments, he said, "Yes. I was there." He spoke with an air of resignation.

She waited.

"How much do you know about what happened between me and Margaret?"

Katie took a moment to answer. "We know that you and Margaret were close. We knew that you were married at the time and that you decided that you wanted to stay with your wife. We knew that you left Margaret when she was pregnant."

He winced. "I'm sorry," he said. "You're wrong there. She left me."

Katie stared at him. She exchanged a glance with William, who seemed to share her incredulity at his answer.

"You see," George said, "I was undecided. She made the decision. She ended it."

William intervened. "Maybe you both wanted it to end."

George looked him with gratitude. "Perhaps."

"But you didn't want anything to do with your children?" asked Katie. How could one not? she thought.

"She didn't want me to," said George.

Katie gave him a searching look. She did not want to believe him—on the surface, this was such an open-and-shut case of male refusal to face up to responsibilities, but she now thought that what he said was credible. Had he been presenting them with a contrived justification, a retrospective acquittal of himself, he would have said more; he would have come up with a more elaborate explanation. He had not done that; he was telling the truth.

"I did as she wanted," George went on. "I never tried to get in touch with her or to see or find out anything about the children." He shook his head—with regret, Katie thought. "She brought them up, and she didn't want me in their lives. I accepted that. And I didn't want my wife to find out about them. I loved my wife, you see, even if I had . . . strayed. I felt bad about—later on, I felt very bad. I tried to make it up to my wife, even if she didn't know that I had let her down."

"I see." Katie did not know what else to say.

"But after her death not all that long ago, I found myself thinking of them. I thought that now I would at least see them, even if I didn't approach them. You may think it odd, but I felt that Margaret had not wanted me to have anything to do with them, and I intended to honour her wishes."

He stopped, and looked at Katie and then at William, as if expecting approbation of his decision. William obliged. "I think I can understand that," he said.

George picked up his teacup. He took a sip, but his tea was cold, and he made a face. "You probably think I'm a coward. I wouldn't blame you if you did." He paused. "I wondered what Margaret was thinking of when she gave George his name. I wondered whether she intended to make me feel guilty. I had friends, you see, who continued to see her after we ended our affair. They told me about the choice of name."

He sighed. "But that's not what we should be talking about. You've come to see me about something, and I hardly dare ask what it is. I'm hoping against hope that you're going to tell me that Angela and George want to meet me. You know, when I went to that Burns Supper, I was worried that Margaret might recognize me—I did everything I could to keep away from her that evening, but there was always a risk. Fortunately, I got away with it, and I was able to see George and Angela. They were pointed out to me by the people I was with at that table. They had met them before.

"I sat there, and I can't begin to tell you how I felt. It was the most extraordinary moment for me. Our marriage was a childless one, you see. My wife had an ectopic pregnancy and couldn't have children. That evening, I sat there and saw my own children for the first time. What can I say about that? How can words describe that experience?"

He stopped. Katie waited to see if he would add anything, but he lapsed into silence. "Your children," she said, "might like to meet you, you know. And they also want you to talk to their mother."

He frowned. "To Margaret? But why? She made it clear she never wanted to see me again."

"That was a long time ago," said Katie. "You said it yourself."

"But why?"

"Because they think it's unfinished business for their mother. They want her to have the chance to express her feelings to you—her anger, possibly, or her regret—who knows? But they think that the two of you should get the past out into the open. That's the way to defuse it, perhaps." She was not quite sure where those sentiments came from, but they seemed right to her. Perhaps psychology and its insights, she told herself, were simply a matter of common sense, applied to human relations, and now she was learning the principles—and the vocabulary to go with them.

He rose to his feet. "I'm going to make a fresh pot of tea. This has gone cold. Then we can talk."

"If you want to," said Katie. "It's not for us to interfere."

William thought: But that's exactly what we've done. Exactly.

"I want to talk," said George. "I really want to talk."

CHAPTER FIFTEEN

A laborer in the vineyard of love

Two weeks later, Emma telephoned to arrange an appointment. William took the call, as Katie had gone to the post office, and he had agreed to answer the office phone while she was out. Ness had insisted on a landline, and initial enquiries from clients often came that way.

"Emma called to speak to you," William informed her when she came back to the office. "And do you like this top?" He held up the garment he was working on, a subdued piece in russets and browns. "I'm calling it Autumn, Opus 3. I've already had four people trying to buy it."

Katie took a closer look. She felt the texture between her fingers.

"Shetland wool," said William. "Natural dyes."

"It's lovely," said Katie. "Somebody is going to be very happy with . . . what did you call it?"

"Autumn, Opus 3," replied William. "Not that I'm being pretentious."

"Pretentious?" said Katie. *"Pas toi!"*

William gave her an appreciative look. "Do you really like it?" he asked.

She nodded. "I really like it. Those colors. And the pattern. It's utterly lovely."

He watched as she ran her hand against the top's front panel, still cast on his needles. "It suits your coloring," he said. "I've always seen you as a russet and brown person. Some people can't take those colors—you can."

"I like them," she said. "I always have. I never went much for blues and greens."

"Then it's for you," said William.

She gave a start. "I wasn't hinting. And you mustn't. There are plenty of your paying customers eager to get their hands on it."

"I don't care," said William. "I'll do Autumn, Opus 4, for them. And 5 and 6. There'll be enough to go round."

She felt embarrassed by his generosity, but she was not going to protest any more than she had already done—and that had been pretty much a token. So, she said, instead, that she would love to have the top when it was ready. "I have a birthday coming up," she said. "It could be my birthday present from you."

"I wanted to give it to you anyway," he said. "But yes, it can be a birthday present. I always find it so hard to choose presents for people."

She wanted to step forward and kiss him. It would be so easy, so natural, but she held back. A thank-you kiss, a peck on the cheek, was not what she had in mind; and even a chaste kiss could so quickly become a passionate embrace from which there could be no stepping back. So she handed the panel back to him with no more than a smile and a muttered word of thanks. He took it, and then said, "Emma called."

"What did she want?"

"She wants to see you."

Katie bit her lip. She had spoken to Angela on their return from Doune, but had heard nothing from Emma, or, indeed, from the younger George. They had given Angela a message from her father, and told her that he was awaiting a call from her. But whether that call had taken place, and whether George McIntyre and Margaret had been in touch with one another, was something about which she was uncertain. And now Emma wanted to see her, which was slightly ominous news. Had something gone wrong in her relations with George? Had Margaret and her former lover met, and had that led to anything positive? Or had everything unravelled? Any of these was possible, and Katie was unsure which outcome was more possible than others.

She called Emma's number, which was answered quickly. To Katie's relief, Emma's tone was warm: nothing untoward could have happened. Yes, said Emma, she was hoping to see her. They could talk over the phone, of course, but a face-to-face meeting would be so much nicer. Was Katie free right now, for instance, or would she prefer a time later that week? Katie replied that if Emma would care to drop into the office an hour later, she would be only too happy to see her.

Hanging up, Katie grinned at William. "She was positively purring down the phone," she said. "I think everything must be going swimmingly."

He was relieved. "I've been thinking a lot about those people," he said. "I think that they're a bunch of liars."

Katie protested. "That's a bit harsh, don't you think? There's a difference, after all, between getting things wrong and lying."

William defended himself. "But look at what we heard. Margaret said she was left in the lurch by George. George said that she ended it. The other George said that his mother was being too possessive—and then she says the precise opposite. Somebody's not telling the truth."

"We'll see," said Katie.

William was not convinced. "Will we?" he asked.

They waited for Emma in silence. William continued to work on Katie's top, counting stitches silently, expertly and effortlessly following the design that he'd sketched out in one of his red-covered notebooks. Katie sat at her desk, working on an invoice that she had been slow to post out to a client. She glanced at her watch from time to time: the minutes dragged. And then the bell rang, and William laid his knitting aside to let Emma in.

There was nothing in Emma's demeanour to suggest that this was going to be a difficult visit. When Katie asked whether everything was all right, Emma simply leaned forward to show her the ring on her finger.

"I see," said Katie. "Well, congratulations."

William stepped forward to take a closer look. "Now that's a ring," he said. "Diamonds, emeralds, white gold?"

"All of those," said Emma, twisting the ring on her finger.

Katie waited.

"It belonged to George's grandmother," said Emma. "Margaret gave it to George to give to me."

Katie and William exchanged glances.

"She . . ." Katie began, but was cut short by William, who said, "She approves?"

Emma nodded. "She was no problem. In fact, I think she's really pleased."

William frowned. "But George thought she'd be dead set against anybody—not just you."

"George was wrong."

Katie asked how the first meeting with Margaret had gone.

"Really well," replied Emma. "Although I was surprised by one thing. She seemed to know that George and I had met through you. Did you tell her?"

"No," said Katie. "But she hinted to us that she'd like us to arrange something for him."

"Odd," said Emma.

"Very," agreed Katie.

"And then Angela told me that Margaret had met up with their father. She—Margaret—said that she had been hoping that this would happen."

Katie held her breath. The perfect ending to this whole tale was within grasp. "And?" she prompted.

"Apparently Margaret forgave him—or so she told Angela. But then Angela said that when she went to see her father, he told her that he had forgiven her mother."

William laughed. "You see?" he exclaimed. "Somebody's not telling the truth."

"William is convinced that we're not getting the true story behind all this," said Katie.

Emma looked thoughtful. "Possibly not. But does it matter? Don't you think the future is more important than the past?"

"Yes," said Katie. "But there are still one or two things that puzzle me. Do you think that Margaret was over-possessive?"

Emma thought for a moment. "It depends what you mean by *over-possessive*," she said.

"Good point," said William.

They looked at one another. There was so much to talk about—to question or to analyse—but all of them had other things to do. William had to deliver a set of designs to a prospective buyer; Katie had an appointment with the dental hygienist; Emma had to get back to the Hutton Hotel, where she was now helping George with the payroll and the tax returns. All of these things were important and relatively uncomplicated matters—rather less complex than the inner workings of the human heart. They took precedence.

⁓

That evening, Katie cooked dinner for William in her flat. She made spinach cannelloni because William had said a few days earlier that that was his favourite dish. She liked it too.

Sitting at her table, they talked about the affairs of Margaret and her family. There was nothing more for them to do, said Katie. Margaret had phoned earlier that day, she told him, and—very politely—thanked them for their help. There was now no need for them to introduce her to anybody.

"She's not looking any longer?" asked William, smiling.

"I imagine she's found what she was looking for."

William looked thoughtful. He liked resolution. It was like casting off when you were knitting.

"They can look after themselves now," Katie continued. "We did what we agreed to do."

"This is lovely cannelloni," said William.

Katie accepted the compliment gracefully. "I'm glad you like it. *Fatto a mano*."

Then William said, "I had an email from Alice today."

Suddenly, the mood of the evening changed—at least for Katie. "Oh yes," she said, guardedly.

"She said that she was sorry," William continued. "She asked me whether I'd forgive her for . . ."

Katie looked down at her plate. She thought: Forgive her for what? Alice must have admitted that there was another man in her life.

"What do you think?" William asked. "Should I?"

Katie continued to stare at her plate. This was a moment of profound moral significance. Every so often in life one is faced with a question that tests one's sense of what is right. It may be tempting to give the answer that is best for you personally, that serves your own interests. But that might not be the morally right answer.

We should *always* forgive, she thought. We have to. Withholding forgiveness can *never* be the right thing to do because it meant that the burden of the past could never be lifted.

So she said, "I think you probably should."

She felt empty. This had been her chance, but in giving dispassionate advice she had done the right thing.

He said, "I'll think about it."

And she took her chance and said, "Yes, these things are best not hurried." She need not reproach herself for that, she thought. And that left a door open for the future.

She changed the subject. "I heard from Ness this evening. Just before you arrived, she sent an email. She's very happy with the life she's making for herself in Canada. I'm not sure that she'll ever come back."

"I'm glad she's found whatever she was looking for," said William.

"She's getting involved with the local community," said Katie. "They've found out she's a matchmaker, and apparently they're flocking to her for advice. Her neighbor and his friend. They're pushing her to take them on, to find partners."

William laughed. "And will she? I thought she was taking a holiday from that sort of thing."

"I think she will," said Katie.

He poured her another glass of wine, and looked at her—with fondness, she thought—or hoped. After they finished dinner, William thanked her and left. He was going out to meet a friend for a drink, he said. She heard him go down the mutual stair, and she heard the sound of the door onto the street opening and closing. She went to the window and looked out on Mouse Lane. It was high summer, and although it was almost eleven, the city was still bathed in that lambent light that made the very stone seem warm and gentle. She watched William set off, and she was still watching when he turned, saw her at the window, and waved. She drew back from the window: men do not like to be stared at, she thought. She sat down and listened to some music. She thought of this strange job she had taken on, which required her to work for the cause of love—to be a laborer in love's vineyard. She was happy to be that because love was more important than anything else, she decided, and if it came our way, then well and good—and if it did not, but if we glimpsed it in the lives of others, then that was consolation of a sort.

PART III

The Girl from Melbourne

CHAPTER ONE

What puts men off

Katie sat in 181, a small delicatessen on the wrong side of Edinburgh. It was on the wrong side, of course, only because she lived to the north of the dividing line that was Princes Street, while 181 was to the south. Edinburgh, though, was not a large city, and she had made her way across town on foot that morning and was now taking a first sip of her latte in the deli's coffee bar. Behind her were shelves of unconcealed temptation: boxes of pasta, tinned olives, packets of porcini mushrooms—all displayed in that classic Italian packaging that she found so enticing. These were things one needed, she thought, but did not *really* need.

Katie had become a regular customer of the deli because of a shopping list she had found in the kitchen of her cousin's flat. Ness must have slipped it months ago into the pages of one of her cookery books, marking a recipe for focaccia. It was headed *181, Thursday* and listed not only things that were called for in the making of focaccia—olive oil, rosemary, rock salt—but also other items that one might expect to find in an Italophile kitchen. It was the name of the olive oil, though, that caught her eye—it was one of those obscure, single-estate oils favoured by people who really knew the subject: *Olio Sant'Angelo in Colle*.

Sant'Angelo in Colle . . . The name resonated somewhere in the recesses of memory; she had been there, she thought, even if she could not remember exactly where it was. It was probably in Tuscany, which was the part of Italy she knew best. Somewhere near Siena? That trip with Michael, the boyfriend before James, whom she had thought might be the one . . . Michael, the graphic artist and enthusiastic cricketer, with his freckles and open-faced innocence. She had felt so secure in his company, yet even as they picnicked in that olive grove near Montalcino, with the sound of bells drifting from the nearby church, he must have been thinking of how he might extricate himself from their relationship—because the break-up came so soon after their return and must have been planned. How wrong we can be, she thought; how wrong we can be about everything, but particularly about how other people really feel about us. The problem is, she said to herself, that we think that others see us as we see ourselves—and they do not.

The name 181 had intrigued her, and she looked it up. She was living her cousin's life, now, she thought, and might as well see the deli she frequented. She was just about to run out of olive oil, she realised—and the thought came to her of fresh focaccia with Sant'Angelo in Colle oil dribbled across the top, and the crunch of sprinkled sea salt . . . She made her way across town, and found the bottle on the shelf in 181. The label confirmed the memory; it showed a small hill town towards which a chalk-white road made its winding way. It was the village she remembered, with its narrow streets climbing up the hill, and the plain stretching out to become, on the horizon, an echoing, empty sky.

She bought the oil, made the focaccia—a moderate success,

she thought—and found herself returning regularly to 181. These outings gave her the chance to get out of the office—which she found she needed—and the time to think about things—not just about what was happening at work, but about her life in general.

That morning she found herself dwelling on the Fane family and the complexities of their relationships. Each complicated family, she thought, is complicated in its own way, as Tolstoy might put it. No nineteenth-century novelist—especially a Russian one—would have been surprised by the weight of psychological clutter around each of the Fanes. At least she had been able to lighten that burden: George had been introduced to Emma, and they had hit it off; Margaret and George Senior planned to meet again; and Angela, having stopped worrying about her mother and her brother, had found their father. All of this constituted a success: emotional logjams could move, and sometimes required only the smallest of nudges to do so. Speaking to one another was the way we started that process, thought Katie; and sometimes only a few words were necessary.

So now she could look back on her first few months running the Perfect Passion Company and conclude that there had been some point to it all. She had taken on the job, offered to her by Ness with so little instruction, without really asking herself whether she wanted to do it. She had been ready to get back to Edinburgh, and Ness happened to be looking for somebody to run the business. She had never really asked herself whether this was what she saw herself doing, and whether she would get any satisfaction from it. But then, she reminded herself, so many of the decisions we make in life are like that: we drift into things; we embark almost thoughtlessly upon courses of action that might decide the whole shape of our lives; we take on commitments that we do not fully understand—and yet so often it all works out. And it was working out for her, she thought. She enjoyed the rather unusual work of bringing people together, and it did not matter if people thought her job to be vaguely comic, or sentimental, perhaps. The value of any job, surely, was what it achieved, and hers, she thought, made the world a slightly less lonely place. What was there to apologize for in that?

Ness had had time now to settle in, and appeared to be content living in the small Eastern Ontario town she had chosen more or less at random. She had sent photographs, including one in which she was standing by a lake with those two new friends of hers, Herb and Jacques. The three of them were smiling—not in the artificial way in which those in a photograph may smile, but over something that must have been genuinely amusing. She saw the photographer's shadow, cast on the ground before the smiling threesome, and she saw that he—and it looked like a he, as far as she could make out—was wearing a hat. It would be interesting, she thought, to collect photographs in which photographers appear as a shadow, and to make a book of them. *The One Behind the Lens* might be the title of such a book, she thought—or perhaps *People Only Partly There*. There were so many books she dreamed of writing, but never would, including one that featured William's knitting. William was unusually photogenic, and there would be photographs of him wearing his creations. He's beautiful, she said to herself. That's all there is to it. He's *achingly* beautiful—an odd word, *achingly*, but it was the right word here.

She would love to do a book like that, but of course she could not, for the simple reason: *William was not hers.* William was there in her life; she saw him every day, or almost every day; they talked; they shared jokes; they went out on the spur of the moment for long lunches; and she thought of him rather a lot. But she did not want to think of him too much—he had his own life to lead, and she did not want to find herself becoming too involved. He would be a friend, but that would be it.

She turned a page of the newspaper, and began to read the latest report on a long-running political scandal. Construction contracts had been improperly awarded, one political party was alleging, while their opponents, standing accused of having given the work to political supporters, were full of injured innocence. *That you could even think we would do something like that* . . . Katie was not particularly interested. She knew that she should be, but it was hard to become enthused over a stretch of road that she would have difficulty finding on the map. She turned to the letters page, where correspondents crossed swords over different issues, but there was more disputing of facts and their interpretation. Only in the sanctum of the personal announcements column, where proud parents told the world of new arrivals, did there seem to be agreement; and also in the neighboring list of engagements . . . She stopped. A name leapt out at her. *Fane.* She might so easily have missed it, because she rarely bothered with that page—although perhaps she should, she thought, now that she was professionally involved in these matters.

She read on. George and Emma were engaged to be married, and were delighted, the notice said, to announce the fact. Her first thought was *good*; and then her second, following closely, was *quick*. How long had they known one another? It was only a matter of weeks, she thought, and surely it was wise to give it a little longer than that. Some people took years to make up their minds, although others, admittedly, were much quicker. Still, even if this was a bit on the precipitate side, they were two people who clearly wanted to find somebody and, having done so, might understandably be keen to formalise matters. She put down the paper, and allowed herself a smile. This was her doing; she had brought this about, and she felt a certain satisfaction. She would get in touch with Ness and tell her. "Knot tied," she might write—if, indeed, an engagement was a knot. It was, she thought, although it was a looser knot than the one involved in an actual marriage.

She took another sip of her coffee. An engagement! Well . . .

"Excuse me."

She turned. She was being addressed from a neighboring table.

"Excuse me, I don't want to . . ."

The person who spoke was a woman in her late thirties, perhaps, who had before her on the table a quiche and a bowl of salad. She had not been there when Katie had arrived, and must have slipped in while she was engrossed in the newspaper. She was attractive, in a slightly theatrical way. Her clothes were chosen with care; and they were expensive, thought Katie.

"I didn't want to intrude."

Katie smiled. "Not at all. I don't mind. I was just . . . well, I was just thinking."

"I'm Jenny."

Katie nodded, and gave her name.

"I thought that's who you were," said Jenny. "And Charlotte over there . . ." She nodded towards one of the women working behind the counter. "Charlotte said that you were who you were. I asked her, you see."

Katie waited. It was that article in the local paper: more people had read it than she imagined; they had looked at the photograph, and remembered.

"Do you mind?" asked Jenny.

The temptation to be direct was too strong to resist. "About people asking me to find somebody for them?" she asked.

Jenny blushed. "Oh, I wasn't going to . . ." She paused. "Well, I suppose I was."

"And I don't mind," said Katie. "After all, that's what I do."

Jenny looked relieved. "I used to sell advertising space in a magazine," she said. "And people sometimes came up to me out of the blue and asked me about advertisements they had seen. Sometimes they complained to me, if something they bought didn't live up to their expectations—which were always high."

"Expectations always are," said Katie.

"I used to point out that I had nothing to do with the things that advertisers sold. I handled the ads, that's all. But they—or at least some of them—seemed unconvinced."

"It's about shooting the messenger," Katie ventured.

She drained the last of her coffee. She wanted Jenny to get to the point, but something told her that the other woman might not be the sort to do that too quickly.

"It's better not to hope for too much," Jenny observed. "I mean, if you don't think that something is going to be terrifically good, then you aren't disappointed, are you?"

She gave Katie a look that suggested that she expected affirmation of what she said. And now, as she replied, Katie felt that her response was begrudging. "Perhaps not," she said at first, and then, in order not to sound discouraging, she added, "No, I think you're right. It's difficult, isn't it?" One might say that about *anything*, Katie thought. Everything was difficult in one way or another.

"Of course, it's hard not to hope for something. You may be realistic; you may be determined not to get your hopes up, but there's always the temptation to think that things are going to work really well."

"Possibly."

"Oh, I think it's often like that," said Jenny.

She looked anxiously at Katie, before leaning forward and enquiring. "You don't mind, do you?"

"Don't mind what?" asked Katie.

"You don't mind my talking to you like this?"

Katie shook her head. "No, I don't mind." And she thought, This is what I do now. If I mind, I will have to do something else. She lowered her own voice. Their conversation was now barely above a whisper, even though there did not seem to be anybody within earshot.

"It's men," said Jenny. "I'm having . . . well, I'm not having much luck."

Katie was about to say that the same might apply to her. But then she reminded herself that this was becoming something more than a casual conversation—she had to be professional.

At last Jenny came to the point. "I wondered if you might be able to help. Your agency—what do you call yourself? The Passion . . . ?"

"The Perfect Passion Company." Katie still felt a certain measure of embarrassment in using the name. Ness was slightly *dramatic*—that was the problem. A person who was not dramatic would not have chosen a name like that.

Jenny smiled. "That's a great name," she said. "Perfect Passion. Who could turn down the prospect of a perfect passion?"

"Well . . ."

"But what I wanted to know is this," Jenny continued. "Could you . . ." She hesitated as she looked for the right word. "Could you *represent* me?"

Katie replied immediately. "That makes it sound a bit formal. But we could try to help. If you want an introduction, we'd try to find one for you." She paused, before adding, "That's what we do, you see."

"I thought as much," Jenny said. "There's somebody I know, you see, who said that you had been really helpful. He said that you'd saved his life."

Katie raised an eyebrow. Had anybody been *that* desperate? "I'm not sure that we've ever done that. Or at least, not since I've been involved."

"But you were," insisted Jenny. "David Bannatyne."

So that was it. "You know David?" asked Katie.

Jenny hesitated, but only briefly. "David's a friend," she said at last. "Not a boyfriend . . . There's never been anything between us. Just friends."

Katie waited.

"Not that I would have minded," Jenny went on. "David is a really good guy, you know, but he and I go back a bit, you see. I was at school with his younger brother. David's quite a bit older than I am, you see. He's in his forties. I'm thirty-seven."

A critical age, Katie told herself. Children were still a possibility, but the biological clock would be ticking down.

"His younger brother is called Tom. I always called him Bill, though. I don't know why. Sometimes people have private names for people, don't they? I called him Bill since we were about eight or nine, I think." She paused. "Do you have a nickname, Katie?"

Katie shook her head. She imagined the conversation drifting off into a discussion of the rights and wrongs of nicknames. "No, I never had a nickname," she said.

"Bill didn't mind," Jenny went on. "He said that he quite

liked the name. So he called me Hyacinth. He still does. He's married, of course. I have no idea why he chose that particular name. Hyacinth. Rather odd, isn't it."

"Nicknames often are," said Katie. Jenny had said that Tom/Bill was married *of course*. There was regret in the words. The nicest men were married—of course.

"Not that I'm saying that Hyacinth is one of those names you'd want to get rid of."

"No, I didn't see anything wrong with it," Katie reassured her.

Katie glanced at her watch. It had not been intended as a signal, but Jenny noticed it, and continued, slightly apologetically, "I shouldn't take up your time."

Katie felt that now she could look at her watch more decisively. "I have to get back to the office at some point," she said.

Jenny looked disappointed. "Could I . . ." she began.

"If you'd like to see me professionally," Katie said, "that would be fine. You could come to the office."

"That's exactly what I'd like to do. Can I arrange something?"

Katie reached for her bag. "Of course." She paused. "You said that David . . ."

"He's pleased with what you did for him. Really pleased. He said that I should think about speaking to you."

"I'm glad that David is happy," said Katie.

Jenny agreed. "He deserves to be. He's a very kind man, you know."

"Yes."

Then Jenny added, "Unlike a lot of men."

Katie looked at her. Yes, she thought. Disappointment. Men run away, she thought. It was a diagnostic moment.

She rose to her feet. "I have to buy olive oil," she said.

"Who doesn't?" said Jenny.

Katie pointed to the shelf behind her. "They have a particular olive oil here that I really like."

Jenny followed her gaze. "That Sant' Angelo stuff? Oh yes. It's wonderful."

A thought occurred to Katie—an anarchic, subversive thought. Was olive oil the way to a man's heart? What a ridiculous thing to think. But she could see the article in some appropriate magazine. *Use olive oil to meet your man*. Ridiculous. Except . . . except . . . David had wanted somebody to cook for him. Sometimes the traditional wisdom, the old sayings, expressed a certain truth.

Now she said to Jenny, "You could drop in on the office the day after tomorrow, if you like."

They agreed on a time. "You make it easy," Jenny whispered. "I thought it would be much harder."

Katie wanted to say that the hard bit was yet to come, but she did not. She thought, though, this is not going to be simple.

She went outside. This meeting with Jenny had tired her out, as any conversation with an incessant talker tends to do. And that, she imagined, was going to be the problem. There were some women who exhausted men—and other women too. They just did. Jenny, she decided, was one of them. She would ask Ness for advice, or William perhaps. William, after all, was a man and might have views on what exhausted men and what did not.

Out on the street—a street of small shops—the sun was upon her face. She closed her eyes briefly, and made the most of it. She was not sure how wise it was to acquire new clients over coffee in a deli, especially ones who might prove difficult. But it was too late now and she would do her best for Jenny. Katie rather enjoyed a challenge, and she thought that was exactly what Jenny might turn out to be.

CHAPTER TWO

Are you pleased?

William did not appear until lunch time.

"You went out," he said.

She set aside the file she had been working on. There was a note of accusation in his voice—but why? Did he expect her to tell him every time she left the office? He was her neighbor, not her minder, she thought; and yet the idea that he wanted to know what she was doing appealed to her because it suggested that he might feel for her in the same way that she felt for him. But she stopped herself: she should not think that because William, as she frequently reminded herself, was engaged to somebody else. William was a *friend*, tout court, and if she began to entertain the possibility that he was something else she would only make herself miserable. That was what so many people did: they made themselves miserable over other people, and she would not do that; she would not.

"Yes," she replied. "I went out."

She watched him. He was staring at her. He wanted to know where she had been—that was clear enough. Simple nosiness?

"I knew you did," he said, crossing the room to the window and looking out onto the lane below. "I saw you from my window."

"I didn't realise I was being observed."

He turned round and grinned. "Oh, I notice these things. I see it all."

"Curtain twitcher," she said.

They both laughed.

"I walked over to Bruntsfield," she said. "There's a deli over there that Ness went to. I've been going there from time to time. I like the walk."

He nodded. "I've got to get more exercise. I used to go to the gym in Melbourne every day." He paused. "Every day, without fail."

"You must have been fit."

"I was. I'd spend hours there. It can get quite addictive, you know."

She knew about endorphins, and was about to mention them, when he went on, "Could we go to the gym some time?"

"Us?"

He looked out of the window again. "Yes. You and me. It's more interesting if you go with somebody. It gives you somebody to talk to."

She hesitated, but then she decided that a trip to the gym was hardly an invitation to go on a date. "Yes, let's," she said. "Perhaps next week—if we feel energetic enough."

William had more to say about the gym. "Have you noticed something about gyms?" he asked.

She shrugged. "The music can be too loud? Everybody else looks fitter than you are? Some people seem to sweat in peculiar places?"

William shook his head. "No. Well, maybe yes to some of

those. But I was thinking of how you can't strike up casual conversations. You don't talk to other people. You work away at whatever it is that you're working away on, and you don't speak."

She agreed. "Perhaps people don't like to be distracted when they're trying to lift weights. You don't want to drop those things. Or perhaps they have to concentrate on breathing, if they're on the exercise bike."

He considered this. "Possible," he said. "That's why it's nice to go with somebody. Then you can talk."

She softened. Why fight it? There was no harm in just going to the gym. "I'll go with you," she said. "Any time you like."

He left the window. "Good. Let's do that."

She stood up. She did not like to sit for hours on end at a desk. She stretched, and then sat down again.

"That's the right thing to do," he said, observing her. "They say you shouldn't sit at your desk for more than twenty minutes without getting up. It keeps the blood circulating."

She sat down again. And it was at that point that he told her.

"By the way, Alice is coming to Edinburgh," he said. "I heard this morning. Alice—my fiancée."

She reached out for the file on her desk. She opened it. She tried to look at the papers inside. The news had had a strange effect on her.

"Katie?"

She looked up.

"Did you hear what I said?"

She tried to pull herself together. "Yes, I did. Yes. You said Alice is coming to Edinburgh." She succeeded in smiling. She had to. "That's great. When?" She wondered whether her voice would give away her true feelings. She had her reservations about Alice.

"In ten days."

She expressed surprise at the short notice. It was all she could think of to say. "What about her course? Isn't she a medical student?"

"They have a break round about now. She's only got two weeks."

"That's a long way to travel for two weeks." Alice must love him very much to cross the world for a few days of reunion. But of course she did—who wouldn't?

He agreed, but it was still worth doing, he said.

Katie tried to sound encouraging. "That's right. It'll be nice for her to see something of your life here—and you can show her the city." How trite, she thought; how utterly bland. *That's the castle up there, Alice, and this is the Royal Mile that goes all the way to Holyrood. And this is where Burke and Hare . . .*

He looked at his watch. "I have to go. I said I'd send her an email."

"Of course."

She watched him go out of the door. She looked at her file. She closed it again. Did she resent the thought that William would be spending time with somebody else? Was this the end of their comfortable, chatty coffee mornings? She tried to put these feelings out of her mind. She had no right to claim a monopoly on his time—no right at all, however strongly she felt about him. And Alice would not be here for all that long; she would leave, and then things could get back to normal. And yet she found that she simply did not want Alice to be here: she just did not want her.

William was not out of the room for long. He came back

ten minutes later, reappearing in the doorway, half in, half out. He looked at her with concern.

"Are you okay?" he asked.

She looked up from her desk. "Yes. I'm okay. I'm fine."

He continued to look at her. "Are you sure?"

She smiled. "Do I look as if there's something wrong?" She paused. "There isn't. I'm just . . . I'm just . . ."

"Yes?"

"A bit tired maybe. I woke up early this morning—really early. And didn't get back to sleep. You know how it is."

He nodded. "You would tell me if there was anything worrying you, wouldn't you? That's what neighbors are for, you know."

"Of course."

"And friends too."

She struggled. She was on the verge of tears, and she thought that if he stood there much longer, she would lose the battle. But he did not; he gave a half-wave and disappeared again.

━━━━

Katie was surprised at the extent to which the news of Alice's visit affected her. Somehow she managed to get through the afternoon, and the evening, too, thanks to a live broadcast in a cinema of *Don Giovanni* from the Met in New York. By the following morning, the crisis—if that is what it was—had passed. As she sat at her breakfast table, she realised that meeting Alice was not something she should dread; she would rise above any feelings of jealousy and do her best to make the other woman feel welcome. It should not be too hard.

By the time she let herself into the office, her mood had lifted to the point where the reservations of the day before seemed absurd. Her life was fine: she had an interesting—if rather peculiar—job. She had somewhere comfortable to live. She had no financial worries. She had friends—no boyfriend, of course—but then did one *need* a boyfriend? The answer to that was probably no, even if a boyfriend might be nice. Somebody might turn up in due course, and she was open to that possibility, but it was not going to be William—that, at least, was certain.

She thought about Alice, and her impending visit to Edinburgh. William must have been missing her—she was, after all, his fiancée—and if it would make him happy to have her here, then Katie would share his delight. She decided that when he came in for coffee that morning she would tell him how much she was looking forward to meeting Alice and how pleased she was that the two of them would be able to spend some time together. Seeing one another on screen was a consolation, no doubt, but it had its limitations. No, she decided that she would not say that—not exactly—but she would say something to that effect. Mind you . . . she remembered seeing a young woman in a coffee bar talking to her boyfriend on screen and leaning forward from time to time to kiss the screen. She had noticed, as she left, that the screen was covered in lipstick, which the young woman sought to remove with a tissue, smiling as she did so.

William came in as usual and wordlessly began to make coffee. He greeted Katie, but he seemed preoccupied with something, and she wondered whether he had taken offence over her muted reaction to the news of Alice's visit. When he brought over her cup, though, he was smiling, and she decided that her fears were unfounded.

"I've been short-listed," he said.

"Well . . ."

He cut her short. "It's a very long short list, of course."

"A long list?"

William said that he thought that there were at least twenty people on the list, and that there was little chance of his winning.

"Winning what?" she asked.

"The Scottish Wool Council Design Award," he said.

Her eyes widened, but he could tell that she had no idea of what he was talking about.

"It's . . . it's really big," he said. "It's the equivalent of the Oscars . . ."

She laughed.

He looked crestfallen, and she immediately apologised. "I'm sure it's really great, William. It's just that the idea of the woollen Oscars . . ."

He burst out laughing too. "I wasn't being serious. It's nice, but it's nothing major. The prize, if you get it, is a plaque, and I don't think they even have an awards ceremony."

"It'll still be an honour," Katie said quickly. "And you deserve it, William. Your stuff's beautiful."

He warned her that he had not got it yet, and probably would not. "You should see the competition. That woman in Glasgow—the one who designed that scarf that the president of France's wife wore. Remember?"

Katie did not.

"Well, it was in all the papers. She was wearing a Harris Tweed scarf—it was purply sort of grey—and she looked stunning. She wore it when she went to Cannes."

Katie shrugged. This was a whole closed world to her—a world of fashion in which she had little interest. She liked clothes and she noticed what people wore, but she never gave fashion magazines anything but the most cursory glance. There was too much narcissism in those glossy pages—too much

concern with things that ultimately were not all that important; too much conspicuous luxury in a world where millions
went to bed hungry.

She glanced at William. Did he *believe* in that sort of thing?
Did he think that fashion was anything but a matter of human
vanity? She liked his work, of course: the garments he designed
were beautiful—they were works of art in the same way in
which a painting was. They said things about harmony and
color and proportion, and these were all important enough in
their own right because they were based on the feeling we had
for what was *right*. But you had to keep a sense of proportion
and understand that there were far more important things to
think about than who wore what and when.

It was as if he had sensed what she was thinking—and
perhaps he did. "Not that it's important," he said, somewhat
sheepishly. "I don't really care who wears what at Cannes. As
long as they're comfortable."

She smiled. That was more like it, she thought.

She thought she might help him. "I agree with you," she
said. "But I suppose that wearing something that is aestheti-
cally appealing helps to make you feel comfortable."

"Exactly." He hesitated. "You don't think my work is . . . is
not the sort of thing a guy should be doing. You don't think
that, do you?"

She did not conceal her surprise. That sort of doubt might
have been expressed in the past, she thought, but we had got
away from those attitudes a long time ago. "Of course I don't,"
she said. "Nobody thinks that way any longer."

He frowned. "Some do, you know. There are still a lot of
men who think that what I do is . . . well, effeminate."

He was probably right, but she did not want to give comfort
to such men, and so she said, "Really? Surely not."

"No," said William, "I can tell you. They make an immediate assumption about me—about my . . . about my being gay because I'm a knitwear designer."

"Well, that's because they're ignorant," said Katie. "They're ignorant and stuck in a whole lot of outdated preconceptions."

"That may be true," William conceded, "but it works both ways, you know." He looked at her, and she saw he was smiling at the recollection of something.

Katie waited.

"I had a friend in Melbourne," William went on. "I was at school with him—same year. He was very good at sports, particularly at Australian Rules Football. He became a welder—I suppose his strength helped him there. He was really tough."

"If I close my eyes," said Katie, "I think I can just see him."

William continued, "But Jez—that was his name—was gay, and he complained to me that there were a lot of gay people who assumed that because of what he did—welding and football and so on—that he was straight. That annoyed him. And I suppose it was just the other side of the coin—an assumption that your job defines you."

"Well, I think we need to get past those assumptions," said Katie. "And I certainly don't think that way." She paused, and then added, "I admire what you do. I love it."

William inclined his head in acknowledgement of the compliment. Katie returned to the competition. "I'm sure you've got as much chance as anybody else," she said.

"It's nice of you to say that, but I should be realistic, tempting as it is to dream."

"Yes," agreed Katie. "But it's good news that you're shortlisted—and it's also good news about Alice coming. That's really terrific."

He looked at her sideways. "You're pleased about that? About Alice?"

"Of course, I'm pleased. Why wouldn't I be?"

He was looking at her intensely, as if he was on the verge of saying something of which he was not yet quite sure. He made up his mind. "It's just that it occurred to me that you might be a bit threatened by Alice." His tone became apologetic. "That's what I thought. I probably had no reason to think that—no real reason—but that's what I thought."

She told herself that she had to be careful. He had picked up her reservations—she should have known that he would: William was sympathetic, and sympathetic people, by definition, often knew what others were thinking.

"No," she said. "I didn't feel threatened . . . It wasn't that at all." She paused. "I suppose it was just—how shall I put it? Concern. Yes, it was concern that you would be off with Alice—and of course you should be—but I've grown used to having you around for advice, if you see what I mean. You've become part of the business, haven't you?"

That was true enough. But there was more to it than that, although she said nothing about it to William. She now felt a growing anxiety over what might happen to him: she did not want him to be hurt, and she feared that Alice would never make him happy.

But William seemed relieved by what she had said about his being part of the business. "I see. Of course. But you know something? That won't stop just because Alice is here for a couple of weeks. Okay, we'll go off to the Highlands for a day or two—maybe up to Skye—but most of the time we'll be here in Edinburgh. I've got work to do. I'll be able to help you. That won't change."

She looked down at her hands. She wished that she had been able to be more honest. "I need to talk to you about somebody," she said.

"A client?"

"Yes. Somebody I saw yesterday. It was in the deli in Bruntsfield. Somebody came up to me. She's going to be coming in tomorrow morning. Ten-thirty."

"Oh yes?"

"Yes. And I've got a feeling she's going to be difficult."

"In what sense?" he asked.

Katie thought for a few moments. "She'll put men off. I'm sure of it. That's why I'd like to get your view."

"You want me to confirm your impression?"

Katie nodded. "Or tell me that I'm wrong."

He smiled. "I suspect that you're right. I think you understand what men want and don't want. And you've decided that they won't want her."

"Poor Jenny," said Katie.

"Let's see," said William. "Let's leave the jury out until we've had a further look."

William walked to the window and looked out onto the road. Then he turned to Katie and said, "I'm so happy, Katie. Alice will be here soon."

She smiled encouragingly. "Good."

"And I want you to feel happy too."

She smiled again. "I am," she said.

"Sure?"

"Yes. Completely."

CHAPTER THREE

I've heard everything

Ness thought about Katie rather more often than Katie thought about her, although Ness was careful not to give Katie the impression that she was watching over the Perfect Passion Company from a distance. So, although there were regular bulletins from Canada, with one or two exceptions, these made only the briefest mention of the agency, so as not to give the impression that Ness was interfering. Katie understood that—and appreciated the tact that lay behind it. In return, she sent Ness occasional reassuring reports about the clients and their successes. The failures were mentioned too, but always with some remark about how Katie believed that something would turn up for them, and it was only a question of waiting. She recalled what Ness had said—that she could find somebody for anybody. Well, that would be her aim too. And she did not forget about patience. "I know we must take the long view," Katie wrote about one very unpromising client. "I know that, but sometimes I wonder if there aren't some people who are just impossible. Fiona Henderson springs to mind. But we shall persist with poor Fiona and will eventually find a man who fits the bill—whatever that proves to be."

This was one of the few occasions when Ness opened up about agency affairs. She wrote back: "I know what you mean about Fiona, bless her. I did my level best, you know. I must have introduced her to six men—possibly even more. But she found fault with every single one of them, you know. There was always something that was not quite right. One man's nose, apparently, was the wrong shape. She said that she did not expect physical perfection, but that some noses were beyond the pale. She had a point, I suppose: he had a very prominent nose, poor man, like Cyrano de Bergerac. But I could hardly believe what I was hearing when she told me that she had even raised with him the possibility of his having cosmetic surgery. Can you believe it? Poor man. I spoke to him afterwards and he was very gentlemanly about it. He didn't say anything about her having said that, but he was sensitive about his nose— I had already picked that up—and I was quite angry with her for being so tactless about it."

There was more. "On another occasion," Ness wrote, "she objected to a man's breath, which she said she found unpleasant. She said that he had asked her for a second date, but that she had refused. I asked her why, and she told me about his breath. 'I'm not fussy about many things,' she said, 'but that's one of them. Personal freshness. It's a red line as far as I'm concerned.'

I was at a loss what to say. That was the first time a client has said something like that, and she brought it up almost as if it was my fault. Perhaps she thought that I should vet the clients in that respect before arranging a meeting. Did she expect me to conduct a sniff test? It almost seemed like it. And her comment put me into a bit of a spin, as I was not sure whether there was anything I should do about it. If what she said was true—and the poor man did have slightly sour breath—then was that something that I should point out to him. What do they say about body odour?—sorry to be so direct, Katie—but there's no way round it. Hasn't that always been one of the big questions: Does your best friend tell you? In most cases, I think people won't tell other people that they smell—sorry, again—but, surely, it's kinder to do so—in the long run. Yet how do you raise the subject? Do you say something like, "I've just found a new deodorant and I'm really pleased with it." That's an old trick, isn't it? You try to give the impression that you're talking about yourself, when you're really talking about the other person.

I didn't say anything, and I'm glad I didn't, because he was not particularly confident, that man, and I don't think it would have helped to make him anxious about his breath. And, anyway, the next introduction we arranged for him worked. They were married about four months later and they're very happy. I still hear from them. They bought a house in France and spent a lot of time doing it up. They send me pictures of it from time to time. There's an old barn on the grounds of the house, and they're keeping chickens in it. The chickens are outside during the day, and then they put them in the barn at night because there's a fox who has been making it his life's work to polish them off. They sent me a photograph of the fox crossing the lawn outside the house. They wrote underneath it, "Here's Monsieur Reynard in broad daylight, bold as brass, utterly unrepentant."

So—Fiona: I don't know what you can do about her, short of telling her that there's nothing more that can be done. Perhaps you should have it out with her. Perhaps you should say, "Look, you find fault with *everyone*—have you ever considered what might be wrong with *you*?" Give her a taste of her own medicine. But perhaps that's a bit cruel. Yet, remember that you have a duty to your other clients. You have a duty not to waste their time introducing them to people who are simply going to find fault with them whatever. It's up to you, though, Katie. You're the boss.

And another thing: How is William doing? Are you seeing much of him? I like to imagine the two of you having coffee together—just as he and I did—talking about this and that. Give him my love, by the way.

~~~~~

She sent the message off shortly after breakfast one morning, with the sun streaming in her kitchen window. The weather was unusually warm, or so she had been told in the local store. It was mid-summer and high pressure had settled over that part of Ontario, bringing unclouded skies and unmoving, somnolent air. In the garden of a neighboring house—the house beyond Herb la Fouche's—children could be heard shrieking with excitement under the spray of the hose; a dog lay on the driveway of another, panting for the heat, even at this hour of the morning. It was a day, Ness thought, on which she would be not at all surprised if nothing much happened.

She had become used to that since her arrival, and had taken to the slow pace of small-town life. The saliences in her day were minor ones now—a chat with a neighbor, a trip to the store, a slow, observant hour spent in the coffee bar that catered for the stream of visitors who stopped in the town on their way to the nearby provincial park. The volume of those visitors had increased since Ness had first arrived, and she found herself beginning to resent them, in the way a local, the hardy annual, surveys summer incomers. They were a reminder of the world outside, of the busy life of Toronto, only a few hours' drive away but seeming to be on an entirely different planet when viewed from these quiet woods. She knew she should not feel this irritation with visitors—she was, after all, a visitor herself, even if a longer-term one. But she sensed that there was something precious in a small community—something fragile that would not necessarily withstand the pressure of people seeking rural peace and quiet. It was the same everywhere: the local, the tucked away, the old-fashioned was struggling in the face of the sameness of the modern world.

She had a few purchases to make at the store—she had run short of the tinned smoked oysters that were her secret indulgence, and she needed to buy potatoes too. Those purchases made, she went on to the café and settled herself into the window seat that gave her a view of the main street with its passing cars and pedestrians. It was from this vantage point that she saw Herb la Fouche drive down the road and manoeuvre his truck into a parking place directly outside the café. Herb saw her as he switched off the ignition. He waved, got out of his truck, and came into the café.

"Busy?" asked Herb, as he accepted Ness's invitation to join her.

Ness shook her head. "I used to answer that question with a yes. And I was—I used to be busy. But now? No. Not really. And you?"

Herb shrugged. "It's a quiet time for me. I don't do much until September. Some fishing, maybe. Fix the truck. Paint the porch, but not just yet. I'll do that in August."

"I'm forgetting what it was like to be busy," said Ness.

Herb ordered a cup of coffee. As he waited for it to be

served, he looked at Ness and cleared his throat. "The other day," he began, "you were telling me about what you used to do over there in Scotland."

"My business? The agency?"

"Yes. What was it called again? The perfect something."

"The Perfect Passion Company."

Herb smiled. "Some name, that."

"I suppose so."

He frowned. "You didn't find some folks getting the wrong idea? A name like that . . ."

She assured him there had never been a misunderstanding on that score—as far as she knew. "We were very respectable, you know. We didn't take on just anybody. Especially the men—we were very careful to make sure we didn't get the wrong sort of man."

Herb looked concerned. "A lot of that sort around," he said. "Always have been."

There was a brief silence. Then Herb continued, "I don't know if you remember, but I asked you whether you might be able to do something for us—for me and Jacques."

"I remember," said Ness.

"I felt a bit embarrassed asking you," Herb continued. "It's not easy to talk about these things. They're kind of private, I guess."

She said that she understood, but that it was best to be frank. He waited.

"I don't know if I'm the right person for this, though," she said. "I'm not a local. I don't know anybody round here." She paused. "You must know everybody. Surely you or Jacques will know if there's anybody suitable. Local knowledge, you know."

He considered this. "We know who everybody is, sure, but we don't mix much," he said. "There's a lot of people I hardly ever see—what with me being away trapping so much. And Jacques kind of keeps to himself." He paused. "Maybe we're just a bit shy."

Ness looked at him. She had spent enough time in rural Scotland to understand the rules of living in a small community. Favours were exchanged. You did not turn down requests for assistance if you possibly could as you never knew when you might need help yourself. People in cities had forgotten these things because life had become impersonal, and you might never know who your neighbor was. That was not the case here.

Ness relented. "I could keep an eye open," she said.

"And let me know?"

"Of course. But, as I said, I'm not sure if there's much I can do."

He looked at her gratefully. "Every little bit helps."

"It might just be . . . how shall I put it? Advice. It might just be advice."

She was relieved to see that he seemed satisfied enough with that, and she relaxed. It had not been part of her plan, that she should start doing here the things that she used to do in Edinburgh, but if all she would have to do would be to give advice, then she could manage that. After all, you never escaped the role you were allocated in life. If you were a doctor, then people would view you as a doctor in all circumstances, and expect of you what they normally expected of a doctor. If you were a mechanic, then they would expect you to advise on mechanical matters. Roles persisted.

She gave Herb a searching look. "I normally need to know a bit about the people I help," she said. "I know a little bit about you, but not much."

He nodded. "You and I haven't known one another all that long."

"No, we haven't. I know what you do for a living now. But what about before? Have you time to tell me a bit more?"

"Right now?"

"Yes."

He sat back in his chair. "You won't laugh at me?"

She reassured him. "Herb, I've heard everything in my job. Everything."

CHAPTER FOUR

Meeting Jenny

Katie observed Jenny's reaction to William. She had noticed it with other women, and now she saw it once more. It took different forms, of course, but there was always something that could be described as *interest*—a reaction to the beautiful that was almost impossible to conceal. And here it was once more, as William handed Jenny the cup of coffee he had prepared and she took it, looking up at him briefly, before she turned back to Katie. Jenny had noticed William, which was not surprising, Katie told herself, because everyone did. But it told her something, at least: that Jenny appreciated men, which was not very much, perhaps, because that was why she was here in the first place. And for a brief moment, Katie imagined herself saying, *Actually, how about him?* and pointing to William as she said this.

But then she saw something else—a fleeting look on Jenny's face that suggested regret. She had noticed William, but with the eyes of one who knew that what she saw was what she would never have. And for a few moments, Katie felt sorry for this woman, who had confessed to her that she had not been having much luck with men—as she put it. We had only one chance at life, and sometimes that chance did not seem to be working out, and time was slipping away, as time always did.

She tried to put Jenny at her ease. She explained that William was her assistant. Jenny turned, glanced at him, and nodded. "And he, like me," Katie went on, "is very careful about confidentiality."

Jenny smiled. "Oh, I'm not worried too much about that."

Katie was surprised. "Most people are, though. It's important."

"If you've got something to hide," said Jenny. "If you're embarrassed about something. But I'm not, you know. I don't mind telling people about what I'm thinking."

Katie glanced at William, who met her gaze with a slight movement of his head.

"I think people are too buttoned-up," Jenny continued. "They keep everything to themselves. They never discuss their issues. That's all wrong. It means that people go around as if the little details of their lives are some great state secret—as if they were bound by some duty of omertà—you know, like members of a Sicilian crime syndicate." She paused. "Have you been to Sicily?"

Katie shook her head. "I never got that far south."

Jenny turned to William. "And you, William? Have you ever thought of going to Sicily?"

Katie said, "William's from Melbourne. He hasn't had the chance to get to Italy yet—as far as I know. Is that so, William? You haven't been to Italy?"

William shook his head. "I'd like to," he began. "There are some friends who . . ."

Jenny did not let him finish. "Italy is the most wonderful country. I simply *adore* Italy. I went there first when I was sixteen, you know. I went on a school trip to Florence. I thought I'd gone to heaven—I really did. Imagine being sixteen and coming from a rather sleepy little town in Scotland, and then, suddenly you're in Italy, and you're standing there in the Piazza della Signoria in Florence, or you're in the Uffizi looking at the *Birth of Venus*, which in my view is the most beautiful painting in the world, easily, by far. Oh, I know some people say it's the *Mona Lisa*, which I quite like, incidentally, but as between Botticelli and da Vinci, give me Botticelli any time. There's something about him—a delicacy.

"But there I was at sixteen, seeing all that. You can imagine. There were twenty-five of us, all girls, because I went to an all-girls school. I didn't mind, and it was more common in those days. Not now, of course. I don't think teenagers stand for it, you know, but that's another question."

William put down his cup. "I went to an all-boys school in Melbourne."

Jenny looked at him, but only briefly. "Did you?"

"I didn't . . ."

"No, boys don't like it," Jenny provided.

". . . mind it," said William.

"We didn't get to the south that time," Jenny continued. "It was just Florence. But I went back when I was a student, and again when I was twenty-three—no, I was twenty-four, I think—I went to Naples for the first time. That's another country, you know. Completely different, and full of criminals. No, I'm not making that up. I read somewhere that over half of the local economy in Naples is based on crime. Can you believe it? Over half. But what a city! I prefer the north," Jenny said. "I loved Siena. Have you been to Siena, Katie?"

"Yes. A couple of times. I—"

"That cathedral. That striped marble. And I love, I really love the Sienese school of painting. It was pretty early—sixteenth century, I think—something like that. But they use those lovely blues to depict the sky. And they put in silver stars, and the buildings in the background are not quite in proportion, but look like little building-block castles. I love those paintings. They're Italy to me, you know."

Katie took a deep breath. Why had Jenny asked her if she had been to Siena if she was apparently uninterested in hearing anything she had to say about it? It was because *she* wanted to display her knowledge of art. This woman was definitely not a listener.

Well, two could enthuse about things Italian. "Italy," she began, thinking, I must try not to shout. "Italy . . ."

Jenny raised her voice accordingly. "I must tell you. I visited a monastery there once. It was a place where they had some very well-known murals. I forget who the artist was, but he was very important at the time. I think he studied with Mantegna, or somebody like that. Well, we went there, my friend Ellen and I—she's a partner in a law firm, but her real interest is art. She knows so much about it. Anyway, we went to this monastery, and there was this terrifically fat monk. He was the abbot, I think, because I noticed that the other monks all treated him with deference. They were all pretty thin—it was remarkable—whereas he was, as I've said, pretty large. And Ellen whispered to me, 'I bet he eats all the food and the others get none.' She thought she was whispering, and she was, I suppose, but we were standing in the chapel, and there was a very strange acoustic effect, and her voice seemed to be amplified. And the thin monks heard what she said—and they understood English. I suppose that being monks they would have studied it—they probably knew quite a few languages. Anyway, they heard it, as did the abbot. It was so embarrassing. But do you know what? He didn't seem to mind, and he simply beamed—as if he was proud of eating all the food. He didn't bat an eyelid—not an eyelid. Some of the thin monks started to giggle. They thought it very funny. Perhaps they'd been hoping for years that somebody would say something like that, and now it had happened."

She paused. Katie decided that Jenny was marshalling her thoughts for the next instalment, and so she said quickly, "That was unfair on the thin monks."

William took his cue from her, and joined in before Jenny could resume. "I thought they took some sort of vow about not eating too much. Or would that be part of the vow of poverty?"

"I don't think those monks . . ." Jenny began, only to be interrupted by Katie, who said, "They're meant to live a simple life. But I suppose that's the ideal, and often people don't live up to the ideals they set for themselves."

"No," said Jenny. "That abbot was probably . . ."

"On the take," interjected William. "He was probably using the gifts of money that people left to buy food. Expensive stuff. Hampers from that shop in London—you know the one—Fortnum and Mason."

"It was in Italy," muttered Jenny.

"Well, the equivalent," said William, rather quickly, his voice showing his irritation.

Jenny became silent, and Katie realised that they had overstepped the mark. She glanced at William—a signal for him to stop. "I'm sorry," she said. "I didn't mean to be rude." She glanced again at William, who now looked abashed. "Nor did William."

William nodded. "I'm sorry too."

"I talk too much," said Jenny. "I know I do."

Katie hesitated. "I wouldn't necessarily say that."

Jenny looked at her. "But you just have," she said.

Katie made a decision. Jenny was an intelligent person—that

was obvious—and would have realised that their diverting of the conversation was a not very subtle way of getting the message across that she was overwhelming them. She could deny it again, as she had already done—rather unconvincingly—but it would be better, surely, to be honest.

She leaned forward. "Jenny, I'll confess that I don't have all that much experience of . . . of this . . ." She gestured towards the filing cabinets. "All this is relatively new to me, and I'm no expert. But I suppose I have as much experience as anybody else of human relationships and know as much as they do about how these things work. And since I'm sitting on this side of the desk and you're on that side, I feel I have a duty to tell you if I see a problem." She paused. "Would you agree with that?" She was concerned that she sounded pedantic—rather like a lawyer talking a client through a contract.

Jenny did not speak, but nodded almost imperceptibly.

"And I think," Katie continued, "that there might be a bit of a problem here—one that you've just raised yourself." It was the lawyer's voice again, and she tried to moderate it. "You said, didn't you, that you talked too much?"

Again, Jenny nodded. "It's a fault I have."

William said, "We all have faults. All of us." He gave Katie a warning look.

"Of course, we do," Katie said hurriedly. "I . . . I . . ."

Jenny was looking at her, waiting for the disclosure. But Katie could not think of any faults she had. *I must have; I must have* . . . But she could not think of anything—at least not in this moment of being put on the spot.

William said helpfully, "Katie has so many she doesn't know where to begin."

She looked at him gratefully. "Yes, that's probably right. Whereas William . . ."

"Don't get me started," said William. "I procrastinate. I leave the washing up until the next morning—actually, the next afternoon. I let the towels fester in the bathroom. I put too much butter on toast. I pull the whole duvet onto my side of the bed so that . . ." He did not finish. Katie looked at him. Her heart gave a lurch.

Jenny did not seem to be paying much attention.

"So, you see," Katie said, "none of us is perfect. We just aren't. And it can help if somebody is able to point out to us where we're going wrong. And men, I think, can be intimidated by women who have . . . who have a great deal to say." She paused. "Women too. They don't like men who talk *at* them all the time. It works both ways."

Jenny looked up, and Katie saw that there were tears in her eyes. She drew in her breath sharply; she had not expected this. "Oh, I've upset you. I'm so sorry. Oh, Jenny . . ."

Jenny wiped at her eyes with a handkerchief. "I'm all right. It's okay."

"But it isn't," said Katie. "It's my fault."

Jenny shook her head vigorously. "I've asked for it. It always happens like this."

Katie wondered what she meant. Did this happen in all her dealings with others? Did people regularly become impatient and reproach her for speaking too much? When Katie had taken over the agency from Ness, it had crossed her mind that she might be taking on responsibility for people who, for one reason or another, were inadequate. People who were confident in themselves did not need help in meeting others—they simply went out and met them—and that left those who had psychological difficulties. Yet her experience, for the most part, had been otherwise. Most of the clients she had dealt with so far had seemed relatively normal. Perhaps it was inevitable, though, that sooner or later she would have to cope with some-body who would be weak and dependent, or overly fragile. And now she wondered whether she would know how to deal with the challenges that would bring.

Jenny looked down at the floor again. Katie exchanged glances with William. Neither of them seemed sure what to do or say next. Jenny, however, settled that: she had begun to sob.

William stood up and moved forward to stand beside her. He bent down and put an arm around her. Katie watched; he does it so naturally, she thought.

Jenny turned so that she was facing William. She looked up at him. "I feel so foolish," she said.

"No," said William. "We're all human."

Katie continued to watch. She felt a surge of affection for William then, in spite of her determination to distance herself. He was being so kind to Jenny; he was being so gentle.

I made her cry, thought Katie. Ness would never have done that—but then Ness was a professional, and Katie was only learning. I have a long way to go, she told herself.

William had a call to make, and he went off to do this from his studio after Jenny had left. Ten minutes later he returned and immediately asked Katie what she thought of their meeting with Jenny.

"Interesting," Katie replied.

"And?" he prompted.

Katie sat back in her chair. "You tell me what you think."

William leaned against a filing cabinet. "All right," he said. "Not good."

"In what sense?"

William looked thoughtful. "She's nice-looking. No problem there."

Katie agreed. "She's thirty-seven, but could pass for thirty, don't you think?"

He agreed. "She's probably one of those people whose genes don't fray—or whatever happens when you get on a bit. Or she uses a good moisturiser."

"Could be both," suggested Katie.

"So, she's attractive," William continued. "We're agreed on that. And yet—no men, you say?"

"She told me she hadn't had much luck with men. That means not very many, or they don't last very long."

"Probably the latter," William mused. "They run a mile, I imagine."

"So you agree with me in assessment?" asked Katie.

"Yes, you're right." He paused. "And there's probably not much anybody can do."

William looked regretful. That was his kindness—once again—Katie thought. And now he added, "Unless . . . unless you feel it's worth a try."

Katie hesitated. She felt that by agreeing to see Jenny, she had indicated, even if only implicitly, that she would at least try to come up with somebody for her. She owed her at least that, and so she said to William, "We have to." And he, relieved, said, "Good. I was hoping you'd say that." But then he said, "But who?"

Katie looked up at the ceiling. "The most tolerant man we've got on the books? The nicest?"

William brightened. "Who also just happens to be the one who's been most unsuccessful?"

Each knew whom the other had in mind.

"Robert Macleod?" William asked.

Katie nodded, and smiled. "It's funny we should both have thought of him."

"I felt so sorry for him," said William. "His eighth try?"

"Seventh, I think," said Katie. "Ness arranged five dates for him, and then there was the one we set up. Yes, this will be the seventh."

William had been leaning against the filing cabinet; now he came and sat down in the chair in front of Katie's desk. He had been smiling; now he looked serious. "Should we?" he asked.

Katie sighed. "I know what you mean," she said. "Perhaps it's not such a good idea."

"I liked him so much when we met him," William mused. "And yet there's obviously a problem. Does Ness say anything in the notes?"

Katie had spent some time going through the file. Ness had become increasingly voluble in her notes on the introductions arranged for Robert. *I can't understand it*, she wrote. *Third introduction, and nothing doing. Robert says that she simply declined his invitation to see him again. No reason given.* And then, after the fourth failure, she had written, *Robert says that Rose agreed to meet him a second time, but she didn't show up. He contacted her and she claimed to have forgotten. She said she would get back to him, but never did. Must speak to her. Simple politeness required.*

"I don't think Ness could work it out," said Katie. "There's a note in the file that she spoke to two of the women and asked them what had gone wrong. They said that they liked him. They said he was obviously a good man. But then one said that she thought he was *too* good. Ness wrote in the notes: *too good?*"

William winced. "That'll be it," he said. "Too decent. People don't want a saint."

Katie smiled. "It's no fun going out with St. Francis of Assisi? Is that what you're saying?"

"You could put it that way," William replied. "They like a bit of . . ." He struggled to find the word to describe the quality. How did one describe the seasoning we like in food?

"A whiff of danger?" Katie suggested.

William said that was not what he had in mind. "No. I'm not talking about the *bad boy* problem—although there are some women who like a bit of spice."

"More than you can imagine," Katie said. It was true, she thought. Men like that seemed to have no difficulty in finding partners.

"But Robert?" asked William. "Is it because he must be desperate and will put up with anything—even somebody who never draws breath?"

Katie denied that it was desperation. "Yet he obviously wants to find somebody. He's decent—we're agreed on that. He'll be kind to her. The two of them are, in a sense, a lost cause. If we bring them together, it might just work."

William considered this. "No harm in it," he said at last.

"No," said Katie.

"And it might turn out to be the perfect match."

"Exactly," said Katie. And for a moment at least, she believed it possible, and imagined the triumphant message she might send to Ness. "Robert Macleod placed. Very happy." She would not have to say more than that. It was a pity, she thought, that telegrams no longer existed, because they lent themselves to the terse message in which every word was made to count, and could carry a whole hinterland of meaning.

She looked up at William. "Have you heard of that famous telegram?" she asked. "Somebody sent it from Venice. *Streets full of water. Stop. Please advise.*"

William looked at her in astonishment. "What's that got to do with anything?" he asked.

"Nothing," she said.

"Streets full of water . . ."

"I was thinking of what I might say to Ness."

He shrugged. "Sometimes I find you inexplicable," he said. And smiled as he said it, which made her heart miss a beat.

Thinking of William, she said to herself, imagining the drafting of a telegram to Ness. *Stop. Please advise.*

Of course, she knew what the advice would be. *If somebody is with somebody else, back off. Stop. Don't fall in love with somebody who can't reciprocate: it's pointless. Stop. Just stop. Stop.*

It was the right advice, and Katie knew it. So, now she said, "I'd better get on with my work." And William nodded, and said, "Me too."

CHAPTER FIVE

Herb la Fouche narrates

Ness noticed that Herb la Fouche was one of those people who, when he spoke at any length, seemed to be addressing an invisible audience. That was what he did now, as they sat together in that small café, and he responded to her invitation to tell her more about himself. She had never been embarrassed to ask people to do that, as it was, for most people, both a flattering and a tempting question to which they responded willingly. Few among us, it seemed to her, were reluctant to spend time on that most intriguing of subjects—ourselves. And Herb was no exception, although he seemed to be addressing somebody just to the right of Ness, rather than Ness herself.

"Me?" he began.

Ness encouraged him. "Yes. You."

Herb hesitated before beginning. It was as if he were weighing up the advantages and disadvantages of accepting or declining an invitation. "Well," said Herb, "I don't need to say much about the early part. It's not that it was difficult, or anything like that—it was just plain dull."

He paused, and Ness wondered whether they had reached the end of such account as he would be prepared to give. But now he continued, "I was born not far from here, and we lived in the same small town—a bit bigger than this place, of course—until I was sixteen. Then we went to Kingston, and everything started to happen. But before that, I don't think anything important happened—at least not to me."

Again, he stopped.

"Please go on," said Ness. "I'm listening."

He closed his eyes briefly, and then opened them again, looking slightly surprised that memories should float to the surface. "My father fixed lawnmowers and agricultural machinery. He had his own business, and he did well enough, although you'll never get rich fixing lawnmowers and tractors. You know that?"

She nodded. "I think you're right. You hardly ever get rich from honest work like that."

He was amused by that. "I guess that's why we're all still poor."

"There's nothing wrong with not having money." She was not sure if she believed that—but it sounded almost right. There was no *shame* in being hard up—that is what she really meant.

"But you won't necessarily get poor either," Herb went on, "because people are always wanting you to cut their lawns or plough fields or whatever, and the one thing you can count on with machinery, as my father used to say, is that it'll break down. You can be one hundred per cent sure about some things: the sun rises in the morning; machinery breaks down.

"My father wanted me to go into the business with him. He said that we could expand, and maybe take on heating systems as well, but I wasn't keen on that. I had an uncle who was a part-time trapper, and I wanted to go off and work with him, but my father was dead set against that. He said that the day would come when you wouldn't be allowed to trap any more, and I think he also didn't like the idea of it all. He said that artificial fur would take over from real fur in due course, and that that would mean an end to the cruelty involved in setting snares for animals.

"We moved to Kingston, where he set up a new branch of his business. He got by, but never made much money down there. We were often left a bit short, as people didn't always pay their bills on time. Some never paid them at all. They pretended not to see you if you came across them in the street. There was always a lot of that, but the business somehow survived and was doing well enough to be sold to somebody else when my father reached an age to retire.

"When I left school, I went to work in a shoe shop. It was not much of a job, as I was never allowed to deal with the customers. I would unpack the crates when the shoes arrived from the factory, and I would stack them on the shelves, according to size. I also had to keep the shop clean and mail shoeboxes back to the makers when there was something wrong with a pair. You'd be surprised at how many boxes we had to send back because they contained two left shoes or two right shoes. That happened all the time. We sent them back to the agents, who imported them from Mexico. They would replace them, always with a note inside saying, *SORRY*, in capital letters, and then a Spanish name, because the agents themselves came from somewhere down there. Sometimes they added kisses—*xx*— and sometimes they slipped in one of those religious cards with a picture of a saint on it and a prayer in Spanish. I had a little Spanish—not much—and I was able to make out roughly what the prayer said. Usually, it referred to illnesses, which those people thought were a punishment for evil deeds and thoughts. They really did. And that suited the priests, I guess: do as we say or get sick. A simple message. There was still a lot of that in those days.

"I worked in that shoe shop for six years, and became quite an expert in shoes. But even in my early twenties, I still thought that life had not started for me, and so I signed up to go to sea. I worked as a member of the crew of a freighter out of Halifax. We used to go over to Europe—to Rotterdam and Hamburg, and places like that—but we also went down to South America, to Rio and Montevideo. I did that until I was forty.

"When I was thirty-five, I met my first wife. She was Cuban, from a family who lived in Miami, but she was working in Montreal at the time. I am not sure whether she loved me— she needed to marry a Canadian, for the paperwork, and she found me. I was happy enough that she did not seem to mind my being at sea for months at a time. She wanted to have children, and one eventually arrived. But looking at the dates, I knew I could not have been the father. The child was conceived when I was away—there was no getting round that, although I said nothing. It was a boy, and he didn't look like me: he was the image, though, of a firefighter called Ernest Badge, who lived down the road. I wasn't the only one who spotted that. All the Badges had that sort of neck.

"We were married for only six years. Then she left Montreal with Ernest. She left a note on the kitchen table—that was all. She took the boy. He was Ernest's, I suppose, more than he was mine. These things happen, and you have to accept them. My mother was still alive in Kingston, and so I moved back home to look after her. I had had enough of being at sea, and so I got a job with an outfit that fixed refrigerators. They called me a refrigeration engineer, but I was just an ordinary guy with the right wrenches. Anybody can fix a refrigerator. Anybody. Even you.

"My mother died. She was ninety-three and didn't want to be around much longer. One day, she looked at me and said, 'Herb, you want to know something? I think I should go ahead and die—no point putting it off.' I said, 'You've got years ahead of you, Mom,' but she shook her head, smiled, and died about fifteen minutes later. That's the way to go, I reckon.

"I wanted to make a new start. I met a guy called Louis Bouchard. We were in a poker game together at a friend's place—Terry Singleton, who sold industrial flooring. Louis was his friend. He came from Sault Sainte Marie. No eyebrows. He was visiting cousins in Kingston. He had a company in Guadeloupe that serviced refrigerators. He was a big tennis player—one of the top players in that part of the country, although he had an arthritic knee, see, that stopped him playing. He said it came from having to work on his knees when he was fixing fridges. It stopped him doing a lot of the work he used to do, and so he was keen for me to go and help him out. I was not quite sure where Guadeloupe was, and so I looked it up on the map and saw some pictures of it in a book about the Caribbean. I liked the look of it. I liked the idea of living on an island, especially a French one. I always thought I might live in France, and this was next best thing, I suppose.

"So I went to Guadeloupe. Louis had found me a place to live and a car that the company paid for. He helped me settle in and invited me to a barbecue at his place every Friday evening. Sometimes we would play poker afterwards, or just drink beer and listen to his wife singing to her karaoke machine. She did

Edith Piaf songs. If you closed your eyes, I swear you'd think it was Piaf herself. What did they call her? *La môme Piaf*—the little sparrow?

"That's where I met Hélène. She was a friend of Louis' wife, and she came from Normandy. She had two sons by a husband back in France who had gone off with another woman. She came out to Guadeloupe with her two boys—they were twins of seven then—because her brother, Antoine, was the local police chief. He had been in the police in Calais, but was getting nowhere with his career and decided to try his luck in Guadeloupe. He was very lazy, and so it was no surprise that he wasn't being promoted in France. He liked the idea of going to a place where there would be no pressure and he could be lazy without worrying about anything.

"Antoine was overweight. He liked fried seafood, and you'd often see him in his car, parked by the side of the road, eating fried conch or lobster. He got this stuff from fishermen—free—in exchange for turning a blind eye to their illegal activities. He only arrested innocent people and then let them out again if they paid a bribe or if it looked like they might get hold of a lawyer. People said that he had never arrested any real criminals, although he once did that by mistake. In that case, he quickly realised his mistake and offered to drive his prisoner home in his own car—with a couple of fresh lobsters thrown in to compensate him for the inconvenience.

"He was very conscious of his appearance. He had undergone a hair transplant—or the beginnings of one—in Miami, but it hadn't worked very well. Louis told me that Antoine was saving up for plastic surgery in Boca Raton, but it was taking time, as the surgery was very expensive.

"Antoine was good to his sister. 'He paid for me and the boys to come over,' Hélène said. 'He got us this house. He's a good man—even the criminals round here like him, which is a big compliment, if you ask me.'

"You can probably see which way this story is going. If you think—*he's going to fall in love with Hélène*, then you're right. People do the things we think they're going to do. They never surprise us—except sometimes, I suppose, when they do the opposite of what you expect. That happens, you know, because of something they call free will. You heard of that? I read about it once, and it made me think. People imagine that guys like me don't think about these things, but they're wrong. When you're out on the trap-lines or fishing, maybe, you have to think of something, and sometimes the things you think about are pretty deep. You can think about free will for hours and hours and never get anywhere, you know. There are people in colleges that do just that—they think about these things all day and never come up with the answer. So, the next day, they start thinking again, and so it goes on. Rather like fishing, maybe. Catching a fish doesn't stop you trying to catch another one."

Herb paused. Ness looked at him, fondly. Dear Herb, and the things that made up his life: fishing; trap-lines; refrigeration; the problem of free will. We fill our lives with things that have no necessary connection—other than that they happen to have been given our attention and our time.

He was looking away, as if embarrassed by the intimacy of the long recital of his past, and so he did not notice her gaze. She found herself thinking, No woman will want to take on a man like this. She did not want to reach that conclusion, but it seemed to her that this was inevitable. Herb la Fouche was destined to remain single, because that was the fate of men like him. They were nice enough, in a masculine sort of way— which meant that they evoked one's sympathy—but there was not much that could be done for them. That, thought Ness, is the uncomfortable truth. Poor Herb la Fouche—his story, it seemed to her, was a small tragedy. Not a big one, nothing worthy of Euripides or Aeschylus, but a slow, rather minor-key one, of the sort that is more common than one might imagine, one of the many tragedies that are all about us, with no Greek chorus to draw our attention to them.

CHAPTER SIX

Robert Macleod reports

It was six days later that Robert Macleod came into the office of the Perfect Passion Company. He rang the bell before announcing himself through the intercom, "It's only me, Robert." As she went to the door, Katie thought about people who said, *It's only me*. Robert was not the only one; she had met others who spoke in those self-deprecatory terms: *only me*. And now here he was, *only Robert Macleod*, coming into the office in his unostentatious Harris Tweed jacket and his brown brogue shoes, that were so assiduously polished and at once so low-key and so unfashionable. Everyone else, it seemed, was wearing trainers now—William certainly did, although his were the fashionable sort that had supple leather uppers attached to trainer soles. But not Robert, who was also wearing a tie, Katie noticed.

She had been in touch with him about Jenny only a few days earlier, and he had lost no time in contacting her. Katie had offered to arrange a meeting over coffee—as was the standard company practice, inherited from Ness—but Robert had said that he would prefer to invite Jenny out to dinner, just the two of them, and he would let Katie know how things went.

"I like the sound of her," he had said, which made Katie try to remember exactly what she had said about Jenny. She had not misled Robert with misdescriptions, she hoped, but she could hardly be expected to put him off with some sort of warning. She had said very little, as she now recalled—something about Jenny being vivacious, or even interesting. And that was true: Jenny was definitely lively, and she was interesting too—if you wanted to be spoken to at length and you were not averse to long monologues.

She invited Robert to sit down. "I didn't expect to see you quite so soon," she said.

He grinned. "I don't let the grass grow under my feet, you know."

"No, I'm sure you don't."

She asked him whether he had been busy. He was a tax accountant, and Ness's notes had said that his business was a successful one. *Solvent*, she had written. *But very nice about it. Not flashy in any way.* And she had underlined *in any way*, which was code, thought Katie, for . . . She thought about it after she had met Robert for the first time, and had realised what Ness must have meant. Robert was utterly decent, utterly respectable, and utterly uninspiring. *There are hundreds of men like him*, Ness had written—and now, as she looked at him over her desk, those words in the file came back to Katie, and she pictured, in her mind's eye, those hundreds of Robert Macleods, gathered in a mighty throng, all with their brown brogue shoes and their well-barbered look, all waiting for the romance that their lives had always lacked, and probably always would. Why did women not sense the opportunity here? Why didn't women refuse the advances of the contrasting legions of unsuitable men to whom they often felt so fatally drawn—

alluring men—and encourage instead these uninspiring men who would never excite anybody but who would be completely trustworthy, who would pay the mortgage, help with the household tasks, and be largely unobtrusive?

She saw that Robert seemed cheerful, and she allowed herself to think that the introduction had been a success. She had been right after all: both were looking so hard that any defects in either of them might be seen as of secondary importance or even as irrelevant.

"Well, Robert," Katie began, "you look happy. It went well?"

Robert Macleod shook his head. He was still smiling, but the shaking of his head told a quite different story.

"I'm afraid not."

Katie could not help herself from sighing.

"Oh dear."

This made Robert look concerned. "I'm very grateful to you, though," he said quickly. "It was an interesting experience."

Katie sat back in her chair. "I hope you don't think I'm prying, but . . ."

He did not let her finish. "Oh, I don't mind telling you. We went out for dinner. There's a seafood restaurant down in Leith. It gets good write-ups."

"A good start," said Katie. "But things didn't work out?"

Robert met her gaze. Katie wondered whether she should confess that she knew all along that Jenny was difficult. She was concerned that he might think that she had taken a deliberate risk in introducing them—that she had even done so in order to amuse herself. That was not true, of course, but it was possible that he might reach that conclusion.

"Did you think they would?" asked Robert quietly. "Did you think the two of us would get on?"

Katie shifted in her seat. "I thought there was a chance," she said. She hesitated, and then added, "Not a very big chance, but still . . ."

Robert smiled. "You mustn't reproach yourself," he said. "As far as I'm concerned, I'm happy to try anything." He paused. "I'm not very picky, I'm afraid. You can't be picky in my position."

Katie swallowed. She was concerned about Robert—she did not want to add to his disappointments.

"I'm very sorry," she said. "I thought it was worth a try, but I should be more discriminating. I need to find you the right person."

He looked at her pleadingly. "Do you really think so?"

She nodded. "I do. You're a good-looking man, Robert. You're kind. You've got a lot going for you."

For a few moments he seemed to bask in her compliments. But then he said, "I wish women would take that view."

"One will. Eventually."

He smiled again. "Eventually? Am I in the bargain section?"

She assured him that this was far from the case. "You've had bad luck, that's all. Compatibility is an odd thing. It's not your fault."

He thought about this. "Would you tell me if I was doing anything wrong?"

"If you wanted me to. Yes, I would." She paused. "But not everybody wants to have that sort of critique."

"I would," he said quickly.

She steered the conversation to the date with Jenny. "Do you mind my asking if anything specific went wrong?" she asked.

"She talked," said Robert.

"She talked?"

"Yes. Non-stop. I couldn't get a word in edgeways. I really couldn't."

Katie looked out of the window. "Talked about what?"

"You name it," answered Robert. "She had views on . . . well, everything." He paused. The recollection seemed to amuse him. "And by everything, I mean *everything*."

Katie transferred her gaze to him. "It might be nervousness on her part. Sometimes that happens. People are nervous, and they talk to conceal it."

He nodded. "Possibly. But I'm afraid it drove me up the wall." He looked at her enquiringly. "How can anybody sustain a conversational barrage that long? It was three or four hours—at least."

Katie sighed. "It's odd, isn't it? I suspect that she doesn't realise the effect she's having on people."

Robert shrugged. "Possibly not. But that doesn't make it any easier."

"No," said Katie. "It doesn't."

Robert was staring at her. "Is there anybody else?" he asked. "Have you got anybody you think might be right for me?"

Katie pointed to the filing cabinet. "There are people in there who might be just right. I'll need to look again." She imagined opening the cabinet and allowing various women to jump out, ready to go on a date with Robert—people for whom brown brogues were neither here nor there. People who could see beyond the beige pullover that he had been wearing when she had last seen him. William had noticed it too, she remembered, but had said nothing. William *must* disapprove of beige, she thought. Beige is such a confession of failure . . .

"I'm not fussy," he said, fingering the crease of his corduroy trousers.

"I know that."

"And I'd be so grateful if you found somebody for me. I really would."

She wondered, for a few moments, whether Robert could simply be *redesigned*. Could a makeover somehow transform him? That happened, of course, but she was not sure whether it would work here. And why could he not do something about this himself? Other people managed to find people without the assistance of something like the Perfect Passion Company. Why was Robert so *dependent*? She felt a wave of irritation—the sort of feeling that sometimes came when she saw people failing to do something for themselves. If the rest of us managed to get by socially, why were there some who required their hands to be held through the process? But then she stopped herself. Not everybody was strong. Not everybody had confidence in themselves. And that was where help came in—help that it was now her job to provide however she might feel privately that people should make their own way in the world.

She decided on reassurance. That was what the job required. "Robert," she said. "I shall leave no stone unturned."

That, she thought, was an unfortunate metaphor in the circumstances. It was as if she would have to look under stones to find somebody who would be prepared to take him on. That was not what she meant, but that, she thought, was how it came out.

She looked at Robert. She was not sure whether Ness had ever asked him to tell her exactly what he was looking for—she must have, and yet there was nothing in her notes about such a conversation.

"Tell me, Robert," she said. "What sort of woman would you like me to find for you? Who's your ideal companion?"

He seemed taken aback by the question. "I told Ness. Didn't she tell you?"

Katie explained that Ness had been unable to tell her everything before she had gone off to Canada. "We didn't have time," she said.

He appeared to understand. "I suppose it's hard for you. You have to deal with rather a lot of people."

"We do. But we like to keep our service personal. That's why we exist, I suppose. Otherwise, people could . . ."

"Go online?"

"Exactly."

He shook his head. "I wouldn't like that. I tried it once, but I couldn't find anybody suitable."

"Then tell me who you would like to meet. Describe her."

Robert looked up at the ceiling. "She's about my age," he began. "Maybe a bit older, but not by too much. She's tall—stately, even. You know how there are some women who seem to *drift* rather than walk? They drift. I like that."

Katie closed her eyes—and imagined Athena. She opened them and saw that Robert was looking at her expectantly. "Like Athena?" she said. "You know—the Greek goddess of wisdom. Like her?"

Robert hesitated. "If I'm thinking of the same one," he said. "Yes. She doesn't say much, does she?"

Katie was unsure about that. But she suspected that Athena was largely silent. "No, she doesn't."

"Her then," said Robert. "Somebody in the background. Somebody quiet."

Katie nodded. Jenny had been a mistake.

"But not too mousey?" she asked.

He hesitated. "Mousey's fine," he said at last. "In fact, anybody, Katie. Anybody will do, except . . ."

"Somebody who never stops talking?"

"I'm afraid so."

She knew that William was busy in his studio, and tried not to think about him that day, as she attended to various office tasks. There were two other people to see that day—one a new client, and the other a woman who had just had her third unsuccessful introduction. She dealt with both of these, and then, since it was time for afternoon tea, she decided to see whether William would join her. He was happy to do so. He had been working all day on a new design, he said, that was going wrong and would have to be scrapped.

"I can't concentrate," he said. "I'm too excited. You know how it is. Your mind wanders."

She was puzzled. "Excited?"

But she knew the answer even as she asked the question. Of course—it was today. She had thought of it as being not just yet, but it must be today, or perhaps tomorrow. Katie had put it out of her mind because she did not want it to happen. Now it was imminent. Everything one dreaded became imminent sooner or later.

"Alice?" she said.

He nodded. "Tomorrow. She arrives tomorrow night—at about ten. From Frankfurt. She found a flight from Melbourne to Frankfurt, and then from Frankfurt to Edinburgh. She will have been travelling for twenty-one hours, or something like that. Poor girl."

"It's a long way," said Katie. She felt a stab of pain. It was physical.

"I'm going to the airport to meet her," William said. "I have to go up to Aberdeen in the morning. There's a trade show up there that is showing some of my designs, but I'll be able to get away by five or six. I'll drive down."

William had recently acquired an ancient white Volkswagen that seemed to Katie to make more noise than a small car should ideally make. He was inordinately proud of it.

"You could go by train," she said. "Wouldn't that be simpler?"

"I have to take samples with me," he said. "I can't manage those on the train."

Katie understood. Now she concentrated on the piece of paper in front of her. The letters swam; they made no sense to her. When she spoke, it was not her, but somebody she barely recognised; another voice altogether. "You must be counting the minutes."

William nodded. "I am. It's always like that," he said, "when you're waiting to meet somebody . . . somebody important. Time drags its feet."

Katie noticed something: William had hesitated before he said *somebody important*. That suggested that he had been about to say something else, and that, she thought, was likely to have been *somebody you love*. But he had not said that, and that might point to his being uncomfortable about talking to her—Katie—about his feelings for Alice. Or it could mean that he did not really love Alice. Could that be possible? He would be wasted on somebody he did not love and who probably did not love him. She wished that she could protect him in some way from that, but the truth of the matter was that she was powerless. She could not interfere: he would not welcome that, and it could destroy their friendship. So she would have to watch—and hope; realistically, that was all that she could do.

Fortunately, Katie was busy the next morning, and had little time to brood. She thought about William from time to time, though—over her morning coffee, when she sat by herself in the office, and again just before she went to meet her friend Laura for lunch. She and Laura had known one another since childhood, although they had not seen one another in the later years of high school, when Laura's parents had moved to Frankfurt for three years. It was only now that Katie was back in Edinburgh that they were beginning to pick up the threads of what had been a close relationship. Now, as they sat together in the café of Valvona & Crolla, Katie felt the easy intimacy of this ancient friendship embrace her, like an old and familiar garment.

Laura soon picked up that there was something wrong.

"You're tense," she said. "I can tell there's something wrong."

Katie replied automatically. "I'm fine."

Laura shook her head. "You could say that to somebody you don't know very well, but not to me. We go back too far."

Katie smiled. "To the age of three? To that first day at nursery school?"

"Yes. Not that I remember it, and you won't either, I suppose. But I do remember something you did to me when we were just five. You took an ice cream I had—a cone—and you ran away with it. You dropped it on the ground and then pretended it had nothing to do with you. I've never forgotten that."

They both laughed. "And you've never forgiven me?" said Katie.

"You've never said sorry," countered Laura. "It's the least you could have done, but you never did."

"Is it too late now?"

Laura laughed. "Of course not. Although sometimes a late apology serves to remind people of something they've forgotten. You don't want to open old wounds."

"No," said Katie. "Some things, I suppose, are best forgotten."

"But the point I wanted to make," said Laura, "is that you shouldn't tell me that everything's all right, when I can tell that it isn't. So, what's going on?"

Katie looked down at the gingham tablecloth on their table. The bistro liked gingham, and somehow it seemed right. The menu was a no-nonsense one, and gingham was a no-nonsense cloth. She raised her eyes, and saw her friend looking at her with concern.

"You're not ill, are you?" Laura asked. She asked that because she had just met a friend who had undergone a scan and had been given sobering news. People became ill—we all did—and sometimes, when we were fit and healthy, we forgot that other people might not be. Human health—and all life, when one came to think of it—hung by a hair, it seemed.

Katie shook her head, and reassured Laura that there was nothing wrong with her. "With me, that is. There's nothing wrong with *me*, but *my life*, well, that's another matter." She looked slightly abashed. "I don't like talking about my problems. I'm not a moaner."

"I know you aren't," said Laura. "You never have been. That's why I wondered . . ." She paused. "A man? Is that it? A relationship not going well?"

Katie met her gaze. "Why do people assume that if one's feeling a bit low, it's down to some man somewhere?"

Laura had a ready answer. "Because nine times out of ten, that's what it is," she replied. "Or maybe eight times out of ten. People have money problems too, and problems at work. But so often it's because a romance isn't going well that they feel as if the world's not right."

Katie thought about this. "I suppose so," she conceded. "We

could argue about the numbers, but you're probably more or less right."

"So who is he?" asked Laura.

She waited for the answer. Katie looked away. She had told nobody about William; this would be the first time she had said anything about him.

"Perhaps I am worried about a man—but not in the way you think."

"What's his name?"

"He's called William."

Laura smiled encouragingly. "A solid name. I'm very suspicious of the fancy names that some men have. Give me the Bills and Johns."

"He's not a Bill," said Katie. "He's a William. It's different."

"If you say so. But tell me about him."

"He's Australian," said Katie.

"Lovely. I like Australians. They're still making men out there."

Katie laughed. "They're not all like that—the Australian stereotype. William is different. He's . . . he's artistic."

"Plenty of them are," said Laura. "I've been in Sydney. Everybody's a painter or designs studio apartments, or the things you put in studio apartments. That sort of thing. There's nobody there who breeds sheep. Not any longer." She looked at Katie enquiringly. "What does your William do?"

"He's not *my* William," Katie said defensively.

"You know what I mean," said Laura. "*This* William. What does he do?"

"He designs knitwear," Katie replied. "And knits."

Laura could not conceal her surprise. "I see."

"I can see you're surprised," said Katie.

"Well, I was—a bit. It's unusual, isn't it? Of course, there are people who design knitwear; it's just I don't seem to meet them. That's all. Is he nice? I know that sounds trite, but there are times when that's the question you have to ask: Is he . . . kind? Maybe that's what I mean."

Katie nodded. "He's lovely."

"Well then . . ."

"And engaged to somebody else."

Laura groaned. "Oh." She stared at Katie. "Seriously?"

"Yes, I'm afraid so."

"And he *wants* to be engaged to this other person? It's not an arranged marriage?"

"There aren't all that many of those," Katie said. "At least not here—or Australia."

"I just thought I'd ask," said Laura. And then, leaning forward, she took Katie's hand. "Katie, I'm sorry—I'm really sorry. This is not good, is it?"

Katie shook her head ruefully. "Well, you asked me if there was something bothering me. There it is. I'm worried about a friend—who happens to be a man. I like him—I like him a lot, but he's involved in a relationship that I think isn't right for him."

"Well, may I offer you some advice?"

Katie waited. "Go ahead."

"Stop fretting over things that you probably can't do anything about. Let him get on with his own life." She paused. "And anyway, are you sure about your own feelings for him? Are you sure you're not just a little bit in love with him yourself?"

Katie shook her head. "He's a friend. I like him . . . but that's all there is to it. I told you that."

Laura looked doubtful. "Sometimes it's what people don't

tell you that's most important. Anyway, I think you may feel something more than you're admitting, but, if you are, you'll get over it."

Katie said nothing.

Then Laura continued, "These things are hard. And don't listen to anybody who says they aren't hard. They are."

Katie said, "I feel so worried about him. It's awful. And it's all happening in front of my eyes."

Laura was looking at her with concern. "Have you thought of going away?" she said. "Just get away from it."

"We work together." Katie sighed. "In a sort of way. It's complicated."

"Then you're going to have to be philosophical about it. Stop worrying. Look after yourself—not others."

Laura gave her hand another squeeze. Touch was important, thought Katie; it was how we underlined what we felt—a punctuation for the language of the emotions. "Sorry to be so direct," Laura said. "I don't think you *should* tell friends what they want to hear. I suppose you shouldn't tell *anybody* what they want to hear."

"But do we always have to tell them *everything*?"

Laura said, rather quickly, that she thought we did not. "You should never criticise people's clothes, appearance, family, city, country, taste, or political views. Not to their face. Not if you want to stay friends."

"That doesn't leave much, does it?"

Laura laughed. "You can still get the message across. You have to use tact. And often it's the things you haven't said that do the work. Damning with faint praise. That requires a bit of thought."

Katie looked away. This conversation had not cheered her up. She would do her very best to regard Alice as a new friend.

This is an important day for William, she told herself. I'm pleased that William is happy.

There: it was not too difficult to think that—and it did make her feel slightly better. She looked at Laura. She told herself that it was a good thing that she had Laura's friendship, even if she squeezed her hand a little bit too often over lunch and on occasion was a bit too direct. Every friendship, though, came with its drawbacks, its historical baggage, its litany of set expressions and familiar conversations that gave it its texture, its place in our lives.

She went back to the office and was sufficiently distracted by the task of the making up of the month's accounts as not to think either of William, or of Alice. Alice, anyway, was a blank in her mind: William had shown her a photograph once, but she had not paid much attention, and now she had little idea of what his fiancée looked like. Making sense of the accounts was a complex task—she had never had much of a head for figures, and there were tax issues here that she had never mastered. But she did what she had to do—enough to satisfy the accountant to whom she passed the books over—and then left the office to make her way back to the flat.

She had not prepared anything for dinner. On the way home, she called in at the small local supermarket round the corner from the flat and looked at the ready meals section. This was encroaching on the shelves previously occupied by fresh food—almost everything seemed now to be pre-packaged and ready for the oven or the microwave. She glanced at a cauliflower and cheese pie in its alluring wrapping, and then at the nutritional information on the back of the wrapping. There was the carbohydrate and the sugar count. Sugar—in a cauliflower pie? Apparently so. And then there was the number of grams of salt per hundred milligrams. This small pie, it was revealed, contained thirty-one per cent of an adult's recommended maximum daily intake of salt. This information, at least, was printed in red—a forced concession to legislation that required people to be warned about what they were eating.

She replaced it on the shelf and reached for a small packet of spinach and ricotta samosas. These were less salty, it turned out, and she bought them. She thought of the dinner that lay ahead of her: heated-up samosas, and a bean salad. The salad at least would be fresh, and would do as a meal in itself if she decided that she could not face the samosas; somehow it seemed less poignant to be sitting by oneself in one's kitchen, eating a bean salad rather than prepared samosas, even if they were low-salt. Of course, many people ate their evening meal by themselves, and thought nothing of it. But now she asked herself whether it was time for her to try to find somebody with whom to share her life. She had not felt the need for anybody while William was around, but Alice's impending arrival had made it clear to her that William was *temporary*. William would not remain in her life—he was not the answer to any prospect of loneliness—indeed, he made it worse because his presence, in a curious way, reminded her that his eventual absence was inevitable.

She had barely sat down to her dinner when she received the phone call from William. His voice was stressed, his relief that she had answered only too apparent.

"Thank goodness," he said. "It occurred to me you might have your phone switched off."

She asked him if anything was wrong. She thought: Alice's

plane has gone down. And she immediately put the thought out of her mind.

"Is something wrong?" It must be, she thought. Alice was not coming: she had decided against the trip. Or, there had been a fire in his studio, and it had spread to the Perfect Passion Company. Everything was lost.

"My car's broken down."

She relaxed. "Oh, I'm sorry. Where are you? At the airport?"

"I'm twenty miles north of Dundee. At the side of the road. There's a garage just outside Dundee that does rescues for the RAC—they've said they were on their way, and they told me to stay with my vehicle until they arrived. And then they called about ten minutes ago and said that they would not be with me for another forty minutes."

"Oh, William, I'm sorry."

He explained that he could not possibly get to Edinburgh Airport on time. He had tried, but failed to contact Alice because she was either in a plane or had her phone switched off. "The last thing I want is for her to arrive in Edinburgh and not be met," he said. "She has no idea where to go—it would be a terrible start to her trip."

"I'll go," said Katie. She looked at her watch. "I can easily get out there for nine."

"Angel," said William.

"It's no problem." And then she added, "I'm not one hundred per cent sure I'd recognise her. How will I know?"

"I showed you a photograph—remember?"

"Yes, but I'm still not sure."

He assured her it would be obvious. "Most of the people on those Frankfurt flights are businesspeople. She'll stand out. You'll know."

"All right. There won't be many people looking as if they're expecting to be met."

"Right. And then, could you take her to my place. You know where the key is."

She said she could do that, and he said, "I don't know how to thank you."

"It's nothing much. Don't worry. She'll be met."

His voice was full of self-reproach. "I shouldn't have gone to Aberdeen."

"It was work; you had to go up there. It's not your fault."

"If I had a better car . . ."

"Your car's all right. Just don't worry about it. Alice will be met. She'll be back in your flat when you arrive home."

"After midnight, I imagine," he said.

She told him once again not to worry, and then the call ended. She returned to her bean salad and samosas. She had time for some yoghurt and honey after that—a dish that she often had to round off a meal. Then she went into her bedroom, brushed her hair, and put on a fresh top. It was warm, and she thought she would get away without a cardigan.

She drove out to the airport and parked her car. It was still light, since in summer, it never really got dark until much later. The sky was empty, as there were a few more planes to land that evening.

A man was wandering around the airport car park, looking for his car. He said to her as he walked past: "Remember to make a note of where you left your car. Write it down. Don't trust your memory."

She laughed.

"No, I'm serious," he said. "All cars look the same. Look at them. They're all the same. The anodyne world of cars."

She smiled. "Press the button on your key and look out for lights flashing somewhere."

He stared at her. "Of course." And then added, with a grin, "I should have thought of that."

He pressed the electronic key. Less than a row of cars away, tail-lights flashed obediently.

The man looked at her with admiration. "Thank you." And then he added, "Come and work for me—anytime."

She smiled, and waved goodbye as she started into the terminal.

"I mean it," he called out. "Serious invitation."

CHAPTER SEVEN

Arrivals

She stood in the entry hall, watching the automatic doors that would open to release the newly arrived passengers. The flight before had cleared, and the doors remained closed for ten minutes before the first of the Frankfurt arrivals appeared. A suspended screen had announced the flight's arrival, and a dozen or so people were already waiting to greet friends and family. A uniformed driver, placard at the ready, stood to the side, ready to pick up his client.

Katie looked around her. She had always disliked airports. She objected to the endless arrays of duty-free goods past which you were corralled, irrespective of your interest, or otherwise, in doing any shopping; the cabinets of sunglasses, the expensive watches, the milling crowds of people who were on holiday, but not quite yet; the artificiality of the great waiting rooms between one place and the next; the sense of being nowhere in particular. Railway stations were different. They were less detached from the world about them. They were more obviously functional, and they did not detain you unnecessarily. They had a smell, which airports lacked: that was a real difference.

There was a young couple standing next to her. She was wearing a light red fleece top across the back of which the word *Committee* was printed. He had an open-necked shirt, and she saw that he had a bangle made of twisted animal hair—the sort of thing that visitors returning from East Africa brought back with them and became attached to. She thought: They climbed Kilimanjaro once. They were in a group. She was a member of the committee.

They were talking German, which Katie understood imperfectly. The young woman said that she was glad that she could stay at home the following day and talk to Danie. Her friend replied that Danie sometimes did not like talking. "Let him rest," he said.

Katie caught the young woman's eye, and they both smiled. They were strangers united by a common experience of waiting—circumstances in which people often felt they could talk to one another.

"Sometimes the luggage takes forever, doesn't it?" said the young woman.

Katie nodded. "It can do. But what counts is whether it arrives."

"Sure. That's the most important thing."

"I sometimes feel like kissing my suitcase when I take it off the carousel," said Katie.

The young man said, "I kissed the ground once when I got home to Munich. Our flight had been diverted, right across Africa, and we had spent thirty-six hours at Djibouti airport."

His friend confirmed the story. "He did. He bent down and kissed the terminal floor. One of the other passengers told him off. She said that that was the way to spread germs."

Katie hesitated. Then, "What were you doing in Africa?" she asked. "Did you climb Kilimanjaro?"

The young woman stared at her. "Kilimanjaro? The mountain? No. I get . . . what do you call it in English?"

"Vertigo," said the young man. *"Gleichgewichtsstörung."*

"Yes, I get vertigo, and Kai, here, is diabetic. He can't do that sort of thing." She paused. "No, we were helping to build a school. Kai is really good at plastering. He used to work with a plasterer during university holidays in Bonn."

"That's a good thing to do," said Katie. "I mean, there's more point to it than climbing Kilimanjaro."

"The school was very pretty," said the young woman. "It had a green tin roof, and Kai's friend Thomas painted a mural all across the veranda wall. Flowers, dogs . . ."

"A bus. Remember the picture of the bus, with the people in it—the children. Waving from the back."

"Yes. Thomas was very good. He did lots of murals."

The door hissed open, and a woman with a child of four or five, came out. The child hung on to her skirt. An older woman stepped forward and embraced her. She picked up the child and kissed him. A man wearing a suit came out and strode off purposefully towards the exit. Katie watched. There was a constant stream of arrivals now. She thought of the school in Africa, with its green tin roof, and the young Germans who had arrived, created it, and then left. And Thomas, going off, she assumed, to paint murals on walls and verandas elsewhere.

A group of golfers came out, each struggling with an outsize bag of clubs. Alice was behind them, and at first Katie missed her. Then she saw her, and knew immediately that this was Alice.

Katie moved forward. "Alice?"

Alice looked startled. "Me?"

"Yes. You're Alice, aren't you? William was going to meet you, but his car's broken down. He asked me to come instead."

Alice looked at her as if trying to take in what had just been said. "I see," she said. "And you're . . ."

"I'm Katie. My office is next door to William's studio."

She became aware of Alice's questioning stare. "He couldn't get back to Edinburgh in time. He was very upset."

"He should get a new car," muttered Alice.

Katie caught her breath. She rarely took an instant dislike to anyone, but she decided that she and Alice were not going to get along. And it was not her fault, either. She had been prepared to make the effort, but there had been nothing warm or friendly from Alice, no word of thanks for having come out to the airport to meet her. And that unsympathetic remark about William's buying a new car—perhaps it was meant to be funny, but it did not strike Katie that way.

Katie offered to help Alice with one of her bags.

"They've got wheels," said Alice. Once again there was no thanks.

They walked towards the exit in silence. Then, as they left the building, Katie said, "You must be tired after that long flight."

Alice nodded. "I slept a bit. Not much—but a bit."

"It takes a few days to adjust. You'll be all right."

"I hope so."

They followed the signs for the car park. Outside the terminal, Katie noticed a man standing beside his suitcase. He was tall, somewhere in his late twenties, and good-looking in a rugged sort of way. He was facing them, and his eyes briefly met Katie's. Alice looked round, and she followed Katie's glance, before quickly lowering her gaze.

"My car's not far away," Katie said. "If you forgot where you left your car, it could take hours to find it—hours."

"Best not to forget," said Alice.

Katie found herself beginning to feel irritated. She was doing her best to make conversation, but was getting no encouragement from Alice. She was not quite being rebuffed, but Alice clearly had little intention of being friendly.

She tried again. "William told me you're a medical student."

"Yes."

Katie waited for more, but it was not forthcoming.

"How many more years before you're qualified?"

"Three."

Katie bit her lip. She would try—for William's sake.

"What do you want to specialize in?"

"I don't know," replied Alice, not looking at Katie as she spoke. "Maybe infectious diseases. Maybe gastro-enterology. Not surgery."

That was at least something.

"Why not surgery?"

"Because it's not for me," said Alice curtly. "You may as well do needlework."

Katie laughed. "What does William think?"

"William doesn't care what I do."

"Are you sure?"

Alice stopped in her tracks. "I think I know how my own fiancé thinks about things," she said sharply.

They were almost at the car. Katie was struggling. She was tempted to say something to Alice about how inconvenient it had been to have to drive out to the airport. She wanted to point out that parking there, even for a short time, struck her as outrageously expensive, and that she—Katie—had paid for the privilege herself. She wanted to tell her that of all the ways in which she could spend her evening, going out to the airport to meet somebody whose behaviour was cold, if not actually churlish, would have been her last choice. She could have said any of that, but instead, once they had put Alice's bags in the car, she took her mobile phone from her pocket and offered it to her. "You might like to call William and tell him you've arrived." She paused. "Unless you want to use your own. This won't cost anything. An Australian mobile may be . . ."

Alice did not let her finish. "Thanks," she said. "Yes. I'll call him."

Alice took the phone, now switched to the keypad.

"I'll give you his number," said Katie, and began to recite it.

Alice keyed it in, and then looked up at Katie. They were seated in the car—Alice in the passenger seat and Katie at the wheel. Katie had begun to reverse out of the parking bay. She said, "These spots are always too small. They don't give you enough room. They try to cram as many cars as possible into as little space."

Alice was watching her. "Good memory," she said.

Katie frowned. "Sorry?"

"Good memory for telephone numbers. Most people find it hard to remember mobile numbers. You remembered William's."

It could not have been clearer: this was an accusation, or, at the least, an implication. Katie was not sure how to reply. This must be the explanation for Alice's attitude: she suspected that she was being met by a competitor. It was as simple as that. She had said nothing, though, about William, other than that her office was next to his studio, and that his car had broken down. There had been nothing more, and that, surely, was not much upon which to base an assumption of emotional rivalry.

William answered almost immediately. Alice half-turned in her seat, so that she was addressing the window, but Katie could not help but hear their conversation.

"Oh Als, it's you . . ."

Als, thought Katie. That must be his fond name for her. It was almost unbearable . . . *Als*.

"Yes, I'm here."

"Katie met you? She was there all right?"

"I'm on her phone. We're in the car."

There was a slight pause. Then William said, "Als, I'm so sorry. I feel awful. I had to go up to Aberdeen, you see, and then on the way down my car stopped. It just stopped. Died. You know that feeling when machinery lets you down? It just stops. It did that."

"Yes, Katie told me. Is it fixed?"

"They're doing something right now. The guy says that he thinks he knows what the problem is. He seems to know what he's doing. He's almost finished, I think."

"I may be asleep by the time you come. I'm pretty wrecked."

"Of course you are. Poor Als. All those planes. You go to bed. Katie knows where the key is."

That, thought Katie, is an unfortunate detail.

Alice turned to glance at her, but they were at the barrier, and Katie had to busy herself with inserting the ticket into the machine. The barrier swung up obediently, almost courteously.

"Okay," said Alice. "We're on our way, Will. I'd better go."

She did not hear what William said; she tried not to. She had been an unwilling, embarrassed eavesdropper on that conversation, and was relieved it was over.

"Thanks," said Alice, handing her back the phone. "It looks as if he's being fixed up."

"Yes," said Katie. "These motoring organizations are terrific."

Silence now descended on the car as they joined the light traffic back into the city. Alice stared out of the window, and Katie concentrated on her driving. In the distance, floodlit against the night sky, was Edinburgh Castle.

"That's the castle," Katie pointed out.

"Yes," said Alice.

Katie thought: I must remember, she's been travelling for twenty-something hours. She has crossed about as many time zones as you can cross without ending up being back in the day before yesterday. She has been sitting in an economy seat on a cheap flight, eating meals from little plastic containers, while a child whined next to her and the man behind her had his knees in the back of her seat. She had flicked through the menu of movies and perhaps had found nothing she wanted to watch. She had tried to sleep and had failed. Katie thought: I should remember all that. And then she thought: I wish I didn't know that he called her Als.

Soon they were parking outside the flat. Katie thought, as she switched off the engine: Alice's problem is a simple one. She may be jet-lagged; she may be exhausted, but her problem is that she has no manners. Some people just don't have manners. Jet-lagged and exhausted people who have no manners behave, on the whole, very much worse than jet-lagged and exhausted people who do have manners. There were no surprises there, thought Katie: that was what one would expect.

An idea occurred to her. She would go away while Alice was here. It was only two weeks, but it would be unbearable. If she went away—right away—to Prague, perhaps, which she had always wanted to visit, she would not have to be here and think about William being with this . . . this *awful* person. There was so much to see in Prague, and it would take her mind off everything. Yes, Prague it would be, as soon as she could arrange it. She had seen Prague on the arrivals screen at the airport. A plane had landed from Prague, and if planes arrived from a destination, there was always return of service. She would go.

But when, having left Alice at William's flat, she returned

to her own flat, Katie realised that she could not run away to Prague—or anywhere else. She had made appointments for clients. She had a business to run. She would have to get through the next two weeks somehow—perhaps by just not thinking about it.

She took some time to go to sleep that night. And when she awoke the next morning, she was aware that she had dreamed of William. He had been standing before her, and she had felt as if she had been bathed in warmth and light—golden, gentle, all about her.

CHAPTER EIGHT

Herb's barbecue

Herb and Ness were comfortable sitting in the café, while the life of the town, the comings-and-goings, continued on the main street outside. Ness reflected on the fact that she had nothing to do, and that she could sit there all day if she wished. This was freedom—something that so many of us surrendered on the first day of our working lives and only recovered—if we ever recovered it—a whole career later. It had taken some time to sink in, but now she felt it, and its effect was heady.

"I shouldn't keep you with this story of mine," said Herb apologetically. "You'll have things to do."

Ness shook her head. "Not today," she said. "Nor tomorrow, for that matter."

"Sometimes it's like that when I'm up north," he said. "In my place up there. Nothing happening on the lines. Everything fixed."

"Nothing happening except time," Ness mused.

He looked at her. "I guess that's right. Time happens, I suppose, whatever we're doing."

Ness remembered that she had read an article about time and about how physicists explained it. She had tried to grasp the argument, but she had been unable to do so. Few people did, she imagined.

"You were in Guadeloupe," she encouraged him. "You'd met Hélène through . . ."

"Through Louis Bouchard's wife, Dominique."

"She was the one who sang Edith Piaf songs on her karaoke machine?"

"Yes, that was her. She and Hélène used to see one another most days. She was in and out of the Bouchard house. They had a pool, you see, and Hélène brought her boys over to swim. She used to worry about them swimming in the sea—she said you never could tell what was beneath you."

"Of course. Sharks and so on."

"Though it's sometimes the things you can't see that are the peskiest," said Herb. "Sea itch. Camouflaged stonefish. You don't see them until you stand on them."

Ness signalled to the woman behind the counter that their coffee needed to be refreshed.

"You and Hélène? You took to each other?"

Herb looked out of the window. "I don't know what she thought. I guess she thought I was okay, but I know I was very keen. She was attractive. She had a sense of humour. Everybody liked her. You went into the shops with her, and everybody talked to her—told her what was going on, asked advice. She knew everything that was happening on the island."

Herb hesitated. Then he continued, "We were happy—I think. At least, I was. Maybe she wasn't quite so happy. She was pleased that I got on with the boys—I know that. I used to take them fishing every weekend. I used to do a lot of babysitting for Hélène when she did her voluntary work. She helped at a young mother centre, where they taught girls how to look after their babies." He sighed. "Some of those girls were pregnant by sixteen. They had the baby, and the father would be strutting around all pleased with himself, and then next thing you knew he was off. The girls had to do the bringing up—with their own mothers, of course, who would have their hands full with other things. Hélène said they should make the young men pay for the baby, but they never did. They never took them to court, and even if they did, they never got any money out of them.

"So, I looked after the boys while she was helping these young women. I took them for hamburgers, and they loved that. They needed a father, those boys, and I discovered that I liked that. It could have worked out pretty well if only Hélène had not . . . well, I think she got tired of me."

The woman behind the counter brought them a fresh cup of coffee along with an unordered chocolate-chip cookie. Ness thanked her and took a bite of the cookie. She made a face. "Too sweet."

"We have a sweet tooth in these parts," said Herb. "Maple syrup, you see."

"I'm sorry to hear that things didn't work out," said Ness. "And are you sure she got tired of you? There can be all sorts of reasons. Sometimes people just drift apart. That happens a lot, you know. Nobody gets tired of anybody, they just . . . go down different paths."

"You've seen that in your work?" asked Herb. "Back in Scotland?"

"Yes. And it's the same everywhere you go. Human nature is pretty much the same. I hear people's stories, you see, when they come to us. Everybody has had disappointments in their lives—everybody."

Herb looked thoughtful. "True." He added, "This was a big disappointment for me. Really big. We'd been together eight years, you see, and the boys were teenagers then. Everything was settled. Nice house. Friends. I was making good money. The company was doing well. There wasn't a cloud on the horizon—except Hélène decided that we didn't have anything more to say to one another."

"She told you that?"

"Yes," said Herb sadly. "She said that she still liked me, but that she felt that we both needed to branch out."

"Branch out?"

"That's what she said. She could have said *move out*, because that's what she did. She rented a house for herself and took the boys with her. She said I could still see them, but they would be living with her.

"Antoine was pretty cross. He came to see me and said that he was ashamed of his sister. This was because she had started an affair with another man. He said that he would deal with this person. If he ran him off the island, then there was a chance that Hélène would come back to me. He said it was easy for him to get his men to plant stolen goods in the coach's place and then threaten him with prosecution if he didn't leave. He said nobody would believe him if he protested his innocence.

"I told him I wanted no part of that. I said that I was thinking of coming back to Canada. I didn't want Hélène to be unhappy, you see. I guess I still loved her. It wasn't her fault that she got bored—more my fault, really. I should have read a bit more, maybe—found a bit more to talk to Hélène about, you know. Women don't like you to talk about fishing all the time."

Ness shook her head. "Oh, Herb," she said. "You mustn't reproach yourself. These things happen. It's nobody's fault—most of the time."

They sat together in silence. Then Herb said, "You're very kind. I can tell that."

Ness smiled. "You don't know me all that well. I can be as mean as the next person."

"I doubt it," said Herb. He hesitated. "You're not going away, are you?"

"Me? No, not in the near future. I have nothing planned."

"So, you might stay here . . . indefinitely."

Ness shifted in her seat. "I wasn't thinking of living here for the rest of my life."

He thought about this. "You'll be going back to Scotland?"

Ness said that she had made no plans. She was on a gap year, but gap years could expand.

"You like Canada?" asked Herb.

"Very much. I like the scale of it. I like the sense of having a lot of space behind me—all the way up to the far north. I like the way people treat one another courteously. That's very important. The world is full of inconsiderate people. Not here."

Herb looked pleased. "We do our best."

"Well, your best is pretty good."

He toyed with the teaspoon that had come with his cup. "Could I make you dinner some time?"

She answered immediately. Later, she realised she should have given it more thought. But now she said, "Anytime."

"This evening? I've got this new gas barbecue. I caught some wide-mouthed bass up in Frontenac. They make great eating. I could barbecue the fish."

"I'd like that."

He sat back, and looked pleased. "It's fine weather," he said. "It won't be cold."

"No."

"And the fireflies will be out."

Herb had prepared the fish in a marinade.

"You'd be surprised," he said, "how many people put the fish on the barbecue without doing anything to it. Jacques does that, you know."

He looked at Ness from behind the outside table on which the fish lay in their dishes of sauce.

"I've got a lot of time for Jacques," he said. "He's a good friend. But he has his faults—like the rest of us."

Ness shrugged. Herb had prepared her a long, cold, minty drink, with what he called "a hint of gin." It was just right for the warm evening, and she took a sip of it now through a straw. "I like Jacques too," she said.

"Yes. He's had to put up with a lot since he lost his arm. That was bad luck. You lose an arm and there's a whole lot of things you can't do."

"I can imagine. And yet he copes pretty well, doesn't he?"

"Yes, he does," said Herb. "He says he doesn't really notice it any longer. And neither do I, I suppose. I don't think of him as having only one arm. Sometimes I forget. I say things like, 'Jacques, you row the boat,' and then I realise that it's not all that easy to row if you have only one arm. He's worked out a way, though. You've got to give him credit for that. He puts a leg over one oar and holds it in position that way—then he uses his arm to pull the other one. Then he does the same thing, the other way round. It works." He paused. "He can be pretty methodical, but you know something? This isn't me crit-icising Jacques—I'm just telling you about it. He's untidy. You should see his place! Nothing put away. Everything lying about like a teenager's room. You see the way teenagers live? Clothes on the floor. Plates all over the place. That's teenagers for you."

Ness was amused. Old friends were often more aware than

anybody else of each other's faults. "So, Jacques' house is a mess?"

"Big time," said Herb.

Ness laughed. She said that people chose to live in different ways. "If he's happy with the way things are, then that's all right, don't you think? He might not see it as a mess at all. He might even think it's tidy."

Herb seemed disappointed with this. Perhaps he had been expecting disapproval on her part, thought Ness, and she had not shown it.

"No woman would put up with it," Herb now said. "A single man might get away with it, but no woman would tolerate it."

Ness said that she knew some very untidy women—and some scrupulously tidy men.

Herb was silent for a few moments. Then he said, "I don't like to eat at his place. I've often had an upset stomach afterwards. You've got to keep your kitchen clean. You have to throw out time-expired food. Clear the fridge. You have to."

"I'm sure Jacques is careful about these things," she said.

Herb shook his head. He was in no doubt about this. "No, he ain't," he said. "He's not careful at all."

Herb started the barbecue, gingerly lowering fillets of bass onto the sizzling grill.

"I caught these on a lure," he said. "I was using one of those small ones that look like fish—they're very realistic. They're articulated, you see, so that the lure moves like a fish when you trawl it through the water. Mine was green—green with a bit of yellow. It works really well, although fish can't resist worms, you know. You put in a juicy worm, and you'll get interest, even when a lure doesn't seem to be attracting much attention."

He had prepared a rice salad. Wild rice and white long-grain were mixed with onions, mushrooms, and chopped celery. Ness gave her verdict: perfect. Herb was flushed with pride. "I've always cooked," he said. "Some guys never step inside the kitchen—I always like to pull my weight. Hélène was a great cook, you know, but I still cooked three days of the week—all the time we were married."

"You'd make a great husband for somebody," Ness said.

It slipped out. It had not been intended seriously, but its effect on Herb was immediate.

"Do you really think so?" he asked.

Of course, she had to say yes. "I think you would," she said. "Men who can cook are at a premium."

He took a sip of beer. "Who knows?" he said. "One day I might find somebody."

He glanced at her as he spoke, and then quickly looked away. Ness swallowed hard. She had wandered into this. She liked Herb, but if he was imagining that she might be suitable for him . . . No, she told herself—he can't be. But then she looked at him again, and she saw the smile with which she was rewarded, and she knew that she would have to handle this very carefully.

The fireflies came out in the darkness, small points of light in the darkness of the surrounding trees. Above them, the night sky's display of stars dipped and swung from horizon to horizon; a blinking light described an arc—a plane dropping down towards Toronto in the distance.

Ness shivered. The night was getting cooler. "I mustn't stay too long," she said. "I've got things to do."

"It was great having you over," said Herb.

"I enjoyed it, Herb. And your marinade was to die for."

"Anytime," he said.

She thought that he looked regretful—even sad. A few

days ago, apropos of nothing, the thought had occurred to her: What was it like to be Herb la Fouche? What it was like to be another was, Ness thought, a question we all should be prepared to ask ourselves. She had learned to ask it in her work: she could only help people, she had long since realised, if she could put herself in their shoes and know how they viewed the world and what they wanted in this life. Now she felt that at last she had some idea of how that question might be answered. After their conversation in the coffee shop, and their meal together that evening, she had been brought closer to Herb, and she had been touched by the fact that he had opened up to her. But this was going to be a friendship—nothing more—and she sensed that she would have to make this clear sooner rather than later, before any misunderstandings deepened. And he would be hurt—she sensed that already; no matter how tactful she was, Herb was going to feel rejected.

CHAPTER NINE

A mild optician

Katie hoped that jet lag might keep Alice out of sight the following day, and that she might be spared the sight, so long dreaded, of seeing William and his fiancée together. She knew, of course, that this feeling was both petty and unrealistic, and she was trying to overcome it, struggling to put a brave face on the situation, when William put his head round the door at the usual coffee time.

"My heroine," he greeted her, smiling. "The neighbor who saved the day."

Is that all I am? she thought. Your neighbor?

She returned the smile. "It was no trouble."

He closed the door behind him. At least he was alone. "You can imagine how I felt when the car died on me. It just did. It gave a sort of sigh and just stopped going."

"Altogether?"

"Yes, a complete loss of power. I managed to get it off the road—there was quite a broad verge at that point—and I phoned for help. But . . ." He shrugged. "They had had several emergency calls, and they were responding to them in strict order. One of the cars had small children in the back, though, and they got priority—quite rightly. Then they attended to the rest of us."

She listened while he narrated the rest of the saga—the waiting; the alarm at the thought that Alice would arrive and there would be nobody to meet her; the anxiety while the mechanic investigated the fault; and the relief, of course, when the interrupted journey was eventually resumed.

"I can't tell you how grateful I am, Katie," he said. "You really saved the day. You were a complete star."

He moved forward, grinning, his arms held out in a gesture of gratitude, and then, quite suddenly leaned forward and embraced her. "Thank you so much," he whispered. "Thank you."

And Katie became aware that the door had opened and that Alice was there. She pushed William back, and he turned his head. For a moment, nobody moved, but then he disengaged from the embrace and turned round.

"I was thanking Katie," he said. His voice was even. "She put herself out last night—she really did."

Alice looked on impassively. "Yes," she said. "Thanks, Katie." Her tone was flat, devoid of the warmth that normally accompanied real gratitude.

Katie felt her face flush with embarrassment. She glanced at William, who seemed to be taking the awkwardness of the situation in his stride.

"I wasn't going to wake you," he said to Alice. "You seemed soundly asleep."

"I was," said Alice. "But then I woke up and you weren't there."

She was looking about the room, but her eyes did not rest on Katie: Katie sensed that she was not there. *Blanked*: she was being blanked.

"This is Katie's office," said William. "I come in from next door to make coffee most mornings." He gestured towards the kitchenette. "Through there, you see."

"Handy," said Alice.

Katie, who had been standing up beside her desk—where William had put his arms about her—now sat down. She felt momentarily dizzy.

"I might as well make coffee," said William breezily. "Coffee, Alice? Katie?"

Katie said, "Yes, please," and Alice simply nodded.

William went into the kitchenette. Alice's eyes followed him; she was uncertain, it seemed, what to do. The kitchenette was very small—there was hardly room for two.

"It's a nice day to take a look round the city," said Katie. It was all she could think of to say.

Alice looked in her direction, although she still seemed not to focus on her properly. The door to the kitchenette clicked shut. It did that; it had been badly hung and sometimes would not stay open.

Katie waited. Then, after a brief moment, Katie said, her voice lowered, "William was just saying thank you for last night. That's all."

Now Alice looked at her. There was a ghost of a smile on her lips. "Oh, I know that."

"He and I are neighbors, you see. William sometimes helps me with the business. Neighbors. There's nothing . . ."

Alice held up a hand. "Listen, I never thought there was anything. Seriously, I didn't."

Katie felt relieved. "Good. I wouldn't want you to . . ."

"I didn't," Alice interrupted her. "I told you, I didn't think."

The door behind her opened, and Alice turned to face William. He handed her a mug of coffee and then passed one to Katie.

"You should sit down," Katie said to Alice. "You'd be more comfortable." She pointed to the client's chair.

Alice seemed to relax. "It's nice here," she said, whether to Katie or William, it was not entirely clear.

Katie said, "I love this part of town. And William, you like it too, don't you?"

"I do," said William. "I've felt at home in Edinburgh since the day I arrived. It's a bit like Melbourne, you see. There's a similar sort of feel."

Alice took a sip of her coffee. "Interesting," she said. Then she turned to Katie. "So, you're a dating agency?"

"Sort of," said Katie. "We introduce people who don't want to meet online for one reason or another."

"They may have had bad experiences," William added. "Or they don't have the confidence. There are plenty of people who find online dating a bit daunting."

Alice considered this. "Yes, I suppose so." She frowned. "How much do you charge?"

Katie hesitated. "It depends."

Alice waited for an answer. William looked embarrassed.

"There's a fee at the beginning," Katie said at last. "To register costs eighteen hundred pounds. Then, for each introduction it's four hundred pounds." She resented being called upon to spell this out. She had not set these charges: she had inherited them from Ness. The business had overheads, and although it made a profit, it was not an inordinate one. Moreover, there were several clients who were charged considerably less because they did not have the means to pay the full charge. Her conscience was clear on that score.

Alice raised an eyebrow. "That's not cheap. Does each client pay four hundred? Both of them in a match?"

"Yes. We spend a lot of time with our clients," Katie

explained. "It's a very personal service. That's why people come to us." She felt growing irritation: she did not have to account to Alice. This was none of her business.

William intervened; he had sensed Katie's resentment. "Look at it this way," he said. "You can go out to dinner at a really good restaurant. The bill could come to two hundred pounds for two—quite easily. So, four hundred is two good dinners out. That's worth it, surely." He paused, waiting to see if Alice was convinced. "And remember what's at stake here. It's a person's whole life we're talking about. The person you choose as your partner could be with you for your entire life. You want to get it right, I would have thought. You don't want to end up with somebody you can't stand."

Katie was not sure how Alice would react to what William had said about marriage. She glanced at William. He was looking at Alice.

Alice now stood up. She yawned. "I'm going to have to crash," she said. "It's two in the morning or whatever—according to my body clock. Or yesterday. Or something."

"I'll come," said William.

Alice shook her head. She stifled another yawn. "No, you stay and finish your coffee. I'm asleep on my feet." She looked at Katie, and just managed a smile. It seemed that she was now making an effort. "Thanks for the coffee."

⁓

Left alone, Katie looked at William across her desk. She was not sure what to say, but at last she offered, "I'm glad that Alice has managed to get here. You must be so pleased."

"I am," he said. "I can't wait to show her round. I've got a lot planned." He paused. He was looking at Katie intently, as if trying to work out what she was thinking. "Alice can be a bit abrupt. You've probably noticed."

Katie reassured him that she had noticed nothing of the sort.

"You're being kind," said William. "You don't have to hide anything from me."

"She must be tired," said Katie. "If I'd flown halfway round the world, I'd feel a bit abrupt, I think."

"No, it can't be easy," said William. "I was hoping that she'd sleep on the flight. She had a business class seat. Fully reclinable. A bed. But she says that she hardly slept at all on the plane."

Katie frowned. "Business class? Not many students fly business class." She stopped. This was no concern of hers.

William looked embarrassed. He started to say something, but stopped. "Well . . ." He sighed. "I didn't mean to say anything about that. I suppose I'm going to have to explain."

He gave her a look of entreaty—as if he was particularly keen that she should agree with what he had to say. "Alice is very bright, you know. She's modest about her academic abilities, but she comes out top of year at medical school—regularly. The uni has an anatomy and physiology prize, and she won that, and another prize too. She's going places in medicine."

"I'm not surprised," Katie said.

"And she's worked hard to get where she's got to," William continued. "Her old man was a bus driver. He couldn't work because he had a head injury. Money was tight—really tight. Alice trained as a radiographer and gave money to her mother each month because her mother was looking after a sister whose husband's business had gone bankrupt—and then he went off to Western Australia and was never heard of again. Alice helped from her salary, which was a bit tight anyway."

"I see."

William hesitated, as if weighing up whether to make a further revelation. At last he said, "Can I tell you something else in confidence?"

"Yes, of course. Of course, you can."

"I don't think I ever told you much about my family, did I?"

He had not. "I think you said something about your father being a farmer. I think you said that."

"He is," William said. "As was my great-grandfather and my grandfather. They were what we call graziers in Australia. In a big way. And they had other businesses. They were livestock dealers."

Katie smiled. "You're telling me they were well-off."

"Well, yes, they were. And still are. Very. And although I don't talk about it, it means that there's a trust. There are lawyers in Melbourne who control it. They hand out the cash to me and to my cousins, and a couple of other relatives. We're the beneficiaries, as they call us."

"Useful," said Katie. She had wondered how he afforded the rental of the studio, although with the success of his designs he must have brought in a reasonable income.

"Anyway," said William. "Under the terms of the trust, the lawyers in Melbourne can pay the educational expenses, including living expenses, of any beneficiaries, or their spouses, who are at university. They can pay the lot. I took it up with them and argued that they had a discretion to extend that to anybody to whom a beneficiary was engaged."

"Ah."

"Yes. At first, they said no. But I argued the case with them, and they caved in. They said that it was probably within the terms of the trust—just—and so they have been covering everything for Alice ever since she got the place at medical school. Fees, textbooks, rent, living expenses—the lot. Even this trip to Scotland. And the trust can easily afford business class travel. Easily."

"She's very lucky," said Katie.

"Yes," agreed William. "But there's something else. I feel pleased that all this money, which was made back in the days when there was a lot of exploitation—made on the backs of a lot of people, to be honest—at least some of it now is being used to support somebody who comes from an ordinary background where there was not much money. There's a sort of justice in that, don't you think?"

At first Katie did not answer. Then she nodded. "Yes, I can see that," she said. She glanced at her watch. She had work to do: Jenny was coming to see her later that day, and she wanted to be able to propose an introduction.

"Will you give me a hand with something?" she asked William.

"Of course," he said. "Alice needs that sleep, and I'm free."

"Let's look at some of the possibilities for Jenny. I want to help her, you know—I really do."

He sat down beside her. He was very close. She caught her breath. People said it became easier; they said that if you came to terms with what it was you could not have, it became easier. It was all about attitude, and acceptance—they said. But they weren't going through it themselves, when they said that, were they?

She spread the files out on her desk. William looked at her expectantly.

"These are?" he asked.

"These," Katie explained, "are from the difficult section. Bottom drawer over there. Labelled by Ness, with her usual style, *circolo problematico*. A reference to Dante, I imagine."

William grinned. "I like people who have a flourish to them."

"She has that," agreed Katie. "There are thirty files down there at the moment—thirty hard-to-place men. Some have been there for ages, I've discovered. There's been occasional activity as a possibility emerges, but then they're filed away for the next time. There's a file labelled *Completely Hopeless*. It's the sad end of our business, I'm afraid."

"So why these four?" William asked.

"I had an idea," Katie replied. "All these men, I think, are probably looking for a woman who's more forceful than they are. All of these would be described as rather milquetoast."

William frowned. "Milquetoast?"

"Caspar Milquetoast was a comic book character who was a bit insipid."

"Ah."

"And I thought that men like that might just fancy a woman who's the opposite of themselves."

William looked doubtful. "But that may simply emphasise their inadequacy, don't you think?"

"Perhaps," said Katie. "But there again, perhaps not. People are funny. Their preferences are unpredictable. Let's do a bit of random chemistry—throwing two very different elements together."

William picked up one of the files. "May I?" he asked.

Katie glanced at the file. "We'll come to him in due course. Let's go through them one by one."

She told William that she had extracted four clients who were in the age bracket Jenny had stipulated. "I applied another filter," she said. "When she came to see me, Jenny mentioned that she particularly liked tall men. She said that twice, in fact, and so I think we need to take it seriously."

"Does it make much difference?" asked William. "She's going to give both short men and tall men the benefit of her views—and both sorts of men are going to run a mile."

"I won't give up before we start," Katie responded.

"Casting bread upon the waters?"

"Exactly. You never know."

He gave her an admiring look. "You're right. And I like your optimism, I really do."

Katie reached for a file. "All right," she said. "Now this is a man called Andrew McIntosh. He owns a string of filling stations in Lanarkshire. He lives near Biggar in a former manse. He's a widower, but a comparatively young one. He's fifty-two, and Jenny said that she would be happy to see anybody up to fifty-five."

"And height?" asked William, with mock seriousness.

"Six-foot-three." Katie paused. "Ness said something about men exaggerating their height. She said they all do it. She said she used to take two inches off as a matter of course. Six-foot, according to her, is usually five-ten."

William laughed. "And waist size too. I had a job when I was at uni working part-time in an outfitters. When men asked to see trousers of their size, they always asked something smaller than what they actually needed. Forty-inch waists were always claimed to be thirty-eight. I remember one guy came in and asked to see the thirty-two-inch waists. I tactfully suggested I measure him—and he was a good forty."

"Aspirations," said Katie, opening the file. "We all have them."

William peered over her shoulder to look at the photograph on the first page. "He looks nice enough. Nice smile. Kind face."

Katie turned the page. "Ness is quite polite about him," she said. "She says here: 'Andrew lost his wife after twenty-two years of marriage. He tells me he was pretty devastated and kept to himself for almost two years. Now he feels strong enough to think about finding somebody. He makes a very positive impression. He should be easy to place.'"

Katie read on. "The next note Ness makes is not so hopeful. This is what she says a few months later: 'We have had four introductions, none of which has been a success. The women report back that they like him, and there have been follow-up dates. But then they all complain that his children get in the way. One used the word *sabotage* to describe what his daughter had done, but she did not reveal exactly what happened.'"

Katie looked at William. "That's not uncommon, I believe."

"Kids not wanting their parent to remarry?"

"Yes." She paged through the file. "Here it is. There are two of them—a daughter and a son. One late teens, another early twenties. Children can resent a stepparent. They continue to need parental attention, and here's somebody threatening to take that from them. Classic."

"I wonder what the children did?" asked William. "Does Ness say?"

"No. All there is here is a cryptic note saying, *Jean says that the son made her feel very unwelcome when she went round to the house. Unbearable.* That's all she says, but *unbearable* is pretty strong, I would have thought."

William asked whether anything would have changed.

"Possibly not," Katie replied. "But anyway, let's leave him in the pool."

William was still thinking of the stepmother problem. "They get a very unfair press, don't they?" he said. "Look at Cinderella. It's hard to think of any story where the stepmother is anything but wicked—putting the kids to work, moving them to the attic or basement, spoiling their lives in every possible way. It's a very powerful myth."

Katie agreed. "I imagine that most stepmothers go out of their way to get on well with their partners' children, even if it's heavy going. I've seen that with one or two friends. One of my friends had to persist for a long time in the face of a couple of resentful young teenagers, but got there in the end. She won them over."

William looked thoughtful. "Stereotypes. The wicked stepmother is just another stereotype, isn't she?"

"Yes." And as she spoke, Katie thought: And the unworthy fiancée?

She suppressed that thought, and picked up another file.

"Stuart Ross. He's a good bit younger—forty-one. He's a microbiologist. Divorced. Ness writes: 'She left him—definitely not his fault. I knew her myself—vaguely. Niece of a friend. A real number. Can't resist anything in trousers. Felt *very* sorry for Stuart. Problem: very marked stammer. He finds it almost impossible to complete a sentence. Has had years of treatment—to no avail. I like him a lot. Would love to find somebody for him, but it's just not happening.'"

William winced. "Oh dear. Poor man."

"Yes." Ness put the file to one side. "Let's keep him anyway, though, and we'll see."

"Who's next?" asked William.

Katie reached for the third file. "This is Christopher Powell. He's . . ." She opened the file. "He's forty-three. Never married, but had been in two long-term relationships. The last one ended when she was sent by her company to work in Zurich. It petered out. Long distance relationships usually do."

As soon as she had said this, she realised its tactlessness.

But William appeared not to have noticed. "And his problem?" he asked.

Katie consulted the file. A smile spread across her face. "You're not going to believe this," she said.

"Try me."

"Trains," said Katie.

"As in . . . railway trains?"

She nodded.

"Christopher loves trains. He loves them a lot."

"Model trains?" William asked. "Those layouts people have in their houses? I had a friend whose father was like that. He played with his train set every weekend. The track took up an entire room—tunnels, sidings, and so on. My friend was embarrassed. He said the set was his, but it was really his dad's."

"There's a boy within every man," Katie said.

William gave her a sideways look. "Even me?" he asked.

"I don't know you well enough," Katie replied. But she thought: Yes, of course; of course. You're a boy. You've got the enthusiasm that boys have. And innocence—which meant, she thought, that you can't see what Alice is really like.

She returned to Christopher. "Not model trains in his case. Real trains."

William looked disbelieving. "He's a train spotter?"

Katie laughed. "It's not that bad."

William shook his head. "I've never understood how grown men can stand at the end of railway platforms and write down locomotive numbers. Do you get it?"

William did not. "Especially since most trains look the same these days. Old steam trains—yes, I can imagine they're interesting. But not modern trains."

"Christopher likes train journeys. He knows everything there is to know about famous trains. He has a library of books on the subject. The Trans-Siberian Express, the Orient Express, the Ghan. He's done those famous journeys, but he's happiest on these hobby-lines they have—the old steam trains they keep going. He lives and breathes trains."

"Right," said William briskly. "Next candidate."

Katie reached for the final file. "We may not be able to be too fussy," she said. "I'm not going to discard Christopher just yet. We'll keep him in our pool."

"A rather shallow pool," observed William.

Katie was not going to give up hope. She reached for the final file. "Now, I've met this one," she said. "And I like him. Peter Wilson, who's . . ." She opened the file. "Who's fifty-three. Scrapes in. And just makes it in height grounds—he's five-eleven, but a genuine five-eleven I think."

William asked what he did.

"He's an optician," replied Katie. "You've probably walked past his premises—just off Dublin Street. I don't know what's gone wrong. He's had four introductions, and none of them worked. They all declined a second date, although none of them had a word to say against him. Ness made a note here saying that one of the women described him as 'very sweet,' and another as 'inoffensive.' *Inoffensive* sounds like faint praise to me, but there we are."

"Is there anything more on him?" asked William.

Katie referred to the notes. "Personality—tolerant. No strong views."

William raised a finger. "A potential problem there, surely. Jenny has very strong views—on just about everything, Robert said."

"Opposites can attract," countered Katie. "A cliché, but sometimes clichés are absolutely true."

"As are stereotypes?"

"Sometimes," was as far as Katie would go with that.

"Anything else?"

Katie went back to the notes. "Ness has written one or two other things. 'He says that he gets hay fever if the pollen count is particularly high. He says it can be bad enough to stop him working or going out of the house. Also, he's hard of hearing. Wears a hearing aid—discreetly.' That's all."

She closed the file and sat back in her chair. She smiled at William. "So?"

He shrugged. "Not a very distinguished field," he said.

"Maybe not . . ." Katie began, but then stopped. She looked up and smiled at William. "Let's give them a try. No harm in seeing what happens."

CHAPTER TEN

A shocking thing to see

Over the next few days, Katie saw little of William, and nothing of Alice. William had told her that he was going to take three or four days off—"I've not done that since I came to Edinburgh," he said, and she, of course, agreed that he was entitled to that—and more.

"I want to take Alice to St. Andrews," he said. "And the Borders too. There's so much I want to show her."

On the fifth day of her visit, William was back at work. There was a trade fair in Manchester that he had committed to attending well before Alice's trip had been planned, and he would have to get various pieces ready for that. Attendance at that would require him to be away for two days and three nights, but Alice, he said, had been understanding. She had plenty to see in Edinburgh in two weeks, and it was important that he should go.

Katie busied herself with work. A number of new clients had registered, and she had interviews to conduct and paperwork to process. It suited her to be busy, as it took her mind off the fact that Alice was next door with William.

She had watched him to see whether he was different now that Alice was there. There were times when she thought he was—when she felt that he was quieter than he normally was—but she could not be sure. Was he slightly moody? He had a lot on his mind, of course—not only was there work to do for Manchester, but there were the complications of having a guest staying with him, particularly as he had hinted that Alice was not particularly domestic and he was doing most of the cooking.

William left for Manchester on a Friday afternoon, the trade fair being due to take place on the Saturday and Sunday. He came in to say goodbye to Katie, and she wished him luck.

"Is there anything I can do for Alice while you're away?" she asked.

"I think she'll be all right," William replied, adding, almost apologetically, "I did invite her to come with me to Manchester, you know, but she wanted to stay here. She said that she could do with a few low-key days."

"I can understand that," said Katie. "She's been packing a lot in."

"But she can call you if she needs to?" asked William anxiously.

"Of course, she can," said Katie. "I'm going nowhere this weekend."

He seemed relieved. "Manchester's very important," he said. "All the top European buyers will be there. It's *the* weekend for knitwear."

On Saturday morning, Katie did her main supermarket shop of the week. In the afternoon, she went to an exhibition of jewellery and ceramics at the Scottish Gallery in Dundas Street, before returning to the flat. There a text came through from Laura, asking her whether, in spite of the short notice, she would like to go out for a drink. Laura knew about Alice's visit, and wanted to help. "I know this week won't be the easiest time for you," she said. "There's a wine bar that does great tapas, and there's usually a singer on a Saturday night. How about it? Girls' night out?"

Katie hesitated. She did not feel like going to a wine bar because it would be crowded, and she was not in a mood for noise and crowds. But if she stayed at home, she suspected that she would end up going to bed at nine and reading for twenty minutes before dropping off to sleep. The evening would be wasted, and so she accepted Laura's invitation.

Laura was already there when Katie arrived. She had found an unoccupied table at the back of the bar, and had ordered a bottle of Chablis.

"You do like Chablis, don't you?" Laura asked. "You used to."

"Nobody dislikes Chablis," said Katie.

A large plate of tapas arrived, and they settled in to watch the wine bar fill up with its Saturday evening crowd.

"Surviving?" asked Laura.

Katie nodded. "I'm keeping busy."

Laura leaned forward, "What's she like?"

"Unfriendly," Katie replied. "A bit too pleased with herself for my liking."

"I don't like her already," said Laura. "Does she resent you?"

Katie considered this. She did not think that Alice believed that she and William were anything but neighbors and colleagues, but at the same time she had no doubt in her mind that Alice was unhappy.

"I think that she would prefer it if I weren't there," she said. "In fact, I'm pretty sure of that."

"She's obviously insecure," said Laura. "You're a threat to her, you see."

Katie sighed. "I've done nothing to justify that. I've tried my best to be polite to her. I went to fetch her at the airport."

Laura was amused by that. "Frankly, that must have been the worst possible start. But there we are." She paused. "And William? What's he like with her?"

Katie took some time to answer. It was not simple. "He seems protective of her. It's odd. He's very concerned that everything will be just as she wants it. He fusses. And yet . . ."

"And yet?"

"And yet, he doesn't seem entirely relaxed in her company. It's as if he's slightly in awe of her."

"Does he behave as if he's in love with her?" asked Laura. "That's the real issue, isn't it? Are they in love?"

Katie wondered how it was possible to tell whether people were in love with one another. Was it obvious? She knew what it *felt* like to be in love—it felt . . . well, it felt indescribable, and the only thing to do was to experience it. Then you knew.

She thought about Laura's question. She had not dared to ask it herself, perhaps because she could not bear to think about it. And yet it was so obviously pertinent. Did William and Alice love one another? The answer, she thought, was no. They did not.

And yet they were engaged.

Laura was waiting for an answer.

"I don't think so."

Laura was unsurprised. "Well, there you are. I think you'd be able to tell. If you love somebody, you know whether they love somebody else—you can tell. It's not the conclusion you want. It's painful. It's awful. But you just know."

She gave Katie a searching look before continuing. "I told you to put William out of your mind, didn't I? I said that you should try to keep out of his life. But now . . . well, I'm not so sure."

Laura now said, "I'm thirsty. I'd like some sparkling water."

"I'll get it," said Katie. "You got the wine. I'll get it."

She got up from the table and made her way to the bar. More people had arrived, and the barman was busy. She stood waiting. She picked up a bar menu and looked at it. A voice beside her said, "Popular place, isn't it?"

She had not noticed the man standing beside her. Now she did, and for a brief moment she thought that she might know him. She had seen him before, she thought; or at least thought that at first, then she decided that she had not.

He sounded Australian.

"Yes, the whole town gets busy round about now."

She gave him another look. She had seen him—somewhere. She said, "You're Australian?"

He smiled. "Yes. I'm visiting. Not for long. I'm with a friend who had to come over for a couple of weeks. I came for the ride."

"From?"

"Melbourne. Do you know it?"

She did not have time to answer. The barman had appeared, and she indicated that the young man had been there first and should be served first. She looked at her hands, and then she moved away and went back to her table—without the sparkling water.

"Problem?" asked Laura. "No sparkling water? Still would be okay."

Katie looked over her shoulder. The wine bar was large, and there was another section to it altogether. She could see the people at the tables there, and she was able to make them out through the throng. She drew in her breath. She leaned forward and whispered to Laura. "I want to go somewhere else."

Laura frowned. "What's wrong with this place?"

Katie looked over her shoulder, and then back again to Laura. "We have to," she said, and added, "please. Right now." She glanced across the room once again, and then turned away quickly. "I'm sorry. I don't know what to think . . ."

Laura did not argue. "Right," she said, pushing her chair back. "Let's go."

Katie turned her head as they left so that nobody, looking across the expanse of the bar, might see her.

"Talk about furtive," commented Laura sotto voce.

They quickly found a taxi. Katie gave the driver the address of her flat, a relatively short distance away.

"I'll make dinner," she said to Laura. "Something simple, if you're all right with that."

Laura replied that it would help if she were to know what was going on. Katie glanced towards the front of the cab. "Later," she said.

They were soon there, and Katie invited her friend into the kitchen. She had pasta she could serve with a parma ham and mushroom sauce. There was fresh mixed-leaf salad.

"Perfect," said Laura. "But now please tell me what spooked you back there. I feel as if I've fallen down a rabbit hole."

As Katie prepared the pasta, she told Laura about her conversation at the bar.

"I had a feeling I'd met him before," she said. "I couldn't put my finger on it, but then I remembered. I'd seen him outside the airport when I collected Alice."

"So?" said Laura.

"He spoke to me at the bar. We chatted for a few seconds, that's all. But I realised that he was Australian, and he confirmed that. He said that he was over here with a friend for a few weeks."

Laura shrugged. "Nothing sinister in that."

"But then I looked across the bar—there was a whole section at the other side—and I saw her."

"Who?"

"Alice. She was sitting by herself. When I got back to you, I managed to see her again. He had joined her with their drinks—the man I spoke to—and he was sitting right next to her. He had his arm about her. They were an item. There was absolutely no doubt in my mind. Then we left."

Laura was silent.

"I'm not imagining this," said Katie. "That's what I saw."

Laura shook her head in disbelief. "I didn't think you were imagining it, but what I'm doing is trying to make sense of it."

"She's seeing somebody else," said Katie. "There was a question of that earlier on. They patched it up."

"But maybe she didn't stop," said Laura.

"It looks like it. And now she's brought her lover with her on holiday—keeping him tucked away, presumably meeting now and then during the day, snatching opportunities. Until William obligingly goes off to a trade-fair in Manchester. And then they can hit the town together safely. Nobody knows her here—nobody knows him. Except I know who she is, and I happen to wander into a wine bar where I recognise the man I saw outside the airport."

"Who must have been on the same flight in as she was," Laura added.

"Yes. And so they're spotted, and we come back here and

scratch our heads, and I ask myself the question that I'm sure you're thinking of too: Why does she bother to be engaged to William if she has this other man?"

Laura had not got that far, but she agreed with Katie that it was an obvious question.

And that was the moment that the answer came to Katie, suddenly, and with clarity, as the solution to a cryptic crossword clue may suddenly come to mind, or the way out of a maze may reveal itself, or scales may fall from one's eyes. It was obvious.

But it took her breath away, and she felt she had to sit down before she could put it into words.

"I think . . ." she began, and then trailed away.

"Yes?"

"I think I may know what's going on."

Laura reached out to touch her wrist. "I'm listening. Come on."

Katie told her what William had said to her about Alice's situation. "She gets everything—and I mean everything—paid for by William's family trust—on the grounds that she's his fiancée and is engaged in full-time education. Medical school fees, living expenses, travel—the lot. So, is it in her interest to remain engaged—even if she never loved him in the first place, but saw him as a walking financial solution; or if she started off being keen on him, but then met somebody else? That might be plausible, I'd have thought—perhaps the most likely explanation."

Laura's astonishment was evident. "But, of course," she began. "All very convenient."

"And then," Katie continues, "once she graduates and everything has been paid for, she'll be in a position to go off with her real boyfriend." She paused. "That is, assuming that she's as calculating as all this suggests."

"Oh, I suspect she could be," said Laura.

"I'd like to think otherwise. I'd like to give her the benefit . . ."

"That's because you're charitable," Laura interjected. "I'm more inclined to take a sceptical view of why people behave as they do."

Katie returned to the task of preparing the meal. "Of course, this raises a big question: What do we do? And by that, I mean: What do I do? I'm not trying to drag you into all this."

"I am involved," said Laura. "And I don't mind. I gave you advice. I became involved at that point. You can say *we* as far as I'm concerned."

"Do we tell William?" asked Katie. "Do we warn him?"

Laura looked uncertain. "If you see a friend walking towards a cliff edge, what do you do?"

"Warn him?"

Laura gave Katie a quizzical look. "Well, is that the position we're in? Is William a friend walking towards a cliff edge?"

"Or has he already walked over it?" asked Katie.

CHAPTER ELEVEN

Irregular showers

Jacques came round to see Ness the day after her fish barbecue with Herb. He drove up at eleven in the morning, to find her sitting on her screened porch, reading a copy of *Maclean's* news magazine that she'd bought in town a few days earlier. She was halfway through a review of a book on what the ancient Greeks could teach us about happiness, when she heard Jacques' truck pull up outside the house. She had always listened to the ancient Greeks, and was toying with the idea of ordering the book when she heard Jacques slam his cab door and saw him make his way to her front door.

He was carrying a bag filled with vegetables: cucumbers, tomatoes, a cauliflower, several large bulbs of garlic. He placed the bag on the table beside her chair.

"I grew this stuff myself," he said. "You like garlic?"

She picked up one of the bulbs. "Who doesn't? Especially when it's like this."

"That's twice the size of garlic in the supermarkets," Jacques said. "And twice as succulent. Garlic likes water, you see. I water mine every morning and again in the evening. And fertilizer. I put liquid seaweed on mine. It likes it."

"So I see." She smiled at her visitor, and gestured towards the other chair on the veranda. "You're very kind, Jacques." She waved a hand in the direction of the town and of the houses round the lake. "Everyone's kind round here."

Jacques grinned. "We reckon that if we're kind to folks who visit, then they might stay. We like people to stay."

"I'm not going anywhere fast," said Ness.

She offered him tea, which he accepted, and she went off into the kitchen to prepare it. Through the kitchen window she could see him sitting in his straight-backed chair, looking out over the yard.

She went back to the veranda and passed her visitor a cup of tea.

"I saw Herb yesterday," she said.

Jacques took a sip of his tea. "He's around," he said. "I saw him the day before. He's been helping me with a fence."

"He cooked me fish on his new barbecue. It's a nice piece of equipment."

Jacques stared into his teacup. "What sort of fish?"

"Bass," replied Ness. "He called them wide-mouth bass, I think."

Jacques thought about this. "They make good enough eating," he said. "And there are plenty of them. You can haul them out at the right time."

"I liked them."

"I prefer trout," said Jacques. "Nothing against bass, of course, but if I have a choice, it's trout." He paused and then said, "Poor Herb."

Ness waited.

"He's a great guy—don't get me wrong—but things haven't worked out too well for him."

"His marriages?"

Jacques nodded. "Some people aren't cut out for marriage, I guess. They try—sure, they try—but maybe they try too hard, or they're difficult to live with. You never can tell."

"You think Herb would be difficult to live with?" she asked.

Jacques hesitated. "Could be," he said at last. "Nice guy— definitely. He's my friend. But I don't think I could live like him."

Ness raised an eyebrow. "Why's that?"

"His place is a mess. You were outside, I take it? He has the barbecue on that patio of his, and maybe you didn't see inside his place. Just as well. It's a mess. It'd take months to clean that place up."

"I see."

Jacques sighed. "Poor Herb. He goes off in the winter—up to those trap-lines of his. We never see him for months. He has a shack up there, as he may have told you. But I'll tell you something, there's no running water. No shower. No bathtub. Nothing."

He gave her a meaningful look.

"So, he doesn't take a shower for months?" Ness felt that this was the question he was hoping she would ask.

And she was right. "That's it," he said quickly. "Now I know that there are more important things in this life, but I reckon that taking a shower is up there. After all, cleanliness is next to godliness—I had that drummed into me when I was a boy, I recall. I've taken a shower every day since then— every day. Sometimes I take a shower in the morning, and then another in the evening. Regular. Never miss it."

She had ignored her tea, and it was getting cold. She lifted the cup to her lips and watched him over the rim. She was struggling to maintain her composure. Herb had spent some time yesterday warning her of Jacques' shortcomings, and now

Jacques was doing the same thing about Herb. What had provoked all this?

And then it came to her. Herb was interested in her, and so was Jacques. They both wanted her attention, and both had independently come to the conclusion that the best way of clearing the field was to point out the shortcomings of the other. She closed her eyes as she struggled with the full comedy of the situation.

"Oh well," she said. "We all have our failings."

"Yes," said Jacques. "We do."

"That's what keeps me single," Ness went on. "I decided some time ago, that I would never expect anybody to put up with my failings—they're that bad. So, I took a vow—rather like the vows that nuns take. I vowed that was it. No emotional involvement with anybody. Friendship yes; anything beyond that—no."

She wondered whether she should be even more direct, or whether he would take from this what she wanted him to take.

Jacques was impassive, his eyes downcast. Then he looked up and smiled. "Garlic keeps people away," he said.

CHAPTER TWELVE

There were wolves

Katie arranged to meet Jenny and Peter later that week at the Valvona & Crolla café. They had now had three meetings: the initial one at which Katie had introduced the two of them, stayed for a quick cup of coffee, and then, after proffering a diplomatic excuse, had left them to get on with it. Jenny had sent an email a couple of days later to say that their first solo date—a trip to the Dominion Cinema in Morningside, followed by dinner in a nearby Indian restaurant—had gone particularly well. That was followed by another dinner date, this time in Leith, and that, once again, had proved a success.

"You're brilliant," she enthused. "How did you know that we'd get on so well?"

Katie had not intended to try to answer this, but Jenny waited for a reply. So she said, "Profiles. The two of you ticked similar boxes. On the basis of that, I concluded that you would have things to say to one another."

"Oh, we do," said Jenny. "I feel that there's so much I want to share with him."

Katie thought: Yes, I can imagine.

Jenny expanded on this. "You know how there are some people you just want to confide in. You may not know them very well; in fact, you may have just met them. But you discover you need to tell them so much about yourself, about your life, about how you feel about things."

"Taxi drivers," said Katie. "Hair-stylists. These are the new confidants. They've taken over from priests."

Jenny would not be distracted. "That may well be, but Peter is none of these. He's an optician—as you know. You don't normally feel the need to confide in your optician. It's Peter's personality that does it—his manner. You want to confide in him because he's sympathetic."

Now, at Jenny's suggestion, the three of them were to meet for lunch. "Peter is keen to say thank you too," she said. "He's as grateful as I am."

Katie accepted the invitation, but hoped that Jenny was being realistic in her assessment of how things were going. Ness had warned her that some clients misjudged the success of introductions, claiming—and even believing—that all was going well when in fact it was not. "People see what they want to see," she had said. "And that applies across the board—not just with relationships. Economists do it. Politicians do it. It's called wishful thinking."

Now, having arrived early and having been shown to a table in the café, she looked about her at her fellow diners. A party of middle-aged women at a nearby table were listening intently to one of their number revealing a choice item of gossip; there were expressions of astonishment, disapproval, and delight. Katie smiled; people loved to hear of the weaknesses of others.

Peter and Jenny arrived together. They both looked cheerful, and both exchanged kisses with Katie. The waitress, a willowy young Italian woman, arrived with the menu. In the background, from the small function room behind the café, came the sound of an accordion playing a traditional Italian tune.

Jenny drew attention to the music. "There's something so jaunty about those Neapolitan songs," she said. "That one, for instance. Do you recognise it? *Comme facette mammeta*. I love that one. Do you know the lyrics were written by a waiter? They were. He was called Giuseppe Capaldo, and he fell in love with the woman for whom he wrote those words. *How did your mother make you? She took a basket of strawberries; honey, sugar, and cinnamon, she kneaded all that to make your fine lips* . . . It's such a romantic idea."

Katie agreed. "It's lovely."

Jenny looked at the menu. "I suppose we should choose something. I must confess, I'm hungry. I didn't have breakfast, and that means by lunchtime, I'm ready for something." She turned to Peter. "You like mozzarella, don't you, Peter? I thought you said you did? I wouldn't mind a caprese salad, but I think I'll need something more substantial as well. Would you like a salad, Peter. *Caprese?*"

"*Capisce?*" said Peter. "Do I understand? Understand what?"

He smiled benignly. "No," said Jenny. "*Caprese.*"

The waitress intervened, and pointed to the menu. Peter followed, and nodded.

"Well, that's two of us then," said Jenny.

Katie looked at Peter, who smiled back at her. He did not say anything.

"I've been reading the most fascinating book," Jenny said. "It's all about olive oil. I thought of it when I came in here a few minutes ago. I mentioned it, remember, Peter? Remember? It's amazing how complex the olive oil industry is. It's not a question of simply picking the olives and crushing them. There's a lot of art that goes into it. You have to get so much right." She paused. "Some of them have quite a peppery taste, you know. I don't know where that comes from—the variety of olive, I suppose. Maybe the soil. There's so much to learn about olive oil."

Katie looked at Jenny, and then at Peter. Jenny was extremely attractive—that was indisputable—and Peter was nothing special to look at. He was a bit mousey, in fact, and many people might be surprised at seeing this glamorous woman with this rather unexceptional man. He appeared pleased, though, to be in her company—flattered, perhaps, that she would take an interest in him in all his modesty and homeliness.

And then she saw something that confirmed what she had suspected—indeed, in a sense, engineered. She saw Peter reach up and touch his left ear. The gesture was practised—and tactful. He was adjusting the volume.

Peter sat back in his chair. Jenny talked on. Katie thought: I was right. This would work. Jenny could talk at length, and he would tolerate it because he would hear very little of it, and what you didn't hear, you did not, as a general rule, object to.

Katie half listened to Jenny's monologue. She half listened because she was busy composing in her mind the email she would send to Ness telling her of this unusual solution.

"It's funny how things work out," said Jenny to Katie as they left at the end of the lunch. "Peter and I are very happy. I suppose we're on the same wavelength."

To a limited extent, thought Katie. But did not say that. Instead, she said, "You obviously are."

"Thanks to you," added Jenny.

Katie returned to the office. She had been tickled by the success of her unlikely matching of Peter and Jenny, and she was looking forward to telling William about it. She felt more cheerful now—Alice's arrival in Edinburgh, and the churlishness that she had shown, had depressed and saddened her. That might have been her reaction even if Alice had proved to be a very different sort of guest—there was a certain optimism about many Australians, and she could have been like that—but as it turned out, her behaviour had quickly confirmed the bleakness of the situation. But now, that positive meeting with Peter and Jenny had imparted a warm glow to Katie's day. They were happy, and she had played a part in the bringing about of that happiness. That encouraged her.

She wrote to Ness. "A major success," she said. "Jenny and Peter—remember them? Fixed up. Cooing like turtle doves. I don't want to claim all the credit (actually, I do) but it was, I think, not a bad idea at all to introduce her to somebody who is able to cope with her constant chatter—largely because much of it passes him by. And they seem so happy together. He's got what he wants—a forceful woman, who's also very attractive. He's delighted. And she did say something about a wedding, which is quick work, but then why wait when you've tried and tried and at last somebody suitable has turned up? I'm really pleased, Ness: this is what this business is for, and when things work out like this, it all seems worthwhile.

"But one cloud on the horizon—or, rather, right over our heads. William's fiancée has turned up. Yes—Alice, no less! She has two weeks off from medical school and has come to Edinburgh to spend it with William. I don't like to be uncharitable, but she's absolutely dire. She's rude and self-centred, and yet William dances attendance to her. I must say that it turns my stomach to see it. And of all people to have somebody like that in his life—William, who's so kind and sympathetic and—well, you know what he's like. He doesn't deserve to have somebody like that to contend with."

Ness wrote back almost immediately.

Early morning here. I heard a loon on the lake—the other night, there were wolves. William's intended: oh dear. I must confess I always had a feeling about that young woman, although I never met her. I never liked the *sound* of her. That's odd, isn't it?—people have a *sound*, an aura, perhaps, although that's more visual, isn't it? I don't believe in auras and all that *imaginative* stuff. I believe in judging on the basis of evidence—preferably the evidence of one's own senses, but, in the absence of any *data*—is that the right word here, as I want to be up to date on these things?—then one may have to go by feelings for which one may not be able to provide much justification.

Are you asking me for advice? I'm not really in a position to say much, not being there, in the thick of it, but what I would say to you is this: don't make yourself miserable over other people's problems. Let them sort it out themselves. You can't protect William from the world—he has to learn how to do that himself.

I'm sorry about Alice, but if he has decided his future is with her, then you probably just have to accept that. She may be unworthy of him, but that's something that you really mustn't think about because it will draw you into a situation that you're best remaining completely detached from. (I've ended a sentence with a preposition there, Katie. You may not have noticed it because you are of a generation where every sort of solecism is perfectly acceptable. I don't. I was taught grammar by Miss Hammond-Brown. You should have seen her. We were just too frightened to end our sentences with a preposition because Miss Hammond-Brown would write, in red pen, on your workbook: *See me about this immediately*. And you went to see her, and she would grab your upper arm in a vise of a grip and say, "Rules exist to be obeyed, young lady—they are not discretionary—they are mandatory.")

Anyway, back to Alice. She's not going to be around for long. Ignore her—keep out of her way. She'll go back to Australia before long, and life will get back to normal. Try meditation. That helps clear the mind and forget things you can't do anything about. And finally, meet somebody else. That's the best cure—it always is. I know that you're being cautious about going back into a relationship too soon after James, but I think you shouldn't leave it too long. But enough said now on that subject.

All love,
Ness

Katie smiled as she read Ness's message. She could just hear Ness saying all that, and for a few moments she felt sad that Ness was so far away. It would be far easier to deal with all of this if only Ness were here, dispensing advice, providing an amusing and often rather erudite commentary to the day's events as they occurred.

She worked at one or two routine tasks, and then decided to get out for a walk around the block. It was a particularly fine day, and Edinburgh was bathed in the slanting gold of a summer day. She had one or two items to buy at the corner shop—she had run out of washing-up liquid in the flat, and she also needed toothpaste. She would go for a stroll and get these things on her way back.

She had just reached Broughton Street when she saw Alice, who was walking down the hill towards her. Katie had no desire to talk to her, but now it was inevitable. Alice had seen her, and if she suddenly turned off into Abercromby Place, it would be very obvious that she was avoiding her. She would have to put a brave face on it.

They came face-to-face. Greetings were exchanged, and Katie then said, "William will be back tomorrow, I believe."

"Yes," said Alice. "Tomorrow morning. He gets in at ten."

"You didn't want to go down to Manchester?" asked Katie.

Alice shook her head. "No, I couldn't face more travel. And William would be working all the time."

"Of course," said Katie. "So, what did you do?"

Alice hesitated, but only briefly. "Nothing. I was catching up on sleep. I didn't set foot outside the flat for the whole time. It was very therapeutic."

Katie's eye narrowed. "The whole weekend?" she asked.

Alice shrugged. There was nothing defensive about her manner. "Yes. I didn't feel like going out."

Katie looked up at the sky. There was something particularly uncomfortable about being lied to. And suddenly, without any presentiment, she felt within her a surge of anger. Alice had a litany of charges against her, and now this. This was just plain *wrong*, and she saw no reason why she should have to tolerate it.

She drew in her breath. She felt her heart hammering within her. She would not let this pass—this tawdry lie. "But

I saw you in that wine bar," she said, nodding in the direction of Frederick Street, further up the hill. "You were there with a man. I saw you."

Alice remained quite still, her features frozen. Then she said, "You didn't."

"But I did," said Katie calmly. "You were there with your friend from Melbourne. I spoke to him at the bar."

Alice took a step backwards, and for a few moments Katie thought that she might strike out. But then she took a step forward again, so that she was right up against Katie. Katie noticed her make-up: the eyeliner, the blush, the powder concealing of a small blemish on the jaw.

"You mind your own business," Alice hissed. "Just keep out—right?"

It was the crudity of this challenge that tipped Katie into a spirited response. "I know about you," she said, struggling to keep her voice even. "I know how your university fees are paid by William's trustees. So it suits you fine, doesn't it, to be engaged to him, while all the time you have your real lover in the background. And you even brought him with you to Scotland—all very nice. Did you exchange one business class ticket for two economy class ones?"

That had just occurred to Katie. That was why Alice had been unable to sleep on the journey—she had been occupying an economy seat.

Alice's jaw dropped, and Katie knew then that she had somehow stumbled across the truth. All that was exactly what had happened.

Suddenly Alice smiled. "You give yourself away, you know."

Katie waited.

"You've got a thing about William, haven't you? I suspected that, you know—right from the word go. I suspected that you were keen on him. You had that look about you—the look of somebody who knows she'll never get the man she wants. Poor you. And you're dead right about that, you know, because William doesn't like women like you. You're way too conventional. Sorry about that, but it's the truth. You'll be okay as a friend, but as a lover—forget it."

Katie did not reply. She saw something like white mist. Was that anger? Was that what rage looked like? A white mist obscuring everything?

"Are you thinking of telling him?" Alice went on. "If you are, then you'd better not. That's all I've got to say to you. Because if you tell him, I shall say that you're making it up in order to put him off me—because you're head over heels in love with him. I'll say that you can't help yourself. And you know what? He'll believe me, because he always does." She paused. "Have you got that?"

The mist cleared, and Katie watched Alice take a step back, give her a last look, and then walk off down the street. She felt herself shaking. She hated conflict—even minor altercations—and this had been a major one. She turned round. She had no idea where she was going, but she walked to the end of the block and then turned. She retraced her steps, not quite aware of why she should do this. In a narrow side street, children played hopscotch on the pavement, the squares chalked in on the paving stones in bright reds and blues. Their voices were high-pitched squeals as they called out their commentary on the game. She watched for a moment, and then continued. She took her phone out of her pocket and dialled Laura's number.

CHAPTER THIRTEEN

Shower him with kisses

Laura was at the front door of Katie's flat exactly fifteen minutes later.

"I dropped everything," she said, her voice full of concern. "Are you all right, Katie?"

Katie nodded. "I'm fine—well, sort of. Thanks for coming so quickly. I feel a bit stupid . . ."

Laura cut her short. "You don't need to apologise for being human—nobody does."

They sat down, facing one another across the kitchen table. Katie told her friend about the unexpected meeting on Broughton Street, and about the exchange that ensued. Laura seemed to relish the story. "It must have been really satisfying," she said, "to tell that piece of work that you had rumbled her."

"I wasn't thinking of that," said Katie. "It all came out rather quickly. I hadn't intended for things to happen this way."

"No, one never does. But when it happens, and you manage to say the things you've been itching to say, well . . ." Laura paused. "Of course, you're not going to pay any attention to her threats."

Katie frowned. "I'm not sure . . ."

"You have to tell him," Laura insisted. "And how can she be so confident that he will believe her rather than you?"

"I know, but . . ." She looked away in distress. "If he did believe her—and he could, you know—then that would be the end of everything between William and me—the end of our friendship."

"But he may not believe her," objected Laura. "I wouldn't."

"I think she has some sort of power over him," Katie said. She sighed. "But you're right—I have to tell him. I can't let him be hurt like this."

Laura agreed. "No, you can't." She gave her friend a sympathetic look. "It's a pity, isn't it, that the right thing is sometimes also the most uncomfortable thing." She paused. "Yet we have to stop her. I hate to see somebody like her getting away with it. It makes me wonder whether there's any justice in this world."

"It often seems as if there isn't any," said Katie. "Except . . ."

"Except sometimes. And this may be one of those occasions." Katie smiled. "It might be."

Laura looked wistful. "I wish I believed in something," she said. "I wish I had a simple faith. I wish that I could say to myself that the scales of justice will always be balanced at the end of the day. I wish I could say that—and actually believe it. I wish I could say that the proud and the bullies and the manipulators will be hounded out of their offices and made to account for what they do, but I can't because that's not the way the world is."

"There's no reason why you can't say things that you know are not strictly true," said Katie. "If it helps you to say them, then there's no harm in it."

"Oh, I know," said Laura. "What you say is right, but it's just not all that easy to convince yourself."

They talked for another half hour or so before Laura had to get back to work. Once her friend had gone, Katie did not go back to the office, but stayed in the flat, where a couple of hours later she made herself dinner. She went to bed early, and lay awake thinking of her conversation with Laura. She was not asleep by eleven-thirty, and so she got out of bed to make herself a cup of tea. As she was doing so, her phone blinked to announce the arrival of a text message.

It was from William.

Katie: Can we meet tomorrow morning? Walk in the Botanics? 8 am? Main gate? I know it's a big ask, but I need to talk urgently. William. XXX.

She sent a reply. *Of course. I'll be there.* Then she hesitated. He had sent three kisses. She sent back four.

⁓

He was waiting for her at the gate to the Botanic Garden when she arrived shortly before eight the next morning.

"I know it's a real cheek," he said. "Asking you here. But I didn't want to meet at work, and I wanted to be someplace where we could talk."

She reassured him that she did not mind. It had been no imposition, and she liked the Botanics.

He gestured for them to go in. "You often have them to yourself this early," he said. "And everything's so fresh—the plants haven't had time to be discouraged by the world."

They began to follow a winding path past labelled shrubs and trees.

"By the way," William said. "I didn't get that award. I came fourth."

"I'm sorry," said Katie. "But fourth . . ."

"Isn't too bad. No, I'm happy enough with that."

They turned off along a path that led towards the large greenhouses. He said, "I imagine you can guess what this is about."

She hesitated. "Not really."

"You sure?"

"Well, I did wonder if it had something to do with Alice's visit."

He nodded. "Yes, that's it." He paused, and looked at her with concern. "We haven't had a row, if that's what you're thinking."

Katie tried not to show her disappointment. "Oh well, that's good."

"I feel terrible," William continued.

"Why?"

"It's not that I had much choice."

"Choice?"

He shook his head. "I've tried my best—I really have."

He had slowed his pace. They were barely strolling now. A man and a woman walked past them on the path. The man said, pleasantly, "What a gorgeous morning."

"Yes," said William.

Katie said, "Of course you've done your best. Of course, you have."

"But I no longer love Alice," he said. "That's what it amounts to, Katie. I don't . . ." He was struggling. "I don't even like her, I'm afraid."

The admission seemed to distress him. She said, "Oh, William, you don't have to be ashamed to say that. It happens. It happens all the time."

"But the fact remains: I was her fiancé," he said. "I made various promises to her."

Katie was struggling too. In her case, it was to contain her wild joy. She wanted to burst into song. She wanted to throw her arms around William and shower him with kisses. She wanted to do something that would proclaim to anybody who happened to be in the Botanic Garden at that hour that she had just received the most overwhelmingly glorious news. Instead, she said with complete solemnity, "The whole point about an engagement is that it isn't marriage. If there are going to be reservations or a change of mind, then have them while you're engaged—not once you're married."

He was staring at her. They had stopped walking now, and were standing with the background of the Edinburgh skyline behind them. He said, "I suppose you're right. But I wanted to talk to somebody about it, and I thought you were the obvious person. I mean, you can give me dispassionate advice. You've met Alice, and you like her. You wouldn't have let me make the wrong decision."

Oh no, thought Katie. I wouldn't do that. And yes, I've met Alice and . . . She reached out for his hand. "Listen, William, I think you're doing the right thing. Alice is great, but maybe she's not for you. And you shouldn't worry too much about hurting her. She'll get over it."

She almost added, "She's already got somebody else," but did not. It could hurt William, she thought, to discover that he had been so comprehensively deceived. And now that Alice no longer represented a danger to him, she saw no point in upsetting him.

"I hope she'll be all right," said William.

"Of course, she'll be all right."

William looked thoughtful. "One of the things that worried me is that business I told you about. Remember? She gets all her university expenses paid. I was worried about letting her down."

Katie remained silent.

"I telephoned the lawyer last night," William continued. "Our last night—their morning. I explained the situation to him. He said there was no problem—that the trust would not change the arrangements they made for her because I'm the one who's breaking off the engagement. In the circumstances, they feel they should honour the terms all the way through to her graduation."

Katie listened to this in astonishment. This was extraordinarily generous, and she felt irritated that Alice should be getting away entirely with her unconscionable behaviour. She made a weak protest. "But surely you don't have to . . ."

William cut her short. "I know I don't have to do it. But it's nothing much to me. I've got so much more than her."

"Yes, but . . ."

He gave her a discouraging look, and she did not press the matter. "Well, you're being extremely kind," said Katie. She was struck by what she saw as an injustice. Alice had behaved appallingly, and yet she was going to continue to benefit from what was, indirectly, William's money. She thought of saying something, but decided not to: kindness often occurred in surprising circumstances—and that, perhaps, was what made it so striking in the first place.

Katie now asked the question she had wanted to ask when William first dropped his bombshell. "What made you change your mind about Alice?"

He hesitated. "She's selfish," he said. "I didn't realise it before, but now I do."

Katie was cautious. "I see."

"And a bit nasty," he added.

She waited. He seemed to be uncertain about saying more, but then he did. "She was nasty about you, actually."

Katie did not have to feign surprise. "Me?"

"Yes. I don't want to go into it, but she said things I didn't like. I hope you don't mind if I don't go into it any further."

"I don't mind—and I don't think I care either."

"And there's another thing," William continued. "I decided I couldn't trust her."

Katie took a deep breath. Then she replied, "Actually, I'm not surprised, William."

"You don't think I'm being unreasonable."

"Not at all. I wouldn't trust her if I were you."

"Really?"

"No," said Katie. "I wouldn't."

They resumed their walk. "I feel much better," said William. "Discussing it with you has really helped."

"Have you told her yet?"

"Yes," he replied. "I've told her."

Katie asked how Alice had taken it.

"She didn't make a scene, if that's what you're wondering about," said William. "I had the impression she might even have been half-expecting it."

Katie nodded. "Perhaps she was."

"Anyway," William continued, "she's gone. She left a bit early. She wanted to break her journey in Paris on the way back. She said it would help with jet lag."

Katie suppressed a laugh. "There's only one hour's difference between here and Paris." She thought: a few days in Paris with one's lover. Of course. She glanced at William, and realised that he knew—of course he knew; yet he was going to overlook the matter.

Now he said, "Well, anyway, she wanted to spend a few days in Paris on the way home. So she left last night."

Katie looked at her watch, and then said, "Let's go and have breakfast. Somewhere nice. Let's treat ourselves. Eggs Benedict. Smoked salmon. Champagne."

She thought: I am so happy being with him. Was that just friendship? Was friendship capable of painting the world with gold? Was it?

Later that day, in her office, Katie received another email from Ness.

"I've been thinking about Peter and Jenny," she wrote. "I've always had a soft spot for Peter, even though he's been hard to place. Now they're both happy—and that's the important thing, isn't it. And I'm happy too, as it happens. I've two admirers here, by the way—my friends, Herb and Jacques. Neither of them is suitable for me, and I've had to make that clear as gently as I can. It's sorted out now. They saw one another as rivals, believe it or not, and each of them tried to convince me he was more suitable than the other. They remain good friends with each other, though.

"I like this place, and I like the people who live here. Life is going well, I think. You don't need to do a great deal to enjoy yourself and be happy—you just have to do the right thing—however you manage that. Of course, that leaves the question of what the right thing is. How much ink has been spilled in attempts to answer that question? Rivers, oceans perhaps. And yet everyone, in his or her own way, knows intuitively what the right thing is. All we have to do is to summon up the courage to act upon our sense of what's right. And we can all do that, I think—and I've always felt that you'll do just that, Katie. I've had that feeling about you for a long time."

Katie sat back in her chair. She thought of her time in the Perfect Passion Company and what she had achieved. It was something—yes, it was definitely something: David Bannatyne; the Fane engagement; Jenny and Peter. That all amounted to something—and there would be more because she would stay on and do more of this work, which was good work, and added to the happiness of the world, which was surely necessary, now more so than ever before perhaps. She looked up at the ceiling, and then out of the window on to the roof of the next-door building. A pigeon had alighted on it, and the sun was on its feathers, on the dark green shimmer of the bird's neck plumage. It was almost time for afternoon tea, and William had announced that he would be coming in to make it.

Suddenly a thought came to her—a thought that had not occurred before. She sat quite still. Surely not, she said to herself; surely not. Ness was a matchmaker: it was what she did. And sometimes when people do something for years, they can't stop doing it—it becomes part of what they are. Ness had invited her to look after the agency; she had introduced her to William . . . *She had introduced her to William.* No, it was highly unlikely. And yet . . .

———

William came into the office later that afternoon. He had designed a new pattern that he wanted to show her. "It's very

Shetland," he said. "It'll make you think of islands, and the sea, and fishermen in sweaters, and gulls in the slipstream of boats, and things like that."

"Beautiful," she said. He was making it for her. He did not say it, but he was.

LA'S ORCHESTRA SAVES THE WORLD

From the bestselling and beloved author of The No. 1 Ladies' Detective Agency comes a heartwarming novel about the life-affirming powers of music and company during a time of war. When Lavender (La to her friends) moves to the Suffolk countryside, it's not just to escape the London Blitz but also to flee the wreckage of a disastrous marriage. As she starts to become a part of the community, however, she detects a sense of isolation. Her deep love of music and her desire to bring people together inspire her to start an orchestra. Little did she know that through this orchestra she would give hope and courage to the people of the community—and meet Feliks, a shy, upright Pole who would change her life forever.

Fiction

TINY TALES
Stories of Romance, Ambition, Kindness, and Happiness

In *Tiny Tales*, Alexander McCall Smith explores romance, ambition, kindness, and happiness in thirty short stories accompanied by thirty-four witty cartoons designed by Iain McIntosh, McCall Smith's longtime creative collaborator. Here we meet the first Australian pope, who hopes to finally find some peace and quiet back home in Perth; a psychotherapist turned motorcycle-racetrack manager; and an aspiring opera singer who gets her unlikely break onstage. And, of course, we spend time in McCall Smith's beloved Scotland, where we are introduced to progressive Vikings, a group of housemates with complex romantic entanglements, and a couple of globe-trotting dentists. These tales and illustrations depict the full scope of human experience and reveal the rich tapestry of life—painted in miniature.

Fiction

Amanda and her daughter Clover live in a close-knit community of expats on Grand Cayman Island, an idyllic place to all appearances. But the comfortable island life can become stifling in hard times. As Clover falls for her first love and allows her heart to chart her life's course, Amanda realizes that she has fallen out of love with Clover's father and that her carefully mapped-out future is actually unknown territory. Through the years, mother and daughter try to navigate their chosen paths as both are torn between the dreams they cherish and the reality they face.

Fiction

EMMA

A Modern Retelling

The summer after university, Emma Woodhouse returns home to live with her widowed father and to launch her interior design business. Apart from cultivating grand career plans and managing her father's hypochondria, Emma busies herself with the two things she does best: matchmaking and offering advice on everything from texting etiquette to first-date destinations. Happily, this summer presents abundant opportunities for both, as old and new friends are drawn into the sphere of Emma's counsel: George Knightley, her principled brother-in-law; Frank Churchill, the attractive stepson of her former governess; Harriet Smith, a naïve but enchanting young teacher's assistant at the local language school; and the perfect (and perfectly vexing) Jane Fairfax. Carriages have been replaced by Mini Coopers and cups of tea by cappuccinos, but Alexander McCall Smith's sparkling satire and cozy sensibility are the perfect match for Jane Austen's beloved tale.

Fiction

CHANCE DEVELOPMENTS
Stories

Inspired by antique photographs, these five stunning short stories capture the surprising intersections of love and friendship that alter life's journeys. "Sister Flora's First Day of Freedom" introduces us to a young nun who makes a difficult decision to leave the sisterhood and finds delightful new riches in the big city of Edinburgh. In "Angels in Italy," childhood friends, separated by circumstance, learn the enduring power of a first love. The enchanting "Dear Ventriloquist" tells of a mishap at a Canadian circus that sparks unexpected magic between a gifted puppeteer and a dapper lion tamer. Changing a tire changes the life of a young Irish teacher in "The Woman with the Beautiful Car," and a young New Zealander learns what matters in life from his grandfather, a WWII veteran, in "He Wanted to Believe in Tenderness."

Fiction

THE GOOD PILOT PETER WOODHOUSE

Val Eliot is working on an English farm during the war when she meets Mike, a United States Air Force pilot stationed nearby. The two become close, and after Val rescues a border collie named Peter Woodhouse who is being mistreated by his owner, she realizes the dog would actually be safer with Mike. Soon Peter Woodhouse settles into his new home on the air force base, and Val and Mike fall deeply in love. When a disaster jeopardizes the future of them all, Peter Woodhouse brings Ubi, a German corporal, into their orbit, sparking a friendship that comes with great risk but carries with it the richest of rewards. Infused with charm and warmth, *The Good Pilot Peter Woodhouse* is an uplifting story of love and the power of friendship to bring sworn enemies together.

Fiction

PIANOS AND FLOWERS
Brief Encounters of the Romantic Kind

Pictures capture moments in time, presenting the viewer with a window into another life. But a picture can go only so far. Who are the people in the image? What are their fears? What are their dreams? The fourteen captivating tales in this collection are all inspired by photos from the *Times of London* archive. A young woman finds unexpected love while perusing Egyptian antiquities. A family is forever fractured when war comes to Penang in colonial Malaysia. Iron Jelloid tablets help to reveal a young man's inner strength. And twin sisters discover that it's never too late to forge a new path—even when standing at the altar. Though at first glance these photographs may appear to represent small moments, they in fact speak volumes, uncovering possibilities of love, friendship, and happiness. With his indomitable charm, Alexander McCall Smith takes us behind the lens to explore the hidden lives of those photographed; in so doing, he reveals the humanity in us all.

Fiction

ALSO AVAILABLE

Fatty O'Leary's Dinner Party (eBook only)
The Pavilion in the Clouds (eBook only)
Trains and Lovers
AND OTHERS

VINTAGE BOOKS
Available wherever books are sold.
vintagebooks.com